FINAL WITNESS

JAMES SCOTT BELL

FINAL WITNESS

A NOVEL

BROADMAN
& HOLMAN
PUBLISHERS

Nashville, Tennessee

0-8054-1842-3

Published by Broadman & Holman Publishers, Nashville, Tennessee
Acquisitions and Development Editor: Leonard G. Goss
Typesetting: ProtoType Graphics, Inc.

Dewey Decimal Classification: 813
Subject Heading: FICTION
Library of Congress Card Catalog Number: 98–43329

Library of Congress Cataloging-in-Publication Data

Bell, James Scott.
Final witness: a novel / James Scott Bell.
p. cm
ISBN 0-8054-1842-3 (pbk.)
1. Title.
PS3552.E5158F56 1998
813′.54—dc21 98–43329
CIP

3 4 5 – 03 02 01

DEDICATION

For Cindy, Nathaniel and
Allegra—Simply the Best

GLOSSARY

AKA—"Also known as"

AUSA—Assistant United States Attorney

CHP—California Highway Patrol

CRI—Confidential, reliable informant

GSA—Security key-card manufacturer

LAX—Los Angeles International Airport

LCN—La Cosa Nostra

MDC—Metropolitan Detention Center, downtown Los Angeles

ME—Medical examiner

OCIS—Organized Crime Information System

OR—"Own recognizance." Release from detention without bail.

RICO—Racketeer Influenced and Corrupt Organizations (federal law)

Shepardize—To research the subsequent history of a legal opinion, to see if it has been overturned or cited as precedent in later legal decisions. Named for the publication, *Shepard's Citations*.

SWAT—Special Weapons and Tactics. A law enforcement team trained for high-risk rescues and potentially deadly situations.

Part One

Inside

To be free is to live under a government by law.

—Lord Mansfield

CHAPTER ONE

"HOW OLD ARE YOU?"

"Twenty-four."

"Going into your third year?"

"Yes."

"Second in your class?"

"Temporarily."

"Isn't it true you have a motive to lie?"

"Excuse me?" Rachel Ybarra felt her face start to burn. That question had come from nowhere, like a slap. She sat up a little straighter in the chair.

The tall lawyer took a step toward her. "Motive to lie, Ms. Ybarra."

"No, sir. I don't lie."

"Never?"

"No."

"Come now, Ms. Ybarra, everybody lies, especially when they want a good job."

Feeling like a cornered animal, Rachel suppressed the urge to snap. *Calm yourself,* she thought. *Don't lose your cool.* "Not everybody," she replied. "Not all the time."

"Can you prove it?" the tall lawyer demanded. "Can you prove you never lie?"

"Why are you asking me all this?"

Alan Lakewood took a step toward her, stopped suddenly, and sat casually on the corner of his desk. "It's just a little exercise I go through. I call it my trial by ambush. You want to know what it's like to grill some witness in court, you have to walk in their shoes once. And you have to be ready to take the gloves off, like I just did."

Rachel nodded, still wondering what to make of the exchange. When she saw a slight smile on the tall lawyer's face, she relaxed a little.

"That's what it's like to be in trial sometimes," Lakewood continued. "You have to be able to think on your feet." Lakewood stood and returned to his chair behind the wooden desk. The corner office on the eleventh floor of the United States Courthouse looked out across Spring Street and the Hollywood Freeway, now jammed with typical Los Angeles traffic. Rachel glanced out the window and, for a quick moment, wished she were on the other side. She was more nervous than she ever thought she'd be.

"So why did you come to work as a paralegal for the U.S. Attorney's Office?" Lakewood asked.

Rachel shifted in her chair, took a deep breath. Finally this was a real interview, the kind she expected when she arrived half an hour before. "Because I want to be a federal prosecutor when I get out of school," she said.

"Why federal?"

"That's where the biggest difference is made."

Lakewood touched the tips of his fingers together and looked at them. "Do you see it as a stepping-stone to a lucrative private practice?"

"I hadn't thought about it," Rachel said.

"A lot of people do."

"That doesn't concern me."

Now Lakewood eyed her steadily. Rachel judged him to be in his early fifties, though he looked younger. His black hair held only a hint of gray, and he didn't have a pronounced thickening around the waist. His soft twang sounded like the heart of Texas. "I find that hard to believe," he said.

"Why?"

"Because money talks."

"Not to me."

"Not even a little?"

"Okay," Rachel said with a smile. "A little. But I try to keep it in its place."

Lakewood looked down at the resumé she had handed him when she first entered the office. He nodded his head slightly then said, "You're helping meet expenses doing paralegal work?"

"Yes," said Rachel.

"And some financial aid?"

"That's right."

Reading, Lakewood asked, "What's the Christian Legal Society?"

"A small group, gets together once a week for lunch and a Bible study. Every now and then we have a guest speaker."

Nodding, Lakewood said, "You take your faith seriously, then."

"Of course."

"Ever think it might be a hindrance?"

"How?"

"I mean, when you have to take the gloves off, as I was saying earlier. If you really had to tear into a witness, let's say."

"I've never thought of it as a hindrance."

"You should."

Rachel didn't respond. The conversation seemed suddenly too personal, but at the same time understandable. He was basically asking her if she had what it took to be a federal prosecutor—to stand inside the federal district courtrooms going toe-to-toe with the worst offenders and the ablest defense lawyers. Maybe he thought a Christian woman wouldn't be tough enough for the task. Like it or not, that would be an attitude she knew she'd have to face in the so-called real world.

"My faith is not a hindrance, Mr. Lakewood."

"I didn't say it was. I only said you should think about it."

Rachel's mouth felt suddenly dry.

Lakewood tossed the resumé to the side of his desk, folded his hands in front of him, and leaned back in his chair. "Where'd you grow up?"

"Montebello."

"Like it?"

"It served its purpose, I guess."

"Hispanic neighborhood?"

"Yes."

"Gangs?"

"Yes."

"Any interaction with them?"

Rachel wiped her hands on her lap a couple of times. Her voice seemed to come from a distant part of her, almost like she was hearing her own echo. "It couldn't be avoided."

"You all right, Ms. Ybarra?"

Rachel tossed her head back. "Shouldn't we be focusing on my work record?"

"Not necessarily." Lakewood picked up a pencil, as if he was suddenly nervous about having nothing to do with his hands. "Life experience counts for something. You have family in Montebello still?"

"My dad lives there. I'm living with my grandmother in Hollywood while I go to school."

"Mother?"

"She died when I was seven."

"I'm sorry."

Rachel put up her hand and started to say something, but the words stuck in her throat. She felt claustrophobic, wanting to get outside into the air.

"You've been working in our Santa Ana office for a little over six months, is that right?"

"Yes."

"I got some very good reports on your work."

"Thank you."

"But this is the big office. The person I hire needs to be ready for long hours. I'll need a lot of help with one major case that is coming down."

"I'm not afraid of hard work."

"No," Lakewood said, "it's apparent you aren't." He stood and offered her his hand. "I'll let you know, Ms. Ybarra. Thanks for coming in."

"Thank you," Rachel said.

"You know your way out?"

"Yes."

"Good. It's a requirement for the job." Lakewood smiled.

Though she was relieved, Rachel felt like the walk out of the office and down the hall to the reception desk was much longer than when she entered. At the reception desk she signed out. The woman at the phone bank smiled at her. "Bye now," she said.

Rachel felt like an empty sack as she walked out of the courthouse on the Main Street side. She paused on the steps and looked back at the building. There was something inspiring about the place, with its majestic bas-relief eagles and World War II ironwork design that still said "United States of America War Office." It was the kind of place that would make her father proud of her, or so she hoped.

She walked two blocks toward the parking lot, passing City Hall on one side and the state criminal courts building on the other. She paused behind the courthouse and looked toward the *Los Angeles Times* building a city block away. At one time she had thought about becoming a reporter, maybe working for the *Times*. But that dream faded the more she disagreed with the paper's editorial policy, which was often.

She entered the lot and paid the extortion being charged, then drove back to the USC campus. She needed a swim. Whenever she was tense, the water never failed her.

The water was the Olympic pool, built for the '84 games. Swimming laps there was not only great exercise, it also allowed Rachel to indulge in a little fantasy about swimming for Olympic gold. She'd been on the swim team in high school and even took second in the city finals one year in the 1,500 meter. Now, when she swam alone, she imagined she was representing the United States, in the lead, with Russia just a stroke or two behind. She always beat the Russians.

Refreshed, she sat at poolside for awhile. The sun was warm but not oppressive. It was one of those days that made Los Angeles so appealing, despite the problems the city still dealt with. Those problems were even more acute here at USC, situated as it was near the Coliseum and Sports Arena, which were sort of landmarks beyond which stretched a terrain known more for its poverty and gangs than anything else.

Maybe that thought started it. Or maybe it was just a link to something deeper, darker. But whatever the trigger was, Rachel suddenly began to feel an icy sweat breaking out on her forehead.

She tried to draw a breath, but it was labored. It had nothing to do with conditioning. Hers was excellent, and she had long since powered down from her swim. But she found she could not breathe deeply without concentrating fully on the actions of her lungs and chest.

Gripping the sides of her chair, Rachel squeezed tight, as if she were on a roller coaster car without sides or seatbelt, as if she might fly off at any moment. She felt a slight sense of dizziness.

For a moment Rachel thought she had been hit by a flu bug—a new, nasty strain that worked fast and hit hard. But this wasn't a physical illness, though it had physical manifestations. What she was experiencing was not coming into her from the outside. This was inside her. She knew it was an anxiety attack, a big one.

She had experienced a similar feeling only a few times before, but in a much milder way. It all seemed related to going to law school. First, she had to gear up for the law school entrance exam. She had studied hours every day, cramming her head full of sample problems, reading until her eyes couldn't continue. On the day of the test she knew one thing absolutely—no one had studied harder than she. But as she drove to the test location, she almost had to pull over because of the anxiety.

Then, during law school, she sweated out the posting of the first semester grades. That was anxious for all the students, she knew, but she wondered if they broke out in cold sweats the way she did.

Now she was getting those same feelings, only worse. Much worse.

Why? She wondered. What was her body or mind—or both—trying to tell her? She sensed that it had something to do with her desire to work in the U.S. Attorney's Office. That had to be part of it.

But she also had some strange sense that this was a mixture of guilt and dread. Guilt because of Stevie. Her brother was still a part of her, his death a constant shadow over her life.

And the dread? What was that all about? Why should she be dreading anything when she had a faith that was supposed to deliver her from fear?

Breathing rapidly, shortly, Rachel closed her eyes and tried to take in as much air as she could, telling her mind to quiet itself. She tried to pray but couldn't. Her mind wouldn't cooperate. She thought for a moment she might lose consciousness.

Then, as suddenly as it had come, the feeling began to go away. It was as if a cold snap had blown across a warm beach, chilling the air for an odd moment before fading. Relieved, Rachel loosened her hold on the chair.

For ten minutes she sat virtually motionless, finally achieving a modicum of relaxation once more. It wasn't total. She still had a nagging feeling hanging on inside her, a feeling she was again familiar with. The feeling was that just when things seemed all right, something bad was about to happen.

CHAPTER TWO

NOTHING BAD HAD HAPPENED to Dimitri Chekhov over the past year. It had been wonderful—the sort of year that made all the clichés about America real to an immigrant who had managed to get out of the Soviet Union before the great collapse.

Over there he had been just another cog in a communist factory machine. Now he was making money hand over fist and living in a house that would have impressed Brezhnev.

His American wife, Sarah, was beautiful. She was forty-nine and looked half that. His limousine business was flourishing, with contracts at two of the movie studios. And if some in the Russian community in Hollywood seemed jealous of his success, what of it? He never bought into that egalitarian stuff in the first place. He was no happy communist. In fact, he didn't know any. He only knew people who wanted to get out, to get to the West, especially to America.

He remembered seeing a propaganda piece one day; it portrayed lazy, foolish American men exploiting their hired help as they indulged in pointless luxuries. Dimitri thought the luxuries looked pretty good. And now, fifteen years later, he had his pick of them.

Yes, America was a good place to grow wealthy, especially if you knew your way around the laws. That was one thing Dimitri had learned in the old country. There the laws could get you killed or exiled. You didn't break them; you bent them and exploited the holes. That was good training for the land of opportunity he had come to fifteen years ago.

So, when Dimitri Chekhov decided to get into the drug trade, he was well suited for the job. Governmental authority hadn't scared him in Moscow, and it certainly didn't here. One simply had to choose wisely the means and ends.

The means was narcotics. The end was a steady income stream from a variety of sources. Chekhov knew that black market items—and narcotics were such an item in this country—needed a way to be moved.

There were various ways to do this, but most of them were obvious to the investigating authorities. So-called "mules" were usually easily pegged, susceptible to what law enforcement called the drug-courier profile. With nothing more than suspicion based upon appearance, agents could stop those who might be moving drugs. They did it all the time.

They also stopped trucks that traveled well-known drug highways, and if the drivers seemed nervous, they would find some pretext to search. It was all getting very predictable. Dimitri Chekhov figured out that limousines were perfect vehicles for transporting drugs. They were the opposite of the profiled vehicles, and so they worked beautifully. From a variety of sources, Chekhov built a brisk business, and that business built the lifestyle he now enjoyed.

Of all the trappings of wealth that were available to him, Dimitri Chekhov loved one simple item above everything—his DVD player. He couldn't get over the wonder of full-length feature movies on little discs. As a child growing up in a little town, movies had been a luxury seldom enjoyed. When he did get to see them he was transfixed, even when movies took the form of lifeless indoctrination put out by the Party. Not even that pabulum could dull the memory of seeing Sergei Eisenstein's 1938 classic, *Alexander Nevsky,* for the first time in his town's opera house. The story of the great Russian hero of the thirteenth century moved him like nothing else in his life before or since.

Now, sitting in stocking feet in the living room of his own stylish home, he could pop in a little platter and watch virtually anything he wanted.

Tonight it was *Independence Day.*

Sarah was out at her weekly social gathering. Dimitri was proud of her accomplishments too. A widow at thirty, she had worked hard at a dress designing business and saw her two children through college. She still had a hand in the business, but after marriage to Dimitri she had turned her attention more to civic causes. She had become a fixture in the upscale community where they both lived. Best of all, she didn't ask detailed questions about his enterprises. They were a perfect fit.

With a vodka in hand, Dimitri clicked the remote and started the movie. The lights in the house were off, save for the kitchen where Sarah would enter from the garage. It would only be him, aliens, and Will Smith for the next couple of hours.

He thought he heard a sound from the garage just after the credits finished. It was a thump of some kind, as if someone had dropped a soft bag on the floor. But no one could be in the garage, fixed as it was with a double security system. No one except Sarah could get inside without tripping the alarm.

Maybe she was home early. No, it was too early. She hadn't been gone more than half an hour.

Another possibility crossed his mind. Lately the Hollywood hills area was having a problem with, of all things, opossums. Several times in the last few months Dimitri had come face-to-muzzle with what he called "giant rats" in his backyard. One of them could have dropped onto his roof from one of the overhanging eucalyptus trees that surrounded his house.

If opossums were causing the noise, there was nothing to do about it. He went back to his movie.

He did not hear a sound, but something told him he wasn't alone. It was instinct, born of the Soviet system where someone was always looking over your shoulder.

Dimitri Chekhov hadn't felt that in a long time, but he felt it now.

"Sarah?" he called.

No answer.

He got up from his easy chair and turned toward the front of his house. Only darkness and shadow loomed. Again his mind told him no one could be inside. He had the finest security system money could buy. He needed it. The business he was in was not free from cutthroat competition—literally. There were people out there who wanted in on the huge profit pie Chekhov had fashioned for himself. They were known to cut themselves pieces with sharpened knives and hollow-point bullets.

But his house was secure. He decided to sweep through the house once, put his fears behind him, and get back to the alien invasion.

He had a .38 in the antique desk in his study. He went for it just in case. As he walked through the hallway, he flicked on the lights. No sudden image of an intruder. Nothing but cold emptiness.

In the study he found his gun in the drawer and quickly checked the chamber. Fully loaded. He couldn't remember the last time he had fired the weapon. Probably last year when he took it to the local firing range. He made a mental note to visit there again. It was time to brush up.

Feeling more confident than fearful, he strode toward the kitchen.

He turned on the lights and, as he expected, saw only the glistening tile and pine of his wife's newly remodeled kitchen. A basket of apples and bananas sat on the breakfast bar. He started feeling a little foolish then. He wasn't going to find anybody, let alone shoot anyone. He laughed, selected an apple, and rubbed it on his shirt.

He raised the apple to his mouth. He never got a bite.

A hand covered his face and pulled his head back. A searing pain shot through his neck. Dimitri felt another hand grab the gun from him, twisting his wrists until he thought they might break. He was pulled backward, off his feet, dragged across the kitchen floor.

The surprise attack had frozen him, but now he struggled. He tried to get his feet underneath him, but the man who had hold of his head was strong. Whoever it was said something in Russian. To Dimitri it sounded like, "Get a chair."

So there were two of them. At least.

Dimitri pumped his arms, trying to hit his assailant with an elbow. He made contact with the body, but with hardly any force. He tried to twist out of the grasp, but the man snapped his head back again, causing incredible pain. In the next instant Dimitri felt himself being shoved in a chair with rope being thrown around him.

The hand on his face released him for an instant. But before Dimitri could turn his head a heavy cloth was snapped over his eyes and pulled tight. Dimitri tried to move his arms, but the rope restrained him. It took only a few seconds more before he was completely incapacitated and blind to the world.

"Who sent you?" he said.

No answer.

"Supevsky?" Dimitri said quickly.

A hand slapped him across the face.

"What's he want?" said Dimitri. "I'll talk to him."

An arm wrapped around his neck like a headlock and started dragging him backward. He tried to speak again but couldn't. He felt like he was going to choke.

His mind traced his direction as he was pulled through the house. He sensed they were going back through the kitchen. He tried to kick out, but his feet had been tied up. He was helpless.

He thought of Sarah. It was some consolation to him that she wasn't there. If this was to be the end, at least it would only be him.

He sensed a door opening—the door to the garage. He felt himself being pulled through the door.

Finally the arm around his neck released. "Let me talk to him," Dimitri said desperately. "I have money! I will pay you more than Supevsky!"

One of the men turned his chair around. He heard activity on the other side of the garage, as if the other man were moving something.

"You can have it all," Dimitri said. "Both of you. I'll leave. I'll take my wife and go back to New York. I won't come back."

The only sound he heard was the tinny knock of a large can of some kind. Suddenly he knew what was going to happen. As he cried out, "Don't do this!" he felt the gasoline being poured on his head, and he smelled the sickening odor.

"No! Don't do it!"

"Quiet," a voice said.

"Don't do this to me!"

"Listen."

"Yes, yes." He was doused head to foot with fuel.

The voice said nothing further. A rough strand of rope was pulled into Dimitri's mouth, tightly, like a bridle bit. He wouldn't be speaking again, at least not now.

Then Dimitri felt the sodden blindfold being lifted from his head. He blinked, his eyes burning from the gas. He coughed as the fumes assaulted his lungs. Shaking his head, he tried to focus. The lights were on, blindingly bright. Sensing his assailants behind him, he turned his head but couldn't see them.

He looked forward, finally able to make out images, and saw someone sitting across from him. Perhaps one of the men, ready to talk, to negotiate. Perhaps they were not unreasonable men after all.

And then Dimitri Chekhov screamed. The scream came through muffled, because of the thick rope in his mouth.

Dimitri screamed again.

In a chair secured with ropes was the lifeless body of his wife. Her head hung limply to one side.

"No!" he cried as loudly as he could, knowing the sound of his voice dropped uselessly to the floor.

He jerked himself violently in his chair, tipping himself over, falling hard on the concrete. His head hit with sudden force. He almost blacked out. He wished then for death. He cried out once more.

Then he closed his eyes and began to cry. When the flames came, instantly covering his entire body, it was almost a relief. Dimitri Chekhov did not scream again.

CHAPTER THREE

ABI HAD MADE her special cheesecake from the "secret" family recipe. "Someday," she told Rachel, "I'll pass it along to you. But not yet, *conejíta*, not yet."

Rachel smiled and kissed her grandmother's cheek. Abi, short for *abuela*, had been using that line for years even though everyone in the family already knew the secret. It was all in the hands. Abi insisted that the ingredients—eggs, cream cheese, vanilla extract, sugar—be thoroughly kneaded and mixed with the bare hands. She said it gave it a silkiness you can't get any other way.

So it would be *pollo* for dinner with a slice of cheesecake tonight, and Rachel would hear some more stories about life in America during World War II. And she would love it.

Rachel was living with her grandmother on Nichols Canyon Road in Hollywood. It was a perfect arrangement. Abi, widowed now for thirteen years, had a large guest room for Rachel and a need for companionship. Rachel had never seen her grandmother enough growing up and relished the chance to get to know her better. And Abi charged no rent. That was a major plus with Rachel attending law school via the student loan program.

The house was lovely. Built in the late '30s by her husband Ernesto, it had wonderful stonework walls, hardwood floors, and the faint smell of mothballs. Abi made rugs, and she'd been fighting the moths ever since Hirohito surrendered to MacArthur.

They sat down at the dining room table, and Abi, as was her custom, asked Rachel to say a blessing. When Rachel finished, Abi said, "How was your interview today?"

"Fine, Abi."

"They will hire you?"

"I don't know."

"I hope they don't."

Rachel paused mid-bite, a piece of chicken hanging from her fork. "Why not?"

"What got into you to become a lawyer, huh? You should be making great-grandchildren."

"Times have changed just a little, Abi."

"Don't like it. And there's too many lawyers. I see them on TV all the time and I don't like them. There is that commercial, have you seen it? The lawyer says getting mad for you is his job. Is that what lawyers do now? Get mad?"

"Sometimes."

"But not you, *conejíta*."

"You can't believe that your little rabbit gets mad?"

"And working with criminals is another thing I don't like."

"Abi, the U.S. Attorney *prosecutes* criminals."

"Like who?"

"Large-scale fraud, drug trafficking, criminal organizations, that sort of thing."

Sighing, Abi said, "I don't like that. Why don't you get married to a lawyer and leave all that to him?"

"There's an idea. Maybe I'll marry that guy who says his job is to get mad."

Abi looked shocked at first, then squinted in mock rebuke. "You! I have a mind to send you back to . . ." Abi looked at her hands.

"It's all right, Abi."

"How is he?"

"The same."

"He doesn't call me. Why won't he call me or see me?"

"I think maybe, deep down, he's ashamed."

"But I'm his mother."

"And I am his daughter. There's no reason to it."

"Is it because of Stevie?"

"I'm sure." Rachel took a sip of coffee. For a moment the only sound she could hear was the distant flow of traffic on Hollywood Boulevard.

"Why did Stevie do it?" Abi asked finally, a small catch in her voice. "I don't understand."

Rachel set her own fork down and put her hands in her lap.

Tears began to form in Abi's eyes. "Why did he?"

Rachel said nothing. She felt suddenly claustrophobic in the small kitchen. She closed her eyes.

"I'm sorry," said Abi.

Rachel reached out and took Abi's hand in hers. The old woman's hand was delicate but warm.

They sat in silence for several minutes until the ringing of the phone jolted them. "I'll get it," Rachel said.

It was Alan Lakewood. "Hope I didn't disturb y'all," he said.

"No, no," Rachel said.

"Just wanted to let you know I expect you in the office at eight o'clock Monday morning."

"Really?"

"Congratulations."

"Thank you!"

After hanging up she turned to Abi. "I got it," Rachel said. "I got the job."

"That's good," said Abi, in a tone that said the very opposite.

CHAPTER FOUR

RACHEL ARRIVED at 7:30 on Monday morning.

"Anxious, aren't we?" said Gina Goodman.

"A little," Rachel answered.

Gina laughed. "It'll pass." She was, Rachel learned later, one of the more valuable workers in the office. She made the best coffee, could wrestle the copy machines into submission, and knew the quirks of every Assistant United States Attorney on each floor. Today her job included guiding Rachel on a quick tour of the office. "I also get to do this with the new externs," Gina explained. "A few of them arrive today, too."

They began on the eleventh floor, where major frauds and major crimes were located. File cabinets were stacked along the hallway walls, testament, Gina said, to the infinite stream of paper that had to be analyzed, categorized, and memorialized for quick reference. "If you're lucky," Gina said, "you won't be stuck going through these drawers all summer."

Rachel shuddered at the thought.

They took the stairs up to the twelfth floor, Gina opening the door by swiping her key card through the security mount.

"This is main reception," Gina said. "Here's where we have the library, the grand jury rooms, and the best coffee. You'll have your Friday meetings down here in the Bob Brosio Room. There's his picture." Gina pointed at a portrait of a dignified, gray-haired gentleman. "Chief of the Criminal Division for, like, thirty years. Knew everything about everything."

"That covers quite a bit," Rachel said.

"Maybe you'll be here thirty years."

The tour continued up to the thirteenth floor, the Government Fraud Division, and finally the fourteenth, major narcotics. This was also the floor where externs and paralegals were assigned either small offices or even smaller cubicles. "Since you're an early bird," Gina explained, "I'll give you your pick."

She led Rachel to the row of offices on the Spring Street side. They were all empty save for a government-issue desk and chair and a phone line. The walls were bare. Rachel shrugged her shoulders and entered one near the end. "I guess I'll take this one," she said.

"The one I would have chosen," Gina said. "It has so much more personality than the others." She laughed. "Why don't you arrange the designer furniture the way you like it, then come on down to the Brosio room at 8:30. Alan Lakewood wants to have a few words with the greenhorns. His word, not mine."

Rachel nodded, and Gina left her alone. Flicking on the lights, Rachel looked around at her new office. It was a shoe box, but to Rachel it was as exciting as a penthouse. She went to the window and looked out across Spring Street at the old Los Angeles Hall of Justice. She'd heard it was empty now, a relic of what some called the "golden age of the city." She wondered what it must have been like to try cases back in those rough-and-tumble days, before discovery rules had taken so much of the surprise out of trials. It was rare enough to have a woman in those courtrooms, but a Latina would have been one for *Ripley's*.

She sat in the chair behind the bare desk and turned it so she was looking out the window. She closed her eyes and whispered a prayer of thanks and asked for the strength and wisdom she knew she would need here.

"Meditating?"

Rachel spun around. A tall, blond man about her age, wearing a gray suit and a wry smile, was leaning in the doorway.

"Just a little," Rachel said.

"Ron Ashby," he said, walking in with his hand extended. "Boalt Hall."

"Rachel Ybarra, USC."

"Ah, University of Spoiled Children." He threw out the familiar barb with good humor.

"You Cal guys are all the same," Rachel countered. "Can't come up with new material."

"Give me some time." He sat down on the only other chair in the office. "You an extern for the summer?"

"I'm a paralegal."

"Oh yeah? You're getting paid? Must be why you have the luxury office."

"Yeah, right. It has that convent feel."

Ashby nodded. "Monkish. But we'll need that for all the grunt work we'll be doing."

"I like legal research."

"I hate it."

"Then why go to law school?"

"Fame."

Rachel blinked. It was such an unabashed divulgence she didn't know what to say. On the surface it sounded arrogant, but it also seemed to be, for him, a simple career choice.

"Shocked?" Ashby asked.

"Not really. People put a lot of stock in fame these days."

"And you don't?"

"No. I couldn't care less."

Ashby smiled again in a half curl, one that indicated a mocking disbelief. "But if it comes your way, you'll take it, right?"

"I don't want it to come my way. I want to do my job, go home, read a good book, go to sleep at night."

"What does your husband think?"

Rachel looked at the ceiling and laughed. "Smooth, Mr. Ashby, very smooth."

"Boyfriend?"

"That was a little clumsier."

Ashby shrugged his shoulders, awaiting an answer. Rachel said, "No boyfriend, not looking."

"I move to strike the last part of your answer as nonresponsive."

"It was exactly what you were thinking, though, right?"

Ashby paused a moment, then said, "Guilty."

Rachel smiled. "I'll let you off with probation."

"Thanks," Ashby said, looking at his watch. "I'll see you at the meeting."

After Ashby left, Rachel unpacked a few items from her briefcase—pads, pencils, blank computer disks. She placed her copy of the *Federal*

Rules of Evidence on her desk. Her trial practice professor had told her that trial attorneys need to know the evidence rules backward and forward. She intended to know them sideways, too.

She spent the next half hour getting settled, making plans, and greeting some of the externs. Several of them took the stairs together down to the twelfth floor for the orientation.

Swivel chairs where grand jurors usually sat were set out in rows in the Brosio Room. Rachel sat between Ron Ashby and an extern who introduced herself as Toni Galvan, a second-year student from Harvard.

Alan Lakewood entered the room carrying a large whiteboard, which he set on an easel at the front of the room. "Good morning. It's good to have you here in the Central District. This office is the second largest in the country, with about two hundred lawyers. We have three litigating divisions—criminal, civil, and tax—and a nonlawyer administrative division. We also have a small branch office in Santa Ana, which handles a wide range of criminal matters. This morning I wanted to give you some insight on how we operate and fill you in on some background on organized crime. Give you a feel. I want to start by focusing on an actual case."

Lakewood turned to the whiteboard and wrote "Mr. X" at the top with a felt-tip pen.

"This is a man we're taking a long, hard look at," Lakewood said. "For security reasons, I can't give you his real name. But we're sure he heads a criminal enterprise that's into theft of high technology and traffic in narcotics. In other words, things that make people a lot of money."

"Unlike government legal work," a man said, eliciting laughter from the room.

Lakewood smiled at the man. "That's Mark Shuie, folks, who's been with the office five years now. He was born tired and raised lazy, so don't pay him much mind."

"Thanks, Chief," Shuie said.

Lakewood nodded. "Unlike Mr. Shuie and myself, Mr. X likes to live in high style. Has an estate in the Hollywood Hills. Likes $2,000 Brioni suits and the L.A. Kings."

"A hockey fan," said a man just entering the room.

"Glad you could make it," Lakewood said. "Folks, this is Agent Jeff Bunnell of the FBI. He's been working this case from day one."

"Hi," Bunnell said to the crowd. Rachel thought him to be in his early thirties. For a moment he made eye contact with Rachel and smiled.

Toni Galvan leaned over to Rachel and whispered, "He could give Mel Gibson a run for his money."

"Shh," Rachel said, embarrassed.

"He can interrogate me anytime," Toni said.

"Is there a question?" Lakewood said toward Rachel and Toni. Rachel felt like a spotlight had suddenly been trained on her, illuminating not only her outside but her mental landscape as well. Like a grade-school student caught talking by the teacher, Rachel looked back at Lakewood and slowly shook her head.

Lakewood said, "I've asked Agent Bunnell to give you an overview of organized crime in this country and explain a little bit about how our man X fits in. Jeff?"

Bunnell stepped forward. "Thanks. For sixty years in this country, La Cosa Nostra, or Mafia, is what most people thought of when they thought of organized crime. It started with a big wave of Sicilian immigrants early in the century. They brought these strong-arm tactics with them from the old country—beatings, leg breaking, the occasional murder. During Prohibition they put these to use to monopolize bootleg liquor, loan sharking, gambling, and prostitution."

"How many families were there?" Lakewood asked.

"Hard to say exactly. There were a whole lot of murders, turf wars, and the like going on. Then along comes Charles 'Lucky' Luciano, the real Godfather. He took charge of the entire underworld back in 1931. He came up with a panel of bosses called The Commission, and they oversaw all the rackets in the United States. The Mob hardly made a move without Lucky's approval. He was the guy who set the pattern. This was the formation of La Cosa Nostra in the States."

Rachel leaned forward, concentrating as if she were in a law school class.

"Luciano was smart," Bunnell continued. "He formed alliances with powerful, non-Italian mobsters, like Bugsy Siegel and Meyer Lansky, the guys who founded Las Vegas. Luciano's family was years ahead of most Mob families in labor racketeering. They had their hands in everything from Detroit's car industry to Hollywood's stagehands' union to textile locals in New York City. Eventually there were about twenty-five families in the American LCN; five of them in New York. In the 1980s there was a lot of bloodletting. It pretty well decimated two of the major New York City families—the Colombos and Bonannos. That left open the door for the Gambino family and a man named John Gotti."

"The Teflon Don," Lakewood said. "Kept beating major raps."

"He took over the Gambino family," Bunnell said, "after he arranged a hit on Paul Castellano in 1985. Castellano showed up at a nice steak house for a meeting and immediately got popped with six bullets to the head."

Bunnell paused, then said, "And sitting across the street in a car, watching the whole thing go down, were John Gotti and Sammy Gravano."

"Sammy the Bull," said Lakewood.

"The very same. The biggest informer of them all. The reason why John Gotti is sitting in a prison cell today. And why Vincent 'Chin' Gigante was found guilty of murder conspiracy in '97. Bottom line is that LCN has been dealt a severe blow, brought to its knees. But crime abhors a vacuum, and newer, deadlier forms of gangland activity have sprouted up around us. We can start with the Bloods and the Crips."

The mention of the notorious gang names made Rachel sit up. Bunnell said, "They were born, of course, right here in L.A. Like all of the modern gangs we're talking about, they had, and have, business sense. That's what makes them so dangerous. They started to establish franchises—what they called 'sets'—all over the country."

"Like McDonald's," Lakewood said, "only they served up murder instead of fries."

"Exactly," said Bunnell. "Our best estimates have them with chapters in sixty cities, in forty states. Main trade is crack.

"Then you got your biker gangs out here on the Coast specializing in methamphetamine. They're a very nice group of guys. Along with the street gangs, they operate much the same as the old LCN, but without the sense of *familia,* which had a feudal code of honor. They use various forms of violence. But nothing like the violence we've seen lately from newer gangs."

He paused. Rachel had the feeling he was building up to something. The agent went on, "You've no doubt heard of the Jamaican posses. In the eighties we had massive incursion of young men from Kingston and the outlying areas, hungry, poverty-stricken youths coming over on agricultural visas. But once they got here, they just disappeared, and suddenly we started seeing a new level of violence that broke all old paradigms. The largest gang is known as the Shower Posse, because the gang members like to shower anybody that gets in their way with bullets. We figure about four thousand murders since 1985."

A collective gasp went up from the law students in the meeting room. Bunnell said, "And now we're seeing other ethnic groups, like Nigerians and Armenians, getting into the criminal act. And each group seems to be more violent than the last."

Rachel couldn't help herself. She raised her hand. Bunnell nodded at her. "Why is that?" she said.

"Competition," Bunnell answered. "It's business. If you're going to scare off your rivals, you need to show them you can take things one step further. It was really a logical progression. Prior to the breakup of the Soviet Union, private enterprise was illegal. The state owned all goods and services. This left the only free market as a black market. You had two ways of securing goods—you pilfered them from the production source or you stole them from the point of distribution. Everyone from factory workers to government officials in the various republics could get involved.

"Criminal enterprises were all over the place, and of course, coercion and violence were part of the price of doing business. Some people got very good at this. When private enterprise became a reality in the former Soviet Union, people did not change the way they did business. And you had a lot of former soldiers and KGB agents looking for work. They found it."

Rachel shook her head.

"These people formed the backbone of the *shabaskniki*, the Russian word for "self-employed." Others called them the Russian Mafia. They started showing up back east, especially in Brighton Beach. They've grown tremendously, especially with regard to narcotics. The Russian Mafia has set itself up all over the Caribbean islands so as to be able to contact the Colombians. Two dozen Russian banks have offices on the island of Antigua alone. A little curious, you might say. They aren't there to get tans."

The room filled with light laughter. Bunnell continued, "And now they're out here."

Lakewood said, "Which brings us to Mr. X."

Bunnell nodded. "The subject runs an import company. On the surface, very clean. But he is probably the biggest single organized crime figure west of the Rockies. His enterprise seems to be into a little bit of everything. Right now we're sure he's partnering with figures in the Mexican military to bring in narcotics. The investigation, as they say, is ongoing. Our job is to collect the evidence and find the legal framework to put him away."

"Which isn't going to be easy," Lakewood said. "He has set himself up as an American success story. Millionaire businessman, two kids, wife. Just like Ozzie and Harriet."

"Ozzie and Harriet from hell," Bunnell said. "Let me just give you an idea. Back when he was living in Brighton Beach, he had a nice little house in a nice little neighborhood. Had his first kid then, a girl. One day she was riding her tricycle. Nobody was watching the kid; they just let her do what she wanted. She rode out into the middle of the street just as an accountant, a neighbor, was driving home from work. Boom. He slammed into the kid. It was not his fault at all. The girl should have been on a leash. She wound up in the hospital in a coma."

He paused, looked around the room, and continued. "The accountant was a family man himself and was torn up about what had happened. He sent flowers to the hospital. Then one day, a couple weeks later, he was missing. Two weeks later a woman found his head on the beach at Coney Island."

Rachel felt a chill on her neck.

"Nobody ever found any evidence that Mr. X put out the contract," Bunnell added. "But he did. We all know he did. And the upshot is his little girl recovered. Good as new. Don't know how the accountant's kids ended up."

A heavy silence shrouded the room.

"This is an example of what we are up against these days," Lakewood said. "I wanted you all to get a picture of it. Any of you who would like to resign now may do so."

No one said anything. Someone coughed in the back of the room.

"Welcome to the United States Attorney's Office," Lakewood said.

CHAPTER FIVE

RACHEL SPENT THE REST of the day in the small library on the twelfth floor. It felt good to have work to do. She'd been assigned by one of the AUSAs to help prepare a trial memorandum, and she dove into the project, eager to please.

Rachel began by reading an important case in the *Federal Reporter.* Usually this was easy for her. She loved the legal arguments, the logic, the flow of a good decision. It was like a puzzle, and she liked puzzles. But now, for some reason, it was different. Reading was a chore.

An image kept interrupting her, flickering in her mind like shadows cast on a wall by candlelight.

It was this criminal, Mr. X. Though his identity was secret, Rachel had formed, after the morning briefing, an image of him. She saw a face of stone and eyes devoid of true humanity. And it was something about the eyes that created in her mind another distraction.

She wasn't sure about it at first, but then it began to click. The eyes she had imagined in the face of Mr. X were eyes she had seen before.

They belonged to Raimundo Montoya.

Yes, that was it. Montoya, the man who had killed her brother.

She was in high school then, a senior, working a job after school to help her father make ends meet. On this night her dad was out, no doubt drinking with his buddies at The Boxcar. It was a school night, and Rachel had just returned from her shift at Skip's Pizza in Montebello. Stevie wasn't home. He should have been. The only reason he ever did any homework was because Rachel hounded him about it. She had to hound him a lot lately, because he was starting to fail some classes.

She looked in Stevie's room. It was a mess—clothes strewn on the floor and bed unmade, and the paper debris of a fast-food meal cluttered the already crowded desk. She went to his desk and looked for the small address book she knew he kept there.

She opened it, thumbed through it, found the name.

She went to the hall, picked up the phone, and dialed the number.

"Hello?" a girl's voice answered.

"Is this Marlene?" asked Rachel.

"Yeah. Who's this?"

"I'm Stevie Ybarra's sister."

A pause. "Yeah?"

"I want to know where he is."

"Stevie and I don't go together anymore."

"Well, would you have any idea where he might be?"

No response.

"Please," Rachel said.

"How come?"

"Because I'm his sister, why do you think?"

"Hey, you don't have to—"

"I'm sorry," Rachel interrupted. "I'm just concerned about him."

Another pause. "Me too," Marlene said finally.

"Why?"

"Well, he's sort of been hanging out with a guy."

"Who?"

"I don't really want to say."

"Please. I won't say anything."

"Promise?"

"Promise."

"Well," Marlene said cautiously, "a guy named Raimundo Montoya."

"Who's he?"

"He's . . . sort of a gangbanger," Marlene said. "Into drugs."

The news sent waves of shock and pain through Rachel. She knew Stevie had been drifting, that he was covering up an inner anger. He would never talk to her about it and now had obviously found his solace elsewhere.

"Do you think Stevie is using?" Rachel said.

A long pause this time, then Marlene said, "Yeah. That's why I broke up with him. We fought."

"Do you think he's with this Montoya now?"

"Probably."

"Can you tell me where?"

"I don't know for sure," Marlene said, "but they like to hang out at the park."

Rachel knew that would be Derry Park, on the far side of town. Not a nice place, even during the day.

"Thanks," Rachel said.

"Hey."

"Yes?"

"Don't say anything, okay? These guys, they do some bad stuff."

"I won't."

It took her ten minutes of excessive speed to reach Derry Park. She drove slowly around the perimeter, looking into the park, seeing only the shadows of trees standing silently like alien life forms on a dark planet. The only light came from the sand area, where a row of swings sat empty and motionless. A single figure, a man in a dirty army coat and bare feet, lay in the sand, passed out or asleep.

Rachel continued around the park until she got to the far side. There she found a cluster of picnic tables. And gathered around one table was a group of four or five men. She paused and watched and saw a red dot glow, diminish, and then a moment later glow again in a different location. A pot party, no doubt.

With a deep breath Rachel turned off her car, got out, and approached the group. The pungent smell of marijuana filled her nostrils.

She scanned the darkened faces as she got closer. At the end of the picnic table was the one she recognized.

"Stevie," she said.

He looked at her with shock, though it seemed a labored surprise that struggled against the fog of his condition.

"What are you doing here?" he spat.

"Who is this *chiquita?*" a voice said.

"Stevie, come home with me," Rachel said.

"Stevie, come home with me," another voice echoed sarcastically.

"Get outta here!" Stevie yelled.

"You're coming with me," said Rachel.

"He don't want to go with you," the first voice said.

Rachel took a step toward the voice. He was sitting on the corner of the picnic table. "Are you Montoya?"

Silence pervaded as all the shadows seemed to look her way. Rachel saw his eyes, reflecting a distant streetlight. They seemed to have no color.

Rachel said, "You the one supplying this stuff?"

"Won't you join us?" said Montoya, holding a joint out to her. The other shadows tittered.

"Leave my brother alone," Rachel said.

Montoya took a drag on the joint. He held the smoke in his lungs for a long moment, then blew the smoke toward Rachel's face.

Rachel coughed at the acrid smoke, at the same time sensing the shadows closing in around her. Her first thought was to run, but her instincts, forged over years of life in the barrio, told her that would be useless. Better to stand and put up a front. Attitude mattered among this kind.

"If you don't leave him alone," Rachel said, "I'll go to the cops."

Montoya's wide mouth opened in a huge smile, his teeth flashing like weapons. "The cops are my friends, *chica*. We get high together."

His friends laughed. Rachel glanced at Stevie, who had his head down. Maybe this Montoya was right. Maybe Stevie wanted it this way, and she should leave him alone. It was his life. But she knew she would never leave him alone.

"Stevie, come on," she said.

"No," said her brother.

Montoya kept smiling. He slipped off the picnic table and, holding the joint to Rachel's face, said, "Chill, baby. Take some."

Rachel pulled her head back in revulsion. Someone grabbed her hair and pushed her head forward. She tried to spin around, but hands like vices gripped both her arms. At least two, maybe three were holding her now.

"Just a little hit," Montoya said. "Come on now."

She felt the soggy end of the joint on her lower lip. Shaking vigorously, she managed only to move her head a few inches. Montoya assaulted her with the cigarette again. He was laughing.

Suddenly Montoya was jerked away. "Leave her alone," Stevie said.

"She wants to play," Montoya answered.

"Let her go."

"Shut up." Montoya put a hand in Stevie's chest and pushed him so hard he fell down. Stevie grunted and then emitted a low, guttural shriek. He scampered to his feet and charged Montoya.

Those holding Rachel let go, rushing forward. Bodies seemed to be everywhere, spinning and jumping like some violent whirlwind, focused on a single target—her brother. Without thinking she threw herself on someone and pulled at him. He struck out with his elbow and hit her ribs, shooting fire through her body. She collapsed on the ground, holding her side and fighting for breath.

The melee stopped as quickly as it had started. Rachel got to her knees and saw a mirror image—Stevie, too, was on his knees, only he was being held down by three gangbangers. Raimundo Montoya was pointing a gun to Stevie's head.

"You want some of this?" he said.

"Don't!" Rachel screamed.

Montoya looked at her. "You want your brother, huh? You want his brains?"

Horrified, Rachel tried to get up. A hot poker jabbed her ribs. She doubled over.

"Don't mess with me when I'm gettin' high," she heard Montoya say. "It makes me a little crazy."

"Come on, man," Stevie said. It sounded to Rachel like he was crying. She looked up and saw Montoya pressing the gun in Stevie's ear.

"Smoke him," a voice said.

Then there was silence, like the quiet before an execution by firing squad. It was broken by a distant siren. Rachel thought she saw Montoya draw back the trigger.

And then he pulled the gun away. "He's my brother," Montoya said. "I don't smoke my brother." He turned toward Rachel and pointed the gun at her, smiling. "But you're not my brother."

Rachel was startled by a hand on her shoulder. "You okay?" Toni Galvan said.

"Yes," Rachel said. "I was zoning there for a minute."

"Good thing I caught you at it before Lakewood."

"What's up?"

"A bunch of us are going to Olivera Street for dinner, sort of debrief the first day. Want to join us?"

"Sure," said Rachel. "That would be nice."

"Great. We'll gather in Ron's office at five. See you then."

Rachel went back to the books, but concentrating was hard. She found herself watching the clock, wanting five o'clock to come.

CHAPTER SIX

JAROSLAV SUPEVSKY took a small piece of *skavar* bread and spread some caviar across it. He held it to his mouth and paused a moment, getting ready to savor it. Good caviar should never be rushed, he believed. It was one of life's greatest pleasures.

A soft evening breeze blew across the bow of Supevsky's yacht, floating a mile offshore. The flickering lights along Newport Beach were dancing in the dark, and the only illumination for Supevsky was a single lamp near the stairs to the fly bridge. He opened his mouth and took a long, lingering bite, closing his eyes as he did.

"Ah," he said. "Nothing like the best."

He finished his morsel, then prepared another. This one he held out to the man sitting in another deck chair. The man took it.

Supevsky lifted a bottle of Dom Perignon out of a silver ice bucket and filled two champagne glasses. He handed one to the man and took the other for himself.

Lifting his glass, Supevsky said, "To America," and then he drank. He meant it, too, in the way that so many of his predecessors would have—not in the patriotic sense, but in the sense of opportunity, as a land with rich, golden soil for those who had the cunning to exploit it. He knew he had that cunning and always had.

Back in the old Soviet system, when he was an underground millionaire in Georgia, Supevsky had risen quickly in the black market as a fabric manufacturer. At the age of only twenty-seven he had already established his safety net—a web of public figures, party officials, and local police whom he bribed regularly.

By the time he was forty, he was ready to use his leverage with these people (the unimaginative might have called this blackmail) to get himself appointed as Minister of Light Industry. He was not only a wealthy entrepreneur but a well-placed politician as well.

Jaroslav Supevsky knew how to get his way.

The Communist party was impressed with him. It obviously knew about his machinations, but he was able to do many favors in furtherance of the party line. One such favor was the quick elimination of undesirable elements.

Supevsky arranged his first murder in 1981. The foreman at a local mill was making a move at becoming a *shabashnichestvo*, a self-employed black marketer. The man had apparently done his homework, as he was approaching many of the same people Supevsky had paid off. One of them was a constable who told Supevsky that this new man was willing to spend a lot of money to make a place for himself.

"We cannot support both of you," the constable warned. "It would not be tolerated. Unless this situation is settled soon we will all be in the queue for the gulag." It was a less than subtle directive for Supevsky to do something.

He did. Supevsky was easily able to find a policeman who, for a price and a nice fur coat for his wife, was able to dispatch the encroacher with two bullets in the back of the head. The body was taken to one of the "disappearing fields" where it became fertilizer.

That had been a particular thrill for Supevsky. It was not simply that he had killed a competitor nor that he got some sadistic pleasure out of it. It was that he discovered he was so good at this aspect of *shabaskniki*. He would prove just how good over the next several years.

Ironically, it was his very success that led to his collapse. When the smell of inevitability hit the air and everyone knew that the USSR would soon become a relic of the past, it was the ensconced establishment that had to scurry for opportunity. And there was one already in place—the black market itself. This would become, under the euphemism of the new order, private enterprise. Private enterprise brings with it competition. The greatest competition came from the previously successful, and not many were as successful as Jaroslav Supevsky.

When one of Supevsky's fabric mills mysteriously erupted into flames, Supevsky knew it was time to spread his wings and fly.

Just two weeks later he alighted in the Russian enclave of Brighton Beach, where he immediately began putting his skills to work once again.

That was over nine years ago. In the near decade since, Supevsky had risen to heights he had never experienced before. And this was only the beginning.

Soon the army of another country would be involved in the enterprise. It made the taste of the champagne sweeter.

"This is how to do business," Supevsky said. "I imagine the czars did it this way, don't you?"

The man, whom Supevsky knew only as Grigory, said nothing.

"Tell me about it," Supevsky said.

Grigory's voice was low, impassive. "It was as you wanted it."

"Did he scream?"

"He tried."

"Did he beg for mercy?"

"He asked to see you."

"And what did you tell him?"

"Nothing. He knew."

Supevsky took another sip of champagne. "If I were sentimental, I might feel sorry for him. You know why he had to be eliminated, don't you?"

"I don't ask why."

"Ever?"

"That's not my job."

"Perhaps that's why you're so good. KGB trained you well. No questions, just results, eh?"

Supevsky prepared another piece of bread and caviar and held it out to Grigory, who put up his hand in refusal. Shrugging, Supevsky popped it in his own mouth. He began to speak before he swallowed. "How long have you worked over here?"

"Four years."

"You still work in Europe?"

"On occasion."

"They tell me, the ones who put us in touch, that you have the ability to disappear. Is that true?"

"Almost."

"What do you mean?"

"I am already invisible."

"I understand," Supevsky said, nodding. "No one sees you if you don't want to be seen."

"Yes," Grigory said.

"Your English is excellent, by the way. Another part of your training?"

"My mother grew up in London."

"Ah."

Supevsky poured more champagne for himself, feeling a warm glow. He said, "The money has been transferred to your account in Antigua."

"Good."

"I've put in a little more, as a retainer."

"Why?"

"I want you to be on call. The federal government has been, shall we say, sniffing around. They have this idea that I am a bad person." Supevsky laughed. "Do you think I'm bad, Grigory?"

"That is a term I never use, except with regard to personal taste."

Supevsky raised an eyebrow. "Now that's interesting. No moral judgments?"

"Moral judgments suppose a moral reality."

"You're a philosopher!" Supevsky said with a certain degree of pleasure.

Grigory seemed to relax a little. "I studied philosophy at university."

"And did you like it?"

"It was as much nonsense as theology. I came to the conclusion that everyone had it wrong, except perhaps the French existentialists."

"They believed life is absurd, didn't they?"

"Don't you?"

Supevsky pondered this for a moment. "I wouldn't call it absurd."

Grigory eyed him remorselessly. "What other word describes a world built upon morality, yet where moral reality does not exist?"

"I like you, Grigory," Supevsky said. "You are exactly the kind of man I can work with. Here, have more champagne." This time Grigory accepted.

Two of Supevsky's bodyguards stepped out of the cabin. "Boat coming," one of them said.

Supevsky nodded and waved his guards to bring the boat alongside. "Our guest," he said to Grigory. In that moment he truly did feel like a Roman emperor aboard his ship, with emissaries from another country coming to him to pay tribute. He liked that idea. He wasn't all that far from being an emperor anyway, he thought.

What, after all, was an empire? It wasn't raw land anymore. That was the old days, when men fought hand to hand with spears and shields, bloodying themselves over tufts of dirt and sod. Now land didn't matter. That was all taken up, distracting politicians who entertained the quaint thought that they actually controlled something other than their own reelection campaigns. Empires now were made of money, and power was exercised by directing its flow.

The boat cut its engine. Supevsky listened to the footsteps as the visitors clambered up the stairs and onto the deck. Without getting up from his chair or even turning around, Supevsky said, "Good evening, General."

General Alejandro Vega stepped into Supevsky's sight line and nodded. He was short and muscular and wore a pencil-thin mustache that arced from one corner of his mouth to the other. He wore a *guayavera*, blue jeans and black boots. Two of his men, dressed in the uniform of the Mexican army, stood behind him.

"Take a load off, as we Americans like to say." Supevsky offered a chair. Then he turned to his bodyguard and told him to take the general's assistants below deck and offer them tequila.

"Nice to see you again, General," Supevsky said.

"The same," Vega said in his terse manner. He looked toward Grigory on his left.

"An associate," Supevsky said. "He just listens."

Vega shrugged. Supevsky poured champagne into a glass. It was only half full before the bottle ran out. Supevsky turned to one of his guards and snapped his fingers. The guard took the empty bottle and disappeared below deck.

Handing the champagne to Vega, Supevsky said, "Appreciate the visit. It's about time we had another talk."

Nodding, Vega drank his champagne.

"I'm a little concerned about our supply being interrupted," Supevsky said.

"What do you mean?" the general asked.

"I mean the pressure in Juarez."

Stiffening slightly, Vega said, "I can assure you, there will be no interruption."

"You have a very ambitious prosecutor down there."

"Trujillo."

"Yes, the woman. She has the support of the people, I understand."

"That situation is being taken care of."

"How?"

Vega took another sip of the sparkling wine. "It will happen this way. She will come to a red light in her American car. A motorcycle with two men will pull next to her. She will be shot. And the blame will be put on the drug cartel."

"You are sure about that?"

"It is the style they use. No one will suspect that these men are from the army."

"And what does the cartel say?"

"They go along with it. What choice do they have? If they want to continue to market across the border, they need our help. This was my plan, by the way."

"I like the way you think, General. But thinking and doing are two different things."

Vega's expression changed, growing hard. "You doubt my abilities?"

"The Mexican army is not the Rockettes."

"Como?" said the general, lapsing into Spanish.

Supevsky enjoyed the moment. He was confusing Vega even as he was angering him. Keeping him off balance. That was what he was good at. His guard returned to the deck with a full bottle of champagne, setting it in the silver bucket. Supevsky dismissed him with a nod.

"The Rockettes," Supevsky explained, "are an American institution. They are the dancers at Radio City Music Hall in New York City. You know, all in a line, kicking their legs at the same time."

The general looked confused.

"Well," Supevsky continued, "you do not stay in line. You mess up."

"Excuse me," Vega snapped. "We do not mess up."

"Perhaps your definition of messing up is not the same as mine."

The two men stared at each other for a long moment. Vega said, "We will continue to provide you with the product. But now I will question you. Can we depend on your people?"

Supevsky shrugged. "Of course."

"You have had legal trouble."

"An investigation, nothing more. Nothing near me."

"I am wondering how long you can hold up against your federal agents. They don't seem to like the drug business."

"I can handle this end. They have no witnesses. And even if they did have one, it would not be for long."

"How can you be sure?"

Supevsky smiled, then nodded to Grigory, who had been silent throughout. Seeing the nod, Vega turned to his left. In that instant Grigory removed a switchblade from his pocket, released the blade, and held it to the General's neck.

Wide-eyed, Vega said, "What are you doing?"

"This is a demonstration only," Supevsky said.

"Enough," said Vega, his head tilting backward.

Supevsky nodded at Grigory, who withdrew the blade. "Now," said Supevsky, "if we can get to the throat of a general of the Mexican army, what trouble will one civilian witness be?"

The juke was pumping traditional Mariachi, and all the tables were filled. The restaurant held an equal mix of locals from the east side and professionals from the west, a sure sign the food was good. Rachel took in a deep, warm smell of the place as she entered with Ron Ashby and

Toni Galvan. It smelled like her home in the days when her mom was alive.

A group of externs waved from a large table in the center. The trio made their way in and joined them. Several conversations were going on at once. Everything blended into the general cacophony of the Friday night dinner crowd.

"So how'd your first day go?" Toni asked Rachel.

"A lot like law school," Rachel said. "Research and writing."

Ashby leaned over from Rachel's right. "The boring stuff," he said.

"We had this conversation earlier," Rachel explained.

"Yes," Ashby said, "I was explaining to Ms. Ybarra here that I intend to make a name for myself. You don't do that writing briefs."

"You can do it *wearing* briefs," Toni said. "How many underwear models have there been from the U.S. Attorney's Office?"

Rachel found herself laughing. It felt good. A waiter appeared at their end of the table. "Something to drink for you?"

"Three margaritas," said Ashby.

"Not for me," Rachel said.

"I'm buying."

"No thanks. Iced tea, please."

"Iced tea!" Ashby practically shouted. "Okay, two maggies and one iced tea. And bring me a shot of Cuervo on the side."

"My, my," Toni said, "the things you get to know about your coworkers."

Ashby held his hands out. "You two want to relax or what?" Looking at Rachel, he said, "You don't drink?"

"No," she answered.

"Anything?"

"Iced tea."

"I mean anything that'll put hair on your chest."

Toni made a sound like air escaping a balloon. "Exactly what do they teach at Berkeley?"

With apparent sincerity Ashby said, "Responsible drinking." He paused and reached for a tortilla chip. "So what is it with you," he asked Rachel, "a health thing or a religious thing, what?"

"Both," she said.

Ashby raised his eyebrows. "So what are you?"

"Excuse me?"

"You know, religious right, Mormon, what?"

"Your tact is amazing," Toni interjected.

"Hey, I learned a long time ago you go right for the jugular vein. It works in court."

"We're socializing," Toni said.

"It's all right," said Rachel.

"So?" Ashby said.

"I'm a Christian," Rachel said.

"Now *that's* fascinating," Ashby said.

"How so?"

"Do you believe only Christians go to heaven?" There was an edge in his voice, almost as if he were closing in on a hostile witness.

"Come on, Ron," Toni said.

He leaned back in his chair and said, "If she doesn't want to talk about it, fine."

"I don't mind," Rachel said, "if you really want to have a conversation."

"I do. So tell me what happens to Hindus, Buddhists, Muslims, and people like that."

"You forgot talk-show hosts," Toni said. Ron Ashby did not laugh. He waited for an answer.

"I don't presume to make God's judgments for him," Rachel said. "Jesus showed mercy to a thief on a cross. I wouldn't have predicted that."

"You're not answering the question."

Feeling testy, Rachel said, "I'm just not giving you the answer you want."

"She's got you there," Toni said.

"Baloney," said Ashby. "I want her to admit it. All Hindus are going to hell, right?"

"I think what you want is a stereotyped answer."

"Just answer the question."

"Look," said Rachel. "What happens when there's a dispute over the law? Where do the judges look?"

Ashby blinked for a moment, then said, "I don't follow you."

"Good thing," said Toni with a laugh.

Rachel said, "When there's a question about the meaning of a statute, where is the argument focused?"

"All right," said Ashby. "Legislative intent. You try to figure out what the lawmakers intended the statute to mean. Easy. So what's your point?"

"You want to read the law, in this case the Bible, in a slanted way. But you have to expand your vision. You have to look at the legislative intent."

"Where is it? I'd like to see it."

"It's found throughout the Scripture. God's intent is mercy. You can't read the Bible without seeing it."

"So?"

"So we can be assured that people will not be lost on some technicality. We can trust God to be a righteous judge who will not make a mistake. And he has given us a way to be assured of salvation."

"Jesus, right? But what if you don't accept that angle? Are you lost forever?"

"That's a question I can't answer. I can only offer the same assurances the Bible offers."

The waiter came back with their drinks. Ashby, scowling, picked up his shot glass of tequila and downed it immediately. Then he took a sip of his margarita. "So it's that way or the highway, right?"

"Let's look at it from another legal angle," Rachel said. "You remember your Contracts Law?"

"I should. I got the AmJur Award."

"All right. Then you know that before there is a contract both parties must agree on the terms."

"Of course."

"So if one party makes an offer, there is no contract until the other party accepts the terms of the offer."

"Yes, Professor."

"But what if the other party, instead of accepting the terms of the offer, changes them, and then says, 'I accept this.' Is there a contract?"

"No. It's a counteroffer."

"And there is no contract unless the original party accepts the terms of the counteroffer."

"So what's your point?"

"God is offering us a contract. He says that if certain terms are accepted, he will provide a certain result. Guaranteed. The main item to be accepted is Jesus."

Ashby took a drink of his margarita and shrugged.

"Now," Rachel continued, "anyone who does not accept Jesus is making a counteroffer to God, changing the terms of God's contract. So is there an agreement? No. Not unless God accepts those changes."

"Will he?" Ashby asked.

"I don't know. No one knows. Every Christian, including me, is acting as an agent for God. An agent cannot change the material terms of the contract. If someone wants to make a counteroffer, there is no way I can say he has reached an agreement with God. But I can say that if you meet God's terms, you definitely *will* have an agreement. And that leaves the ball strictly in your court."

"Hey," Toni said, "that was good. I have never, ever, heard it put that way."

"I don't know," Ashby said.

"Come on," Toni insisted, "she's made a pretty good case here."

"Yeah? What about in a real courtroom?"

Rachel cocked her head. "Meaning?"

"You think a Christian can be a good prosecutor?"

"Of course."

"What about a tough case where meek and mild won't do it then?"

Smiling, Rachel said, "I've never been described as meek and mild."

"I'm serious."

"So am I."

"We'll see," Ashby said. "Rumor has it Lakewood is looking for someone to work with him on this Russian case."

"The one we heard about this morning?" Toni asked.

"Yeah," Ashby continued. "Lakewood wants to start a mentoring type deal, and he's going to let his assistant be involved in practically every aspect of the case. In other words, it's a big deal. And I want in on it."

"I bet you do," Toni said.

"Don't you?"

"I'm more into major frauds," Toni said.

Ashby looked at Rachel. "You?"

"I wouldn't mind helping put a gangster away," Rachel said.

"Sort of a Christian versus the devil thing, huh?" Ashby said, a slight tinge of mockery in his voice.

"Yeah," Rachel said distantly. Her mind flashed quickly back to the face of Raimundo Montoya, the eyes that had no humanity, filled with evil. She had last seen that face up close in a courtroom in Orange County. He saw her that day as he was brought in, saw her sitting with the crowd, and he picked her out immediately, as if he knew she was going to be there. And he smiled at her.

"No," Rachel said, "I wouldn't mind it a bit."

Thankfully the dinners arrived at that moment, and Ashby was distracted from his theological cross-examinations. He got involved in a conversation with an extern on his other side.

Toni said to Rachel, "You did good."

"Thanks."

"I'd like to hear more about your beliefs sometime. I'm interested in all that."

"What's your background?" Rachel said, relieved to be on the questioning side for a change.

Toni took a bit of tostada, then said through the lettuce, "I'm New York Jew by way of Georgetown Jesuit. How's that for a mix?"

"Pretty eclectic. What did that do for you?"

"Not much. My family wasn't religious, but I was always thinking about God. Then I got to Georgetown. I took a freshman religion class called 'The Problem of God.' "

Rachel frowned. "Sounds pretty ominous."

"It was weird. The guy who taught it had some crazy ideas, including stuff I thought was right out of green monster."

"Green monster?"

"Left field. At Fenway Park in Boston, the left field wall is called the green monster."

"Ah."

"Anyway, the guy was teaching something about God having two poles, you know, like the North Pole and the South Pole."

"Excuse me?"

"Exactly. One of his poles is outside the cosmos. The other pole is inside and is part of the cosmic process."

With a shake of her head, Rachel said, "It sounds like your professor was somewhere outside the cosmos."

Toni nodded. "That's what I thought. Anyway, I haven't been real clear about God ever since. Which is why I liked what you said earlier to Mr. Charm." She gave a nod of her head toward Ron Ashby's back. "To be quite honest with you, I haven't known many Christians as articulate as you."

At the moment, Rachel had just stuffed a load of refried beans in her mouth, looking anything but articulate. The absurdity was not lost on either of them. They both laughed.

Rachel swallowed. "I'm back to normal now."

"But you're sold on God, right?" Toni asked, seemingly very interested.

"That's one way to put it."

"Don't you find life a little more uncertain than that?"

"I'm not sure I understand."

Toni munched a chip. "I'm not sure either. Thanks, Georgetown! But I guess what I'm asking is whether your faith makes your life any more predictable than the rest of us."

Rachel thought for a moment. "I think the way I'd put it is that life tests us. Christianity doesn't promise a life without trouble. But it does promise that when trouble comes, we have one who is there to help us."

"Has that turned out to be true for you?"

"Yes. God helped me through a very dark time when my little brother died."

Toni nodded. "Well, keep me posted, will you?"

"About what?"

"The next time God helps you. I'd like to keep tabs."

"You got it," Rachel said, wondering how soon that next time would be.

CHAPTER SEVEN

JEFF BUNNELL said, "Nice neighborhood."

"Nice for a hit guy," Sam Zagorsky commented. "Hardly seems right."

The two agents were sitting in a parked car, a couple of Subway sandwiches on their laps. The afternoon was a pleasant one, with a few fluffy clouds hanging in the sky. If they hadn't been waiting for a killer, Jeff would have thought it a great way to spend a lazy afternoon.

Part of that was his partner. Jeff liked Sam, even though he was his opposite in many ways. Sam was swarthy, almost always looked like he needed a shave, and his clothes hung on him like vegetable sacks. Despite that, Zagorsky knew his stuff. He had almost twelve years with the Bureau. Jeff felt confident being hooked up with him. When it came to street practicalities, Sam would be a good teacher. He might even be a pleasant companion if he didn't always keep to himself outside of work. But Jeff understood. Sam was a family man.

"What made you get into this line of work anyway?" Sam asked.

"I saw the movie," Jeff said.

Sam smiled and took a huge bite of his sandwich. "How old were you?" he asked, though the words were muffled.

"Seven. My hometown station had something called the 'Wonderful World of Movies,' where the same movie would be shown each night for a week. One week it was *The FBI Story.* I watched it every night."

"Seven times?"

"Eight. They showed it twice on Sunday."

"I've never met anyone in the Bureau who's seen it that many times."

"I'll bet Hoover did."

"Hoover did a lot of things I'd rather not talk about."

Jeff took a bite of his spicy Italian sub and thought for a moment. "You know the part that really got to me?"

"What?"

"The very beginning, where Nick Adams blows up the plane his mother is on."

"Oh, yeah, where he gets her to take out an insurance policy right before she gets on the plane."

"Yeah. I thought, man, this guy is cold. And he thinks he's going to get away with it. But then the FBI steps in. They analyze the scraps of metal from the plane, trace the elements, narrow the suspects, and boom, next thing you know they've got Nick Adams. And as they're carting him off, he tells them to send his mail to hell."

Sam laughed. "Great moments in movie history."

"So it was that and the other cases Jimmy Stewart solved. I got caught up in it. I thought it was neat."

"Neat?"

"Really neat."

"And now?"

Jeff paused. He looked out the front window without seeing anything. A haze of images, all of them abstract but plucked from memory, floated in front of him. "It's not like the movies."

"No," Sam said, "it isn't."

The two men ate in silence for several minutes. "What about you, Sam?" Jeff asked finally. "What got you into the Bureau?"

"I was studying economics at Florida State. I thought about going into accounting. A friend of mine, a real gung ho guy, football player, said he was going to apply to the FBI. He asked me to do it too. It was a lark. So we both sent in preliminary applications. We both got interviews. I got the job and he didn't. Go figure."

"Whatever happened to him?"

Sam paused for a short laugh. "He went into sporting goods. The guy is made out of money now." Sam stuffed the last part of his sandwich into his mouth.

"Funny how things work out," Jeff muttered, feeling like an idiot for mouthing a cliché. But he had nothing left to say. He had the feeling Sam wanted the conversation to end.

Twenty minutes dragged by, then thirty. A couple of kids on bikes stopped on the opposite sidewalk and stared at them for awhile. Jeff smiled and waved. The kids rode off without waving back.

Then Sam said, "Here's our boy." Jeff looked up and saw the maroon Nissan, the one described in their report, pull into the driveway at the house across the street. The two were out of their car before the Nissan was turned off.

A thickset man with a mustache got out of the driver's side. Sam said, "Paul Dedenok?"

The man turned quickly and for a moment looked like he might turn and run. Jeff saw a fear in his eyes and then saw it vanish. That alone made him suspicious. An innocent man being approached by two strangers would have kept that look of fear.

"Yes?" Dedenok said.

"My name is Sam Zagorsky. This is Jeff Bunnell. We're with the Federal Bureau of Investigation." Sam showed Dedenok his credential.

"FBI?" Dedenok said.

"We'd like to ask you some questions if we may," Sam said.

"Most certainly," said Dedenok. He smiled, but his cheek quivered.

"May we come inside?"

"Am I under arrest?"

"No. This is purely voluntary on your part."

The man looked from Zagorsky to Jeff and back again. He had his hand in his pocket and was jangling his change. "Of course," he said. "May I ask what this is concerning?"

"I'd rather not talk about it out here," Sam said.

"All right," Dedenok said as he walked toward his front door. The agents followed.

The house was well kept, with blue trim over white. A small flower garden blossomed near the porch. Jeff noticed a gossamer spiderweb spanning a flower to the front window.

Inside the house was dark. Heavy curtains were drawn across the windows. Decoration was sparse. It seemed a Spartan existence, functional but no more. The furniture was basic, like a motel's. Dedenok led the two agents into the living room where he turned and said, "So?"

"May we sit?" Sam said.

"Of course," said Dedenok, motioning to the sofa. He sat himself in a chair by the opposite wall. He placed his hands on his knees, as if he couldn't find a more comfortable spot for them. To Jeff he looked like a nervous man trying very hard not to appear nervous.

"Mr. Dedenok," Sam began, "do you know a man named Jaroslav Supevsky?"

Dedenok frowned. "Supevsky? No, I don't believe so."

"He's quite well-known in the Russian community."

Dedenok shrugged his shoulders. Sam said, "Odessa Importing?"

Dedenok shook his head.

Sam looked at Jeff, then back at Dedenok. "Do you know a man named Dimitri Chekhov?"

Again Dedenok shook his head.

Sam said, "He owned a limousine service that was quite profitable, in Hollywood."

"No," Dedenok said.

"Mr. Dedenok, what do you do for a living?"

Jeff watched as Dedenok's face turned from feigned ignorance to confusion. By switching gears in midstream, Sam was throwing Dedenok a curve. Jeff admired the timing.

"I am . . . a financial consultant."

Sam nodded. "Might you have ever worked for Supevsky?"

"No."

"Chekhov?"

"No."

"You seem pretty certain."

"I am certain about my clients. What is this all about, if I may ask?"

"Two nights ago Dimitri Chekhov and his wife were murdered. Their bodies were burned in a fire. You may have read about it in the papers."

"I don't read the newspapers."

"Makes it pretty hard to keep up on the financial world, doesn't it?"

Dedenok started to say something, stopped, then said, "I read reports."

"I see," Sam said. "Let me try one more name. Kolya Medilich. Ring a bell?"

For an instant Jeff was sure that name recognition flashed through Dedenok's eyes. But he said, "No."

"Medilich is being held in the Metropolitan Detention Center. He's under indictment for murder."

Shaking his head, Dedenok said, "I don't know him."

"He seems to know you, Mr. Dedenok," Sam said.

Dedenok put both his hands on his knees and squeezed them. "I don't understand."

Sam reached in his pocket, pulled out an investigator's notebook, and flipped it open. "I questioned Medilich last night. I asked him if he knew anything about the Chekhov murder." Sam looked at the notebook. "He told us a little story about Chekhov's dealings with Supevsky. And then he mentioned your name, Mr. Dedenok."

Sam looked up from the notebook and stared directly at Dedenok. Jeff glanced over at Sam and noticed the notebook. The page Sam had turned to was blank.

"That's a mystery," Dedenok said. "A mystery."

"Shall I tell you what he said, Mr. Dedenok?"

The man stood up. Jeff tensed, waiting for him to make a move. He didn't.

"This is all very disturbing," Dedenok said. "I am being accused. . . ."

"You are not being accused, Mr. Dedenok," Sam said. "At least not yet."

Dedenok nodded. His eyes darted from one side of the room to the other. Jeff watched him closely, especially his hands.

"Do you wish to revise your statement to us?" Sam said.

Dedenok didn't answer.

"Mr. Dedenok?"

Slowly, deliberately, Dedenok turned his back on the agents, and then he bent over. Jeff's first thought was that the man was sick, but then he saw Dedenok's hands reaching under the seat cushion. Springing to his feet, Jeff charged across room. Dedenok's hand emerged with a pistol. Jeff leapt at him, like a football player at a tackling dummy. Only this dummy could move and was quick. Dedenok's hand, the one with the gun, pounded into Jeff's stomach. As air left him, Jeff was aware of the two of them going down.

Jeff felt a momentary blackness. The butt end of the gun had hit him in the solar plexus. His mind told him to reach out and grab Dedenok's arms, but his body wouldn't let him. Jeff thought he sensed Sam grabbing Dedenok. He felt Dedenok being pulled away from him.

Fighting for air, Jeff rolled onto his back. He tried to focus his eyes and saw his partner struggling with Dedenok. Then he looked down and saw the pistol on the floor. He scrambled for it, reached, and felt it in his grasp.

A body fell on top of him. Jeff wrapped his arms around the body and flipped it over, wrestler style. That's when he saw it was Sam. Blood was streaming from Sam's nose.

Jeff heard the sound of steps running away. Light suddenly streamed into the house, and Jeff knew it was from the open front door. He struggled to his feet and ran toward the door, pulling his gun from his shoulder holster.

When he got out the door he heard a car door slam and an engine rev up. He ran down the walkway to the corner of the garage. Tires squealed. Dedenok was in his car, tearing backward out of the driveway.

Jeff dropped to a knee and aimed at the front tires. He fired once, twice, a third time. The left front tire of Dedenok's car seemed to explode. The car did not stop. Burning rubber, it backed up into the street, almost doing a 180 before reversing direction. Jeff ran to the end of the driveway, dropped again, and aimed at the rear tire as the car sped by. He nailed it on the second shot.

Sam was at his shoulder now. The crippled car continued down the street, weaving. Jeff took off running with Sam close behind.

The street took a curve almost immediately, and Dedenok's car squealed around it, wisps of black smoke shooting up from the tires. Jeff raced across the sidewalk, cutting out the curve, picking up much needed distance on the car, which, inexplicably, was accelerating.

An old man watering his lawn shouted "Hey!" as Jeff ran past. Jeff gave him a quick glance, then saw him drop the hose and run back toward his house.

Dedenok was starting to pull away. Looking beyond the car, Jeff saw the two kids on bikes he had waved at before. They were in the street, peddling toward Dedenok. "Look out!" Jeff yelled. "Get off the street!"

The two young faces looked up. The car headed straight for them, Dedenok not seeing them or, more likely, not caring.

Jeff pushed himself to run faster. But he was helpless as the car, thumping along at increasing speed, shot toward the two frightened boys.

One of the boys veered off toward the sidewalk, hit the curb, and fell on some grass. The other wobbled, not knowing which way to go. He screamed.

Dedenok's car did not even slow. It rammed the boy on the bike with a sickening thud and crunch of metal. The boy was tossed in the air like a rag doll, arms and legs splayed, falling with hardly a sound on the hard asphalt surface.

Jeff felt his breath leave him.

The collision sent Dedenok's car veering left. It hit the curb, jumped it, ran up a nicely manicured lawn and straight into a small orange tree planted in the middle. The orange tree cracked but didn't fall.

"Check on him!" Jeff yelled over his shoulder to Sam, indicating the boy in the street. He ran past the motionless child, eyes wide, lungs bursting. No motion from within the car. He pointed his gun at Dedenok's head and moved toward him.

"Out of the car!" he screamed so loud his throat hurt.

Dedenok did not move. Was he stunned? Or reaching for a weapon? Jeff noticed a few people appearing in doorways in the houses, some coming outside toward the car.

"Stay back!" Jeff yelled. "FBI! Stay back!" Turning again toward Dedenok he repeated, "Get out of the car! Now!"

He saw that Dedenok's eyes were open, staring straight ahead, but the man made no move to open the car door.

Jeff flung the door open, grabbed as much of Dedenok's shirt as he could, and pulled him from the car, slamming him to the ground. Jeff brought his knee down on Dedenok's back with full force. Dedenok grunted weakly.

Jeff reached for the handcuffs on his belt then pulled Dedenok's right arm behind his back. Dedenok did not resist. Jeff cuffed the right wrist, then did the same thing with the left.

Jeff grabbed a handful of Dedenok's hair and pulled the man's head off the ground. Dedenok winced in pain and groaned.

Jeff put his mouth to Dedenok's ear. Through clenched teeth he said, "If that boy dies, I am personally going to blow your brains out. You hear me? I'm going to blow your brains out!" Jeff yanked the man's head back further. Dedenok groaned. Then Jeff slammed his head into the ground.

As he stood, Jeff felt the world spinning around him—a mad, suburban merry-go-round without music. Every muscle in his body was tense and extended, as if he were trying to grab onto the carousel to keep from flying off. He felt his hand twitch on his gun.

He was unaware how long he stood like that. He felt a hand on his shoulder and, with a guttural exhalation, spun away.

"You all right?" Sam said.

"Yeah, yeah," Jeff answered. "The boy? What about the boy?"

"Okay, I think," he said. "Broken arm at the worst. Lady's calling an ambulance."

Jeff nodded and turned. Sam said, "Jeff, you okay?"

Jeff waved his hand, said nothing, and walked slowly back toward Dedenok's car. He slowly placed his gun back in its shoulder holster. Light flashed behind his eyes like an explosion, tearing through his brain, leaving it wounded and exhausted, but most of all, remembering. More than anything Jeff did not want to remember. But he did.

The mall. The hostage.

The images pulsated through him, and he was powerless to stop them.

He balled his hand into a fist and brought it full force down on the hood of Dedenok's car. Then he burst into tears.

CHAPTER EIGHT

AS RACHEL DROVE SOUTH toward Montebello, the five o'clock commuter snarl all around her, she started to fear the talons. That was how she described the migraines she had suffered off and on since high school—like a bird's claws gripping her head. They always seemed to appear, to a greater or lesser degree, when she was going to see her father.

Tonight's visit was planned, though she didn't call first. It was best that way. If she called, her father would tell her not to bother, and if she showed up anyway, he'd be angry. The spontaneous visit at least had a chance to catch him in an even temper. These days that was all she could ask for.

As she got closer to her hometown, familiar landmarks flashed by. She recognized them subconsciously—the old drive-in theater, the Dairy Queen where she worked her first job, and Montebello High School. These were the memory markers of her childhood, the reminders of her childhood. She always felt like a schoolgirl when she drove down here. In this world she was always eight or nine years old, feeling again all the fear and confusion of a little girl whose mother had been taken away too soon.

She got off the freeway and drove five minutes to the small street where she grew up. The house was midblock in a working-class section that was still remarkably free from the blight of most other neighborhoods in the area. The folks here still viewed their homes with a certain pride. In fact, if there was any home that seemed to have worn more than the others, it was her own.

The small three-bedroom house was a faded blue. Rachel couldn't remember it ever being painted. Her father had talked about it, but when her mom died of cancer, he didn't talk about doing anything with the house again. He just seemed to patch things up when they fell apart, and sometimes not even then.

Rachel pulled into the driveway. Her father's pickup was in the carport. At least he was not out at The Boxcar, not yet.

Rachel was met by the strong smell of beans and beer when she walked in the front door. She heard canned laughter from the TV. She closed the door quietly behind her, took a deep breath, and walked into the living room.

Art Ybarra, in boxer shorts and T-shirt, sat on the sofa, a TV tray in front of him. The tray had a plate of food and a bottle of Dos Equis beer on it.

Art suddenly laughed at the TV, along with the taped hilarity of the studio audience. Then he glanced left and saw Rachel. "I didn't hear you come in," he said.

"Hi, Pop. How you doing?" Rachel dropped her purse on a chair and went to give her father a kiss. He didn't turn to her, so she kissed him on the head. She noticed another Dos Equis bottle lying empty on the floor.

"This Erkel, he's a funny guy," Art said, motioning to the TV.

Rachel sat on the end of the sofa. "I've got some news."

Art took a sip of his beer and did not look away from the TV.

"I got that job," she said.

"You know why he's funny?" Art said.

"Who?"

"Erkel."

"Pop, come on."

"Because he keeps trying."

"I'm working for the U.S. Attorney."

He picked up a fork and scooped up some beans.

"It's a great job, Pop, a real opportunity."

"What's so good about it?" He kept his eyes on the TV.

"I get a chance to do some good, solid work for the government," Rachel said. "It'll help me find a job when I graduate." She wanted him to understand, needed him to. He loaded another forkful of beans into his mouth, washing it down with beer. "You've got to eat better, Pop."

"I eat fine."

"When was the last time you had a checkup?"

He slammed his fork down on the tray. "How come you're always at me, huh? I take care of myself. I took care of you, didn't I? And your brother." Art Ybarra quickly grabbed his beer and finished it off with a long pull.

Slapping her knees, Rachel got up and walked quickly out of the room and into the kitchen. What was the use? Why had she even bothered? It was the same old tune, and her father seemed dead set against ever playing another. She knew what the heart of it was, and she despaired at ever getting to it.

A swarm of dirty dishes lay in the sink and on the counter. They smelled of old food and, of course, beer. A row of empty beer bottles lined the floor near the back porch. Needing to do something, anything, Rachel turned on the hot water and prepared to clean the dishes. She filled the sink with water and squirted in a jolt of dishwashing liquid. There was hardly any soap in the bottle, which was probably the only one he'd had in the house for a year. She closed her eyes and thought of how much she loved him and how much it hurt since he put up the wall.

As she washed the dishes, she thought of her mother, a hazy memory now. The kitchen was where Rachel always remembered her mother. It was her mother's domain. Rachel remembered her mother as having a radiant smile and a strong body—strong until the ravages of cancer took over. Rachel also had a memory of her mother as thin and weak and in a hospital bed, but thankfully that picture was fuzzy. The memory of her mother in the kitchen was what Rachel remembered most about her.

Rachel was almost finished with the dishes when she sensed her father in the doorway. He was staring at her. For a moment there was an awful silence, as if two strangers were meeting in the middle of a dark alley, wary and distrustful.

Then Art Ybarra said, "Nobody asked you to."

"Pop," Rachel said, "it needed to be done."

"I can take care of my own house." He stumbled toward the refrigerator, opened it, and grabbed another beer.

"You're drinking too much," Rachel said.

"Not your business." He walked out unsteadily.

Feeling pain behind her eyes, Rachel returned to the dishes and finished them, setting the last in the drip tray on the counter. She wiped her hands on a dishrag and went into the hallway where her old room was. The door was open. The room was empty, except for a bed without linens. It was as if someone had scraped all memory of her away, leaving nothing behind.

She walked further down the hall to the closed door, Stevie's room. She paused there, hearing her brother's voice, a six- or seven-year-old voice, calling to her. She could hear her name in the distant reaches of her memory—*Rachel, come play with me. . . . Rachel, help me draw a picture. . . . Rachel, why did Mama die?*

As if some antidote to despair might be found inside, Rachel opened the door to Stevie's room and turned on the light.

The room had not been altered since her brother died. His bed was made, and the pictures of athletes were still stapled to the wall. She recognized Jose Canseco. He had been Stevie's favorite player, the one he most wanted to be like.

The dresser was lined with rows of trophies from Little League and Pop Warner football, golden treasures of the happiest times in Stevie's life. For Rachel they were icons of another kind, reminders of what is left behind when drugs take hold of a life.

She reached for one of the trophies, the one she remembered Stevie had treasured most. It named him Athlete of the Year for his eighth-grade class. That was the year he socked a grand slam home run in the annual intraschool softball game. She remembered him rounding the bases, his fist in the air, a smile like a lighthouse beacon across his face. He had seen her in the stands and waved.

"Put that back."

Her father was at the door.

"I was just—"

"Put it back!"

Rachel placed the trophy back in its place.

"Why don't you just go now?" Art said.

"How long are we going to do this?" Rachel said.

"Just go."

"What do you want me to do, Pop?"

"Nothing."

"I can't bring Stevie back."

"Don't talk about it." He turned quickly and left.

Rachel followed him out. "Pop, don't walk away."

But he did. Rachel followed him into the living room. "I've got a life, too," she said.

Art sat on the sofa again, took the remote, and began changing channels.

"Can't you forgive me?" Rachel said.

Her father didn't answer. He looked straight ahead.

"Pop, will you talk to Manny?"

He shook his head.

"Can he at least come over?" she pleaded.

That's when he turned to her. "I don't want religion! Keep him away from here. And your grandmother, too!"

"Pop, please."

"Just get out," he said, his voice weak now, like a fighter ready to throw in the towel. Rachel tried to think of something to say, but her voice was paralyzed. No sound would come. She grabbed her purse and walked toward the door. She wanted to say, "I love you," but it suddenly seemed absurd to try.

She made no attempt to stop the tears as she got in her car and pulled away. It was dark now, and driving from the house was like escaping from one dreary place only to arrive at another. It was a place she didn't want to go, but there was no stopping it. It was as inevitable as the night itself.

It was the place in her recall where Stevie died, and where his killer stood trial.

It happened only a few miles from the house, near the all-night market. She was the one who got the call from the detective. She could still remember every word he spoke to her. "There's been a shooting. Esteban Ybarra. Are you related?"

Her father was not home, still out at the bar. Rachel threw on her clothes and drove to the scene. Already it was marked with yellow tape, illuminated by the flashing reds and blues of the police cars.

A detective named Kirby walked her to the body. Stevie might have been asleep, like some wine-soddened derelict, except that the side of his head was wet, next to a pool of dark blood.

Rachel opened her mouth. Only a whisper of a scream came out.

"Is that your brother?" Kirby asked.

Rachel nodded. "How?" she managed to say.

"We're looking into it. We have witnesses."

Rachel knelt by Stevie's feet. She closed her eyes, wept, and heard herself say, "I'm sorry, Stevie. I'm sorry."

Her father was home when she returned, and giving him the news was the hardest thing she had ever done in her life. But it was not as hard as seeing his reaction. His eyes darkened, life rushing out of them even as she watched. He didn't speak. He charged out of the house to go see Stevie's body.

That was the beginning of the wall.

Brick after emotional brick, Art Ybarra erected it over the next several months. It was finished on that last, awful day in the courtroom, the day Montoya walked out smiling.

He was charged with first-degree murder. The story, as it came from the detectives, was that Stevie wanted out of the gang life. Montoya wouldn't let him. They argued. Stevie, who had the same temper as his father, threatened to go to the police. Montoya pulled a gun and shot him twice in the head.

There were two witnesses. One was an old man who lived in the neighborhood. He was walking out of the market with a sack of canned goods when he saw Montoya shoot Stevie point-blank.

The other witness was a twelve-year-old boy who shouldn't have been out that late. He bought some candy and got on his bike, but stopped when he heard the argument. He would have provided the motive, had he been present at the trial to give a testimony.

When Rachel and her father arrived for the start of the trial, they were met in the hallway by Detective Kirby. The look on his face told her immediately that something was very wrong.

"The old man has lost his memory," Kirby said.

Rachel thought it was something medical, but the hard look on Kirby's face told her otherwise. "It's not uncommon in gang cases," the detective explained. "The witnesses are usually neighbors. They have to live with the gangs. If they talk, they can't expect to live."

Her breath almost leaving her, Rachel said, "How can you convict anyone?"

Kirby shook his head. "It ain't easy. I'm really sorry."

"What about the boy?"

"Gone."

"What do you mean?"

"I mean his family took him away."

"Can't you find him?"

"They went to Mexico." Kirby put his hand on Rachel's shoulder. "I'm sorry."

Rachel could almost feel her father freezing over beside her. This was the final insult. When a conviction had been possible, some relief was also possible. If justice had been done, maybe her father would have reversed his emotional slide.

But conviction was not possible.

Her father left the courthouse without a word. Rachel stayed, determined to see it through to the end, wondering if by force of will she could change the result. How could this be called a criminal justice system? How could the known killer be set free without even a trial?

The hearing in the courtroom seemed to her a perverse play, with all the actors walking through their appointed roles, devoid of conviction. The judge looked unmoved, the prosecutor resigned, the defense lawyer astounded, and the defendant, Raimundo Montoya—head shaved, face hateful—seemed to take it all as a joke.

As the judge pronounced the dismissal, Montoya turned to the gallery. That's when he made eye contact with her. That was when he smiled.

And that was when Rachel almost lost it.

She fought despair again and again over the next several weeks. Her father froze her out; the wall was up. Stevie was dead, and she couldn't help blaming herself, as her father blamed her. She gave up on Stevie that night in the park. If she hadn't, if she had turned to someone, maybe Stevie would still be alive.

Guilt roiled in her mind until she thought she couldn't stand it anymore.

Then a friend from school, Lisa Santiago, someone she knew only on a social level but who had always been nice to her, dragged her to a church meeting one night. Rachel didn't want to go anywhere near a church. God wasn't real. If he was, he had been absent. He hadn't stopped the bullets from entering Stevie's head.

But she went, determined to resist, feeling perhaps this would be the last social gathering in her life, a final confirmation that there truly was no hope, no goodness, no reason left in existence.

That's when she heard Pastor Manny Mendoza for the very first time.

Now, after the scene with her father, she needed to see Manny more than anyone else. With eyes like hot anvils—heavy and burning from crying—she pulled up in front of the house. She waved her hand in front of her face for a few moments, trying to generate some cool air for her eyes, then got out of the car.

Lights were on in the house. Lydia Mendoza answered the knock and immediately knew something was wrong. She threw her arm around Rachel and pulled her into the warmth of the house. "What is it, Rachel?"

"I've been to see Pop."

Lydia gently walked Rachel to the living room, a place of soft browns and oranges, and sat her down. "I'll get Manny," she said.

A few moments later Manny Mendoza came in with his characteristic smile, the one that exuded joy. "Hey, Rach," he said, taking her two hands and shaking them gently. "How you doin'?"

Rachel, in spite of how she felt, smiled at her pastor. Manny was forty-seven, stocky and strong, with deep brown skin and hair like black steel wool. If he hadn't had his hair cut short and if he hadn't been wearing the loose Promise Keepers T-shirt over his blue jeans, he would have looked like the outlaw biker he had been for over a decade.

Manny Mendoza had been one of the more notorious of the biker gang leaders, rising to the top of the Bandidos, a gang of nearly 350 members, mostly Latino, that managed to take a huge chunk of the ice trade—crystal methamphetamine—from the larger Hell's Angels network. This did not set well with the more established Angels, and Mendoza, of necessity, became violent, cunning, and, to the frustration of the Feds, nearly invisible.

At the height of his power he was regularly using drugs and slowly descending into a pit of paranoia and depression. One night outside a biker hangout in Diamond Bar, he passed out and had a distorted dream that his girlfriend and her young daughter were planning to kill him. When he came to it was 3:00 A.M. He took a seven-inch knife from his bike bag, placed it in his boot, hopped on his bike, and started off to kill them.

That's when he heard the voice.

It was not coming from heaven, but from the back of the bar. It was a man's voice, and he was talking about *him*. He was talking about a notorious man of violence, a murderer, a gang leader, one who wanted nothing more than to stamp out a rival gang forever. Manny found himself getting off his bike and wandering toward the voice. How did it know so much about him?

The voice said the man was on his way to kill again when the light hit him in the eyes. Manny listened closely as he moved closer and closer toward the voice, finding the source in the open window of the small room in the back. It was obviously a radio. No lights were on inside the shack. Manny stopped at the window and listened.

The voice continued. The gang leader was blinded by the light that hit him in the eyes. He went to a place called Damascus. Manny didn't know where that was, thinking it might be in northern California. And then some guy with a weird name, Ananias, came into it, put his hand on the gang leader, called him "Brother Saul," and said that it was Jesus who appeared to him and that he was going to be filled with the Holy Spirit.

Scales fell from this guy Saul's eyes, and he was baptized, and then he started preaching that Jesus was the Son of God. And people were amazed.

Manny was amazed, too. More than amazed. He was frozen in place, feeling a jolt pass through his body like nothing he'd felt before—not from speed, not from grass, not from acid—an incredible, light-filling torrent of warmth that rushed through him from his feet to his head so that it felt like his head might explode with a sort of strange ecstasy no pharmaceutical could ever approach, no human act could ever approximate. He started pounding on the door of the shack until a little Mexican guy, groggy and scared, opened the door. Manny asked him who was on the radio, and the guy struggled out of his drowsiness to tell him it was a pastor who had a church in Huntington Beach, and this was one of his sermons and . . .

Manny rode that night not to the house of his girlfriend and her daughter, not to commit murder, but to Huntington Beach, until he found the church. He curled up in the doorway and slept there until a confused church secretary encountered him in the morning. He told her he had to talk to that pastor who was on the radio. It might have been half out of fright, but the secretary ushered him in, gave him coffee, and called the pastor at home, asking if he could come in a little early.

He did. Pastor Bill Gillis spent four hours with Manny Mendoza, then the two of them went down to the beach and, in front of several dozen curious beachgoers, Gillis baptized Manny Mendoza—leader of the Bandidos, trafficker in drugs and human lives—into the family of God.

That was fourteen years ago. Mendoza was mentored by Gillis and eventually led a Bible study at the church. The study was soon packing the church to the max. With Gillis's blessing, Manny planted a sister church in Rosemead—the church where Rachel Ybarra had found hope again.

"You been crying," Manny said, sitting on the sofa next to Rachel. Despite, or maybe because of his outlaw background, Manny was as gentle as a dove when counseling one of his flock. It was as if he had been through a hell no one in his congregation would ever experience, and, therefore, his compassion would always be more than sufficient.

"I was with Pop tonight," Rachel explained, "it's worse than ever."

"Hey, hey," Manny said, his favorite phrase, something that could mean almost anything depending on the moment and how he said it. Now it meant comfort.

Lydia came back in the room with a tray of milk and homemade cookies. Lydia majored in chocolate chip. "I'll let you two talk," she said.

"No, stay," Rachel said. Lydia sat down. "I just didn't know who to turn to. I can't get through to him. He still blames me for Stevie's death."

"That's wrong," Manny said.

"Is it?" Rachel looked Manny in the eye. "I still blame myself."

"You can't."

"I do. It doesn't go away. Why doesn't it go away?"

Manny placed his strong hand on her shoulder. "It sticks like tar on the bottom of your shoe, doesn't it?"

Rachel nodded.

"I know all about it," Manny said. "My hands hurt a lot of people. My heart doesn't let me forget it. My head tells me, 'Hey, it's okay, you're forgiven by Christ,' but that doesn't always do it. I know about guilt, Rach."

"What should I do?"

"Use it."

"What do you mean?"

"You remember the first time we met?"

"I'll never forget it."

"You were angry, baby"—*baby* was another of his favorite words, peppered throughout his speech—"I mean you were burning up. I thought you'd set our building on fire just by the way you looked."

Rachel laughed. "Yeah, I didn't want to be there."

"When I shook your hand I thought I was connected to the electric company. You remember what I said to you?"

"Yes. You said God could use my fire."

"You spent the next hour telling me about what happened, almost challenging me to tell you God exists. You remember?"

"Yeah."

"And I said I thought God was preparing you to do a great thing. That's why you went to law school, right?"

"Right."

"God's still preparing you, baby. Don't you feel it?"

Rachel paused, then slowly nodded.

"And Stevie's death, and your dad, that's all going to be part of it. That's Romans 8:28 up and down. If you love God, all things work together for good."

"I've got to believe that."

"You do. I know you do. You've still got the fire. God's going to use that. Something big is going to happen, and you'll be ready."

"Pray over me, will you?"

He did.

CHAPTER NINE

ALAN LAKEWOOD closed his office door and offered Rachel a seat. "Coffee?" he asked.

"Thanks," Rachel said. "Black."

Lakewood had a coffeemaker on a table near the window. He poured two cups, handed one to Rachel, then sat down behind his desk.

"How do you like it so far?" he asked.

"The coffee?"

"The office."

Rachel smiled. "I like it a lot."

"It shows." Lakewood picked up a sheaf of papers and held it up for Rachel to see. "Your trial memorandum in the Hunter case. Excellent."

"Thank you."

"I mean really excellent." He dropped the memo on his desk. "One of the best I've seen, and I don't ladle out the praise too often."

Rachel swallowed. "Thank you again."

"I think you've got what it takes to be a great prosecutor."

"Thank you."

"Don't thank me yet. I want to take you through an entire trial with me in a front-row seat. I'm talking about investigative conferences, going into the judge's chambers, being in court, that sort of thing. It will involve extra hours. Long hours. I'll keep you busier than a cat in a room full of rocking chairs. You understand that?"

"Yes," Rachel answered.

"You'll have other assignments around here, but mine will be top priority."

"I understand."

"You'll be in on official meetings and hearings. I'll also have you in the courtroom with me during trial. You've got the security clearance, and I want the help. How's that sound?"

"It sounds," Rachel said, almost short of breath, "just great."

"You'll do it?"

"I will. I want to."

"Just remember, this one's going to get ugly."

"Which one?"

"You didn't hear? The Grand Jury just handed down an indictment against Jaroslav Supevsky."

"Supevsky? Who is that?"

Lakewood steadied his gaze at her. "Remember Mr. X?"

Eyes widening, Rachel said, "Him?"

"The very same. We finally got the break we were looking for."

"What break?"

Lakewood picked up the phone. "Let Agent Bunnell tell you about it," he said to Rachel. Into the phone he said, "Is Bunnell still here? Send him in."

A few moments later Jeff Bunnell knocked and entered Lakewood's office. Lakewood introduced them. Jeff shook Rachel's hand. His grip was warm and firm.

"I remember you," Jeff said, "from the meeting."

"Right," said Rachel.

"You were the one paying attention." Jeff laughed.

Lakewood laughed, too. "Rachel is going to be my legal assistant on this one and liaison between you and me. Why don't you fill her in on why the indictment came down now."

"Sure," Jeff said. "We found ourselves a key witness. He could be just as important to the Government as Sammy 'The Bull' Gravano. You heard of Sammy?"

"I've seen his book," Rachel said.

"Yeah. *Underboss*. Gives a whole new dimension to 'Don't buy books by crooks,' doesn't it? Anyway, our guy put a hit on a local couple a few weeks ago, Supevsky's orders. We found him, and we also found out he's very afraid of one thing."

"What's that?" Rachel asked.

"The gulag," said Jeff. "He's a former Soviet. And he's scared of prison. Well, he's going to do time, but it's a question of how hard and how long.

We're going to make it easier on him, and he's going to testify against Supevsky. That's the deal."

"Your FBI dollars at work," Lakewood said.

"Congratulations," said Rachel.

"Thanks," said Jeff. "Same to you."

"Okay then," said Lakewood, "now that we're all giddy with each other, let's get to work. Bail is going to be an issue at the arraignment. Rachel, you get me a memo on the latest bail cases by the close of business today, okay?"

"Right."

"And you," he said to Jeff, "take care of our witness."

"He's in good hands," Jeff answered.

"Zagorsky?"

Jeff nodded.

"And Rachel," Lakewood said, "you'll be in good hands with Agent Bunnell. I think you two will get along famously."

Jeff smiled at that, and Rachel, seeing his smile, felt something she immediately wished she didn't. Jeff Bunnell was attractive all right. She wasn't blind. But this was business, big business, and physical attraction to an FBI agent was not going to help matters one bit. She quickly excused herself and walked out of Lakewood's office.

On her way back to the fourteenth floor, Rachel got her mind on track. She had a lot of work to do, and it was best to get right to it. Halfway down the hall to her office Ron Ashby stepped in front of her.

"So you got it," he said.

"Got what?"

"You're going to be Lakewood's puppy."

"I'm going to be working with him, yes."

"What did you do?"

"Excuse me?"

"To get it. What did you do? Pray?" He pronounced the word *pray* with dripping sarcasm.

Rachel started by him, but he moved slightly, enough to obscure her path. "Don't be juvenile," she said.

"Just interested in what the good Lord can do."

Rachel slipped past him and walked quickly to her office, feeling his eyes on her back. She closed the door and then her eyes. It was her first brush with professional jealousy. Shaking it off she grabbed a legal pad and a pen, then headed out of the office.

Even though the U.S. Attorney's Office had more than an adequate library, Rachel still liked to do her legal research at USC. She was used to the school's library, having navigated its shelves for two years, and she had a favorite corner on the third floor, with a study carrel by a window facing the north side of the campus, where trees obscured the urban tangle that surrounded the university.

Here she was usually undisturbed and found she could work three, four hours straight. And when she needed to take a break, she had the chapel.

Rachel had been attending USC for nearly six months before she discovered it. There was no mention of it in any of the catalogs, and it was off the beaten path for the law students. Most entered the Law Building through the front doors, which faced the business school at one angle and the center of campus at another. There was no need to enter the law school through the breezeway passage on the side.

Rachel had taken this route on a few occasions, noting only that the buildings seemed to be of the old style, probably originals, built of brick and covered with the proverbial ivy of the venerable institutions of higher learning.

One day she noticed a wooden door, partially hidden by bougainvillea, in the side of one of the buildings. She wondered what it was, and finally, the third time she walked by, she went to investigate.

The door was shaped like a smaller version of a cathedral entrance, with a small cross in the middle. Rachel tried the handle, found it unlocked, and went inside.

What was there delighted her. It was a chapel—a small, quiet sanctuary smack in the middle of the bustle of a secular university. Soft light from a stained glass window gave the place an amber hue. Four sets of wooden pews lay empty, and a maple stand at the front held an open Bible. No one was in the place, and the heavy walls tuned out the noise.

After discovering the chapel, Rachel frequently went there to relax and meditate. It was almost always empty. Every now and then another person was in there, but never more than one or two at a time.

And that's where Rachel went after three hours on her bail memorandum. She was alone and took a seat in one of the front pews. She prayed, thanking God for the opportunity he had given her and for the strength to do a good job.

Later, when the evil began, she would remember this moment and this prayer. She would remember and wonder if her prayer had been earnest enough.

If it had, she thought, would the evil have come at all?

CHAPTER TEN

MUTED SUNLIGHT hit the closed curtains of the hotel room. Jeff Bunnell leaned back in his chair, pulled back a curtain with his finger, and glanced down nine floors to the street. "Looks hot today," he said. "Who's going for lunch?"

"Depends on the next five minutes," said Sam Zagorsky. "Shake and roll."

Jeff let the curtain drop and came back to a full sitting position at the card table. Zagorsky, sitting opposite, eyed him suspiciously. Jeff smiled and looked at his score sheet. Then he looked back at his fellow FBI agent. He picked up the blue cup, threw the five dice in it, and slowly began to rattle them around.

"You realize," said Jeff, "that if I throw a Yahtzee, you get lunch for the next five days."

Unsmiling, Zagorsky said, "Just roll."

With a flick of the wrist, Jeff tossed the dice on the table. Three of the dice showed two spots. "I guess I'll work on my twos," Jeff said, noting that Zagorsky sat back now with an air of confidence.

"Work on whatever you want," Zagorsky said. "I'm sitting pretty."

"Pretty is one thing you're not." Jeff rolled the dice, picked up another two. He rolled again, without success. He marked his score sheet and said, "I'll check Dedenok."

"I'll be waiting," said Zagorsky.

Jeff got up and walked into the bedroom. Paul Dedenok was propped up on the bed with five or six pillows, in boxer shorts and white socks, tossing peanuts in his mouth as he watched a Cubs baseball game on TV.

"You okay?" Jeff stayed at the doorway, allowing Dedenok at least the illusion of having his own space.

"Time of my life," said Dedenok. His hair, as always, was perfectly coifed, solidly slicked back with some sort of gel that gave off the faint scent of gardenia.

"What's the score?" Jeff asked, motioning with this thumb to the TV.

"What do I care?" Dedenok answered. "I hate this baseball."

"Don't watch it then."

"What else do I do? The game shows, they are even worse. Soap operas? Bah." Dedenok shoved a few more peanuts in his mouth with his left hand. His right half-cradled the can of nuts on his lap.

"You never told me what happened to your hand." Jeff asked.

"A factory accident when I was a boy."

"And you still made KGB?"

"I am deadly with my left."

"Tell me about it." Jeff rubbed his stomach in the place where Dedenok had slugged him.

Dedenok smiled. It seemed a point of professional pride. Then the smile left and he said, "Did you really mean what you told me?"

"What's that?"

"That if I killed the little boy you would kill me."

"I believe I said I would blow your brains out."

"I think you would have done so."

Jeff looked at the carpet and said nothing.

"Ah, yes," said Dedenok. "There is something going on behind your eyes."

"Forget it."

"Something that haunts you maybe."

"Never mind."

"I am haunted too."

"By what?"

With a shrug, Dedenok said, "I will never find rest either. They will find me."

"Who is *they?*"

"Supevsky."

"You're going to put him away."

"You think that will stop him? Not while The Man is outside."

"Your mythical partner?"

"No myth!" Dedenok said, slapping his leg. The can of peanuts spilled on the bed. "He's out there."

"Why can't you tell us where?"

"He's invisible. I do not even know what he looks like, where he comes from. We wore masks when we did the job. I do know he is former KGB. It was said that he could kill anyone, and he would not even leave a footprint in fresh snow. You think I'm crazy, yes?"

Jeff shrugged. "You may be telling the truth. But no one's that good."

Dedenok threw back his head and laughed—a deep, Russian laugh. "You are naive! He is out there, my friend. I will hand you Supevsky. But he will still be out there. And I will never be at peace."

"Our witness protection is pretty darn good," Jeff said mildly.

"That is not good enough." With vacant eyes, Dedenok turned his face back toward the TV.

Jeff returned to the living room. "How's our boy?" Zagorsky asked.

"Hanging in there, I guess."

"You guess?"

"He's convinced his life is over."

"It may well be."

"He's still stuck on being found out."

"By that hit man?"

"Yeah."

"Ah, it's all based on fear."

"Well, it's working."

"I'm ready to roll." Zagorsky shook the dice cup and poured out the dice. The two agents played in silence for the rest of the round. When they tallied the scores, Zagorsky claimed victory. "Your turn for lunch," he said. "You want to run out, or shall we have Lakewood's assistant run it over?"

Jeff snapped a look at his partner, who was smiling. "What's that supposed to mean?"

"Come on, pal, I hear things. She's supposed to be a looker. I'd give her a look myself, only I'm married, and my wife doesn't like me window shopping."

Jeff smiled and nodded.

"But she's probably not right for you," Zagorsky said.

"Why's that?"

"She's smarter than you."

"Thanks." Jeff tossed his pencil and hit Zagorsky in the chest.

"She's religious, they tell me," Zagorsky said.

"So?"

"I mean, real religious, you know, like she takes it seriously."

"Zagorsky, what are you trying to say? That religion is only good when you don't take it seriously?"

"Come on."

"No. I mean it. You sound like a bigot of some kind."

"Hey, I'm no bigot. I'm a realist. If she wants to believe that stuff, fine. But you better keep it in mind."

"Why?"

Zagorsky shrugged. "All I'm saying is, she's not gonna be some easy conquest, you know?"

Jeff felt his face heating up. "You think that's what I'm looking for?"

"Hey, you're a guy, like me."

"Oh, man!"

"Hey, cool off."

"Why should I cool off?" Jeff snapped, noticing he had both his hands balled into fists, resting on the table. "You make her out like some piece of meat."

"When did you suddenly get religion?"

"Shut up!" Jeff stood, almost knocking the table over. For a long, tense moment the two partners stared at each other. It seemed so off the wall, Jeff didn't know what to say. Why was Zagorsky needling him like that?

There was a knock at the door. Jeff stomped over and checked the peephole. It was the maid. He turned the bolt and threw the door open.

"Housekeeping?" the maid asked, almost sheepishly.

"No thanks," Jeff snapped. She looked at him strangely for a moment, then turned away. Jeff closed the door and bolted it. He turned around and saw Zagorsky standing there.

"Hey, I'm sorry," Zagorsky said. "I didn't know."

"Didn't know what?"

"You were sweet on her."

Jeff shrugged. "Forget about it."

Zagorsky stuck out his hand. Jeff took it. "Yeah," Zagorsky said, "let's forget it. We got a lot of Yahtzee to play together."

Jeff nodded.

From the bedroom Dedenok shouted "Hey!" The two agents hurried in and saw Dedenok pointing at the TV with his good hand.

On the screen was a live news feed from the steps of the federal courthouse.

"Supevsky!" Dedenok said.

Supevsky it was. Dapper in his blue suit and red tie, with sunglasses giving him a movie-star look, he was standing next to a striking woman in red. The pair faced a mangled bouquet of microphones as they got ready to speak.

"I don't believe it," Jeff mumbled. "Jessica Osborn Holt!"

"The very same," Zagorsky laughed. "This is going to be some fun."

"Fun?" Dedenok said incredulously.

"Watch," Zagorsky said.

Supevsky spoke first. "The federal government has run a sword through me, my family, my friends, my associates, and my business interests. I am proud to be an American, but I am not proud that my government is conducting this witch-hunt. I am an innocent citizen. I have worked hard. I have had success. Is this what America does to you if you are a success? I am ready to answer all charges, and in the end I know I will walk out of that courtroom a free man."

"Dream on," Zagorsky muttered.

Then Jessica Osborn Holt stepped before the microphones. She was in her mid-forties, with raven-colored hair and taut features. Jeff had seen her often enough on the TV news and talk programs. She was a publicity generating machine, and as much as that rubbed Jeff the wrong way, he had to admit one thing—she had charisma. She was part of that select pantheon of actors and celebrities for whom the camera lens is a loving and submissive paramour. News cameras were no exception.

"In addition to defending Mr. Supevsky from these false and defamatory charges," Holt said, "I will be filing a formal protest with the Attorney General's Office in Washington, and I will do everything in my power to hold it accountable for this vendetta against my client. In addition, I'm issuing this challenge: If, when the trial is all over, and my client is found not guilty, I will call upon Alan Lakewood to resign from the U.S. Attorney's Office."

"Nice touch," said Zagorsky. "Maybe she should ask God to step down from heaven, too."

A reporter shouted a question. "Are you denying any complicity in the death of Dimitri and Sarah Chekhov?"

"Complete denial!" Supevsky shouted. "It is an outrage!"

"Do you have any interests in the narcotics trade?" another reporter asked.

"I have legitimate interests in several businesses, all legal, all protected by the United States Constitution."

Zagorsky shook his head. "He's wrapping himself in the Constitution!"

Jessica Osborn Holt raised her hand to stop further questioning, repeating, "No comment, no comment," and hustled her client off to the courthouse. The field reporter came back on camera.

"Turn it off," Dedenok said.

Jeff clicked off the TV. Dedenok sat on the bed, a look of unremitting fear on his face.

"You okay?" Jeff asked.

Dedenok slowly shook his head.

"Let me clue you in on the first rule of trial preparation," Alan Lakewood said. "Always expect the unexpected."

"Always?" Rachel asked. They were sitting in his office, files and law books piled on the floor around them, balls of crumpled yellow legal paper scattered here and there.

"Yes," Lakewood said. "And the unexpected turn, what I call the bombshell surprise, can turn a trial right around on its head."

"But if it's unexpected, how do you prepare?"

"You anticipate. You form contingency plans. You think, if this happens here, I'll do this. If that happens, I'll do such and such. And you must know your opponent."

"Jessica Osborn Holt."

Lakewood nodded. "She'll do anything to win. She has no qualms. She'll skate as close to the ethical edge as she possibly can without going over. Sometimes she does go over, but because she's a defense lawyer, the judges will treat her like a disobedient little kid instead of a professional who deserves to be sanctioned."

"You speak from experience."

"The Elliott case. It still sticks in my craw."

"That was the land developer?"

"Yep. Wanted to build a huge mall in West Hollywood but couldn't raise the money. At least, not legitimately. Thought he could make a big score on a cocaine deal."

"Wasn't he on tape?"

"Slightly. He's sitting in a hotel room looking at a suitcase full of snow and saying, 'This is money in the bank.' Could it get any clearer?" Lakewood raised his arms, as if arguing to a jury.

"Doesn't seem like it."

"The jury bought the entrapment defense."

"Unbelievable."

"Holt put the guy's wife on the stand as her last witness, after telling us she wasn't going to call her."

"Why did the judge allow it?"

"Because the judge was afraid of Jessica Osborn Holt."

"Afraid?"

"Afraid of being reversed on appeal, afraid of appearing to be a sexist, I don't know. I still can't figure it out. But the wife ends up crying on the witness stand, and I made a stupid blunder."

Rachel waited for his explanation.

"I went after her," Lakewood said. "I tried to grind her up, show she was performing. Bad move. Juries side with grieving spouses."

"You think that turned the tables?"

"Probably."

"Has she pulled stuff like this in other cases?"

"All the time. So in addition to your other duties, I want you to keep an eye on Jessica Osborn Holt. I want you to pore over every piece of paper she sends us. I want you to watch her on the news, listen to radio reports, keep her in the forefront of your mind. By the time we get to trial, I want you to know her like a wayward sister. We'll keep our heads together and be ready for anything she might try."

"I'll do my best," Rachel said.

"Do better than your best." Lakewood seemed almost to be pleading with her. She nodded.

"Okay then," Lakewood said. "You might start with a Nexis search on Holt. That'll give you a little background." He handed her a piece of paper. "Then read and Shepardize this case for me. Tomorrow morning is the arraignment. I don't want any surprises."

Rachel went immediately to the computer station and logged onto Nexis, the news database. She pulled up several articles about Jessica Osborn Holt, printed them out, and took them to her office to read.

The articles made up a fascinating account. Holt started as a prosecutor in Mobile, Alabama, quickly becoming the star of the office, trying three murder cases in a row and winning them all. She married and divorced the scion of a rich Southern family, and that event signaled a change in her career.

She left the Mobile prosecutor's office and moved to New York City, joining two other female lawyers who had a small firm. They specialized in federal criminal defense with mixed success. Jessica Osborn Holt's record was less than stellar. She apparently hit the club and drug scene for awhile. She checked into a rehab center, got clean, got out, and started winning some cases.

Then, inexplicably, Holt disappeared from the scene for a period of five years. It was speculated that she went to India to seek spiritual enlightenment. No one knew for sure, because Holt never talked about it. The only thing that was certain was that when she returned and opened up her own law office, she began her ascent to national prominence as a defense lawyer.

Her first big win came when she defended a doctor in New Jersey who had assisted the suicide of a forty-year-old woman with Parkinson's Disease. After that she won several drug and racketeering cases.

At one point she was retained by Paul "Candy Man" Ciardelli, a high-ranking member of the Gambino crime family, to fight a RICO charge brought against him. After a spectacular victory, she went to work for him almost exclusively. She won another acquittal for him in a case brought by the Manhattan District Attorney. It seemed like nothing was going to stick against the Candy Man.

But then the federal government figured out a way. Wiretaps had picked up certain conversations in the hallway adjacent to Ciardelli's favorite hangout. Jessica Osborn Holt was part of several of those conversations, offering her advice on dealing with the Feds. When Ciardelli was indicted in federal court for another RICO violation, government prosecutors argued that Holt should be disqualified as his defense attorney. She was not only "house counsel" to this criminal enterprise but a potential witness as well. The judge granted the motion. Holt was out. And Ciardelli was convicted and sentenced to life.

The setback, if one believes the articles, seemed to strengthen Holt's resolve. She moved her offices to a refurbished Victorian building in Santa Monica and immediately won a big case involving an accused narcotics trafficker. She bought a huge home in an exclusive section of Brentwood and began dating David Leonard Goss, one of Hollywood's most prominent leading men. She was feature material in both print and TV tabloids. Through it all she kept winning cases, including the Elliott case against Alan Lakewood.

As Rachel read on, she felt an increasing inner anxiety about her own abilities. Jessica Osborn Holt was ambitious, perhaps ruthless, but above all she was good. Good in the courtroom, good on television, good at everything she set her mind to. And Rachel was part of the legal team that had to defeat her.

"Mind if I join you?"

Rachel snapped out of her reverie and saw Ron Ashby standing at her elbow. "Didn't mean to wake you," he said.

"I'm working," Rachel said, gathering up her notes randomly, wanting to look busy.

"Sure, so am I. I've got a real swell bank fraud issue." His tone was full of sarcasm and derision.

"That can be interesting," Rachel said.

"Not as interesting as Russian Mafia."

"Look, Ron, I didn't make the decision, okay? I'm just doing what they tell me."

"Good dog."

Rachel's jaw dropped half open, and she just stared at him. This was unbelievable. It wasn't that the talk was anything she hadn't heard before. Much worse banter had been the norm in her school days, especially in the part of town where she grew up. But this was the United States Attorney's Office. This was one of the most august federal institutions in the country. The people who came here were supposed to have a certain maturity about them. Now one of the externs was pursuing an obvious strategy aimed at making her ill at ease, like a sixth-grade bully upset that someone got a higher grade on a test. Unbelievable.

"I have to get back to work," Rachel said, turning to the computer monitor.

"Hey listen," Ashby said, leaning closer to Rachel and lowering his voice. "I'm not such a bad guy. Why don't you give me a shot?"

"What?"

"A shot. You know, a chance."

"I think we can get along fine."

"No, I mean more than that. How about dinner?"

"I don't think so."

"Come on, a chance to get to know me."

"I'm not dating, Ron."

"How come?"

"I'm too busy."

"You've got to have a social life. Don't Christians have social lives?"

He had slipped back into semimocking tones. "This isn't the time," Rachel said.

"Then let's make time."

"No."

Rachel tried, with a motion of her head, to indicate that the conversation was over, she was back at work, and she wanted to be left alone. It didn't fly. She felt Ron's head next to her ear. And then he made a suggestion so crude that Rachel's entire body chilled. She was frozen in place, feeling shocked, embarrassed, and violated. At this point the anger rushed in.

She stood up and whirled on Ashby, who had a half smile on his face. "Get out of here," Rachel said, barely holding back the intensity of her anger. "Don't talk to me again."

"Hey," Ashby said, taking a step back. "Take it easy."

Rachel wanted to take it easy by knocking him over the head with a copy of the Federal Code. The smile on Ron's face fueled her already flaming temper. Her face must have been quite a sight, because at that moment Alan Lakewood walked in and, seeing Rachel, said, "Whoa!"

Before Rachel could speak up or even gather herself Ron Ashby said, in a calm and cool way, "Hi, Mr. Lakewood."

"Mr. Ashby," Lakewood answered with a nod. "How goes it?"

"Great," Ashby said. "Got a great bank fraud issue I'm working on."

Rachel felt like a figure in a wax museum. Lakewood finally turned to her and said, "You okay?"

She glanced quickly at Ron Ashby, unable to control the clenching of her jaw.

"Overwork," Ashby said with a laugh before turning and walking out.

Lakewood, a concerned look on his face, said, "True?"

"No," Rachel said quickly.

"What's wrong?"

"Nothing, nothing." She was sure the opposite answer was written in bold letters all over her face.

"I need you to hang in there with me," Lakewood said. "If something is upsetting you I want to know about it."

She considered, for a quick moment, telling him about Ashby, but stopped herself. It would be a mistake. This was a personal problem. Yes, it happened in the workplace, but it would be her rendition of events balanced against Ashby's, and his farewell act just now convinced her he wouldn't think twice about blaming her.

"I'm fine, really," said Rachel.

"Maybe you do work too hard. Maybe you should take a break every now and then."

"I will."

"Good." He handed her a page from a yellow legal pad with notes scribbled across it. "Check these out, too, while you're at it."

"Right."

"And remember, I don't ask that much. Just perfection." Then he smiled, which was a great relief to Rachel.

She got back to the computer and started to work again. But the research went slowly for the rest of the day. As much as she tried not to be bothered by the incident, she couldn't shake it off. Ron Ashby was a problem, and she was sure he was going to be one as long as she was in the office.

CHAPTER ELEVEN

ARRAIGNMENTS IN THE MAGISTRATES' courtrooms on the tenth floor of the courthouse were mundane and almost always *pro forma*. Defendants marched in with their attorneys for the initial appearance before a judicial officer. The officer explained the charge against the defendant or read the actual indictment. Then a copy of the indictment or information was given to defense counsel, and the defendant entered a plea. After that some haggling over bail took place, and the next case was called. Nothing very exciting.

Given the normal sequence of events, Rachel did not expect the mini-media circus on the tenth floor, hovering outside Magistrate Wayland Deering's courtroom like a swarm of hungry bees. As soon as she and Alan Lakewood stepped off the elevator, the buzzing began.

Several reporters tried to ask questions, and each time Lakewood responded with, "No comment." Lakewood liked to do his talking in the courtroom and not the hallway, feeling it was unseemly for a prosecutor to make public remarks about pending cases. He kept walking straight for the courtroom.

Rachel, carrying a file holder, tried to keep up, but a female reporter quickly stepped in front of her and began talking faster than any human being Rachel had ever met, "ExcusemeI'mSusieAkersChannel7newsare youconnectedwiththiscase?"

Rachel blinked then quickly shook her head, not in denial but in confusion. The woman had said something in English even though it didn't sound like English. Then the reporter stuck a microphone with an attachment that had a big "7" on it in Rachel's face. Rachel made an attempt to move around the reporter, but the reporter refused to give ground.

"Can I get a comment from you on the Supevsky case?"

"Excuse me," Rachel said.

"Channel 7 news!"

"Please."

Suddenly the way was clear. A man shoved the reporter to the side. He smiled at Rachel and gave her a nod of his head, indicating she should pass by while the passing was good. She did and made it into the courtroom without further incident.

Lakewood was waiting for her. "They get you?"

"They tried," Rachel said.

"Get used to it. Have a seat by the rail."

Rachel sat on a bench near the prosecution table and close to the wall, placing the file pocket on her lap. The courtroom was starting to fill up with attorneys, journalists, and, through a side door, detainees from the Metropolitan Detention Center.

One of them was Jaroslav Supevsky.

Rachel flipped through her own memo and tried to look busy, hoping to deter any inquiries from the press. She was not successful. She sensed someone slipping into the spot next to her. She kept her eyes on the page.

"So you made it."

Rachel glanced to her right and saw the man who had run interference for her in the hallway. He was dressed in a crisp, blue suit. He smiled charmingly.

"Yes," Rachel said, "thank you." She looked back at her memo, hoping the conversation would end there.

"That's not my real job," the man said.

"Excuse me?"

"Blocking for attorneys. You just seemed like you needed it."

Rachel nodded.

"Name's Stefanos, Fred Stefanos."

"Nice to meet you," said Rachel tersely.

"You're not offering your name?"

"Are you a reporter?"

"Sort of. You an attorney?"

"No," Rachel said. "I'm just a lowly paralegal."

"Nothing lowly about that," Stefanos said. "You're the ones that keep people like that—" he nodded toward Alan Lakewood—"going."

Rachel gave him a quick smile and, once more, tried to go back to her reading.

"I'm a freelance writer," Stefanos said. "I write a lot about true crime, the legal system, that sort of thing. I don't name my sources unless they want to be named. Would you mind if I asked you about this case?"

"I really can't offer you anything," Rachel said.

"You'd be surprised. I take it you're assisting Mr. Lakewood there."

"You know him?"

"By reputation."

"Then you know he doesn't like to give out information to reporters."

"Freelance writer," Stefanos corrected with a smile. He was easy to talk to. Rachel could see him charming information out of many sources, especially female ones. "And I'm not just after a story. I'm after more than that. I like to focus on real people. Someone like you, for instance, seeing a case from your point of view. How would you like to be the subject of a book?"

For a moment Rachel wondered if he was serious. The prospect of being a character in a book was actually intriguing to her. She had read Jonathan Harr's book, *A Civil Action*, the summer before. That was a masterful account of one lawyer's obsession to get compensation for several citizens of a small town whose water supply had been poisoned by a big company. The story was thrilling and exhausting, better by far than most legal fiction.

"I don't think so, Mr. Stefanos," Rachel said.

"Call me Fred."

"I really don't feel I can be a source for you on this."

"Well, you can't blame a guy for trying, can you?"

"No. No harm done."

"One last question?"

"Sure."

"Are all the clerks in the U.S. Attorney's Office as good-looking as you?" It could have been a crude and clumsy line, but coming from him it sounded unforced and natural. He was just one of those people who was not offensive, even when being a little pushy. He must be, she thought again, very good at his job.

"Yes," Rachel said, "every one of them."

Stefanos smiled. "Then I'm going to law school. It was nice to meet you Miss . . . I didn't get your name."

"Off the record?"

He nodded.

"Rachel Ybarra, anonymous and loving it." She offered him her hand. He shook it and smiled.

"I'll let you get back to work," he said. "It was a pleasure." He stood and exited the row.

At that moment the magistrate, Wayland Deering, entered the courtroom and took his seat on the bench. He was a slender, dignified looking jurist with wavy gray hair and a pencil-thin white mustache. After a clipped "good morning," he read the litany of constitutional rights that every accused is protected by. Then he called the Supevsky case. Jessica Osborn Holt stood, walked to the lectern in the center of the courtroom, and motioned for Supevsky to join her.

Rachel examined Supevsky from behind. Even though he was dressed in government-issue coveralls from the MDC, he looked somehow dapper. His hair was perfectly combed, and his bearing was almost regal. He didn't seem to have an ounce of concern. He was obviously a man who was used to getting his way, no matter what the circumstances. A federal indictment was just another obstacle to be removed and dumped.

At one point he glanced back toward the gallery, as if looking for someone. Or maybe he was just showing his face to the media. Rachel noticed a sketch artist from one of the news stations busily trying to capture Supevsky's profile. Maybe Supevsky just wanted to make sure the guy had a good view.

Deering looked out over his courtroom. "In the matter of the United States versus Jaroslav Supevsky," he began, "is the defendant present in court with counsel?"

Jessica Osborn Holt said, "He is, Your Honor."

"State your appearances," said Deering.

"Jessica Osborn Holt for the defendant, Jaroslav Supevsky."

Alan Lakewood stood and stated his name for the record.

"All right then," said Deering. "Mr. Supevsky, did you hear and understand the rights I just read here in the courtroom?"

Supevsky glanced at Holt, who nodded. "Yes," Supevsky said.

"And has a copy of the indictment been given to you?"

"Yes."

"Do you wish the indictment to be read?"

Holt said, "We will waive a reading of the indictment, Your Honor, and enter a plea of not guilty."

"All right," said Deering. Without pause he reached for a large envelope and pulled out a piece of paper. "Your case will go for trial before Judge Montross. You're ordered to appear at one o'clock this afternoon."

Rachel looked for reactions from the two lawyers. The naming of a judge was always a suspenseful moment, like the opening of the Oscar envelope. Lakewood and Holt remained impassive.

"On the matter of detention," Deering said, "I've read the Pretrial Services Recommendation. Any further argument?"

Lakewood stood and said, "We request that the defendant be held without bail, Your Honor. There is a significant flight risk here. The defendant is charged with a crime that can get him eighty years in prison. That, of course, is a life sentence. He has the means and the motive to flee the country, Your Honor."

The magistrate said, "Ms. Holt, do you have a response?" That question brought a titter of laughter from the gallery. The obvious implication of the laughter was that no one in the press had ever known Jessica Osborn Holt *not* to have a response, to anything.

With a slight smile in acknowledgment to the press—*She knows how to work a room,* Rachel thought—Holt went to the lectern.

"Your Honor," she began, "I would first like to begin with the obvious. My client, Mr. Supevsky, gave himself up. He did not wait to be arrested. He came in voluntarily, and has, as of now, given up his passport."

With a dramatic flair Holt took a passport out of her briefcase and held it out for the court clerk. Looking mildly bemused, the clerk, a young African American woman, took it.

"That should speak volumes, Your Honor," Holt said.

"It can also be a ploy," Lakewood added.

"Mr. Lakewood," Deering said, "I'll hear a rebuttal from you when Ms. Holt is finished." To Holt he said, "Continue."

Jessica Osborn Holt said, "It is the Government's burden to show, by a preponderance of evidence, that Mr. Supevsky is a flight risk. We do not have to present any evidence to the contrary, but we just have. In addition, Your Honor, let us remember just where Mr. Supevsky came from. He wanted to get *out* of the Soviet Union. He came here, at great risk, to start a new life for himself, to build a business by the sweat of his brow, to find the American dream. Why should he want to flee? He has nothing anywhere but here."

Holt paused for a moment, then said, "Mr. Lakewood has referred to the seriousness of the charge, but that, I submit, should not carry any weight."

Deering said, "It's one of the factors listed in section 3142, is it not, Ms. Holt?"

"Indeed, but my argument, Your Honor, is that the government is free to bring any charge it wants. The defendant should not be prejudiced because of the whims of the prosecutors."

Lakewood stood up. "Objection, Your Honor."

Deering looked at him sternly. "This isn't a trial, Mr. Lakewood. Do you have anything else?"

"Yes," Lakewood said. "We believe the defendant also poses a significant danger to the community."

"Based on what evidence?"

"The nature of the killings, Your Honor. And we can show easy access to weapons."

"Ms. Holt?"

"Mr. Lakewood knows he has to provide you with clear and convincing evidence on this issue, Your Honor. But this danger he concocts is as imaginary as the charges. There is not one shred of evidence that Mr.

Supevsky poses any harm at all. Indeed, the very opposite is the case. He has worked hard to establish a successful business in this city and deals with numerous entities, public and private. That he has strong ties to his community is quite clear, which brings me to the two most important factors in this proceeding, factors that Mr. Lakewood has conveniently ignored."

As Holt flipped a page of her notes, Rachel looked at Alan Lakewood. She could see his jaw twitch. It was quite apparent that Holt's jabs were finding their mark.

"First," Holt continued, "the history and characteristics of the person must be considered. Your Honor, Mr. Supevsky has been an honored member of the community, both here and in New York, for nearly twenty years. He has in that time built a substantial import business with never a hint of any scandal, lawsuit, violence, or misdeed. He has worked hard, raised a family, contributed to society. To have him subject to detention pending an outrageous witch hunt of a trial is preposterous."

Wayland Deering looked like he almost smiled at that point. "Ms. Holt, I would advise you to save your overcharged rhetoric for a jury. This is a pure matter of law."

"I understand that, Your Honor," Holt said quickly. "It's just a little difficult to swallow the pill Mr. Lakewood is forcing on the court."

Another small wave of laughter rippled through the courtroom.

"All right, all right," Deering said in mild rebuke. "Anything else?"

"Yes, Your Honor," Holt said. "You are also called on to consider the weight of evidence against the accused. Since we have no idea what the evidence is, the inference must fall in favor of the defendant."

Rachel felt her insides do a small dance. This was the major issue in the case she had researched for Lakewood. He had anticipated Holt's argument, and she had walked right into the little snare she had helped him prepare.

"If I may?" Lakewood said. Deering nodded at him. Lakewood carried a copy of the case with him to the lectern. "Ms. Holt is apparently unaware of a case from the Tenth Circuit, the Whitney decision. I have it here, Your Honor."

Lakewood held out a copy of the paper to the court clerk, who handed it to Deering. "Directing your attention to page 307," Lakewood said, "the court holds that the weight of evidence factor is not something to be looked at in isolation but in conjunction with the charge in the indictment or information. It states here specifically that the factor is *not* to be viewed in favor of the defense."

Short, crisp, and clear. Rachel admired that. No reason to devolve into the same verbal pyrotechnics as Jessica Holt. He had the law on his side. Rachel quickly glanced at Holt to see what her reaction would be.

She was, to Rachel's surprise, completely composed. Rachel thought she might at least be nervously scouring her head for an answer. Holt had a reputation for wearing her heart on the sleeves of her designer suits. That was why juries responded to her. She was just like them, like real folks.

So why was she so cool?

Deering paused momentarily while glancing over the copy of the decision Lakewood had given him. He nodded a couple of times then looked at Holt. "Are you familiar with this decision, Ms. Holt?"

"I am, Your Honor," Holt said.

The answer surprised Rachel. This was a narrow point in a decision out of another circuit. Unless Holt had herself anticipated this issue, why would she be familiar with the case?

"Looks pretty clear to me," Deering said.

"Oh, it's clear all right," Holt said. "It's just not good law."

"And why not?" Deering asked.

Holt reached for a sheet of paper from her table. "Because the case was overruled two weeks ago by the entire panel of the Tenth Circuit."

To the reporters in the courtroom that might not have sounded like much more than a small point in an otherwise arcane legal argument. But to Rachel it sounded like what it really was—a legal bombshell, an explosion that completely destroyed Alan Lakewood's argument.

And it was her fault. After the upsetting exchange with Ron Ashby in the library yesterday, she had made a crucial mistake in not Shepardizing the case—seeing if it was still valid or had been modified in any way.

Federal appellate decisions were rarely overturned, but Lakewood had directed her specifically to check up on the case. She hadn't, and now he was standing in court looking like the legal equivalent of a fool.

Deering looked surprised. "Mr. Lakewood, I think you've been tripped up."

Ashen-faced, Lakewood said nothing.

"Is there anything further?" Deering asked.

"No, Your Honor," said Holt. She didn't need to say anything else. This was the perfect place for her to stop. Alan Lakewood sat down like a deflated balloon.

Deering said, "The court will set bail at one million dollars, with the following conditions. Mr. Supevsky has given up his passport, but I am going to require him to report every day to Pretrial Services. In addition, I'll require a surety on the bail. And Mr. Supevsky, you are ordered not to talk, intimidate, or otherwise attempt to contact, yourself or through associates, any potential witness in this case. Is that understood?"

"We understand, Your Honor," said Holt.

"All right," said Deering. "Next case."

Rachel saw Supevsky pat Jessica Holt on the back. Alan Lakewood's reaction was of another sort. He glared at Rachel.

"You lose again," Sam Zagorsky said.

"Those dice loaded?" said Jeff.

"You use the same dice as I do."

"Do I?" Jeff narrowed his eyes like a sheriff sitting across a card table from the most notorious cheat in the Old West.

Laughing, Zagorsky said, "I'll take pastrami on rye today, light mayo, heavy mustard. And a cream soda."

Jeff stood up and walked to the bedroom where Paul Dedenok was watching a soap opera.

"Look at her," Dedenok said to Jeff. "She thinks she can have an affair with a priest and God won't judge her!"

Jeff looked at the tube and saw a stunning blond woman throwing her arms around the neck of a handsome young man in a Roman collar.

"No respect for the church," Dedenok said with disgust. "Me, if I was that priest, I would knock her teeth out."

"I guess you went to church in a pretty rough neighborhood," Jeff said.

Dedenok nodded. "My family did not attend the church. But we always showed respect for the priest."

"What do you want for lunch?"

"What are my choices?"

"White bread or rye bread, mayo or mustard."

"Pastrami again?"

"Check."

Dedenok shrugged. "The rye bread," he said.

Jeff turned and was about to leave when Dedenok stopped him. "Agent Bunnell?"

"Yeah?"

"I want you to know something."

"What is it?"

"No matter what happens, you have been fair with me."

It was odd, being given a compliment by a Russian killer. They were on opposite sides of the fence, as far apart as two people could ever be, yet somewhere Dedenok had a code, a sense of honor, twisted though it was. Jeff had honor of a different sort, but somewhere in the middle, in this dim hotel room in the center of downtown L.A., the two codes met and found a mutuality, if only for a single moment in time.

"Thanks," Jeff said, then walked out of the bedroom. He gave Zagorsky a wave and went to fetch lunch.

It was hot on the street. Even in the valley of the shadow of the Bonaventure Hotel, with neighboring buildings rising like cliffs and cutting off direct sunlight, the air was heavy and moist, like a blanket dipped in boiling water. Jeff immediately started to sweat under his crisp white dress shirt.

He turned south on Figueroa and started for the deli four blocks away. Normally he didn't mind this run so much. It got him out of the hotel room and gave him a little exercise. But it was too hot to enjoy the walk, and something Dedenok had said just before he left had stayed in his mind.

No matter what happens . . .

It was a strangely portentous phrase, like it was coming from a condemned man. Well, in a way, Dedenok was condemned—he was going to die to his old life, take on a completely new identity in some undisclosed spot in the midwest, and begin all over again.

But was that all? There seemed some larger subtext in his phrase and in the look on his face. Did he believe they might try to get to him before he took the witness stand? Of course that was why he was being watched at all times by two agents. But Jeff knew Dedenok would never really be at peace. Even with the cloak of a new identity, there would always be that part of him looking over his shoulder, wondering what lay in the next shadow, what that odd sound might mean.

Jeff crossed 5th and almost got clipped by a Cadillac racing through the intersection. Now that would have been an irony. FBI agent on a protection detail can't even protect himself. Gets taken out while going for pastrami sandwiches.

Wonderful.

No matter what happens . . .

And what if something did happen to me? Jeff wondered. *What would I leave behind? Mom and Dad, a sister in Eagle Rock. A couple of social friends. But no one really close, no wife.*

The deli was crowded. Jeff took a ticket with "29" on it. The little sign behind the counter said "Now Serving: 15."

Sighing, Jeff leaned against a back wall and watched the parade of hungry and disgruntled humanity before him. It took nearly twenty minutes for him to finally place an order. Another ten minutes went by before he was handed a white sack with the sandwiches.

He walked back to the Bonaventure and took the elevator to nine. He slipped the coded card into the door lock and went in.

"I hope you like *hot* pastrami," Jeff said as he entered, "because it got hotter on the way back."

Jeff stopped.

Sam Zagorsky lay sprawled on the floor.

"Sam!" Jeff dropped the sack and ran to his partner. Even as he did, his agent instincts told him to duck, take cover, and watch for movement.

The room was empty. But Dedenok could be behind a door, a curtain, anywhere.

Jeff quickly checked under Sam's coat. His gun was still in its holster. Jeff took it, ran to the bedroom, and looked in.

Empty.

"Dedenok!" he shouted, the weapon ready.

No answer. Then he heard a groan. It was Sam.

Slowly, Jeff backed toward the agent.

Zagorsky moaned and moved his head slightly. At least he wasn't dead. But he wasn't going to talk anytime soon.

Dedenok must have knocked him out and taken off. But that made no sense. Still, what other answer was there?

Jeff grabbed the phone and called the desk. He told the clerk to call an ambulance immediately.

Sam was moaning again. Jeff didn't want to move him, but maybe he could make him more comfortable with a washcloth and cool water.

Jeff hurried through the empty bedroom, past the bed where Dedenok had been sitting not forty-five minutes ago, and into the bathroom.

He stopped cold, his breath leaving him. He put a hand on the wall to keep from falling.

Dedenok was in the bathtub, unmoving, up to his neck in water dyed a deathly red. Both his wrists were sliced open.

Disbelief rolled over hysteria in Jeff's mind. He sucked in air to compose himself, looking around the bathroom as he did. Dedenok had left a neat pile of clothes on the bathroom floor. Around the pile were some pieces of broken glass.

An ugly, jagged, blood-stained shard lay on the rim of the bathtub.

Feeling like he might get sick, Jeff backed out of the bathroom and sat heavily on the bed.

CHAPTER TWELVE

RACHEL KNEW FROM THE LOOK on Alan Lakewood's face that this wasn't going to be a pleasant conversation.

"The case against Supevsky may be over," he said, sitting behind his desk.

"Why?" Rachel asked, hoping it had nothing to do with the blown bail hearing.

"Dedenok's dead."

Rachel felt her heart jump. "What?"

"He planned it out. He waited until he was alone with one of the agents, hit him from behind, climbed in a bathtub, and slit his wrists."

"Was there a breakdown in the security?"

"Slightly!" Lakewood pounded his fist on the table. "We had two agents protecting him."

Rachel swallowed. "Who?"

"Zagorsky and Bunnell."

"Who . . ." Rachel hesitated. "Who was hit?"

"Zagorsky. Bunnell was out of the room."

A feeling of relief spread through her. "What about Bunnell? Is he all right?"

"Oh, he's fine, physically. But this happened on his watch. There's going to be hell to pay."

"But it wasn't his fault, was it?"

Lakewood looked at her with a curious expression. "Like I say, it happened on his watch."

Rachel could hardly draw a breath. "Is that it then?" she asked finally. "Supevsky walks?" Visions of Montoya filled her head.

"Probably," Lakewood said. "We have only one thread. It's a thin one, and it's a long way from here. But it's all we have, and you're going to pull it."

Rachel blinked but said nothing.

"There's another witness."

"Where?"

"In New York. Evan Hansborough knows. He's an Assistant U.S. Attorney in Manhattan. We went to law school together. He's sort of been helping me with Jaroslav on the side. A lot of what we have comes from Supevsky's New York days."

"Who is this witness? Will he testify?"

"She. I want you to fly to New York tonight."

Lakewood looked deeply into her eyes. "I have a good reason for sending you. I'll let Hansborough explain everything to you. But you don't have to do it. I have to tell you that there's a little bit of risk here. You'll be doing more than researching legal questions for me. You'll be doing some hands-on work. You don't have to do it if you don't want to."

Lakewood's expression was troubled. Something was going on, something not right.

"Of course I will," Rachel said. "But. . . ."

"Yes?"

"After yesterday."

Lakewood paused for a long moment then said, "You blew it, you absolutely did. You left me hanging there like a Catholic at a Baptist convention."

Rachel looked down. "I'm sorry."

"But I'm more Baptist than Catholic. I believe in grace. You're still raw. I also believe in works. What I'm sending you to do is work. But it's more than that."

Rachel waited.

"It's our last chance," Lakewood said.

At one time in his life Jeff Bunnell envisioned rising to the top in the FBI. He would do his time in the field, distinguish himself in everything from far-reaching investigations to local stakeouts. His service would culminate in promotion to the head office in Washington, where he would eventually be named director. The cover of *Time* or *Newsweek* would cap the ascendancy and seal his place in the history of the Bureau.

That, at least, was the dream. It was a dream that started with his first assignment to the Bureau's suburban Los Angeles office in Westwood. He relished the learning experience—how to track fugitives, the basics of surveillance, the intricacies of fraud, the machinations of organized crime. Soaking it all up, Jeff became one of the stars of the office, well liked by colleagues and supervisors alike.

Next he moved into the hostage-rescue and antiterrorism SWAT unit and became what some jokingly called an "urban commando." The moniker was amusing to Jeff, the work exhilarating. He even started to consider making this his specialty, operating and rising within the unit for an entire career.

But that was before the mall.

A skinhead in full military armor had held up the Bank of America two blocks away at the Third Street Promenade. When he rammed his getaway car into a fire hydrant, sending plumes of gushing water into the sky, he tried to make his escape on foot. Running down Third Street with his Czech Vz.58 assault rifle firing randomly into the sky, it was no wonder screaming pedestrians split open for him like the Red Sea did for Moses. The skinhead, whose name was Charles Wiggate, ran into the Macy's store in the mall and took a woman from the perfume counter hostage.

Jeff's SWAT team was called into action and, according to plan, Jeff took the point. It was a tense two-hour standoff. Wiggate was only one man, but he had a weapon that could average eight hundred rounds per minute in full-auto mode, and reports from witnesses made it likely that he had plenty of ammunition with him.

Finally progress was made. Wiggate agreed to come out with the hostage and said he would give her up in exchange for an airliner to Cuba. Arrangements were made at LAX.

When Wiggate finally stuck his head out the entrance, the terrified hostage in a headlock in front of him, the first thing he did was raise his rifle with one arm to his hip and fire.

An armor-piercing .50 caliber bullet ripped into Jeff's flesh. It lodged just under his left shoulder, barely missing his heart. The pain and bleeding were intense. Jeff was dragged by a team member out of harm's way. He blacked out in the process.

Jeff underwent delicate surgery for the removal of the bullet and began a successful physical recuperation.

His mental recovery was another matter. As soon as he came out of the anesthesia he asked a nurse what the outcome of the hostage situation was. She responded by bringing him a newspaper. There he learned the worse. Wiggate had shot the hostage before turning his weapon on himself. An editorial in the paper was already questioning the SWAT team's "frontier tactics."

Devastated, Jeff fell into a dark hollow of despair that lasted several months. He started seeing a Bureau psychiatrist regularly. He was assigned to a less stressful desk job where he remained for two years. Finally he requested and was granted a field job again, this time in the drug trafficking division.

Slowly and painfully, Jeff started working his way back. Sam Zagorsky was a big help during that time, inviting Jeff over to spend time with his family, taking him to dinner, but mostly just being a sympathetic ear.

Jeff finally got a degree of confidence back. Maybe his career would get back on track.

Now agent Jeff Bunnell, badge number 6075, was wondering if he would have any career at all.

He had never seen Emmitt Jefferson so steamed. His boss was usually the picture of reserve—smoldering when the circumstances justified it but never out of control. This was as close as Jeff had ever seen him to losing it.

"You undermined one of the most important cases we've ever had in the organized crime unit!" Jefferson screamed, not at all concerned that his voice was carrying through the glass door and out over the floor where several agents sat motionless, listening. Out of the corner of his eye Jeff could see his colleagues, rapt at the soap opera of vituperation raining down upon him in Jefferson's office.

Jefferson pounded his desk with a fist so tight his knuckles threatened to break through the skin. "You should have known Dedenok was ripe to try something! You should have been on red alert the day after the indictment was handed down! Instead, you treated everything like business as usual! It borders on criminal negligence!"

Pausing for a breath, Jefferson turned his back on Jeff and put his hands on his hips.

Jeff did his best to compose himself. He had never had any disciplinary problems with the Bureau before, never anything that questioned his competence or ability. A hearing on the Wiggate hostage situation had cleared him of any wrongdoing or negligence. Now he was standing there like some boot-camp lackey being ripped apart by a drill sergeant with an attitude. Tears of defensive anger were welling up in his eyes. He took a deep breath and battled them back.

Whirling, Jefferson put his hands out in a gesture of total confusion. "Well what have you got to say for yourself? Can you give me any good reason why I shouldn't send you to a desk and keep you chained there?"

"Sir," Jeff began carefully, "as you know, I work closely with Agent Zagorsky. We had an arrangement that had been working just fine."

"Leave Zagorsky out of this," Jefferson snapped. "You were the one who left him alone and vulnerable."

A burst of anger fractured Jeff's thoughts. He felt his hands ball into fists and his arms tense with coiled rage. Jefferson was accusing him of endangering a fellow agent, something Jeff would never allow himself to do. The accusation was all the more debasing because Zagorsky was becoming a friend.

Jaw clenched, Jeff said, "Sir, neither one of us had any idea the witness would do this. Our conversations with him gave us no indication. He was ready to testify and to go into witness protection. He seemed nervous about people finding out where he was. He wanted to keep breathing, sir."

"Obviously not. He pulled a fast one on you. And you took it like a two-bit rube at a country carnival! Negligence like that is what tears the Bureau down and gives the ACLU types the chance to rip us apart. I'm appalled, Bunnell. I'm appalled I have to be having this conversation with you. You're off field duty until further notice."

"But, sir—"

"That's all, Agent Bunnell. You'll be notified." Jefferson again turned his back, this time in obvious dismissal.

Without another word Jeff walked out the door and into the central office. Stares met him on all sides. Without meeting any of the looks, he proceeded to reception, then out of the building onto the street.

He tried to take a deep breath, but his chest was tight, and he couldn't open it up. His pulse was throbbing in his neck, and he felt sick. That would be a fitting end to the afternoon, wouldn't it? Throwing up on the sidewalk in broad daylight. Great public relations for the Bureau.

But he held it in. He managed to start walking, without immediate destination, down the street.

A couple of blocks later he ducked into a diner, a little hole-in-the-wall that still served hot coffee and loose banter. He wanted nothing of the latter and headed for a booth in the corner. He ordered a glass of water and coffee from the waitress and tried to put his thoughts together.

It looked like Paul Dedenok would be his undoing as an agent—at least as an agent with a bright future. The way it was being played out, Zagorsky wouldn't receive any of the blame. He was a victim, a victim of Jeff's negligence, and he'd received a blow on the head as a result. And yes, the most important federal witness since Sammy "The Bull" Gravano had slipped through their collective fingers.

That still puzzled Jeff. As he sipped his coffee and drew patterns on the condensation of his water glass, Jeff reviewed everything about his time with Dedenok. He had never hinted of suicidal intent. Dedenok talked for hours about the new life he'd be starting in witness protection. Sometimes he'd seem like he was grateful for a clean slate, a new lease on life. At other times he expressed a certain fear that he would be found eventually by the family. But never had he spoken of a desire to check into the great beyond at his own hand.

Indeed, on a few occasions, he seemed eager to bring down Jaroslav Supevsky. "I would kill him myself if I had the chance," Dedenok had said on more than one occasion.

So why the sudden change? It was possible Dedenok had been bluffing all along, awaiting his chance to die by his own hand. But if that were true, he was one great actor. You don't spend the equivalent of three weeks in the same room with a person and get a performance that good, unless the guy is Laurence Olivier in another life.

Something just didn't seem right. But Jeff didn't have any other answers. Dedenok must have been waiting for his chance, and the moment Jeff stepped out of the room, he took it.

Jeff played the picture of leaving the room over and over in his mind, as if he might force his way back in time and reverse course. He could have been right there to stop Dedenok from cracking Zagorsky's head, from breaking the water glass, from slicing his skin. Maybe this was the sort of torture he needed for absolution.

It had been a long time since he'd prayed. He had never been very religious, had never adopted his parents' Presbyterian ways. He had an ambivalent belief in God, something he told himself he'd resolve one day.

Now, facing censure from the organization he had dedicated his life to, it seemed like a good time for a first step. He closed his eyes and held the water glass against his pulsating temples and whispered, "Oh God, help me, please."

CHAPTER THIRTEEN

NEW YORK CITY SEEMED READY to explode. It wasn't just the stifling heat or the mass of humanity pummeling against itself on the sizzling sidewalks. It was something almost indefinable. Rachel merely felt it, sensed it around her. The city was like a giant headache on the verge of a massive stroke. Something was going to burst and cripple the borough for the rest of its days.

As bad as L.A. was, Rachel thought, it was ten times better than New York. At least in L.A. you had some open spaces—beaches, mountains, parks. In Manhattan everything seemed squeezed together. And the green rectangle in the middle they called Central Park was less famous as a refuge than as a mugger's happy hunting ground.

The sooner she could get out of there, the better.

Evan Hansborough, Assistant U. S. Attorney for the Southern District of New York, seemed to sense her unease. A large man in his fifties, looking like an ex-football player in an ill-fitting suit, he greeted her in the offices at Foley Square with a promise that he would send her back to Lakewood as soon as possible. "I know you probably have some suntanned lifeguard to go back to," he said.

"Not really," Rachel answered.

"Oh? Is he a movie actor then? Maybe surfer?"

Laughing, Rachel said, "Your cultural stereotypes are showing."

"That's how I get through life. Putting people into easily identifiable categories. Works wonders with a jury. It's hard to believe you haven't got some kind of boyfriend back in the land of fruits and nuts."

"Well, I don't."

"All business?"

"For now."

"Good. Then shall we get down to it?"

Rachel removed a legal pad from her briefcase and prepared to take notes.

"What do you know about the Russian Mafia?" Hansborough asked.

"A little, I guess."

"Let me make it a lot. Organized crime is a one-hundred-billion-dollar-a-year business. Untaxed. Out here the mob has major clout in construction, food distribution, textiles, garbage hauling, and even the fish trade. That's not to mention narcotics, prostitution, loan sharking, Las Vegas and Atlantic City entertainment, and pornography. The list goes on."

"This is La Cosa Nostra influence."

"Right. That's traditional. With the Russian émigrés, new horizons are being explored. Technology theft, stolen computers, counterfeit software, that sort of thing. But there is still one enterprise they all want to be a part of."

"Narcotics?"

"You got it. They have some of the strongest ties to the Colombians we've seen, even stronger than LCN. That does not bode well for the future."

"And Supevsky is part of that?"

"Almost certainly. Your office knows more about that aspect of it. The reason you're here is . . . do you *know* the reason you're here?"

"Mr. Lakewood said you'd explain it to me."

Smiling, Hansborough said, "That's Alan for you. The silent, cowboy type. Yes, I'll explain it to you. There is one witness left who might be able to make Alan's case for him. Her name is Deanna Natale. At one time she was Supevsky's mistress. She was a pornographic movie actress, and Supevsky set her up in a nice apartment with a nice car and all that money can buy, including drugs. Supevsky got her hooked, used her for awhile, then dropped her. I think he figured she would self-destruct, and she almost did."

"How did you find her?"

"She actually found us. She came back here—to Connecticut, actually—and got herself cleaned up. She apparently got a little angry at the way she was treated by Supevsky. So she placed a call to an FBI agent named Stingley and told him she had something on Supevsky that might prove very interesting, something that had to do with Supevsky, drugs, and threats against competitors, including a man named Chekhov. Stingley contacted me, and we set up a meeting. She never showed."

"Why not?"

"Fear. It's the common plight of witnesses to organized crime—for obvious reasons. They see the pictures, the blood-soaked bodies. That gets in their heads. So we had to try to find her. She had only given a first name over the phone, calling herself Sheba."

"Sheba?"

"Odd name, right? We ran it through the computer, crossing it with files on Supevsky. It didn't take long to find out that Sheba was one of her porn names. A little more digging and we figured out who she was and where she was. Her mother owns a farm in Connecticut. That's where she's holed up."

"She's there now?"

"Right now. We interviewed her and tried to get her to come forward, but she wouldn't. Finally she said she would only come forward if we needed her. We got some helpful information from the interview, although her past makes her a questionable witness."

Rachel nodded. Drug addiction and pornographic movies were not exactly the pedigree of a reliable witness. She could imagine what Jessica Osborn Holt would do with Deanna Natale on the witness stand.

"Unfortunately," said Hansborough, "she's the last link. And that's why you're here. Well, there are actually two reasons. First, you know what the case is about since you've been working on it. Second, you're a woman. Alan thought, and I agreed, that the witness is fragile and might better respond to a woman's touch." Hansborough frowned suddenly. "Do I sound completely sexist?"

Rachel smiled. "No. I happen to hold a quaint belief that men and women are actually different."

Returning the smile, Hansborough said, "Imagine that. Well, you're going to ride out with Agent Stingley and see Deanna Natale. Your job is to convince her that she is needed for this case. You understand that?"

Rachel nodded.

Hansborough said, "And one more thing."

"Yes?"

"No one is going to know you're seeing her. No one but me and Stingley. We're going to take you to her in secret."

Rachel's breath almost left her. "You think we could be followed?"

"Let's just say I'm not taking any chances."

Deanna Natale looked like a ghost—no, like a skeleton draped with ghostly skin. Rachel had been briefed and knew she was forty years old. She looked sixty. The ravages of her past stood out across her haggard face. Her eyes, which may have once been dazzling, were dull and vacant. It was an odd contrast as the two women sat on the porch of the farmhouse. They were surrounded by the smells and colors of rustic innocence, of gentle repose. But inside the head and body of Deanna was a deadness of spirit that seemed to envelop her in a cocoon of condemnation.

Rachel felt like an intruder. Deanna had come here to escape from her past, perhaps hoping against hope to find some benefit in remaining alive. What right did she have to disturb this last dream of peace?

However, that peace might be attainable only if Deanna confronted her past and purged it from its consequences, through a right action in the name of justice. If Rachel could be a part of that, she would try to be. That was, after all, her assignment. She was not here on her own. While Deanna's mother served lemonade to Agent Stingley and Evan Hansborough inside the house, Rachel listened to Deanna's story.

"I was with Juri about eight months," Deanna said. Her voice was small, like a little girl's. "It was party time all the time."

"Did he takes drugs with you?"

"No way. Never did any of that. Just let everybody around him. Another way he controlled people."

"Like you?"

"Exactly."

"And he was married?"

Deanna let out a short, derisive laugh. "Course he was married. He had the family thing goin' over here and all the girls he wanted on the side. Some setup."

"Did his wife know?"

"Yeah she knew. But she can't do nothin' about it."

Rachel sighed and shook her head.

"How about you?" Deanna said.

"Me?"

"You got a man?"

"No, not yet."

"How come?"

"I've just been too busy, I guess."

Leaning closer, Deanna put a hand on Rachel's knee. "Listen to me, honey. Don't do that to yourself. You find yourself a good man, a straight-up guy. Don't do what I did, 'cause look at me now."

Responding to the deep sense of loss in Deanna's voice, Rachel said, "It's not over for you."

Deanna sat back in her chair. "Oh, yeah, it is. Damaged goods. But hey, you dance, you gotta pay the band."

For awhile, the two women listened to the breeze. Then Deanna went back to her story. "So anyway, one night we was all partying downstairs at the club, one of Juri's hangouts on Sunset, when he says he has to take a phone call upstairs. I'm gettin' high and kind of frisky, you know, and without him knowing it I follow him up the stairs."

Rachel scribbled notes. "He didn't see you?"

"No way! He would've broke my nose if he'd seen me. We was never to go upstairs at his places. That was off limits. Even to his girlfriends. But we'd been gettin' along real nice for a couple of weeks, and I figured he'd be funny about it, laugh it off or something and spank me and send me back. I was loaded, so I wasn't really thinking."

Deanna, sitting in an old rocking chair with a rhythmic squeak, looked out at the chicken coops thirty or so yards away. "Anyway, I'm up the stairs, I walk through the door, and I hear voices. It's Juri and Paul."

"Dedenok?"

"Yeah. Been with Juri since back in the New York days."

"And you could hear their conversation?"

"Oh, yeah. And Juri's screaming, and he keeps mentioning a name."

"You remember the name?"

"Yeah. Dimitri Chekhov."

"Did that name mean anything to you?"

"I only knew he had a big limo company, and the limos were used to carry more than people."

"Drugs?"

"Right on. So I hear Juri scream at Paul to subtract Chekhov."

"Subtract?"

"His way of saying *kill*. Juri says he wants it done, and the sooner the better. Juri tells Paul to go with 'The Man.'"

"Which man?"

"Just, 'The Man.' Another guy, I guess. And Juri says to make it brutal; he wants to send a message."

Deanna looked at the floorboards on the porch. Her dull eyes shone with a sad wetness. "Anyway, I was one of Juri's girls for another couple of months, but by then I was so hooked on coke I couldn't get through the day without three or four blows. Last time I saw Juri he hit me across the face and gave me a bloody nose. He told me I was a worthless pile of . . . well, you get the idea. He threw me out of the apartment he was giving me. I guess he figured I was gonna go ahead and die all on my own. I almost did."

"I can't begin to imagine what you've been through."

Deanna shrugged. The expressionless look in her eyes returned.

"And I don't have anything I can say," Rachel continued, "even though I want to."

"You want to?" Deanna said.

"Yes. Desperately. I wish I could somehow make things better."

"Thanks. I don't have no friends these days. I got Mom, but it ain't the same."

There was a long pause. Rachel noticed the wind blowing through the white cypress trees, shaking the leaves into a kaleidoscope.

Finally Deanna said, "You did come out here to get me to testify, didn't you?"

"Yes," said Rachel.

"I don't want to go back."

Rachel waited and said nothing.

"You gonna try to convince me?" Deanna asked.

"No."

Deanna seemed surprised and puzzled. Rachel said, "It's true it was my job to convince you to come forward. Without you we have no case. It's as simple as that. And I was all ready with a bunch of good reasons why you should, why it's the right thing to do. I was going to give you every one of those reasons. But Deanna, I just can't do it. It has to come from you."

For a moment it looked as if Deanna would burst into tears, but then Rachel saw a hardness—no doubt a defense mechanism forged over hard time—descend over Deanna's face. "What I got to say ain't much," Deanna said. "But any way you look at it, it ain't worth putting my life on the line, what there is left of it."

Rachel nodded. The arguments she had prepared and rehearsed in her mind over and over again on the ride out to the farm crumbled to dust. "Would you mind if I did something?" asked Rachel.

"What?"

"Would you mind if I said a prayer with you?"

Deanna's forehead tensed into a deep frown. It was a look of surprise, not derision, as if that was the last thing she had expected to hear. "I'm not religious or nothin'."

"You believe in God?"

"Well, yeah, there's gotta be somethin'."

"That's enough. Just hold my hand." Rachel reached out, and Deanna took her hand. It was trembling. Rachel put her other hand on top and squeezed gently.

She prayed aloud. And as she did, Deanna's trembling stopped.

CHAPTER FOURTEEN

THE TV DINNER, supposedly a Salisbury steak with potatoes, seemed more like a shoe with wallpaper paste. Jeff Bunnell poked at the meat with his fork and noticed that it wasn't fully cooked.

Can't even heat up a frozen dinner, he thought. *So how am I supposed to catch criminals?*

He only half heard the TV. Nickelodeon was showing *Green Acres,* the inspired mindlessness he thought might take his mind off things for awhile. But he couldn't get into it as anything more than background noise.

The image of Paul Dedenok kept going through his mind.

He pushed the Swanson dinner away, grabbed the phone, and dialed. "Sam? It's Jeff."

"Jeff?" said Zagorsky.

"How's the head?"

"Throbbing. I got a feeling I'm gonna clean out the local Sav-On of its aspirin supply."

Jeff wanted to laugh along with Sam but couldn't. "I been thinking about Dedenok."

"Ah, Jeff, give it up, will you?"

"I can't, Sam. Haven't you thought of anything? Anything he may have said to you?"

"I went through all that with Jefferson. And I even told him, just today, that he was being too hard on you. But his mind's made up. I think you should appeal."

"What good will that do? I'll just be branded a malcontent, and that'll really finish me."

A pause. "I wish I could help you, Jeff."

"Just wrack your brain, will you?"

"I have been. There was nothing there. No way you or I could have known what he was gonna do."

Jeff's head felt like a motordrome with a loud cycle of thoughts spinning round and round, going nowhere. He'd had this conversation before, with Zagorsky and with himself, looking for a crack where light might shine through.

"Listen," Jeff said, "one time I was talking to Dedenok, and he was telling me about The Man."

"Who?"

"You remember, his partner in the Chekhov hit."

"So he said. I never believed him."

"Well, it sure looked like *he* believed it."

"What's your point?"

"He said he didn't know what The Man looked like; he was invisible."

"Yeah, right."

"Just hang on." Jeff noticed his hand, gripping the phone, was moist with sweat. "His eyes got real glassy."

"Jeff, I gotta go—"

"Hang with me a second! Please, Sam. Help me out here."

"I don't remember any of this."

"Maybe this guy, whoever he is, has something to do with all this."

"All what, Jeff? Dedenok committed suicide."

"I know, I know, but maybe there was a threat of some kind, you know? Something."

Zagorsky sighed on the other end. "Jeff, you've been taking this all too hard, man. I don't want you to start wigging out. Just do your job, and you'll work your way back in. But not with cockamamie theories. That'll just get you a psych report."

"Can't you think of anything?"

"Nothing, Jeff, I told you. Now get some sleep, will you?"

Zagorsky hung up. Jeff knew sleep would not come. His mind was swirling like a whirlpool in a rocky shoal, a mental tempest that ebbed and flowed but never fully ceased.

Alan Lakewood's frustration was evident. Rachel knew he had spent years trying to get Supevsky, and now there appeared to be no hope. He had his face in his hands, elbows on his desk, for at least a minute—the longest minute Rachel ever had to sit through.

Finally, without looking up, Lakewood said, "I shouldn't have sent you. You're just a law student." The disappointment in his voice cut through Rachel like sharp blade. "I should have gone myself. I just thought . . ."

"Thought what?" said Rachel.

"I thought you might have been able to relate to her, to get through. I don't know. I just think I should have gone."

"I don't think that would have helped," said Rachel. "I think she trusted me."

"But not enough to testify."

"No."

"You pressed her?"

"I . . . not really. I didn't think she would respond to that."

Lakewood rubbed his eyes and looked at the ceiling. "I should have gone."

Rachel felt the sting of his frustration again. She wished there was some way she could help him, some way she could dig up another witness. But she knew Deanna had been their last hope.

"Why don't you go ahead and gather up all your files," Lakewood said, "and put them in a storage box. I'll let you go work with some of the other lawyers now."

"The Supevsky case is over?"

"Until further notice."

There was nothing left to say. Rachel slowly walked back to her office and started pulling all her files on Supevsky. It was bitter work. She had let down her boss and perhaps the entire community. What had begun as a job in one of the finest offices in the entire Department of Justice had suddenly become a dose of astringent reality.

Her phone rang.

"Hi, it's Fred Stefanos."

At first Rachel didn't remember the name. He said, "From the courtroom last week. I got you inside."

"Oh, yes, yes."

"Sorry to disturb you."

"What can I do for you?"

"It's what I can do for you."

Rachel paused.

"I can't discuss this by phone," he said. "Will you meet with me for a few minutes?"

"If this is about the case, I already told you I can't talk about it."

"I'll do the talking. But it is vital that you come tonight, and it is vital that you tell no one about the meeting."

Rachel shook her head slightly at the cloak-and-dagger urgency in his voice. "I'm not sure it's a good idea."

"It concerns Supevsky. I have information."

"Why don't you come in and talk to an agent about this information?" Rachel said. "Why do you want to give it to me?"

"Because part of it concerns you."

"How so?"

"Because," Stefanos said, "your life may be in danger."

Rachel arrived at the marina at half past six. She parked on the street near the Red Lobster, grabbed her briefcase, and checked it. She had a legal notepad and a hand-held tape recorder inside.

Stefanos had told her they would meet at his office but would have to connect first by the seafood restaurant. Wind was whipping off the ocean as the sun set in the west, casting an orange wake across Marina Del Rey and the entire southern California coast. Rachel thought momentarily how nice it would be to live near the beach. The glory of creation, the cleansing of the sea breeze, the purity of it—what a lovely contrast it would be to the cold lines and dark corners of downtown.

The thought of peace brought on a sudden urge to jump in her car and drive away. What was she doing here? She had no business getting involved at the investigatory level on a case as big as Supevsky.

But she gave herself two reasons for staying. The first was to find out why she was in danger. The second was to see if Stefanos really had something to help the Supevsky case. In her mind, the latter reason was the most important. She wanted to help Lakewood get his case back. She wanted another chance.

Her chance came walking up from the side of the restaurant a few moments later. Stefanos wore a dark red windbreaker and blue jeans, looking more like a weekend sailor than anything else. He smiled and waved, then indicated to Rachel to walk his way.

"Thanks for coming," he said, shaking her hand.

"Where's your office?" Rachel said.

"Down here." He led her past the restaurant to a set of stairs. The stairs led down to the marina, which was fully packed with boats of various sizes. Stefanos walked her to a slip that held a boat she guessed was almost fifty feet. "This is it," he said.

"A boat?"

"A boat! You wound me. This is my home away from home. Come on aboard." He jumped on and extended his hand to her. "You'll find this one of the more comfortable offices you've been in. I guarantee you."

She stepped over the side and onto the deck, then nodded approvingly. If one had to have a home away from home, this would do nicely. More than nicely, in fact.

Stefanos began pointing as he said, "It has three staterooms, a pilot-house, twin diesels inboard, two bathrooms, a galley . . . let's see, what have I left out?"

"A symphony hall?" Rachel said.

"That's next," laughed Stefanos, "complete with symphony."

His easy charm was at once comforting and disconcerting to Rachel. She liked him. In other circumstances she might like to spend some time getting to know him. But this was not the circumstance, and his social grace was at odds with the reason for her coming here.

"I like it," Rachel said. "But I—"

"Can I take you for a tour of the harbor?" Stefanos said.

"Maybe another time. I'd like to hear what you have to say about Supevsky."

"Can we at least have a bite to eat first?"

"A meal?"

"You didn't expect to skip dinner, did you?"

"Well, I didn't really think about it. I want to get down to it. You told me I might be in danger or something, and I'm a little anxious to find out about it."

Stefanos smiled and nodded. "Of course you are. Forgive me. Let's go down to my humble office." He led her aft, then down a small set of stairs into a comfortable room with a kitchenette, table, and soft chairs. On the table was a closed laptop computer and a cell phone.

"Have a seat," Stefanos said, indicating a chair by the large, square window that looked out on the marina. "At least let me offer you a drink. The bar is fully stocked."

"I'm all right, thanks," Rachel said, sitting.

"How about one of my famous vodka martinis?"

"Please, just business."

Stefanos sat in a chair opposite Rachel. "You're a curious one," he said. "How did you get into law?"

"Mr. Stefanos, I'd rather get—"

"I have my reasons for asking."

"I just became interested in criminal justice, that's all."

Stefanos nodded. "I share your interest. It's why I do what I do. It's also why I know what I know."

"Can we talk about that now?"

"Sure." Stefanos placed both his hands on the desk. "Let's start with what we know so far. The government secures an indictment against Jaroslav Supevsky, a man who looks, on the surface, like a successful American citizen. The question is why? Why does the government take such an interest in this man?"

"For obvious reasons," Rachel said.

"Perhaps. Perhaps not. But the government is basing its case in large part on the testimony of a key witness, who is being placed in what the government charmingly calls witness protection. Only they can't protect him from himself."

Stefanos raised his eyebrows, as if to invite a reply. Rachel said, "How much do you know?"

"Most of it," Stefanos said.

"But how?"

"Stay with me. So it looks like your case is dead. But then Alan Lakewood sends you to New York to confer with his colleague out there."

"How did you know that?"

"This isn't rocket science. Why else would a law clerk go to New York in the middle of summer at the behest of her boss? It's obvious this is a last-ditch effort to put the case against Supevsky back together. Am I right or am I right?"

Rachel looked at Stefanos without comment. She was amazed.

"Now my guess," Stefanos continued, "is that there is another witness back there. A witness you may have talked to. How am I doing?"

Rachel shivered slightly. "I can't answer your question."

"And that's answer enough."

"Please tell me how you know this and what this has to do with me."

"I know this," said Stefanos, "because it's my job to know. It's how I make my living. And as for your life, what do you know about the Russian Mafia?"

"I'm still learning."

"Well, I have the advanced degree. And you need to know one thing—when it comes to a case like this, they will do everything they can to find out who this witness is. Everything. And if that means a threat to the life of a law clerk, so be it."

Rachel shook her head. "I can't believe this. Are you serious?"

"Absolutely."

"I've got to get back. I've got to tell someone. The FBI."

"No, no. You don't want to do that."

"Why not?"

"If they've targeted you, and you go to the Feds, that will just give them a reason to kill you."

"*Kill* me?"

"I'm afraid so."

Rachel shook her head. "This can't be right."

"It is."

"But . . . what am I supposed to do?"

"I'll tell you." Stefanos stood and looked out to sea. "But first you have to know something about Supevsky and his network. Are you sure you wouldn't like that drink now?"

"No. Please."

"All right. The Russian 'mafiocracy' has roots that go back to the Soviet system. It also has roots in KGB. Deep roots. You know about KGB, don't you?"

"Only what I've read in the papers."

"You haven't read anything then. *Komitet Gosudarstvennoy Bezopasnosti*."

"Excuse me?"

"That's KGB. Translated, Committee for State Security. At its height it employed five hundred thousand people. Think about that. Half a million. And among its employees was a group of superassassins overseen by Vladimir Kryuchkov himself."

"Who is he?"

"The KGB chief, who led the coup to overthrow Gorbachev in '91. It failed. And with it KGB came to an end as the world knew it. But that left an employment problem for many, including those who had been trained so expertly to kill. Many of them moved to, for want of a better phrase, private enterprise."

"Mercenaries?"

"Some. Others became connected to multinational corporations. The best worked freelance. And that brings us to Jaroslav Supevsky."

"He employs these men?"

"One in particular. Within this KGB unit I spoke of was one man who became the best of the best. He was like the Kasparov of the system."

"Kasparov. The chess player?"

"The greatest chess mind of all time, yes. What this assassin could do was incredible. He could appear and disappear. He could change identities, even nationalities. He spoke several languages and was adept at all technologies, including weapons, communications, and computer systems. In fact, his identity was so cloaked in mystery that he was referred to only as 'The Man.' That is how he is still referred to by those who employ him. Jaroslav Supevsky employs him now."

Rubbing her eyes, Rachel said, "I just can't believe this. It's like something out of a novel."

Stefanos shook his head. "The novels don't come near it. The movies? Forget about it. Did you see *The Jackal?*"

"No."

"Bruce Willis? Are you kidding me?"

His light tone was lost on her. A deep, dark sense of fear began to gnaw inside her. If what he was describing was the truth—and his authoritative manner indicated it was—she was locked in a nightmare. "What can we do?" she said. "Is there anything?"

"There is," said Stefanos. "Fortunately, there is."

"Tell me."

"It's really not complicated," Stefanos said. "You have the power right now to assure yourself and the ones close to you of absolute safety."

"How?"

"Information."

"What kind of information?"

"Case information. Information that can help us prepare a defense."

It was the look on his face, more than the words, that gave him away—the calm and assured coolness of his reply. Rachel stood up, the grip of fear tight in her stomach, her head light. She took one step toward the stairs, but then he moved, quicker than any man she had ever seen, so that he was like a ghost, appearing here first and then there, suddenly next to her, twisting her around and pulling her head back. Then she felt the rope pulled tightly into her mouth, almost choking her, and making all sound muffled and pointless.

Part Two

Deeper

Only he who feels that God is his rival
Can feel himself a man on this land.

—Yevgeny Yevtushenko
Russian poet

CHAPTER ONE

THE NIGHT AIR WAS like needles of ice, thrown by an impatient and unrepentant sea upon all those who would forget what part of nature ruled the world. It didn't matter that they were within the sight lines of the shore—the ocean didn't care for land. Land was a hindrance, an afterthought, as were all who dared to venture out upon her.

Rachel's wrists chafed against the nylon rope in the cold. Her shoulders ached, pulled back against her will. She found that if she relaxed them the pain would stop for a moment, until the tension came back of its own volition and reminded her, with searing thrusts, that she was nothing more than a prisoner.

After tying her up in the cabin, he had taken the boat out to sea. Lying on the floor, she was aware only of the engines churning and her inability to move. She gave up trying to free herself when, a short time later, he cut the engine, came back down, and pulled her up into the night.

As he had tied her up to the chair on the deck, she made the first effort to calm down. *Don't fight back,* she told herself; *it may only set him off.* Whatever his intentions, a struggle would do no good.

He tightened the ropes, not enough to cut off her circulation, but more than enough to discourage all movement. His motions were crisp and practiced. He had done this before.

By the time he finished tying off, some semblance of thought had returned to her, and the first thing she did was say a prayer. Eyes closed, she merely said to herself, "Lord, protect me." She opened her eyes but repeated the phrase in her mind. She said it over and over, until he disappeared from the deck with a smile and a promise not to be too long.

Rachel became aware of a distant sound, a *chut-chut-chut* over the mainland. She scanned the shoreline and saw the flashing lights in the sky. A helicopter. A police helicopter. And as far away from her as the North Pole.

What was it looking for, she wondered. Was there a report of some violence on the shore? Or was it merely a routine survey? Would it shine its search beam soon? Would it catch a glimpse of a boat at sea? The contemplation of these things gave her an eerie mix of hope and despair. She'd always had confidence in law enforcement. But it did no good if the law didn't know where you were, knew nothing of the iniquity being practiced under cover of darkness.

The water was black all around her, malevolent. She found herself wondering, if somehow she were to get loose, how long it would take her to swim to shore. The ocean was cold and unyielding, nothing like the amiable pool at USC.

Would she make it? Could she? Or would some voracious life-form under the inky surface reach up and gorge itself on her, smelling her fear?

Gather yourself, she thought. *Take a few deep breaths.*

The smell of salt air filled her nose.

Strength. Pray for strength. She remembered something Manny Mendoza once said in a sermon. He was preaching about expectations. He said that new Christians sometimes had the expectation that life with Christ was going to be smooth and happy and without obstacle. That there would be no major problems, no confrontation with evil, no valley of the shadow ever again. Not so, he said, not so. There would be tribulation in the world. That was certain. But the other certainty was that Jesus has overcome the world.

She was praying when Stefanos, or the man who called himself Stefanos, appeared on deck, carrying a tray draped with linen and filled with what looked like a meal and utensils.

"Sorry for the delay," he said, pulling up a chair close to hers along with a small table and setting down the tray. "But I wanted this to be a decent meal. You deserve that." He reached behind her head and untied the gag. He then leaned over the tray and started assembling. He placed two small dishes at opposite ends of the tray. Rachel saw two shrimp cocktails on the tray, as nicely arranged as in any restaurant. Stefanos opened a bottle of sparkling water and filled two glasses.

The cold normalcy of this ritual was even more chilling to Rachel than the ignominy of being tied up like an animal. The man was committing his crime without any sense of tension or strain.

"What's your real name?" Rachel said.

"Dinner conversation? I'm in charge of that. We won't talk about names." He placed a shrimp cocktail on each dish, then held one up to her mouth.

"I'm not hungry," said Rachel.

"Eat," Stefanos said in an uncompromising tone. Deciding this was not the time and place for resistance, Rachel opened her mouth.

Stefanos put the shrimp on her tongue, still holding the tail. "Go on, bite," he said.

She did as he said. Stefanos sat back, tossed the tail on the tray, and dipped a shrimp for himself.

"That's better," he said. "Now we can, like the walrus said, talk of many things. You remember the walrus in the Lewis Carroll poem, don't you?"

Rachel nodded.

"He saw the absurdity of it all but managed to put it together anyway. Some say the walrus was insane. But I say he was a genius. He saw things as they really were and expressed it."

Rachel tried to think of something to say. The word made *absurd* stuck in her head. What better word was there to describe what was happening at that moment?

"The walrus," he continued, "taught me many things. One of them is that you can be a walrus or an oyster in this world. You remember what happened to the oysters, don't you? They were eaten. Every one."

Stefanos offered her another shrimp, and she took it like the last. He took another himself, then raised her water glass, allowing her to sip.

"Now that we're all comfortable with each other," he said, "let's talk, shall we?"

"All right," Rachel answered, trying to sound as normal as possible. She was amazed at just how calm she did sound. She felt a small, almost imperceptible current of strength running within her. Maybe it was illusory, but it steadied her nonetheless.

Stefanos said, "Your name is Rachel Ybarra, and you are twenty-four years old. You were born in Montebello, California, attended Cal State, and are going into your third year of law school at USC. How am I doing so far?"

Chilled and amazed, Rachel said nothing.

"Your mother died many years ago, and you had a brother who died, I believe in a violent fashion. Now you work for the United States Attorney's Office, a very good career move, I might add, and you live in Hollywood with your grandmother."

At the mention of Abi, Rachel stiffened.

"Have I missed anything?" Stefanos said.

"Not much." A small fire of anger was beginning to burn inside her.

"Now there is no reason you shouldn't have a long and prosperous career with the U.S. Attorney. Yes, and there is no reason you shouldn't go on living. No reason at all."

Stefanos popped another shrimp into his mouth, this time consuming the entire thing, tail and all. "I'll untie you now." He reached in his pocket and came out with a closed switchblade. The blade snapped to attention with a cold, ominous click. "But you have to promise me," he said, "that you won't do anything foolish. That wouldn't be helpful. Have we got a deal?"

Rachel, her arms tired and shoulders throbbing, said, "Yes."

"Fine." He walked to the back of the chair, and Rachel felt him cut the ropes. She brought her arms to the front of her body with an exhalation of relief.

"There, isn't that better?" Stefanos said. He sat back in his chair, folded the blade, and put it in his pocket. Then he removed a handgun from under his left armpit. "This is a Lorcin L-380, a semiautomatic pistol that is quite effective from short range. I just want you to know that it's here."

Rachel watched as he replaced the gun in a shoulder holster. "If you're trying to scare me . . ."

"Yes?"

"You're doing a good job."

"Well that helps. It makes my job that much easier, don't you see?"

"No, I don't see."

"Let me try to explain. We're not unreasonable people. That part you don't have to worry about. We're fair. We set up the terms and tell you exactly what you need to do. But we do insist that the terms are carried out. If they are not, that's when you have to fear us."

"So you are this 'Man' you were talking about."

"I am."

"Just an old-fashioned hit man."

"I prefer the term *craftsman*."

"You call killing people a craft?"

"Why not? What's the difference? You do something well, you are a craftsman."

"How many people have you killed?" Even in her fear, Rachel felt almost like he was inviting her to a conversation. It was the strangest thing, but she went with her feeling. Maybe if he talked enough he would forget about everything else. Or slip up. Or something, anything. Having never been in such a surreal situation before, Rachel was flying by the seat of her pants.

Stefanos cocked his head a little, as if Rachel were a curiosity to him. "Time is slipping away from us." He pulled a cell phone from his coat pocket and opened it. "You need to call Grandma," he said.

"Why?"

"To tell her you're not coming home."

Rachel's pulse quickened. "I'm not?"

"No. We have much more to talk about."

"You're going to keep me a prisoner?"

"Guest."

"For how long?"

"However long it takes." He handed her the phone. "Now call and say you had dinner with a friend, a girlfriend from law school, and you're going to spend the night. You'll get back to her in the morning."

"You want me to lie to her?"

"Of course."

"I can't do that."

"Sure you can."

"I can't."

"It's easy. Just move your lips."

"I can't lie to my grandmother."

"You want me to make the call?" He held the phone to his ear and feigned conversation. "Hello, is this Rachel's grandmother? I don't want to alarm you, but your granddaughter is dead, and you're next. Hello? Hello? Are you there?" He snapped the phone shut. "Must have had a heart attack."

The man's gaze was like wind over frozen tundra. If Rachel had any doubts before about his willingness to do just as he said, they were erased by his glare. In that moment a confusion of thoughts and considerations rumbled through Rachel's mind as she tried to be rational in a completely irrational situation.

Rachel took the phone from Stefanos and dialed the number. Abi picked up on the first ring.

"It's me, Abi."

"Oh, I've been worried. Are you studying?"

"No," she said. Stefanos was leaning slightly forward, listening intently to her every word and nuance. "I'm with a friend."

"A friend?"

"From law school. One of my study partners."

"Then you *are* studying."

"We had dinner together."

"What time will you be home?"

"It's a long drive. I think I'm going to stay with her tonight."

After a slight pause, Abi said, "Are you sure?"

"Yes. We'll be up late, and it's better if I just crash at her place."

"Well why don't you leave me a number where I can reach you?"

That was a query she had not been ready for. Her mind scrambled to formulate an answer. "Um, we're not at her place yet, and I'm on a pay phone."

"But what if I need you?"

"I'll call you in the morning. Don't worry. I've got to go."

"Are you all right?"

"Of course I'm all right, Abi. Sure. Good night."

"Don't stay up too late, dear."

"Right."

Rachel waited until Abi hung up, then handed the phone back to Stefanos. Her head felt heavy. She wanted to cry, not for herself but for her grandmother, who was now pulled into this noxious charade.

"That was very nice," Stefanos said. At that moment Rachel wanted to jump on him and scratch his eyes out, wrap a rope around his neck, and pull. The anger inside her was like an eruption of molten lava. It was primeval, raw, the base part of human nature crying for expression without thought or reflection.

"Just what is it you want from me?" Rachel asked.

"I told you, information."

"What kind?"

"The kind that helps."

"And you're prepared to kill if you don't get it?"

"It's a simple calculation, isn't it?"

"Why do you do it?"

"Do what?"

"Kill."

The question seemed to give him pause, though only for an instant. But in that instant Rachel thought she saw a hint of vulnerability, like the thin light that escapes through the crack of a boarded-up window.

"Because," Stefanos said, "I'm well paid."

"Is that the only reason?"

"What other reason is there?"

"To take away a life? How do you justify that?"

A smile creeped onto Stefanos's mouth, like a rat slowly poking its body out of a hole in a dank wall. "So it's philosophy you want to discuss." He seemed, in a perverse way, to lighten up at the suggestion. "I know about you."

"Yes?" Rachel answered, not knowing exactly what he meant.

"Yes I do. You're part of a Christian group at the university."

"That's right."

"And you take that nonsense seriously?"

"Yes."

"Here at the close of the twentieth century? Someone with your obvious intelligence? Why do you cling to it?"

"I believe in it."

"Like a child believes in Santa Claus?"

"No. Like someone who trusts his parents."

"You intrigue me."

"You intrigue *me*."

Stefanos issued a short laugh. "Then we intrigue each other. This should be the start of a beautiful friendship."

Picking up on the ironic tone in his voice, but heartened by the fact that he was at least talking to her, Rachel said, "Have you ever thought about giving it all up?"

Stefanos looked at her as if she were an odd-colored snake in some glass enclosure. Rachel was surprised at how directly she was speaking to a man who moments before had wielded both a knife and a gun in her face.

"You mean," said Stefanos, "should I inform? Like Dedenok?"

"More than that," Rachel pressed. "Turn your whole life completely around."

He stood up. "The conversation is over for now. You better get some sleep."

"Sleep? Where?"

"Below."

"You expect me to sleep here?"

"You're my guest."

"How long are you going to keep me here?"

"I haven't decided yet." He moved away from his chair and toward the port bow. "You'll find a bed in the first cabin, all made up and ready."

Rachel stood up, feeling her lower back rebelling against staying in one position too long. He had his back to her. For a moment she thought about running at him, knocking him over the side, commandeering the boat, and making a miraculous escape. The fantasy disappeared as he turned around to face her.

"I want to go home," she said.

"You can't. You're spending the night with a friend, remember?"

CHAPTER TWO

THREE O'CLOCK, and still sleep would not come. Jeff had suffered bouts of insomnia before, especially in the months after he'd been shot. Night visions of guns exploding and innocent people dying had haunted him in those days. Mercifully the visions had become less frequent over time.

In these early morning hours, though, it wasn't images from the past but of the future that beset him. What future? His. What kind of future? The kind without closed ends, where the things done and not done in the present are never fully healed, or rectified.

Something was wrong, but he didn't know what. Something stunk, but he couldn't identify the smell. Was it incipient paranoia? Was it only the interplay of the wild imaginings of his own mind?

Yes, one side of him said.

No, said the other.

The argument continued, chasing away sleep.

He rolled out of bed for the third time, walked through the darkness to his refrigerator, and opened it. He pulled out the gallon of milk, half full, and drank from the jug. From the cupboard he took a bag of shelled peanuts and tramped to his sofa, grabbed the remote, and clicked on the TV.

He wanted the dull mindlessness of whatever was being broadcast at that hour.

The first thing he landed on was an infomercial for some product that took leftovers and converted them, "*as if by magic,*" into lovely garnishes and hors d'oeuvres. Dully he watched as two effervescent hosts, a man and woman both in the grips of terminal cuteness, effused enthusiastically around a rotund man in a chef's apron. This, Jeff surmised, was the inventor of the thing.

What a worthy achievement in life. Smiling bitterly, Jeff clicked the remote and landed on a news station. He didn't pause. He didn't want anything to do with the reality of the news shows—a reality viewed strictly through a lens that filtered out stories with anything redeeming in them.

He flashed by a religious station—some guy in a tie behind a desk talking about Bible prophecy—then he hit a cartoon channel. Popeye was in trouble, Bluto had him by the neck, and Olive Oyl was doing her usual wail of despair. This was a comfortable place to stop, a place where Jeff could predict an outcome. Popeye would pop his spinach can, and all would be right with the world.

Jeff wondered if there was a spinach can waiting around for him somewhere. Some force, some *deus ex machina*, an Aladdin's lamp. Anything to get him out of this grip of disheartenment.

Popeye had to use his pipe to suck up the spinach.

Something is wrong.

He got up and turned on a light. On a small table, under the bowl he'd used for breakfast cereal the day before, was a sheaf of papers. He picked up the bowl and grabbed the papers, then sat in a chair and looked through them. They were the notes he'd been making, during odd hours, of his interactions with Paul Dedenok.

Where was that page he was looking for? He found it. In his own lousy handwriting—always too flat, looking like the letters were smashed—Jeff recounted some of the last words Dedenok had spoken:

I am haunted too . . . .

I will never find rest . . . They will find me.

The Man is outside . . . .

Jeff tried to remember the look on Dedenok's face when he said these things. It wasn't the look of a man who was *frightened.* It was the look of a man *resigned,* who had accepted his fate.

Was this the sort of man who would commit suicide? Perhaps. But then again, he had seemed prepared to testify. He did not seem prepared to die.

So why did he kill himself? No one got to him, no one talked to him. No one threatened him or his family. How could they? Jeff and Sam Zagorsky were his only family.

Did someone else kill him?

The thought jumped into Jeff's mind out of nowhere. It was crazy, and he knew it, but he entertained it for a moment because nothing else made any sense.

What if it was somebody else?

Who? And how could he have gotten in the hotel room without Sam knowing it?

There were several problems. First, the assassin would have to know where they were hiding Dedenok. Next, he would have to know when one of the agents was going out to get lunch. Then, somehow, he would have to overcome the normal security of the hotel—video surveillance, coded key card—though in this day and age nothing was truly secure. Finally, if he managed to get in the room, he would have had to do so with such stealth—or such stunning rapidity—that Sam never knew, literally, what hit him.

Then there was Dedenok. What was he doing all this time? Standing idly by? Watching Vanna White turn letters while a federal agent was being slugged just outside his bedroom?

There was no sign of trauma on Dedenok, save for the ugly slits that began in the middle of his forearms and ended, like jagged deltas, at his wrists.

No visible signs.

Jeff grabbed a piece of scrap paper and jotted a quick note to himself—one word: *Coroner.*

He rubbed his eyes and sat back in his chair. He needed more information. There had to be more information out there he had not yet tapped and which might somehow form a pattern.

Who could he speak with about these things?

Well, the choice was obvious. She would be the one to start with, because it would be a matter of the proverbial two birds with one stone.

He had found himself thinking about her more and more these past few days, between the tortured thoughts about himself and the Dedenok matter.

He would call Rachel Ybarra in the morning.

A fog had drifted in from the open sea, enveloping the coastline and waters in a soft obscurity. He could hear the periodic sounds of a foghorn, like in the old movies about the wharf at midnight, when gunrunners or bootleggers transacted their business while the law slept.

But he couldn't sleep. The woman below had disturbed him more than he cared to admit. There had to be a reason, one looming, obvious reason, and he had to find it. Find it so he could eliminate it, much as he would eliminate a target with two slugs to the back of the head.

What had done it?

Was it the fact that she was a woman? Yes, he was attracted to her, in a different way than with his other women. He had no trouble getting women, and he knew why they were drawn to him. It was pure, animal magnetism. The less he cared, the more ruthless he became, the more they seemed drawn. And in return he gave them what they sought.

The woman below was different because she never would be attracted to him in that way. And that made her dangerous.

The waters lapped quietly against the hull. The boat rocked easily, like a lullaby. He thought for a moment that the sea was calling to him, gently, like a mother, even though he had never known a mother's call. Not a real mother, but a series of stand-ins, the last of them dressed in black.

Blackness seemed suddenly vivid to him, as he sensed the fog growing thicker. The lights on the shore had long since faded away, like the stars and the moon, but now it all seemed so much darker, and closing in.

And the darkness was inside him.

He shook himself and growled audibly, as if in rebuke of his own weakness. He needed a healthy jolt of anger and hatred, and he got it.

The woman below would have to be dealt with harshly. She would have to be shown her place. He would have to break her down, not just mentally but spiritually. She believed in spirit. He would disabuse her of that belief.

She was getting to him in a way he did not like. He would have to stop that from happening. In a few hours, it would begin.

Rachel awoke without knowing how long she had slept. She knew her sleep had been in fits and starts, and that it had taken hours before she found any relief. As she groggily pulled herself into wakefulness, her senses began to remind her where she was and whom she was with.

The smell of sea air was palpable, even in the closeness of the small cabin. She heard movement and the sound of an engine. Gray light labored through the curtained window.

Rubbing sleep from her eyes, Rachel pushed back the curtain and looked out at the fog. She had no way of knowing what time it was.

But it was a new day, and mornings had always given her hope. She closed her eyes and prayed, as she would at the start of an ordinary day. Then she got up, put on her shoes, and climbed the stairs to the deck.

Stefanos was at the wheel on the upper pilot station with his back to her. With the drone of the engine and the swoosh of the sea, he would not hear her. She could silently creep up behind him, grab any blunt instrument available, and smash the side of his head.

She wouldn't do it, of course. He had accomplished his initial goal and put a healthy fear into her, not only for herself, but for Abi. He was a professional, after all. She reminded herself of his use of the word "craftsman." It made her shiver in the morning mist.

As if on cue, Stefanos turned around and saw her. He nodded and motioned her up. She ascended to the pilot station.

"Nice morning," Stefanos said.

"Where are we going?" Rachel asked.

"I'm taking you home."

Relief washed over her. Then just as quickly it receded, replaced by the hard, dry recollection that Stefanos was not through with her, that this was only the start of their aberrant relationship.

"You do want to go home, don't you?" he said.

"Yes."

His voice became a glacial monotone. "Home to Grandma?"

He didn't need to say anymore to remind her of the fullness of his menace and the vehemence of his intent.

For several minutes Stefanos guided the boat in silence.

"Our arrangement will be like this," he said finally. "I will contact you. You will never try to contact me. Ever. I will know where you are, and you will know that I know. Are you with me so far?"

She nodded.

"I will tell you what information I need, and you'll provide it. It's as simple as that."

A vice seemed to enclose her throat, making it difficult to breath easily, like some medieval torture device. He had her in his control. She was powerless.

"Of course, you won't mention our little arrangement to anybody. That would be very bad form and result in certain consequences. Also, don't even think about leaving your job. That would be the easy way out, but it isn't acceptable. Do you understand?"

Again she nodded, her head light.

"Out loud," he demanded.

"What?"

"Tell me out loud that you understand."

"I understand."

"Good. We can begin right away."

No, she thought, not now. Not without a chance to get away from him and find some sort of respite from the last twenty-four hours.

"You spoke to someone in New York," he said flatly, looking straight ahead at the enshrouded waters. "Who was it?"

"What do you mean?"

"Don't play games. Not now. Not after all we've meant to each other."

The threatening playfulness of his tone filled Rachel with even more dread. "There's nothing to report."

Sighing impatiently, Stefanos said, "Don't lie to *me*. Others you may lie to, but not to me."

"I am not lying. I am telling you there is nothing to report."

He studied her face. "You did meet with someone. . . ."

Rachel tried to keep her expression neutral.

"But it didn't pan out. That's it, isn't it?"

She answered with her silence.

"So you did meet with a potential witness, but he decided not to testify. A good career move on his part. But I'll have to know who it was."

"Why?" Rachel pleaded, her voice sounding to her like it did when she was a little girl and told she would have to perform some unpleasant task.

"I've told you. It's information."

"But there is no need. She's not going to—" Rachel stopped quickly, closed her eyes, knowing she had blown it.

"She?" Stefanos said slowly. "Now that's a twist."

Tears of rage and frustration erupted under her eyes. She battled them with only partial success. She heard the moan of a foghorn and saw a shaft of light struggling through the blanket of fog.

"Who was it?" he said.

"Don't."

"Come now, this is no way to start. Give me the name."

"I'm telling you she will not testify. What more do you want?"

He turned then to look at her. "You," he said.

She was too shocked to reply.

"I want you," he explained coldly, "completely and utterly. I want you to know that I own you. And I want you to know something else."

She waited.

"I want you to know there isn't a thing your God can do about it." He paused to let the words sink in. "Now tell me," he said, looking back toward the sea, "that you understand. That you understand I own you. That you will do exactly as I say from this time forward."

The foghorn groaned against the morning invisibility, like a mournful matin from a distant church. Without thought, Rachel slipped off her shoes and said, "I understand."

"Good," said Stefanos. "And now the name, the name of the one you met with."

Inching toward him, Rachel said, "Her name . . ."

"Yes."

He waited, looking ahead, hands on the wheel—but not on the throttle. Rachel, fully in the throes of emotion, reached out, grabbed the throttle, and pushed it.

The boat lurched forward with an angry growl.

She sensed Stefanos stumbling backward as she, facing the stern, allowed the force to carry her. She felt his hands strike out wildly, grabbing for her, catching part of her dress. Her momentum freed her from his clutch. She heard the thud of his body against the rail and a curse escape from his mouth.

Force of motion propelled her out over the stairs. This she had anticipated. She did not anticipate the deck, how hard it would be, and her right ankle turned on impact, sending bolts of pain up her leg. She wondered if she had broken it but did not pause in her wonder. Struggling to her feet she made for the side. Her right foot couldn't support her, so she hopped, and as she did the boat pounded into a swell and knocked her flat.

With the little presence of mind she had left, she glanced back up at the bridge and saw Stefanos standing up, wobbly, finding balance. Something told her she had to get up now, or it would all be over. Forever. She pushed against the deck and up onto her left leg. The roll of the pleasure craft went her way, and with a little push off her good leg she propelled herself off the side and into the cold ocean waters.

Engulfed in the churning anger of the wake, Rachel struggled for breath and composure, steadying herself by treading, and watching as the yacht disappeared quickly into the thick soup of fog that was now her ally. She listened to the sound of the engine as it grew fainter, then as it seemed to cut, slow, and prepare for a new direction.

She thought she heard the sound of a voice, laughing.

Then the foghorn gave its warning, and Rachel turned toward the sound. Braced by the cold waters, she struggled out of her blouse and dress, discarding them more easily than she would have expected, and began to swim.

CHAPTER THREE

THE RESIDENT MEDICAL EXAMINER was maybe twenty-six or twenty-seven. Jeff thought he looked a little like Ray Bolger, the scarecrow in *The Wizard of Oz*. He had the same hook nose that was a tad too large for the tapered face and the gangling arms and legs. The only thing missing was the grace. He didn't move like a dancer. He moved like a skeleton on a pole.

"You wanted to see me?" the ME said. They were in his office, a small affair with some standard medical tools scattered about and a computer terminal. The ME was in his scrubs, which hung on him loosely.

"I'd like to see the autopsy report on a Paul Dedenok," Jeff said.

"Dedenok . . . sounds familiar. You sure there was an autopsy?"

"He was reported as a suicide. I assume it's *pro forma*."

"Sometimes. You never know. We get eighteen thousand bodies a year through here. Not always room for everyone."

"You want to check the records?"

Looking as if this was a novel suggestion, the ME said, "Oh, right. How do you spell the last name?"

Jeff told him. The ME pecked away at his computer terminal. A moment later he turned around and said, "Yep, we have the report. I remember it now. I'm doing some work on it."

Nodding, Jeff waited for the guy to move. He didn't. Jeff said, "May I see it?"

"Oh, right." The ME stood and walked out of the office.

Another shining example of bureaucratic efficiency, Jeff thought. *If this is to be my fate, remind me not to die.*

A few minutes later the ME came back with a 12 x 14 envelope and handed it to Jeff. "You'll have to read that in here," he said.

"I'm not going anywhere," said Jeff.

"Just in case you were wondering."

"I wasn't."

"Right."

Jeff opened the envelope and removed the contents, which included a photograph of the body, fingerprint card, property check, an ID record, and an autopsy report. Jeff picked up the report and read the summary of findings.

It listed the cause of death as a three-inch, jagged fragment of glass, producing lacerations on the forearms and wrists, resulting in massive hemorrhage and death. Manner of death: suicide.

No surprises. Jeff flipped the page and began scanning the full report. Dedenok had been sliced open with a Y incision, his organs removed and weighed, his skull sawed through so they could get to the brain. Nothing unusual reported. Paul Dedenok had, apparently, been just like the rest of us underneath.

Jeff tossed the report on the desk with a huff of disgust. But what had he expected to find? Everything there was to know about Dedenok's death he had probably already observed when he found the body. No mystery about it. Dedenok had sliced away his own life. As hard as that was to accept, that was just the way things were.

The ME was looking at the photo of Dedenok, like a bored shopper might scan the front page of the *Enquirer*. "You have anything to do with this autopsy?" Jeff said.

"I got to watch is all," the ME replied. "I watch two more and then I get to do one."

"Won't that be a treat?"

"Better than running tests on the clothes. Makes me feel like a laundry worker."

Jeff raised an eyebrow. "You test the clothing?"

"Right now I do," the ME said defensively.

"But there weren't any clothes in this case, since the victim was in a bathtub."

"No," the ME said, "they picked up his clothes. They were in a heap on the floor."

"I didn't see that in the report."

"It's not in the report." There was sort of a twinkle in the ME's eye.

"And why not?" Jeff asked.

"Because I'm not finished with it yet. . . ."

"Well, have you done any of tests?"

"Not yet."

"What's your name, by the way?"

"Palmer."

"Your first name, I mean."

"Palmer," the ME said with a slight rebuff. "Last name is Froug."

"All right, Mr. Froug," said Jeff, trying to sound respectful. "I would greatly appreciate it if you would share with me the results of your findings."

"Sure," Froug said. "When it happens. I've only given the clothes a quick scan."

"Any blood on them?" Jeff asked.

"Nope. They were clean."

"Any rips or other signs of struggle, maybe?"

"Nope," said Froug.

"No violence at all?"

"That horse won't run," said Froug with a chuckle.

Jeff ran his fingers through his hair, feeling tired all of a sudden. His lack of sleep the night before was catching up with him. He thought seriously about getting back in his car, driving home, and climbing into bed for the rest of the day.

"Well," Jeff said finally, "thanks anyway." He started to get up.

"There is one thing," Froug said, his eyes still glued to the screen.

Without much enthusiasm, Jeff grunted.

"I want to confirm this first," Froug said, "but I did notice a little odor on the shirt."

"Odor?"

"Like cologne."

"Yeah," Jeff said, "the guy was partial to cologne, even when he was sitting around the hotel room. We allowed him that little indulgence."

"But I don't think it's cologne. At least not any kind that's going to attract many women." Froug smiled wryly at Jeff.

"Well, what was it?" Jeff said.

"I'm not a hundred percent sure, of course, but I think it may be trichloromethane."

Jeff thought a moment. "You mean chloroform?"

"Yep."

"You're kidding."

"Nope."

"Why would there be trichloromethane on his clothes?"

"You remember how they used it in the movies, don't you? As a way to knock people out."

"That's a pretty significant finding, wouldn't you say?"

"It might be, if it's confirmed."

"When will it be confirmed?"

"When I run a test."

"And when will that be?"

"I don't know yet. I've got a lot things I have to do. People are just dying to get in here."

Froug smiled broadly. Jeff wanted to grab him and shake him and tell him to forget everything else and run that test. But professional courtesy prevailed. He took out his card and handed it to Froug. "I would greatly appreciate it if you could get to that test as soon as possible and then give me a call."

"You got a theory?"

"Don't we all?"

"Oh," Froug said flatly. "Right."

As he drove away from the coroner's office, Jeff felt all the fatigue leaving him. Adrenaline pumped through his body. He tried to gather his jumbled thoughts into a coherent pattern, but it was still mostly a mess.

That's when Jeff decided to point his Chevy Blazer toward the hills of Altadena.

Grigory guided the yacht through the early morning fog in a slow, almost contemplative fashion. He would reach the hidden dock up the coast in good time, but he was in no hurry. He wanted to give the events of the last few hours some thought.

Would he kill her? He wasn't sure, though her religious beliefs gave him an added incentive. The last time he killed a man of God was in 1990. Sergei Znosko had not only defected, he had gone crawling back to God by way of the Orthodox Church. Didn't help him with his drinking, though. When Grigory caught up with him on the lower West side of Manhattan, he smelled of cheap bourbon.

Znosko was an officer in the KGB's Second Chief Directorate, handling counterintelligence inside the Soviet Union. Specifically, Znosko surveilled officers from MI-6, British Intelligence. Grigory didn't know him personally but always heard Znosko was an exceptionally good agent. There was something about his background, though, that was troubling. He'd been raised Orthodox, and when he first tried to join the Communist party he was rejected. That only seemed to spur him on, because he eventually became a well-regarded KGB agent. Until the defection. First, Znosko quit the KGB in 1989. Grigory heard it was out of disgust with Moscow's worsening political drift and the paralysis it was causing inside the KGB. So he went off to start a new life in the oil business in the emerging private sectors.

Late in 1989 he traveled to New York on business, got drunk, and was hauled in by the local police. An officer turned Znosko over to the FBI. They convinced him to defect.

This itself wasn't news. By that time the U.S. government was getting very selective about which Soviets it accepted into its defector program. So many ex-KGB officers were trying to jump off the sinking Soviet ship—nearly one a month—that the CIA had to start turning them away. Communism was in full retreat, and to many inside the KGB, the final collapse of the Soviet empire seemed inevitable.

But Znosko knew something. A KGB mole had penetrated the CIA's Moscow station. That's why a spate of American agents had been and would be executed.

Grigory was at this time working directly under Leonid Shebarshin, the legendary leader of First Directorate in the final years of the KGB.

Shebarshin held a great hole card in the poker game with the United States—Aldrich Ames. He was convinced that Znosko would eventually identify him.

That's when Grigory went to work. He arrived in New York at Christmastime. As usual, the holiday trappings repelled him. The lights, the false gaiety, the hypocrisy of city dwellers singing songs of cheer while knocking each other senseless in F. A. O. Schwarz—all of it was commercial worship of a nonexistent deity.

Znosko was back to worshiping that deity. The early concerns of the Party had been correct. Once the corrosive fluid of religion was inside you, it could come back at any time.

Grigory found Znosko easily. He picked him up coming out of a nondescript church on First Avenue and followed him to his small flat—they called them apartments here—on Delancy Street. The building was filthy, marked by graffiti and peeling plaster. That was just as well. The people here would probably care even less about unfamiliar noises than the uptown crowd.

Znosko's apartment was in the rear corner, another benefit. If Grigory had believed in fate or luck, he would have chalked it up to that. It was good, too, when Znosko answered the knock on the door with only the chain lock separating him from his imminent demise.

"What is?" Znosko grumbled through the crack in the door.

With a swift kick, Grigory broke the chain lock and sent Znosko sprawling backward on the floor. Before Znosko could scream, Grigory was inside, kicking the door closed at the same time he pulled his Makarov 9mm and placed the barrel in Znosko's mouth. The look of fear on the hapless traitor's face was most interesting.

"Do you want to pray?" Grigory asked.

Zonosko's face grew even more afraid, and he shook his head violently. Perhaps he meant only that he wanted to buy time, but Grigory found it disgusting that even the man's insipid faith was not meaningful enough to him to make any difference.

He dispatched Znosko immediately, feeling no particular rush. He had expected more of a challenge.

Now, thinking about this Rachel Ybarra, he detected a difference. She also had seemed fearful, yet her fear was only a surface fear. She had more defiance behind the look than Znosko had. Was it because her faith was stronger? He would have to find out about that. He would have to get to the root of Rachel Ybarra, the better to strip her of her pretensions and prepare her to be used.

He also noted, deep in the recesses of his mind, barely giving the thought much attention, that she was, very definitely, an attractive woman. He had not felt that way about a woman in a long time. Perhaps it was time to think that way again.

Abi had just about busted a blood vessel when the cab dropped Rachel off and she entered the house dressed and smelling like a fisherman from Nova Scotia. She was wrapped up in an old blanket, and her hair had all the allure of dead kelp washed onto a windswept beach.

"*Que pasó?*" was all her grandmother could say.

"Don't ask. Just pay the cab driver, will you?"

When Abi returned from the street she said, "What happened to you last night? You look like you fell in a sewer."

"I feel like it," Rachel said, trying to sound nonchalant.

Abi was fidgeting around her neck with her fingers. "I was worried."

"I called you, remember?"

"And then when you show up like this. *Dios mio!* What happened to your clothes?"

"Abi, if it's all the same to you, I'd rather not talk about it now."

The old woman frowned. "Are you in some kind of trouble?"

"Me?" Rachel almost laughed.

"You can tell me, *conejíta*. We have never had secrets."

Outside the window a bird was chirping, as if this were the first morning in heaven. "I just—" Rachel hesitated, searching for words. "—I just don't want to talk about it right now, okay?"

"It is not man trouble, is it?"

"No!"

"I'm sorry," Abi said quickly, "but I have never seen you like this before."

Rachel closed her eyes. "I'm sorry I yelled like that, Abi. Can you trust me on this? Can you just drop the subject?"

Abi looked sadly down at her hands. "I suppose."

"Thank you. Listen, I think it might be a good idea if I got an apartment close to the school."

The look of sadness that swept across Abi's face stabbed Rachel in the heart. "You . . . want to move?"

"For now."

"But that will cost money."

"I've got some."

"Don't you like it here?" Her voice trailed off, like a child's.

Rachel jumped up and went to her, throwing her arms around her grandmother's neck. "Of course I like it here, Abi. But for a number of reasons, I've got to go."

"If you feel that way," Abi said. "But I'll be so lonely without you."

Abi's eyes filled with tears, and Rachel could do nothing but hold her tighter, closer. The bile of hatred rose once more in Rachel, hatred for what The Man was making her do and say to the woman she loved more than any on earth.

The Zagorsky house in Altadena was like a postcard from the world of Norman Rockwell. It even had a picket fence—Sam had put it up himself, slat by slat, he was proud to say—and Janie had tended to the rose garden that bloomed in beautiful colors around the yard. From Sam's front yard Jeff could see the San Gabriel Mountains, which on this Saturday morning were clear of the usual weekly smog layer that was commuter L.A.'s gift to this outlying community.

As Jeff let himself in the front gate and walked toward the house, he heard the kids' voices squealing in the backyard. They were playing and obviously as happy as kids should be. All seemed right, in this world at least, as Jeff pressed the doorbell.

Janie answered, dressed in paint-spattered clothes and holding a roller brush. "Jeff!"

"Hi, Janie."

"Come on in."

"Am I interrupting anything?" He stepped into the foyer.

Janie closed the door. "I'm only painting the kitchen. I can grab you a roller."

"I didn't bring a thing to wear."

"I've got an old dress you can use."

"My size?"

"Touché. Sam's in the family room, helping me out by sorting through the newspaper. Coffee?"

"No, thanks. I won't be long."

"Any trouble?"

"No, no trouble. Just doing some thinking, and I wanted to bounce it off Sam."

"Well his rubber head is good for that. Go on in."

Jeff knew the way to the family room and found Sam seated in his recliner, reading glasses propped on the end of his nose, scanning the *Times*.

"Helping your wife I see," said Jeff.

Sam looked up, startled. "Jeff, what are you doing here?"

"Hey, it's a Saturday. I didn't have anything to do."

For a moment Sam regarded him oddly, as if he didn't pick up the obvious joke. "Well come on in," he said. "Sit down."

Jeff sat on the sofa as Sam folded the paper and tossed it on the floor next to his chair. "Head doing okay?"

"Yeah, much better." Sam rubbed his temples. "It doesn't feel like they're tunneling through anymore."

"Good." Jeff rubbed his thighs. An uncomfortable silence hung in the room for a long moment.

"So," Sam said tentatively, "what's the real reason you came out here?"

"I wanted to talk to you about something."

"Dedenok?"

"Yeah."

"I thought as much. I told you to give it up."

"I can't."

"You have to."

"Not until I'm clear in my own mind."

"Look, what's there to be clear about? He iced himself. He couldn't go through with it. Who knows why? You can never tell with those guys, with their backgrounds. But there it is. He did it. He's gone. What more is there to think about?"

"I have some new information."

Sam frowned. "What new information?"

"I went down to the coroner's office and saw the autopsy report on Dedenok."

"They did an autopsy?"

"Routine in suicide cases."

This looked like it was news to Sam. "And?"

"Well, this guy who assisted in the autopsy, an assistant ME, he examined Dedenok's shirt."

"Why his shirt?"

"Routine again. See if anything was on the clothes. Blood, whatever."

"So was there?"

"None of that. But he thinks there was something."

Sam leaned forward in the recliner. "What?"

"Chloroform."

The house filled with shrieking. Sam almost hit the ceiling. Two seconds later a boy and girl came scampering into the living room. Sam reached out with one of his beefy arms and grabbed the boy, who was in hot pursuit of his sister, lifting him off the ground.

The boy giggled, like it was all part of the game. Jeff smiled at the horseplay. He knew Sam doted on his kids, Michael and Rebecca, and never gave up an opportunity to play with them. Then Jeff realized something was wrong. Sam wasn't playing.

"I thought I told you never to scream in this house!" he yelled. The boy in his arms went suddenly limp, and his eyes widened in fear.

"I was playing," pleaded Michael, who was seven. Rebecca had stopped in the doorway and watched in silence as her older brother faced the wrath of the father.

"Not here!" Sam bellowed, his face red. Michael burst into tears.

Janie appeared immediately at the door. "What's going on?"

Sam plopped his son on the floor on top of the newspapers. The boy quickly ran and attached himself to his mother's leg.

"He's running through here screaming his head off!" Sam said.

"Did you have to yell like that?" Janie asked.

"He's got to learn!"

Jeff said, "Look, I should probably go and—"

"No," Sam insisted. "It's all right. Janie, take the kids in the other room, will you?"

"Come on," Janie said, squiring the children out.

Sam rubbed his eyes and stood up. "Sorry, Jeff. Let's go outside, huh?"

The backyard was large and neatly landscaped, the green grass spotted by random toys and the shade of a large eucalyptus on the west side of the property. Sam walked slowly toward the far end of the lawn, his hands shoved deeply into his pockets.

"What do you make out of it?" Sam asked, looking at the ground.

"I don't know what to make out of it exactly," Jeff answered, "except to say that maybe Dedenok did not kill himself."

"Doesn't that sound crazy to you?"

"On the surface."

"You're saying that someone else, some third party, got in the room, bashed me, and took care of Dedenok?"

"I guess that's the implication."

Sam stopped. They were in the shade of overhanging trees in a neighbor's yard. "That's not the only implication."

"What do you mean?"

"Think about it."

Jeff thought, but nothing came to mind at first. Then it suddenly did. The look on Sam's face confirmed it. "You?"

"Me. If what you're saying turns out to be something, what's to stop them from thinking I did it? I put Dedenok away, set it all up, then hit myself on the head to cover my rear end."

"That's absurd."

"Stranger things have happened. Don't you see that? If this comes out, I won't be a victim anymore. I'll be a suspect."

Jeff knew Sam was right. These days the public was so used to the weirdest scandals that there would be nothing at all unusual about a case involving an FBI agent gone berserk.

"I certainly don't want that, Sam," Jeff said. "I just thought you might have missed something."

"Like what?"

"I don't know, some strange fact or other, a sound, a scuff, a whiff of air—anything."

"Jeff, there's nothing."

"Will you do me a favor, Sam?"

"Like what?"

"Will you go over it again for me?"

"Jeff—"

"Please."

Sam let out an exasperated breath. "Look, it was like this. I was sitting in the chair, right? The one with its back to Dedenok's room."

"Like when we played Yahtzee."

"Right. I was reading a newspaper."

"The *Times*. I saw it."

"And I heard something like the bed squeaking in the bedroom, you know, like somebody getting off it. . . ."

"Yeah."

"And so I said, 'What's up?' You know, like we would sometimes. I didn't look up from the paper."

"Did Dedenok say anything?"

"Yeah. He said he was going to the bathroom and did I have a problem with that."

"He said that?"

"Yeah, you know, in a kind of sarcastic way."

"Then what happened?"

"Then I heard Dedenok saying something like did I have a problem if he took a bath. And I said, 'No problem,' and then I started to turn around."

"You turned around?"

"I started to turn around. I went like this—" Sam turned his head a little toward his left shoulder—"and that's when he hit me." Sam put his right hand on the right side of his head.

"When you turned around?"

"Almost turned around. I didn't have a chance to do a thing."

The information crept into Jeff's mind, destroying the delicate edifice he had begun to create there. There was no one else in the room, or Dedenok would have screamed.

"But what about the chloroform?" Jeff said.

"That's got to be a mistake," said Sam. "You know how hard it is to test that stuff. Who was this guy?"

"A guy at the coroner's office."

"Who knows?" Sam said. "All I can tell you is that I was there; I know what happened." He looked back toward his house. "Jeff, you know what it would do to my family if there was a stink about this." He stated it as a fact, not a question.

"Yeah, Sam."

"That's why I'd appreciate it if you'd drop the thing, like I told you in the first place. Just let it go. It wasn't your fault; it wasn't anybody's fault. Dedenok knew what he was going to do, and he waited for his moment. That's all."

Jeff nodded. "I guess you're right. I feel a little better. I want this thing off my back."

"Good. So, is that it? Or do you feel like staying and hanging out for awhile?"

"Gee, thanks anyway, Sam. Maybe I'll just go catch a movie or something. Get my mind clear."

"Yeah, go see one of those action things where the city gets blown up every ten minutes. That'll relax you."

Sam put his arm over Jeff's shoulder and began walking him back toward the house. "I got a feeling," Sam said, "that you're going to be all right. Things'll only get better from here."

"I hope so, Sam," Jeff said.

Rachel finished packing the suitcase with what she thought would be essential. She could leave the rest of her things at Abi's.

There would be trouble; she knew it. She tried to be rational, but the situation was out of her reality and experience. Try as she might, she could not come up with any sort of plan except one—get out of Abi's so no trouble would come near her grandmother.

It was Saturday. She could spend the rest of the day hunting for an apartment or a room. If nothing else, she could check into a motel for awhile. Anything but stay here.

She heard the phone ring, and it sent cold spikes through her body. It was him. She knew it was him.

"Phone for you," Abi said at the bedroom door. "A young man."

There was no avoiding it. Rachel told Abi she would take it in the kitchen.

"Yes?" she said coolly.

"Ms. Ybarra?" It was not The Man's voice. "This is Agent Bunnell."

A sudden wave of relief washed over her. "Oh, hello."

"I'm sorry to call you at home."

"No, it's all right."

"And on a Saturday, when you could be kicking back."

"It's not a kickback Saturday."

"You working on the case?"

"Not exactly."

"I'd like to help if I can."

"Help? In what way?"

"I don't know. Talk about things. Theories. Anything."

"There really isn't that much to talk about."

"Well, I have an ulterior motive."

"Yes?"

"I thought it would be a good way to get to spend some time with you."

That was a surprise, but a pleasant one. But this was not the time. Still, Rachel wished she could cry out to him and spill the whole thing, and let the power of the FBI take over. She wished, but she said nothing.

"See," Jeff continued, "I'm really not so bad once you get to know me. I bathe regularly. I comb my hair. I'm good to my mother."

"I'm sure you are."

"But the key is getting to know me. I thought if we combined business with pleasure, you could have that opportunity. What do you say?"

"Agent Bunnell—"

"And it's Jeff."

"—it sounds like a wonderful idea, and normally I would take you up on it."

"But?"

"It's just not the right time."

"Will there ever be a right time?"

"It's possible."

"I'm a patient man."

"I'm glad." The words surprised her, as if they had come out of some part of her she had been ignoring. She was glad she said it.

"Is everything all right?" Jeff said.

Rachel tightened her grip on the phone. "What do you mean?"

"It's just my agent instinct acting up."

"I've just got a lot of things to do today, apartment hunting, that sort of thing."

"You're looking for a place?"

"Yes."

"Anything I can do to help?"

Closing her eyes, Rachel took a breath then said, "No. But thank you. Thank you for offering."

"I'll call you again sometime, okay?"

"Sure."

They said their goodbyes, and as soon as Rachel put the phone down, she sat heavily on a kitchen chair. Agent Bunnell had picked up something in her voice. Was she that transparent? If she couldn't keep information from creeping into her telephone voice, what hope did she have when people saw her face-to-face?

She began to worry that Bunnell might inquire further. He liked her. That was clear. That might motivate him to help her through whatever he thought was troubling her. But if he did that, Stefanos would find out. And when he found out, who could predict what he would do?

The phone rang again. She picked up. "Hello?"

"Nice swim?"

Stefanos. She froze.

"You must be in great shape," he said. "I like that."

Rachel could not respond. Her throat constricted and her hand shook as it held the phone. She thought for a moment about slamming it down but knew that would be unwise. It would press the wrong button on a deadly man.

"I know what you're thinking," he said, "and I feel for you. I really do. You get tense, you start looking for a way out of this. But there is no way. And you and I both know why. I'm here to help you understand, Rachel. You can trust me. Now listen very carefully. Your grandmother is a very nice lady."

Rachel looked around the room, as if he was standing there watching her.

"Do you catch my drift?" he said.

She did. And it hit her like a slap across the face.

"Answer me, Rachel. I get somewhat perturbed when people don't answer me."

"Yes," she whispered.

"Good. You've probably been thinking of many things. Thinking of going to the police or the FBI. But you haven't yet. You've hesitated because you know what I can do. Right so far?"

"Yes."

"You may be thinking of running away somewhere. Don't do that. If you do, Grandma will be the one who will pay for the trip. Understood?"

Rachel fought back hot tears as the room seemed to recede around her.

"Do you understand?" he repeated.

"No," Rachel managed to say.

"I don't want to do anything bad to Grandma, but if you leave, I won't have much choice. Now do you understand?"

Rachel, eyes burning, couldn't speak.

"Answer me."

". . . Yes . . ."

"And don't try to move Grandma. If you do, I'll find her. And when I find her, well, you fill in the blank. Are we clear on that?"

The tears were starting to stream down her cheeks.

"Answer me, Rachel."

"Yes."

"Now I want you to stay right where you are. You will not say anything to anyone. You will go on with your life as if nothing out of the ordinary has happened. I will contact you. And don't try anything like that Olympic act again. You see, if you make another mistake like that, Grandma and I might have to talk. Do you understand?"

"Yes."

"Say, 'Yes, I understand.'"

"Yes, I understand."

"Good. That's very good. Just remember, Rachel, I'm here to help. As long as you trust me, you have nothing to fear. There's no reason we can't learn to be good friends. Good-bye now. I'll be in touch."

Click.

Rachel stood motionless, holding the phone to her ear for a long moment. When she finally put it down, she was numb. She had no feeling in her hands. She thought she might pass out.

"Is it bad news?" said Abi, standing in the kitchen doorway.

Rachel turned around. "No."

"Are you all right?"

"I'm . . . just thinking about a case."

Abi shook her head. "I think you are working too hard maybe."

Rachel looked at the wrinkled face, the one that had been her comfort many times as a little girl, and she drew strength from that. She got up and went to her grandmother and enfolded her in her arms.

"I'm not going to go," Rachel said. "I'm going to stay right here with you."

"Oh, thank you," Abi said. "Thank you."

Rachel kept her arms around Abi, tenderly stroking the old woman's hair for a long time.

CHAPTER FOUR

ON MONDAY THE CITY STRUGGLED to wake itself up for another run to Friday. The freeway system groaned under the weight of too many cars with too many solitary drivers, the sky filled with the gray-brown exhaust of rush hour, and radio talk-show hosts tried to outdo one another with scandal, outrage, and in-your-face attitude. Another day in L.A.

Rachel pulled into the parking lot two blocks from the Federal Building. Just being there brought her a slight sense of comfort, of normalcy. Maybe, she thought, if she tried hard enough, she could make it just another routine day at the U.S. Attorney's office.

She began by nodding at the security guards and walking through the metal detector. She took the elevator to the twelfth floor and smiled a greeting at Babs, the receptionist. In the hallway, an extern, John Shuie, greeted her and said that Lakewood wanted to see her in his office. She went immediately.

Lakewood said hello with a smile, then added, "I hope you had a nice weekend."

Rachel could only nod.

"Mine was hell," Lakewood said, "but it was worth it. Sit down."

She did, sensing there was news to be told. Lakewood looked haggard but also energized.

"She's agreed to testify," he said simply.

"Deanna?"

"That's right. I was on the phone with her and Hansborough all day yesterday. She finally agreed."

Rachel looked out Lakewood's office window, stunned.

"She had one condition," Lakewood said.

"What's that?"

"She wants you to be there."

"Me?"

"You made an impression on her. She trusts you. She said she'd cooperate as long as you were on the team. I assured her that would be no problem. This is great news. I wanted you to hear it from me."

"Thanks."

"You don't seem overly pleased."

"No, no," Rachel said quickly. "I just know . . . how hard it is for her, that's all."

"But you'll take her by the hand a little for us, won't you?"

"Yes, of course."

"You don't know what this means."

"I think I do."

Lakewood regarded her for a moment, then stepped behind his desk. "Next order of business; we have a pretrial meeting with the judge at 1:30 this afternoon. You haven't met Carl Montross yet, have you?"

"No."

"Well, let me tell you what that means," Lakewood said. "It means we better have our legal ducks in a row at all times, because he likes shooting little wayward ducks. And that's where you come in."

Lakewood picked up a stack of papers and plopped them on the outer edge of his desk, near Rachel. "The first defense motions. Jessica Osborn Holt at her best. Start preparing our responses."

Rachel stood, gathered up the stack, and started out. "Rachel?"

She turned. "Yes?"

"Thank you."

"For what?"

"For whatever you said to Deanna Natale. It made the difference."

With her stomach tied up in little knots, Rachel nodded and left the office.

For the next four hours she tried to concentrate on the task at hand. Holt had filed two motions—a preemptive motion for discovery and a motion to dismiss for outrageous government conduct. And Holt had done her homework. The motions were thick, packed with points and authorities that would have to be read, analyzed, and distinguished.

As she pored over the motions, Rachel picked up on the obvious strategy. Holt's aim was to put the government on trial. She would attack every stage of the proceedings, picking every possible nit, making the government waste valuable time contending with her arguments. And through it all, Jaroslav Supevsky would be presented as a normal, law-abiding citizen who had been singled out for selective prosecution.

In short, this case was going to be hardball, and Jessica Osborn Holt had come out swinging.

Rachel had anticipated that. Ever since she did the background research on Holt, she knew it would eventually come to this. It was Holt's *modus operandi*. Winning through intimidation. The best defense is a good offense.

Rachel remembered one case she had read about in which Holt had defended a lower level Mob figure in a murder case brought by the Brooklyn district attorney. The deputy who tried the case was another woman, Camille Loretti, a hardworking but rather ordinary career prosecutor. She was not prepared for the buzz saw that was Jessica Osborn Holt, eager to increase her own reputation.

From the very start, Holt and the defense team—made up of more than one Cosa Nostra soldier—did everything they could to intimidate and harass Loretti. Someone—no one ever found out who—leaked intimate details about Loretti's personal life to the New York tabloids. So each day Loretti was in court trying to put together a murder conviction, she knew that the citizens of New York were snickering at her over their Chock Full o' Nuts coffee and powdered donuts.

Inside the courtroom it was no better. One of her own witnesses changed his story on the stand and accused Loretti of making a clumsy pass at him (it was rumored that the witness had been bought off by the Mob and said his piece in order to save his life). Each time Loretti seemed to get close to presenting solid evidence, Holt and the defendant would whisper things about her that only she, and not the jury, could hear. Loretti stopped the proceedings several times and asked the judge to let the jury leave so she could complain.

The judge, a tired old geezer, admonished the defense table, but each time Holt would rise indignantly and protest that it was all a product of Loretti's paranoid imagination. Finally the judge stopped admonishing. It was clear that he just wanted to get the case over with. Without his help, Loretti was at the mercy of Holt and her minions.

The physical stress became obvious. Loretti, who spent the nights preparing and not sleeping, began to lose weight. By the time she delivered her closing argument, she looked like the walking dead. Holt, on the other hand, was impassioned and theatrical, and more than once during her own argument, she stood in front of the prosecution table, pointed her finger in the face of her adversary, and accused *her* of trying to intimidate innocent citizens!

The jury took less than two hours to return a verdict of not guilty.

That was what Alan Lakewood was facing. And he was depending on Rachel to help. So she methodically read the motions Holt had filed, highlighting with a yellow marker all the cases cited, and using a CD-ROM database, she began to read the cases themselves. Soon the challenge of legal research, something she loved, had allowed her respite from her despairing thoughts. She scribbled notes, checked cross-references, found promising cases, printed out copies. She worked right through lunch, and by 1:15 had a legal pad crammed with her research and a stack of papers, haphazardly organized, in her briefcase.

Lakewood called to her from the library door and reminded her of their meeting with the judge. He also reminded her it was Judge Montross, a man who demanded punctuality and, if he didn't get it, got very, very disagreeable.

Rachel stuffed her notes in her briefcase and joined Lakewood at the reception desk. On their way down to the second floor, Lakewood told Rachel a little more about Carl Montross. Like all federal judges he was appointed for life, free of the inconveniences of the democratic process, immune from removal except for egregious conduct leading to impeachment. And, like all federal judges, he could stay well below that line while still exercising what many deemed outrageous, idiosyncratic behavior.

"Once," Lakewood said, "a defense lawyer was arguing a motion, and Montross held up the papers he had filed. He held them out over the bench, took his pitcher of water, and poured water all over the papers. 'Your argument is all wet,' he said."

"Incredible," Rachel said.

"That's not the end of it. The next day when that lawyer came into court and started arguing, he pulled out an umbrella and opened it. The whole courtroom cracked up."

"What did Montross do?"

"He held the guy in contempt and ordered him to jail. The only one who gets to laugh in Montross's courtroom is Montross."

When they arrived on the second floor they walked down the hallway to courtroom 8. It was empty inside, save for Jessica Osborn Holt and Montross's clerk, chatting amiably. Holt looked up with an expression made up of equal parts coyness, aggression, and superiority.

"Why, Alan," she said, "welcome to the party."

"Jessica," Lakewood said abruptly.

Rachel felt Holt's glare switch to her. "And this is?"

"Rachel Ybarra," Lakewood said.

Holt did not offer her hand. "New to the office?"

"She's a student and a paralegal."

"Well, listen," Holt continued, "when you graduate, why don't you move to my side of the courtroom, where the real lawyers are?" She tossed a little wink toward Alan Lakewood, who winced. Rachel tried to read the exchange. She knew one thing for certain about Lakewood—he didn't like to lose. And his loss to Holt a few years before still gnawed at him.

"Shall we go see the judge?" Lakewood suggested.

The clerk, a woman named Celine, said, "I'll take you in."

The trio followed her out the door at the rear of the courtroom and across the private hallway to the chambers of Judge Montross. His door was open, and he motioned them in.

He seemed to fill the room. He had a steel-gray beard over a jowly, obdurate face. Stick a harpoon in his hand, Rachel thought, and he could play Ahab, crying out with maddening torment against the white whale that was the federal legal system. Or put a cigar in his mouth, and he could be the quintessential Southern patriarch in some Tennessee Williams play. Either way he appeared larger than life, and his booming voice only added to the image.

"Sit down," he commanded. He was in his shirtsleeves, his tie loosened, his bright red suspenders straining against the opposition of his torso. The bifocals perched on the edge of his nose were the only things that softened his look. That impression disappeared as he snatched them off and flung them on his desk.

"Are we about ready to go to trial?" he asked.

Holt answered quickly. "As soon as we have all our discovery, Your Honor. How can we prepare if they're holding back?"

"We're not holding anything back," Lakewood said indignantly.

"According to Ms. Holt's motion, you are," the judge answered.

"Her motion is boilerplate," Lakewood said. "You can read the same document in every case she tries."

Montross bore into Lakewood with his eyes. "That's not going to fly with me, Mr. Lakewood. I'm interested only in what is before me right now. Ms. Holt, what is it that you don't have?"

Emboldened, Jessica Osborn Holt said, "A witness list, first of all, under section 3432."

"We gave her a witness list," Lakewood protested.

"Incomplete!" said Holt. "They have another witness, and we don't know who it is."

Again Montross made Lakewood the target of his imposing glare. "Is that true, Mr. Lakewood?"

"Your Honor," Lakewood said, "as you know, in a case like this investigation is ongoing."

"I *do* know, Mr. Lakewood. Maybe you've forgotten, but I served as a prosecuting attorney for thirteen years."

"Yes, I know that, Your Honor—"

"And I also know that 'ongoing investigation' is often a euphemism for 'I've got something I don't want to turn over just yet.' You tell me, right here and now, if you've got a witness they don't know about."

Lakewood glanced quickly at Rachel. He looked like a man sticking his head out of a waffle iron as it was being pressed down upon him. He opened his mouth to speak, but it was Rachel's voice that was heard. "Your Honor!" she blurted.

Three heads turned and looked at her, each one with an expression that was some variation on incredulity. Rachel sensed Jessica Osborn Holt was almost seething, and her boss, while shocked, looked like he was relieved to have some time to think.

The judge sat back in his large, swivel chair, almost like he had been knocked backward by a gust of wind. And, for a moment, it seemed as if he might issue a blast of wind himself, like an angry, frozen North. "You have something to say, Miss . . ."

"Ybarra, Your Honor," Lakewood said. "She's my paralegal and assistant in this case."

Montross looked at Rachel. "Well?"

Rachel said, "I think I have something that might help, Your Honor."

"*You think?* When might you be sure?"

Rachel heard Holt issue a derisive snort. Quickly Rachel pulled her briefcase up on her lap, not realizing the top was open. All of the papers she had inside slipped out and fell on the floor around her feet.

"I'm sorry," she said. Out of the corner of her eye she saw Lakewood put his face in his hand.

"Miss Ybarra," said the judge, "I think it would be advisable if you let Mr. Lakewood make the case for the U.S. Attorney's office, wouldn't you agree?"

Rachel reached clumsily down for her papers, pulling them up only to have some slip out again. "I just had . . . one point, . . . Your Honor." Where was that case she had copied? She ruffled through the papers as fast as she could, looking for the cover page.

"Well what is it?" the judge said.

"It has to do with our witnesses, Your Honor." Rachel scurried through several more papers and there it was. "Here!" She handed the copy to the judge.

"What is that?" Holt demanded.

"It's a case, Ms. Holt," the judge said. "And just what is the holding of this case, Miss Ybarra?"

Clearing her throat, Rachel said, "Basically, Your Honor, that we don't have to reveal the names of confidential informants until they testify."

The assertion lingered for a moment, like a firework that hits its apex just before it explodes. The explosion itself came from Holt.

"That's outrageous!" she cried, in what was just short of a scream.

"Miss Holt, please," the judge said sternly.

"But Your Honor—"

"I said quiet. Will you just let me look at this?" He began to scan the case, flipping the pages as he did.

Lakewood turned to Rachel. When their eyes met he winked at her and smiled. It was a mischievous smile, like they had just played a practical joke on Jessica Osborn Holt and were going to get puckish delight out of it. Over Lakewood's shoulder Rachel could see Holt doing a slow burn as she stared at the judge.

Finally Montross tossed the case on his desk, took off his reading glasses, and chewed on one end. Looking at Holt he said, "That's what the case says."

"Let me see that," Holt spat, reaching for the case. She looked only at the first page. "Look, this is a case from another circuit. Who cares what it says?"

"You're right, it is not binding in this circuit," Montross said, "but it is persuasive. If I find its reasoning valid, then I can choose to follow it."

A pause. Montross clicked his teeth with the end of his glasses. Holt leaned so far forward in her chair that it appeared she might slip off.

Then Montross said, "And I find the reasoning pretty compelling."

Holt wasted no time. "I'll appeal! I'll take this thing up right now!"

"No, you won't," Montross said, glaring at her. "You're too smart for that. You'll object on the record and preserve the issue. Then, when you lose, you can appeal."

For a moment Rachel wasn't sure she heard the judge correctly. But then she saw Holt's mouth open wide and freeze there.

Judge Montross waited a beat, like a seasoned comedian with unerring timing, and then said, "*If* you lose, I should have said. Now, we'll do the rest of our arguing in open court. Right now I want to know if everyone is ready to start trial on the twentieth."

Holt and Lakewood opened their calendar books and checked schedules. Both okayed the date. "Fine," said the judge. "Now if everything can go as smoothly as our little conference here today, we should all get along just fine. Alan, that was some good research your assistant did. Take her to lunch."

"I will, Your Honor," Lakewood said, standing. Rachel stood also and almost felt the breeze—a cool one—as Jessica Osborn Holt stormed out of the chambers.

"Wait outside just a second, Alan," Judge Montross said. "I want to have a short word with Miss . . ."

"Ybarra," Lakewood said.

"Yes," said the judge. "Won't be a second."

Lakewood gave Rachel a nod, then walked out. Rachel felt like she had just been dropped at the principal's office by her father, who would rather wait out in the car.

"Nice work," Montross said. "You're a student?"

"Yes."

"Where?"

"USC. The night program."

"Good school."

Rachel nodded.

"Anyway," said the judge, "it's not often that a law student makes an enemy in the legal community, but you just have."

"Miss Holt?"

"Exactly. Now she's a good lawyer, tough, but when she decides she doesn't like you, she does something about it. There was a district attorney in New York—"

Loretti.

"—who almost died trying a case against Holt. Anyway, what I'm trying to tell you is one simple thing."

Rachel waited.

"Watch your backside," the judge said.

Should I tell him? she thought suddenly. *Should I pour it all out to the judge?* Surely if anyone could figure out a way to get her out of this mess it would be a federal judge with all his connections . . . .

"Do you catch my drift, Miss Ybarra?"

"Yes, Your Honor, I do."

"Enough said. Good luck to you."

Without another word Rachel slipped out of the judge's chambers. Alan Lakewood was waiting for her. "So?" he asked.

"He just wanted to tell me to watch my, um, backside."

"As in Jessica Osborn Holt?"

"Something like that."

Lakewood smiled as he escorted Rachel toward the elevators. As they waited, Rachel turned to Lakewood. "Is there any possibility this case may settle?"

"You mean will Supevsky plead to a lesser?"

Rachel nodded.

"No way," Lakewood said. "He's in it for the long haul."

Rachel looked at the floor.

"You wondering if there's a way to avoid a trial?" Lakewood asked.

"Yeah."

"Not on this one."

The elevator doors opened like steel jaws.

CHAPTER FIVE

HE TRIED HIS BEST to make the mundane Monday seem like a fantastic Friday, but sitting at his small desk in the module workspace, his phone flashing its message light, Jeff Bunnell was not exactly in tune with his work.

First he reviewed the phone messages, dutifully jotting each on the steno pad he kept on his desk. Then he checked his assigned computer terminal to see if he had any interoffice messages. There were none.

He next walked from his cubicle to the metal cabinet near the supervisor's office, where he had a slot for mail. He had no mail, only a copy of an office memo reminding everyone of the retirement party for agent Blake Keane at the El Torito in Culver City.

Exciting stuff, he thought. Future brighter than ever.

Back at his desk he tried to get interested in the file on the vanilla-flavored case he'd been assigned. For Jeff it was like trying to get excited about watching paint dry. Being restricted to desk duty seemed worse than outright suspension. He made it about halfway through the first page of the file before he went to get a cup of coffee.

"What's shakin'?" asked Dean Mills, another agent standing by the coffee pot with a fresh cup.

"My hands," said Jeff.

"Huh?"

"In eager anticipation of looking through a box of bank records."

"Ah. The fun stuff."

"You're a sick man, Mills."

"That's what my wife says." Mills's tummy jiggled as he laughed. He had long lamented his battle of the bulge. He was apparently on the losing end.

Jeff poured his coffee. Mills said, "Tough about your wit."

"Yeah."

"I guess Zagorsky got it pretty good in the head, eh?"

"He did. I saw him the other day."

"How's he making out?"

"Fine. He should be back soon."

"I hope so." Mills looked deeply into his coffee, like he was trying to figure something out. "It's funny," he said.

"What is?"

"Zagorsky getting hit like that. Right across the head, wasn't it?"

"Yeah."

"Just like that." Mills raised his right hand and took a playful swipe at Jeff's head. Instinctively, Jeff ducked, spilling a swish of coffee on the floor.

"Hey, watch it!"

"Sorry, Jeff. I just like to reenact crime scenes. Sort of a hobby."

"Really? Well, why don't you recreate Jimmy Hoffa?"

"Hoffa?"

"Yeah. Disappear without a trace."

Mills frowned, then laughed with another tummy shimmy. "Funny guy," he said. Then he added, "I guess it must be pretty hard on you, huh?"

"How's that?"

"Getting pulled back. I know how it is. Listen, if there's anything I can do. . . ."

"Thanks, Dean. I'll be okay."

Nodding, Mills turned and walked back toward his desk.

Jeff returned to his own. He turned once more to the file before him, but Mills's words blurred before his eyes. He kept thinking about Mills and his little game of bat-a-fellow-agent's-head. The incident put Jeff in the hotel room, seeing things through Zagorsky's eyes. Mills's face disappeared and morphed into Paul Dedenok's. What was in Dedenok's eyes? Jeff tried to see it and perhaps would find an answer there.

None came.

Further work was useless. He had a witness interview set up for 1:30. That gave him three hours. He decided to take a run down to the coroner's office again. Maybe Froug would have the results of the test. Maybe somewhere there would be a finality to this thing.

But he doubted it. Deep down, he had to acknowledge to himself that he doubted he'd ever be satisfied.

He tore down the freeway, oblivious to the fact that the California Highway Patrol does not recognize any speed law exceptions for FBI agents who are not in hot pursuit of fleeing felons.

He parked in the side lot of the coroner's office and jogged inside. The woman at the public service desk looked like a career bureaucrat who was bored with life itself. The sight of an agitated FBI agent moved her not at all.

"I'm sorry, sir," she said tonelessly, "I don't see that name in our records."

"Dedenok," Jeff insisted. "Paul Dedenok."

The woman shrugged. "I'm sorry."

Jeff rubbed his eyes. "Let me talk to Palmer Froug."

"I'm sorry—"

"Please."

The woman scowled. "Mr. Froug is no longer here."

"Excuse me?"

"Mr. Froug has been transferred."

"Where?"

"I don't have that—"

"Let me talk to your supervisor."

The woman gave Jeff a sour look, then turned slowly and ambled away from the front desk. Throughout the short conversation she had not changed the cadence or inflection of her voice. It was, Jeff thought, like a zombie voice. Fitting that he should be at the coroner's office interacting with the living dead.

The zombie returned to the front desk and said, "Third door on your right."

The supervisor was only slightly more animated than the woman at reception. She sat at a rectangular metal desk with a small bouquet of artificial flowers on the corner. "Can I help you?"

"My name is Jeff Bunnell, FBI."

"Yes?"

"I spoke to a guy named Froug last week."

"Yes?"

And I'm here yakking it up with you for my health!

"And I've been informed he's no longer here."

"That's my understanding," the supervisor said.

"Your *understanding?* Don't you know about it?"

"I'm not in personnel."

"All right, look. He had a file on a case. He was conducting some tests. I wanted to look at the file."

"Is this an official request?"

"I'm an agent with the Federal Bureau of Investigation. You may have heard of it. Big outfit? We have guns?"

"You don't have to take that tone with me, sir."

"It's a simple request."

The supervisor looked him up and down once. "Do you know the name on the file?"

"Yes! Dedenok. D-E-D-E-N-O-K."

"I'll check." She turned toward her computer terminal as Jeff gave a sigh of relief. After scaling the awesome promontory of a local bureaucracy, he was at last on the summit of relief. Or so he thought.

"I'm sorry," the supervisor said. "We don't have a record under that name."

"What? But you have to!"

"There is no record, sir."

"Check it again."

"Sir—"

"Please."

The woman sighed and swiveled back to the computer screen and typed something. "No," she said finally. "Nothing."

Jeff stared at her.

"You can always check with the—"

"Save it," Jeff snapped, as he whirled and stormed out the door.

Rachel was just about to leave the office for the USC law library when the call came. "How's my favorite law clerk?"

It was Stefanos, and Rachel felt her entire body lock in place.

"Working hard?" he said.

"What . . . do you want?"

"It's going to be a nice evening. I thought we might have dinner together."

The suggestion filled her with revulsion and dread. The way he said it made the event sickeningly inevitable.

"I know a great place in Chinatown," he continued.

"Look, I can't. I was planning to go see my father tonight."

"Father will have to wait."

"Please."

"We have to talk. I'm very anxious to see you. There's a little place called the Flying Dragon, off Broadway near Bamboo Lane. I don't need to remind you to come all by yourself, do I?"

Rachel said nothing, her grip tightening on the phone.

"Good," he said. "I'll see you at six. My best to your grandmother."

He hung up. Rachel slammed down the receiver and looked up at her office ceiling. With more frustration than trust she said, "God, help me!"

"Why bother?" Ron Ashby said. He was standing in her doorway. Rachel, feeling exposed, glared at him.

"What do you want?" she said.

"Just wondering where God is, that's all." He put his hands out. "Why bother God with whatever your problem is? Why don't you let me help?"

Rachel began to straighten the papers on her desk. "I'm busy."

"I was just offering. You seem a little stressed-out lately. Is it about the Supevsky case?"

"I don't want to discuss it with you."

Ashby slapped his sides. "Well, that's just great. Here I am being a nice guy, and what do I get in return?"

"Please leave."

"It's almost as if you didn't like me," Ashby said.

"Get out!" Rachel snapped.

"Now is that a Christian attitude?" Ashby tossed her a wink and then turned away. Rachel walked over and slammed her office door shut. She paused for a moment, her back against the door, hearing Ashby's voice in her mind, replaying the conversation.

And then she heard her own voice. *Where, indeed, is God?* her voice asked. *Where?*

There was someone who would know. Rachel picked up the phone and dialed. Lydia Mendoza answered.

"Is Manny home?" Rachel said.

"Rachel? Are you all right?"

"Not really. Can I talk to him?"

"He's not here. He's up your way tonight."

"Where?"

"He's speaking at the Faith Center in Boyle Heights. Is there anything I can help you with?"

"Just pray for me, will you?"

"What is it? What's going on?"

"I can't tell you now. Just pray."

"You know I will."

The restaurant was small and dark, and, if Rachel had to describe it, seedy. It was not one of the fancier places in Chinatown. It was off the main drag, a little hole-in-the-wall. But it was apparent why he had chosen it. If anonymity was what you were after, this was the place for it.

The small Chinese waiter seemed to know Stefanos and gave him a table that was isolated from the rest of the place.

Now, seated across from the man who had threatened her in several different ways, Rachel felt isolated from reality itself. The cold in Stefanos's eyes was palpably dangerous, especially with the feigned civility he was trying to display.

"I thought we needed this time together," he explained as he perused a menu. "They make a wonderful *moo shoo pork* here."

"I'm not hungry," Rachel said.

"Oh come on, you have to eat."

"No."

"I insist." His tone was coldly charming. He motioned for the waiter and ordered two dinners. Rachel sat motionless, save for her trembling hands.

"There now," Stefanos said. "We can talk."

"Why did you bring me here?"

"This is a nice place. And you can't swim away." He smiled.

"What is it you want to talk about?"

"About us, of course. Our future."

Rachel felt her skin crawl.

"You need to get used to the idea," he said.

"I'll never get used to that."

"Be that as it may, I'm here to stay. Now let's talk about getting along."

"I don't think so."

"Now, Rachel." His tone was mildly rebuking. "You know that's not going to help. By the way, how's your grandmother?"

Rachel's throat tightened like a fist. She gave up any hope of being rational now. Her next words came out on a small stream of emotion. "Why do you do this?"

"My job?"

"Don't you have any fear?"

"What should I fear?"

"Consequences."

"I won't get caught."

"Don't you fear God?"

Stefanos put back his head and laughed. "I can't believe that an intelligent woman like yourself would believe in God."

"I do."

"Really? Well, I believe in nothing except myself and in what I can do to other people."

"I feel sorry for you."

"That doesn't concern me." Even though he had a mocking smile on his face, his eyes were deadly cold. "I want the name of that witness."

Rachel shifted slightly in her chair. "Witness?"

"Yes, witness. The one your side has not revealed to us, no thanks to the judge."

"You know about that?"

"Of course I know. Now it is time for you to tell me."

At that moment the old waiter shuffled in with an appetizer. As if this was just another standard meal between two people on a date, the waiter placed the dishes in front of Stefanos and Rachel, bowed, and left.

Stefanos picked up something with a toothpick attached to it and held it out to her. "You'll like this," he said.

Rachel shook her head.

"Try it for me," Stefanos said.

"No, thank you."

With a shrug of his shoulders, Stefanos popped the item into his mouth, his face showing exaggerated pleasure. "Now, then," he said. "The name."

"No," said Rachel, amazed at her resoluteness. "I can't."

His facial muscles rolled underneath the skin, like a snake slithering under a carpet. "Rachel, don't be stubborn with me."

"I can't. I just can't."

"Rachel, the name."

"No."

"Now."

"No."

"Are you going to make me upset?"

Not quite sure what he meant, Rachel shook her head slowly.

"Name," he said.

"No."

"Well, all right." He stood up. "Don't move." He left the booth like a gust of wind.

What now? Rachel wondered. *Do I scream? Run for the exit? Call the cops?* No, he would only track her down again, and there was one threat hanging in the air that was not yet cleared—her grandmother. She knew it was his trump card. Until that card was removed from the table, Rachel would do what he said.

Except give up the name. She couldn't. She could not sign a death warrant for Deanna Natale.

Three minutes dragged by, and then he was back. He did not sit down but glared down at her. "Unfortunately, you don't take our relationship seriously enough. I'm very sorry for that. And for what I have to do."

"What do you mean?"

"Don't move." He turned his back and walked out of the booth.

Rachel sat still, wondering what to do next, wondering if she had gone too far with him. She did not move, waiting for him to return. By now the smell of the food in front of her made her stomach turn. She was not a bit hungry. She turned away from the table and, by leaning forward, was able to see out to the front of the restaurant.

A few people, mostly older, sat at the small tables eating with chopsticks. One old man looked her way, locked eyes with her for a moment, and turned back to his bowl.

No one knows what's going on here, Rachel thought. *They are all oblivious.*

There was no sign of The Man. Five minutes slogged by, and no one, not even the waiter, came by the booth. She realized then that Stefanos was not coming back.

Rachel got up and started toward the front of the restaurant. The little waiter almost jumped at her from behind a corner, as if he had been waiting. A short exhalation of surprise escaped Rachel's mouth.

"Check please," the waiter said, holding out a ticket.

"Excuse me?"

"You pay check please."

Incredulous, Rachel said, "You've got to be kidding."

"Check please." He shoved the bill into Rachel's hand.

"There's no way."

The old waiter, who had not been a paragon of friendliness before, got mean. He practically snarled. "You pay now, or I call police."

Rachel was aware of other eyes upon her—the patrons of the restaurant looking at her, making her feel like a deadbeat caught in the act.

"But the man I came in with," Rachel protested.

"He gone."

"Gone?"

"You pay."

Rage flared up in her like a blue flame. She had been set up. This was a final humiliation, part of the game. And this waiter, this shriveled-up Mandarin mushroom, was part of it. But she had no desire to make a scene or be part of one. She only wanted to get out, get home, and think.

She opened her purse and took out a twenty-dollar bill. She handed the bill and the check to the waiter, who disappeared wordlessly into the back. Rachel still felt the eyes of the curious and indignant upon her. She wanted to shout something at them all but held back. Why be considered crazy as well as cheap?

The waiter came back with her change on a tip tray. Rachel scooped it all into her purse and handed the tray back. The waiter looked at it with chagrin. "Tip?" he said.

Through teeth that would not unclench, Rachel said, "Sure. Stop doing business with criminals."

The waiter snorted.

Rachel walked across the restaurant, through the gauntlet of stares, and out the front door. The cool night air hit her with a sense of relief. She walked a few steps toward her car, parked at a meter, and then froze.

The rear of her car sagged to the street, giving the vehicle the ridiculous look of a seesaw at rest.

Lightheaded, she pushed to the back of her car and saw the cause. Both her rear tires were flat, lying like blobs of melted rubber on the street. The amber hue of a streetlight gave her just enough illumination to see something else—on one of the tires was a round hole, the size of quarter.

He had done it. She knew that. He left her sitting like an idiot in the place while he came out and shot her tires.

Helplessly, she scanned the sidewalk adjacent to her car. No one was around. A market was open down the block at the corner, and a few people moved around the outdoor produce. But directly in front of her the storefronts were closed up—a cleaners, what appeared to be a fix-it shop (a vacuum cleaner and toaster were in the window), and a place with Chinese script over the door that could have been anything.

No witnesses.

Why? Why had he done this? Just another power display? It was so . . . juvenile. Like some kid in the schoolyard stealing your lunch just to show you he ruled the roost.

Then it hit her. This wasn't a prank. He was going to Abi's house. He was going there now.

CHAPTER SIX

JEFF WISHED HE COULD GET Steve McGarrett on this job.

Yeah. *Book 'im, Dan-oh.* Ol' McGarrett, the toughest of the tough. Tougher than Mannix, and a whole lot tougher than Banacek. The bad guys would cringe when McGarrett got their case.

Jeff sat back on his sofa, a plate with two slices of pizza precariously balanced on his lap, and got lost in another episode of *Hawaii Five-O.* It had been his favorite show as a kid. He had even combed his hair for awhile like Jack Lord, with the little curl over the forehead. A boy at school, one of the toughs, had laughed at Jeff and pushed him against a wall. Jeff slugged the kid in the stomach so hard he doubled over and fell to the ground in the fetal position, gasping for breath. As Jeff was carted off to the principal's office, he looked back at the fallen bully and said, "Book 'im, Dan-oh."

Memories.

And now the reruns were showing on TV. It was like going home.

Jeff munched his pizza, drank Coke, and watched another crime unfold on the unsoiled beaches of Hawaii. Now there was good duty. *Maybe I should put in for a transfer,* he thought, *get out of this stinking city. Maybe I should retire altogether and start writing television shows that take place on Oahu all about the way the real FBI operates.*

A thought intruded, an image actually, one that had been popping into his head from time to time throughout the day. It was the image of agent Dean Mills playfully trying to whack Jeff on the side of the head. What was it about that image that kept it coming back?

Just as before, Jeff pushed the image away and concentrated on the tube. It took some effort, but that's what he wanted. To leave the office behind and get lost in something else for awhile. He needed the relief. The episode at the coroner's office was bothering him big time. Yep, if Steve McGarrett were around he'd know what to do. . . .

His reverie was broken by the sound of glass breaking.

At first he thought it came from the apartment next door, like someone breaking a dish. But it had been too crisp and clean. And too near. The window.

Jeff rolled off the sofa and hit the floor. He crawled toward the lamp, grabbed the cord, and yanked it out of the wall.

The apartment went dark, except for the blues and whites issuing from the television screen. McGarrett was on a pristine beach, with blue sky behind him, and it was all bathed in sunlight.

Jeff reached up on the sofa for the remote control and clicked off the TV.

Like a GI in a foxhole, Jeff slid along the floor, pulling himself by his arms, until he reached the balcony window. He saw the hole in the glass through the soft light, spidery cracks jutting out all around it. A bullet hole, no doubt about it.

Where had it come from? In his mind Jeff pictured the outside of his apartment and saw the rooftops of the neighboring buildings. It must have come from one of those. Someone with a rifle.

Jeff slowly raised his head and peeked out. Glass exploded next to his left ear. He fell back on the floor.

Now Jeff rolled back toward the interior of his apartment, moving around the furniture by memory, like a blind man who knows his own living space. He rolled to one knee then came up crouching and felt for the holster he had hung over a chair. He found it and removed the Smith & Wesson .9 mm.

Another blast through the window, and this time the thud of a bullet entered wood near his right arm. The sniper had barely missed him but had done some damage to the breakfast counter. *He must have a night sight*, Jeff thought. *He sees me*.

Jeff dove toward his door, rolling twice, reached up, and threw it open. He jumped out and closed the door.

The old woman from across the hall, Mrs. Kensington, stuck her head out her door. "What in the Sam Hill is going . . . ?" She stopped when she saw Jeff standing there with his gun in his hand. Only then did Jeff realize what a picture he must be. He was shirtless, wearing only socks and underwear, and holding an automatic pistol at the ready.

"Don't worry, Mrs. Kensington. Official business." He started running for the stairwell.

"I'm telling the manager!" the old woman yelled after him, and Jeff had no doubt she would. He would have some fun explaining this episode to the manager, who liked things quiet around his building.

Jeff slammed the stairwell door open and ran down the stairs, through the hall, and out the front doors. He was now facing north. The shots had come from somewhere on the east side.

Jeff jumped behind a Honda parked on the street. From there he could scan a good portion of the roofs of the apartment buildings on the street. He looked for signs of movement. Nothing. The sound of a pumped-up stereo system echoed through the street. Blondie. "Heart of Glass." *Haven't heard that one in awhile,* Jeff thought, *but I'd like to live to hear it again*.

Something moved on the roof of the Garden Terrace Apartments, two buildings down from Jeff's. It was quick, it was a shadow, and it was clearly a man.

"Do you have a phone?" Rachel asked breathlessly. The Chinese woman behind the old-style counter, with a classic cash register atop it like some antique from the forties, blinked uncomprehendingly.

Rachel put her fist up to her ear. "Phone, phone!"

The woman shook her head and pointed across the street. Rachel looked out of the corner grocery store and thought she made out the form of a pay phone on the opposite corner.

She ran for it, almost knocking a plastic bag of oranges out of the hands of a woman with a baby in a shoulder harness.

An old couple out for an evening stroll with their Pekinese stepped back from her path as Rachel raced to the phone. The man mumbled something incomprehensible, though the tone was unmistakable in its rebuke. The dog barked at her with a piercing yap.

Rachel wondered what she looked like as she fumbled for change in her purse. A madwoman? Some fugitive from a mental hospital where they kept people like her away from innocent pedestrians?

She dropped two quarters in the pay phone and dialed Abi's number.

Busy!

"Hang up the phone!" Rachel cried. She hit the plunger, retrieved her quarters, put them back in, and tried the number again.

Busy.

She began to shake. "Get out of there!" she said to the dead phone.

A vivid picture in her mind played out like a scene from a movie—her grandmother, innocent as a house cat, opening the front door in response to a knock; the hit man blasting the door open; Abi opening her mouth, wanting but unable to scream; The Man slapping his hand across her mouth, holding her head fast with his other hand, whispering, "Don't say anything, and you won't get hurt."

Torture. And she was helpless to do anything about it.

Once more she dropped the coins and dialed, and once more the busy signal assailed her ear.

Now what?

She felt she had no choice. She dialed information, got the number for the Hollywood division of the police department, and placed a call. A man answered, and she said, "Can you send someone to 2124 Nichols Canyon Road?"

"What's the problem?"

"My grandmother. She's in trouble."

"What kind of trouble?"

"Someone is going to hurt her."

There was a pause. "You'll have to be more specific than that. Who is trying to hurt her?"

Suddenly the whole story sounded absurd in her mind. How was she going to sell him on a Russian assassin turned loose on the streets? "I can't be more specific. Please send a patrol car to check on her, please!"

"The address again?"

She gave it.

"I'll put a word out, but that's all I can do. Now if you'll—"

"Thank you. Hurry."

She hung up and knew this wasn't enough. She had to get there herself, but how?

Catch a bus? Not at this hour, and besides, there were hundreds of metro busses serving L.A., and each had its own code that was inaccessible without a schedule or long experience.

A cab? How long would that take? This was not really a cab city, not like New York where you could flag one any time of the day or night. She'd have to call, order, and wait, and even then these companies were notoriously unreliable.

She grabbed the chain-tethered phone book and madly turned the pages. She finally found the number and dialed.

"Faith Center," a friendly, female voice said.

"Hello," Rachel said desperately, "is Manny Mendoza there?"

"Who?"

"Pastor Manny Mendoza."

"Um, I think you have the wrong church. Our pastor is—"

"No, he's speaking there tonight."

"Tonight?" The woman's speaking rate was painfully slow, making "tonight" sound like it had four syllables.

"Yes, a program, are you having a program?"

"Well, I think we are. Can you hold on a minute?"

"Yes. Hurry!"

Rachel heard the phone drop on a hard surface. She could make out the faint voices of a gospel choir. It was an odd counterpoint to the orange and red of Chinatown's lights and the nameless people on the street.

It seemed like an hour until a voice, a male, got on the line. "You holding for Manny Mendoza?"

"Yes! Is he there?"

"I haven't seen him. We have a program—"

Rachel didn't hear the rest of the sentence. Not there! That was her last hope. She was about to hang up when the voice said, "Wait a minute, he just came in."

Heart pounding, she waited, and then heard the familiar, wonderful voice of Manny Mendoza on the line.

"Thank God you're there!" she gasped.

"Rachel? Where are you?"

"I'm in Chinatown, on Broadway and Bernard, at a phone booth."

"What's going on?"

"I can't explain now. Manny, can you pick me up?"

"Now?"

"Please."

"I have to speak in an hour."

Suddenly overcome with the emotion of it all, Rachel couldn't speak.

"Rachel?"

She managed to say, "Yes?"

"I'll be there."

Jeff made his way to the other side of the street, using parked cars as cover. He watched the Garden Terrace building for signs of movement.

A short, fat man pushed out the front doors and paused to light a cigar. He luxuriated in the smoke for a moment, then walked down the sidewalk in a casual stroll, sort of like Alfred Hitchcock appearing in his own movie, of which Jeff was a part.

In the distance, Jeff heard a siren wailing.

Behind him a gate swung open with a jaunty creak. Jeff whirled and saw a Latino man in his late twenties walking toward the street. He jangled keys in his hand like he was going for his car.

"Hey!" Jeff said from his crouch. He kept the gun hidden in front of himself.

The man looked at Jeff.

"Quick," Jeff said, "call the police. I need help."

Frozen now, the man said nothing. Later Jeff would understand what must have gone through the man's mind—it's night in the city, where criminals and wackos and unemployed screenwriters run free, and some guy in socks and underwear crouching behind a car tells you to call the police. Who could blame him for what he did?

What he did was turn and run away from Jeff as fast as his feet could take him. He ran down the street and disappeared around the corner.

No cops would be coming any time soon.

Across the street a shadow moved quickly.

Cautiously, Jeff crept down the street. His gun was at the ready, but he kept his finger off the trigger. He could not make any assumptions. Whoever it was could be an innocent citizen, maybe some teenager heading out for a joyride or a husband running out for ice cream for a pregnant wife. Or it could be a guy with a rifle intent on killing him.

A car with a souped-up engine screamed toward Jeff, its headlights shining in his eyes. Jeff ducked so the lights wouldn't give him away, but he had to give up his observation of the street to do it. He knelt in front of the grill of a Mercedes. *At least I'm hiding in style,* he thought. Then he noted wryly that the hood ornament, a metallic circle with the Mercedes symbol inside, looked suspiciously like the sight on a high-powered rifle.

He waited until the car roared past before sticking his head up again. Halfway down the block he saw a car pulling away from the curb. Jeff didn't have a reason, but he did have a hunch and a strong one. The guy, whoever he was, was in that car.

Jeff started to run.

The car's tires squealed as the rubber burned against the street. The red taillights gleamed in the night like angry, predatory eyes. They looked at Jeff steadily as the car sped away.

No way Jeff would catch it, but maybe he could get the license plate number.

The car tore out too fast for that.

Still, Jeff ran.

It was only seconds before the car would reach the corner and turn toward Ventura Boulevard, where it would be lost for good. The lights at the corner were bright though, and Jeff stopped in the middle of street to get the best look. That's all he wanted now, one good look at the car.

He got it. The car turned right, splashed with illumination, and for a split second Jeff saw it in crisp, colorful detail.

It was sleek and black and sporty, a Lexus he was almost certain. Whoever had tried to kill him had nice taste in cars.

It was taking forever.

Rachel paced back and forth in front of the pay phone, alternately chewing the nail of her right index finger and whispering desperate prayers to God to protect her grandmother.

The image of an attack kept recurring in her mind, making the seconds pound by sluggishly, as if to make sure her anguish was experienced in all its fullness. At one point she slammed her open hand against the phone box, creating a small ringing sound from the shaken bell and a sharp pain in her palm and wrist.

Where was Manny? She looked at her watch for the umpteenth time and noted that time was not standing still. She craned her neck to see every passing car, her heart dropping a little as each one passed her, oblivious to her agony.

Finally Manny drove up in his green Camry and skidded to a stop. Rachel threw open the door and jumped in.

"What is going—"

"Drive!" said Rachel.

"Where?"

"That way!" She pointed down Broadway. "To the freeway."

"Okay," he said, gunning the car. "Rachel, are you all right?"

"No."

"Can I help?"

"You're helping now."

"Tell me what's going on."

"I can't tell you right now. I wish I could, but I can't. I've just got to get home, now."

"It's serious."

"It is."

"I'd like to be able to do more."

"Just pray."

"For what?"

"Protection."

"You got it."

Manny pulled onto the freeway and changed lanes to get on the 101 toward Hollywood. They drove in silence for several minutes. The city was lit up in the variegated colors of the night. More than once Rachel pounded Manny's dashboard with her fist.

"Should we stop and call the police?" Manny asked.

"I did," she answered.

She instructed Manny to get off at Highland, then directed him to Hollywood Boulevard. Thankfully traffic was light around Mann's Chinese, where the latest sci-fi-special-effects-mutants-attack-the-earth blockbuster was playing to sold-out crowds. Rachel urged Manny to greater speed. He did his best to accommodate her. He almost rear-ended a bus.

Finally they arrived at Nichols Canyon Road. Rachel told Manny to drive slowly.

It was half a block to Abi's house. On approach, nothing seemed out of order. No signs of activity or intrusion. But that was just the outside.

"Stop," Rachel said. Manny pulled over to the curb. Rachel turned to him and put her hand on his shoulder. "Do me one more favor and drive back now."

"Back? But I—"

"Please."

"Rachel, I know there's something I can do."

"I'll tell you later. I can't now. I don't want to drag you into this." She started to get out.

"Rachel?"

She turned.

"Go with the Lord."

She nodded and closed the door. After a slight pause, Manny drove on down the street. Rachel waited until he turned at the next corner, then walked across the street toward the house. She looked for signs, anything that might tell her what was going on. The windows gave off a faint light through closed curtains. On the porch Rachel paused and listened.

Nothing.

Rachel slowly unlocked the door and slipped inside.

There was an odd stillness in the place. Not even the sound of Abi puttering in the kitchen. It was still too early for her to be in bed. *Please let her be alive,* Rachel's mind shouted. *Please, oh please, oh please.*

Rachel slipped off her shoes and started across the living room. She had no idea what she would accomplish by sneaking like this, but that's what her instincts told her to do. She would get to the doorway and take a look down the hall. She would see what she would see.

Instead, she heard . . . the tinking of glass or china. Abi having tea?

Rachel took one step into the hall.

"Rachel!"

Rachel whirled around.

"I didn't hear you come in, dear." Abi was holding a photo album in her arms.

"Are you all right?" Rachel said.

"Of course I am. Are you?"

"No one has been here?"

"Oh, yes," the old woman said cheerily.

"Who?"

Eyes twinkling, Abi said, "You never told me."

"Told you what?"

"Oh, you." Abi gave Rachel a playful slap on the shoulder.

"What are you talking about?" Rachel almost screamed.

"I'm talking about that nice young man in the kitchen." She gave Rachel a pixie smile.

"He's in the kitchen?"

"I fixed him some cocoa and gave him a slice of cheesecake."

"You didn't."

"Why shouldn't I? He's very handsome."

Pulling her grandmother closer to her, Rachel said, "Abi, we've got to be very, very careful."

"What on earth . . ."

"He's dangerous."

"Oh, he is not. He is perfectly charming. And he's waiting for us. We need to go in."

"Abi, listen to me. Let me do the talking."

"I will not. He wanted to see pictures of you." She held up the photo album.

"I can't believe this," Rachel said.

"I love the one when you were a *muchachita,* sitting in the washtub out in the backyard."

Rachel grabbed her own head with both of her hands and tried to soften the ache pounding in her temples.

"You don't look well, *conejíta*."

"Let's go." Rachel walked slowly for the kitchen to have it out one more time, silently praying for wisdom and the right words to say.

He stood up from his chair when she walked in, smiled, and nodded at her.

"How you doing?" Jeff Bunnell said.

CHAPTER SEVEN

"YOU ARE THE LAST PERSON I expected to see," Rachel said, plopping herself in a chair and feeling her pulse knocking at the throat.

"Now that's some greeting," Jeff said.

"Rachel," said Abi. "You be polite."

And then, without any warning or intimation that it might happen, Rachel began to laugh. It started as a giggle, then built like a wave into an all-out, sustained eruption of hilarity. Tears started streaming down her face.

"I don't often have this effect on people," Jeff said.

"Rachel, what is the matter with you?" said Abi.

Rachel waved her arms in the air and shook her head. "Oh, you'll never know." Taking several deep breaths, Rachel regained control. "I'm sorry," she said, then laughed again.

"Loco!" Abi said.

"No, no, I'm all right," Rachel insisted. "Jeff, what are you doing here?"

"I came to see you," Jeff said.

There was a momentary pause. Jeff cleared his throat. Rachel stifled another laugh. Finally Abi spoke. "Why don't you two go into the living room and look at some pictures?" She handed the photo album to Rachel, pressing it firmly in her hands as if to tell her to take care of the guest.

Wordlessly, Rachel took the book. Abi began clearing the dishes from the kitchen table.

Rachel led Jeff to the living room, motioned for him to sit on the sofa, and tossed the photo album onto the coffee table. She sat in a recliner across from him, her body falling into its softness, her mind exhausted.

"We're not going to look at a pictorial history of your life?" Jeff asked.

"That's not why you're here, is it?"

"It might be. Something about you in a washtub?"

"Can we change the subject?"

"Why? It was just getting interesting. Your grandmother told me quite a bit about you."

In spite of herself, Rachel smiled. It was nice to have easy conversation for a change.

"I'm sorry," Rachel said. "The evening has been, well, pretty full so far. I haven't been real hospitable."

"Please," Jeff said, holding up his hands. "Don't apologize. I didn't exactly give you notice, did I? This was a spur-of-the-moment thing. I can go."

"No, don't."

Jeff nodded and seemed to comprehend more than what was merely spoken. Rachel had the sense he understood her cast of mind completely and was sensitive enough not to ask about it. Not yet, at least.

"Then I'll stay," Jeff said, smiling. "I was hoping to combine a little business with pleasure."

"This is an official visit?"

"Only in part. It's pleasure, mostly. I hope you don't mind."

Rachel shook her head.

"I told you I was persistent," Jeff said.

"I'm glad."

"Let's start off with a little shop talk," Jeff said. "How's work?"

"Tense."

"The Supevsky trial?"

"Yes."

"Lakewood working you hard?"

"It's not so much that. I don't mind the work. It's just the whole feeling surrounding a trial like this."

"I know. It's a different world, almost surreal."

"That's *exactly* it."

"Especially out here on the West Coast. Back in New York organized crime is structured, like a monarchy or something. Here it's more casual and loose, like everything else. Makes it harder to pin things down. Plus, you have the Mexican connection."

"Drugs?"

"Exactly. It's like fighting two, separate foreign governments. You have a criminal enterprise here and crooked military there. Puts the squeeze on resources."

"I can imagine."

"Drug trafficking brings in over a hundred million dollars a year. Law enforcement has to fight that with a budget one-tenth of that. It's frustrating."

"Isn't there some way to infiltrate?"

"Virtually impossible. The Mexicans sell only to people they know, meaning other Mexicans. Or someone else, if they can make the right showing. If somebody comes in as a prospective wholesale buyer, he has to go through a whole dog-and-pony show to establish his bona fides. If he's approved, he has to put up collateral, cash, or deeds to real property."

"Collateral?"

"Insurance, if he's ever caught. He also has to provide human collateral."

"What does that mean?"

"His family."

"You're kidding."

"Nope. This collateral will pay with their lives if the wholesaler ever turns informer."

"But how does someone like Supevsky fit in?"

"He's a risk-free investment. His sources know that our government has him pegged. He won't turn informer, because he can't make a deal. He's the prize. He also offers the Mexican connection with a solid network of killers, muscle, and cash flow. The Mexicans know they will get paid."

Rachel shook her head. "How great man's wickedness . . ."

"How's that?"

"I'm sorry, I was mumbling. I was quoting Genesis, when the Lord saw how great man's wickedness on the earth had become."

"And every inclination of his heart was evil all the time."

"You know the verse?"

Smiling, Jeff said, "You're looking at a church kid."

"Really?"

"From birth to high school."

"What about now?"

Jeff looked at the floor.

"I'm sorry," Rachel said. "I didn't mean to pry."

"It's okay," Jeff said. "I want to have this conversation."

Rachel waited. He seemed to be looking for the right words.

Jeff leaned forward and swallowed as if his throat was dry. "I was involved in a hostage situation a few years ago," he said. "The hostage died. I don't think I've really gotten over that. Every time I hear about another kid shot in gang cross fire, I think about it all over again. It's like I'm in a dark movie theater and that scene is playing over and over again. And I can't get out. . . ."

Rachel listened, wishing she could say something that would be just right, that would give him some insight or relief. But she realized the words weren't there because, in her own way, she was feeling the same way. In her darkened theater the scene was Stevie's death.

"I don't pray," Jeff said. "Not really. And I'm sick about it. Maybe that's part of the reason I'm here."

"Why?"

"Because maybe you can help."

Rachel paused for a long moment. She was suddenly aware of her hands, that they were moist. She wiped them on her thighs. The conversation had taken a turn she had hardly expected. She hadn't spoken this intimately with anyone for a long time, not even Manny Mendoza. Yet, though she hardly knew him, she wanted to open up to Jeff. She wanted to tell him about her own inner world and about her outer world as well. Everything. To pour it out like a gushing stream.

She opened her mouth, not knowing what words would come out, when a knock sounded at the door. It sent a jolt through Rachel's body. Jeff said, "What's wrong?"

Shaking her head, Rachel stood and walked to the door. She paused. Another knock, and then a voice said, "Police."

Rachel opened it. Two young police officers, a man and woman, stood on the porch.

"We had a call about this address," the male officer said.

"Yes, that was me," said Rachel.

"Everything all right?"

"Yes, officer, it is."

The officer looked over Rachel's shoulder and saw Jeff. "You sure you're all right?"

Rachel said, "Yes," but it must have sounded weak. The officer said, "Maybe we should come in and have a look?"

"That won't be necessary," Rachel said. Suddenly Jeff was next to her. He flashed his credential at the officer.

"It's all right, officer," Jeff said. "I've got it."

The officer's eyes widened. "A federal matter?"

"Might be," Jeff said.

"Well, will you look at that?" the male officer said to his partner. The female officer nodded.

"Thank you for coming by," Rachel said.

"No problem," the officer said and, turning, walked back toward the street.

After closing the door, Jeff said, "Did you call the police?"

Rachel led him back to the living room. "Yes, I did."

"Why?"

"I thought someone might be breaking in here."

"Who?"

"Can we talk about this another time?"

She saw Jeff's expression suddenly become tense. He glanced over his shoulder as if to see if Abi or some unseen other could hear him.

"What is it?" Rachel asked.

Jeff looked back at her. "Somebody took a pop at me tonight."

"Shot at you?" she asked.

Jeff nodded. "Through my apartment window."

"Do you have any idea who?"

"No. But it's got to be connected with the Supevsky case."

"Why do you say that?"

"Because it smells, that's why." Jeff looked at her. "And one of the smells is chloroform."

"Chloroform?"

"There were traces of it on Dedenok's clothes, or at least that was the theory until everything at the coroner's office, including one of the deputy MEs, disappeared."

"Meaning?"

"Meaning somebody could have put Dedenok to sleep before putting him in a bath and slicing his wrists for him."

Stefanos. The name burst into her mind and assembled all the pieces of the puzzle together. He was the one who killed Dedenok. It all fit.

Jeff was still pacing in small circles. He ran the fingers of his right hand through his hair. "So that's what I've been thinking, and that's why I came over here. I don't trust anyone right now, not in the Bureau, not in the U.S. Attorney's Office, no one. Except you."

"Why?"

"Because I know you have no agenda. And I know you'll keep what I've said tonight between the two of us."

"I will."

"I just wanted to know if you've noticed anything on your side, anything going on that is strange, out of the ordinary. I thought maybe we could put our heads together on this."

"I don't know. . . ." Rachel said distantly.

"Not anything? Everything just rosy with you?"

"Jeff, listen I . . ." she couldn't finish. She turned her head and looked at the wall.

"You do know something." He went to her and put his hands on her shoulders.

"Please, Jeff."

"That's why you called the cops."

"Don't . . ."

"You're trying to protect someone." His grip tightened.

"You're hurting me."

"Is it Lakewood? Is he involved?"

"Let go of me!" She shook her body and broke his hands away with her forearms. He stood up straight and shook his head.

"I'm sorry," he said. "I shouldn't have done that. It's just that . . ."

"I know," Rachel said quietly. There was a long silence between them, then Rachel said, "Jeff, please trust me on this for a little while."

"There's a reason you can't tell me, isn't there?"

Rachel said nothing, and that was answer enough.

"All right," Jeff said. "I'll try. But I'm not going to stop looking into this thing. I can't."

"Jeff, be careful. You're dealing with dangerous people."

"I know. And so are you. May I suggest something?"

"Sure."

"Try praying a little harder tonight."

Manny Mendoza checked his watch as he negotiated the traffic. Eight-thirty. He could still make it. They'd have to shuffle the program a little, of course, but he could speak at the end. He knew Pastor Hickey well. They'd joke about this afterward. He'd take a ribbing for years to come about being late for the big revival.

He thought again of Rachel. She was obviously in trouble, but what kind and how bad he couldn't figure. Maybe it had something to do with her job, maybe it didn't. Maybe it involved issues of confidentiality. Manny, as a pastor, knew all about that. But he also knew Rachel and knew this was not like her.

A light in his rearview mirror caught him directly in the eyes, momentarily blinding him. The guy must have had his brights on. An epithet from Manny's past flashed into his head, but he dealt with it quickly. "Forgive me, Lord," he said out loud. "Keep that person from a fiery accident."

He allowed himself a laugh. Then he continued, "Lord, give Rachel wisdom. Protect her and guide her right now."

He made a turn on the dark street that would spit him out two blocks from the church. The sidewalks were eerily empty and the streetlights incredibly dim. It reminded Manny of the many nights he rode in the dark, preferring the night to the day. Back then he hated the light as much as Bela Lugosi did. Now, urban gloom like this triggered a Bible verse, one of the first he had memorized after his conversion. It was John 3:19: "This is the judgement, that the light has come into the world, and people loved darkness rather than light because their deeds were evil."

He remembered how he loved the darkness.

The lights from another car behind him broke through the shadows. He wasn't totally alone, though he felt like it.

He got to the main drag and turned left. Not many cars were out tonight. He spotted a cluster of kids in gang regalia standing on a corner. Spiritually, Boyle Heights was one of the darker spots in the city. Manny sent out a silent prayer to them.

The church was half a block away, and Manny could see already the parking lot would be full. An unbroken line of cars was parked on the street, meaning they had spilled out of a brimming facility. The service was full.

He drove past the church and turned down a side street, looking for a place to park. The car behind him seemed to be in search of the same. It slowed when he slowed, keeping a respectable distance.

Finally, toward the end of the long block, Manny found a spot that would test one of the weaker areas of his life—parallel parking. He never had to learn that with a Harley! Well, tonight he'd get some practice. He pulled alongside the car fronting the spot, put on his right turn signal, and waited for the car behind him to pass.

It didn't.

Manny rolled down his window and waved the car to go past. He waited. The car did not move. It was directly behind him now, making a parking maneuver impossible.

He waved more vigorously. Didn't the guy get the message?

The car behind him shut off its lights.

Now what's this? Manny thought. The guy is double parking and . . .

That's when the thought hit him. It was a flash, an instinct born of his outlaw past, a reawakened sense of danger. There was violence in the air.

A fist, shooting through his window, caught him in the face.

There was an explosion of yellow light, then Manny sensed his door being yanked open. Two strong hands, having the advantage of surprise and attack, pulled him from the car. Dazed, Manny tried to pull free, but instead felt himself spun around. A hand grabbed his hair and then slammed his head into the roof of his car. Manny felt the warmth of blood in his mouth. Then his head was lifted and slammed again, and he lapsed into unconsciousness.

CHAPTER EIGHT

THE APARTMENT BUILDING was in North Hollywood, just off Vineland. It was a three-story, sprawling job, larger than most in the area. In the normal course of events, Jeff thought, it would be hard to spot a single subject. But in this case he had a hole card—he knew the apartment number.

Amazing, he mused, what you can do on the Internet these days. All he did was type in the name in Yahoo's people search, and in seconds he had the address.

When he first arrived, Jeff knocked on number 223. No answer. But it was just four-thirty in the afternoon, normal working hours, so he could wait. Fortunately, apartment 223 looked out on the courtyard and the swimming pool. Jeff arranged a pool lounge on the far side, facing the apartment, made himself comfortable, and started reading the sports section of the *L.A. Times.*

He started getting into a Bill Plaschke column about the demise of the Dodgers when he found himself staring up at the sky. He realized he was thinking about Rachel Ybarra. He realized how attracted he was to her.

It was getting intense. Why? Part of it, he knew, was that she was in trouble of some kind. Jeff always had a white knight streak in him. Probably the residue of watching all those Errol Flynn movies when he was a kid. He always had the idea that he'd scale a castle someday to rescue the woman of his dreams.

That had almost happened once before. He was engaged to be married just after he joined the Bureau. Christina Barlow was from a wealthy family and had all the right credentials—social and professional. She was working as a VP of marketing in one of her father's businesses—cellular phones—while earning her MBA in a night program at Pepperdine. Later he realized that maybe he was less in love with her than with the *idea* of her. But he was ready to march down the aisle.

Six weeks before the wedding, Christina Barlow decided she did not want to be married to a federal law enforcement officer. She couldn't live with the uncertainty, she said. Would he be willing to give it up? For her?

He almost did. But two things kept him from the decision. The first was that this had been his dream since he was a boy, and now that he had finally realized it, he didn't see how he could just toss it aside. The second reason slipped out of Christina's mouth when she told him that as soon as she had her MBA her father wanted her to take over the head marketing position at his cellular company in Louisville. It was more than a little obvious that she wouldn't be able to do so if she had a husband who was not assigned to the mid-South.

Her protestations to the contrary aside, Jeff felt betrayed. It was hard to trust anyone after that. Though he had dated occasionally, he hadn't become serious about anyone. He wondered if he ever could.

Now he had met Rachel. He felt he could trust her completely, without reservation. Part of it was her faith. Growing up in a staunchly Christian family, he was familiar with her set of assumptions. Not that Christians always conformed to their own ideals—indeed, that was partly why he felt he had lapsed—but the odds were certainly better with someone who had an active faith.

He realized, too, that he held out another hope. Perhaps Rachel would bring him back to the fold.

Jeff shook his head and tried again to read the paper. It wasn't any good. He tossed it aside and just looked out at the courtyard.

Ordinary apartment traffic criss-crossed the courtyard and pool deck. Doors occasionally slammed. Some kids came down from the second floor and jumped into the pool. A girl of about twelve gave Jeff an odd look, as if she knew he was out of place here. Jeff smiled at her, and she swam away.

It was getting toward dark when Jeff finally spotted him. There was no mistaking Palmer Froug. He was just as skinny and his hair just as unkempt as the last time Jeff saw him in the coroner's office. He was carrying two bags of groceries and ascending the stairs to the second level. Jeff sprang from the lounge chair and walked briskly to another stairway near the pool.

Taking the steps two at a time, Jeff reached the second story on the opposite side of Froug. Jeff saw him at the door of his apartment, setting the bags down and reaching in his pocket for his keys.

Jeff waited until he had let himself inside. Then he walked around to the door. He considered knocking but decided to try the doorknob. Unlocked. Jeff pushed the door open and simultaneously gave a crisp knock on the door.

"Froug?" Jeff said as he took one step inside the door.

Palmer Froug spun around from the breakfast bar where he had put the two grocery bags. "Hey!" he protested loudly, "you can't just come . . ." He stopped short when he seemed to recognize Jeff.

"Howdy," Jeff said.

Suddenly Froug was seized by a strange and rhythmic paroxysm of fright. He almost danced backwards, his right arm extended toward Jeff, his fingers wiggling in some sort of nonverbal attempt to get Jeff to go away. "You get out of here!" Froug cried. "You get out of here right now!"

Jeff slowly closed the door behind him. "Look, Froug—"

"Get out! I have a gun!"

Jeff almost laughed. Even if Froug was telling the truth, he doubted his hands would be able to work a weapon.

"Froug, listen," Jeff said, in the manner he had been trained to adopt when dealing with agitated suspects. "You don't want to threaten a federal agent."

"I don't want to talk to you!" Froug had reached the back wall of the front room and started acting like a trapped animal. Both his hands came up in an attempt to shoo Jeff out.

"What's wrong?" Jeff asked.

"Get out, will you?"

"I'm not here to hassle you."

"So you say!"

"Somebody's gotten to you."

"Please, leave me alone!" His voice became a wail.

If they had been talking on the edge of a tall building, Jeff would have considered Froug a sure bet to jump. The guy was clearly over the edge mentally.

"Froug, sit down, will you?"

Shaking his head violently, Froug didn't move from the wall.

"I'm here to help you," Jeff said.

"You can't help me. Nobody can." Froug's eyes became watery. "He'll do it to me."

"Do *what?*"

"He said he'd do it to me."

"Do what?"

"What he did to my cat." Froug shuddered, his face reflecting a horrible picture in his memory. "He was here. He took my cat and . . ." Tears erupted.

"Easy," Jeff said.

"You can still see the blood stains!" Froug cried, pointing toward the floor by the front window. "He said he'd do the same to me . . ."

"All right, all right—"

"And he will! Because you're here!"

"Listen—"

"Get out! Get out!"

"Froug!" Jeff's voice sounded like a cannon.

Startled, Froug whimpered, "Yes?"

"You remember what they used to do in those World War II movies when the hysterical soldier started freaking out?"

Froug looked blankly at Jeff.

"Somebody," Jeff explained, "would slap him across the face. And then the soldier would say, 'Thanks, I needed that.' You remember?"

"Uh . . . I guess."

"Well, I don't want to slap you, Froug, but I will if you don't settle down."

The gambit worked. Froug began to breath normally. He sat down in a chair, looking spent.

Jeff put a hand on Froug's shoulder. Froug didn't attempt to push it away. He was silently crying now, wiping his eyes with the back of his hand.

Jeff sat on the coffee table so he could face him. "Let me help you."

"I'm scared."

"I know."

"He said if I went to the police or anything . . ."

"I promise I won't take this to the cops. I'm in this with you."

Froug looked at Jeff as if he wanted to believe that. Then he took a deep breath and began. "It was a couple of days after you came down to the lab. I was closing up when he came in."

"Who?"

"I don't know his name. He had a gun. I thought he was going to rob me. But then I thought, of what? Body parts? He said he wanted the Dedenok file, you know, the one I was working on?"

"Yeah."

"He was scary and cold, like he wouldn't have thought twice about icing me. I got the file, and then he told me to clear it from the computer records. He knew what he was doing. He stood there and watched me while I did it."

"Then what happened?"

"He told me to quit the office and never to say anything to anybody, or else."

"Now listen to me," Jeff said. "You're going to be okay. What you say to me stays with me."

Froug looked at Jeff like he wanted to believe him but wasn't sure. "There's one other thing I need to know," Jeff said. "About those tests you did on Dedenok's clothes."

Froug sniffed loudly. "Yeah?"

"You were trying to confirm if there was trichloromethane."

"Right."

"Did you?"

Looking uncertain at first, Froug slowly nodded his head.

"Thanks," Jeff said, standing up.

"What are you going to do?" Fear crept back into Palmer Froug's voice.

"Don't worry."

"He won't find out, will he?"

Jeff said, "Get some rest," and walked out of the apartment.

This time they were taking no chances. Emmitt Jefferson, special agent in charge, had ordered four agents on the witness watch, two inside, two in another room. Two other agents were on call to take over the watch on a rotating basis.

The location was as obscure as Jefferson could make it. The Sleepy Wheel Motel backed up against the 5 Freeway about a mile north of El Centro. Jefferson had picked it himself, having had the dubious pleasure of being stuck in El Centro on a stakeout several years before and staying at the Sleepy Wheel a couple of nights before setting up a more permanent location in town. It was a U-shaped layout with a row of rooms that was not visible from the street. That is where Jefferson placed Deanna Natale.

"She's comfortable," Jefferson said matter-of-factly as he piloted his car down the freeway. Alan Lakewood sat in the front seat next to him, Rachel in the back. "But the first thing she said was she wanted to see you." Jefferson indicated Rachel with his thumb.

Lakewood turned toward Rachel. "We want to keep her happy. That's your job."

Rachel nodded, and for the tenth time since they'd started out, she looked through the rear window. Even though Jefferson and Lakewood had taken all of the standard antisurveillance steps, and then some, Rachel couldn't shake the feeling they were being followed. It was a feeling she had all the time now.

Last night had been a nightmare. The whole surreal scene at the restaurant, the gripping fear for her grandmother, the race to get home with Manny's help. Yes, Abi had been unharmed, but it felt like the nightmare was just in repose until the next scene, a scene she was powerless to control.

It was a relief to be going to see Deanna. It was a positive move, something she could do for the good of the case. There was, of course, an undercurrent of dread. Deanna was the key witness, the one in place of Paul Dedenok. If Jeff's hunch was true—that it was someone else who clubbed Sam Zagorsky then proceeded to murder Dedenok—that same someone would be after Deanna Natale. And Rachel was quite certain who that someone was.

No one followed off the freeway. Rachel breathed easier when Jefferson actually pulled into the motel parking lot and drove around to the side, where the car would not be visible.

The room was the last one in the row, nearest the freeway. A man Rachel assumed was an agent sat in a lawn chair near a scrubby facsimile of a patch of lawn. He stood up when he saw them approach and nodded at Jefferson. The agent took out a key, walked to the door—marked 108—and gave three quick knocks. Then he unlocked the door.

Jefferson led Rachel and Lakewood inside. Two more agents, one whom Rachel recognized as Sam Zagorsky, stood up in the small room. In the far corner, seated in a chair reading a magazine, was Deanna Natale.

Rachel saw her look up and smile. To Rachel she seemed to have aged since the last time she saw her. Her skin was pale, and her hair hung straight down, as if tired, around her shoulders.

"Hi," Deanna said without standing up.

Rachel looked at Jefferson a moment. He nodded, and she walked across the room and took Deanna's hand. "It's good to see you," Rachel said.

"Same here."

Jefferson said, "I know you two would like to talk alone for a few minutes, so we'll step outside and have our own little meeting." He walked back toward the door, Lakewood and an agent behind him.

Sam Zagorsky lingered and faced Rachel. "I wish Jeff were here," he said.

"I do too," said Rachel.

"I want you to know that I think he's being made a scapegoat. I think it stinks." Zagorsky shuffled his feet. "You know, I think he kind of likes you."

"Well," Rachel said, "I like him."

"He's a good agent."

"Yes."

"Well, I'll let you two talk. I just wanted to go on the record with you, is all."

"Thank you."

Zagorsky nodded, then walked out of the room, leaving the door slightly open behind him.

"Who's Jeff?" Deanna asked.

"An FBI agent."

"You like him as in *like* him?"

"Maybe."

Deanna smiled, and once again it seemed to Rachel to be an old person's smile. Even so, it was like a small oasis in the desert of Deanna's existence. "I'm glad for you," she said.

"What about you? How you doing?"

"How's it look like I'm doing? My hands won't stop shaking. All I can think about is having a cigarette and a bottle of scotch. Am I bad?"

"No," Rachel said.

"I know I ain't been good. That's why I'm here."

"What you're doing is extremely brave."

"Am I going to be all right?" Deanna asked. "Safe, I mean?"

That was a question Rachel wished she could answer. But no easy answer came. She put her hand on Deanna's knee. "The FBI is doing everything it can on this, I know. You are a crucial witness, and they are not going to let anything happen to you."

With a nod of resignation, Deanna slumped back in her chair. "Sure, sure." She put her hands in her lap, folded, and looked at them. "Hey, remember that day you came to see me?"

"Of course," Rachel said.

"We talked a little bit about God."

"Yes."

"And you prayed."

"I remember."

"I had a good feeling about that. Are you a Christian?"

"Yes."

"You're happy with God, right?"

"Yes. That doesn't mean life always goes smoothly—" Rachel paused and looked toward the window, shaking her head slightly, searching for words—"but it does mean I know where to go when I need the strength." To Rachel it sounded like an empty platitude. She wondered why she didn't feel it in the depths of her bones.

"I believe in God," Deanna said quietly, "but I don't feel like I really know who he is. I didn't go to church or nothin' when I was growing up, but I had friends who were Catholic. They'd go to Mass. I remember going once, just to look. The church on the corner was big; it had these colorful windows and statues and candles burning and things. And at the front was this big statue of Jesus hanging on the cross. I remember thinking there was something real mysterious about it all. I remember I asked my Dad if we could go there once. You know what he did? He grabbed my shoulders and shook me and said, 'Don't ever let me catch you near that church!' He had this real mean look in his eyes. It was scary."

Rachel nodded.

"But I never stopped thinking about the church." Deanna's eyes had the beginnings of tears in them. She looked at Rachel. "Can God do anything with me?"

"Of course."

"It's not too late?"

"It's never too late." She wondered what to say, then remembered one of Manny Mendoza's favorite lines. "God is the God of second chances," she said.

"I wish I could believe that."

"You can." Rachel reached out and took Deanna's hand. "We can start right now. You can tell God you're turning your life over to him right now."

"I don't know how."

"I'll help you."

"Can I be baptized?"

Rachel smiled. "Of course you can."

"I wanted this!" Deanna said, leaning forward and throwing her arms around Rachel's neck. "I wanted this so much. Please, let's pray right now."

And so they did. As she prayed, Rachel thought about how incredible this was. Even with all the darkness going on around her, all the incomprehensible evil, she was leading someone to the Lord. It was a minor miracle.

Just before they finished praying, Rachel heard the voice of Sam Zagorsky. "Ms. Ybarra," he said.

Rachel said "Amen," then turned toward the door. Sam pushed it open further as Jefferson walked in, holding a cell phone.

"You have a call from your office," he said, as he handed her the phone.

"Excuse me," Rachel said to Deanna. Jenny, one of the receptionists, was on the line.

"You had an urgent call," Jenny said. "From the hospital."

"Hospital?"

"County USC Medical. They asked for you. Someone you know, a Mr. Mendoza, has been admitted. Apparently he's asked for you. They'd like you to come in."

Jefferson drove Rachel to the hospital. She raced in, got Manny's room number from the front desk, and two minutes later was standing outside a room that smelled faintly of ammonia.

Lydia Mendoza, her eyes red, came out of the room and hugged her.

"Rachel, thank you for coming," said Lydia.

"What happened?" Rachel said.

"We don't know for sure. He was beat up."

"Manny?" Rachel said incredulously.

Lydia nodded. "Near the church in Boyle Heights."

"How is he?"

For a moment Lydia didn't say anything, and then tears began to run down her cheeks. She put her head on Rachel's shoulder. Rachel pulled her close. It was all so unreal.

Finally Rachel asked if she could go in. "Yes," Lydia said, "go. I'll wait for you."

Rachel entered the room. There were three beds, all occupied. Manny was in the last bed. When she got to his side, Rachel recoiled at what she saw.

Manny's head was covered in gauze. His face was swollen. Both eyes were blackened, the whites of his eyes a dull red. His lips were puffy and discolored. An orange tube, inserted in his left nostril, was taped to his upper lip.

"Oh, Manny," Rachel said quietly.

He turned his head slightly. His lips moved laboriously. "Rach . . ."

"Don't talk."

"I . . . s'okay." He held up his right arm limply. Rachel took his hand and squeezed it. How could this be? Who would want to hurt this man? Her mind searched for an answer. There were only three possibilities she could think of. Maybe someone from his past, some old enemy, had finally caught up with him. That was certainly a possibility, considering what he had been before his life changed. But that earlier life was long ago. It was a stretch to think yesterday had intruded upon the present after such a length of time.

Maybe it was just a random act of violence, one of so many in the city at night.

And then she thought of the third scenario, one she couldn't bring herself to accept. Stefanos. Might this have been The Man's handiwork?

That seemed the weakest explanation. He didn't know Manny, and even if he did, why do this to him? What was that going to accomplish? All logic told her this wasn't it. But Stefanos was pure evil, an evil that was capable of anything.

As Rachel pondered these things she felt Manny's grip tighten. She looked down at him. He opened his mouth slowly and said, "Don't be afraid. . . ."

"Of what?" she asked.

"Evil."

It was as if he had been listening to her thoughts. That was so like him. Even when he was suffering through some trial himself, he always focused on the needs of others. He had simply picked up on her fear. And now, virtually incapacitated in a hospital bed, hooked up to tubes and tape, Manny Mendoza was comforting *her*.

"I won't," she said. "I won't be afraid." A small, labored smile formed under his swollen lips.

Rachel patted his hand. "You rest now," she said.

"Go with the Lord," Manny said.

Rachel walked slowly out of the room. Lydia met her in the hallway. "Thank you for coming," she said.

"Is there anything I can do?" Rachel asked.

"Pray."

"I will. Are you doing okay?"

"Manny's doing better than I am," Lydia said, smiling. "I'm the worrier."

Rachel put her hand on Lydia's shoulder. "Can I buy you a cup of coffee or something?"

Lydia shook her head. "I'm going to stay with Manny." Then she leaned over and kissed Rachel on the cheek. "We love you."

"I love you too."

In an emotional fog, Rachel walked slowly to the elevator and took it down to the coffee shop. She was hungry and selected an apple from the cooler and a Snapple Iced Tea. She paid for them and sat at a table in the corner. She put her head in her hands and tried to pray.

She stayed like that for several minutes, with only the vague sounds of a few people coming and going in the background. The noise in her own head was louder. She kept coming back to the image of Manny Mendoza, one of the strongest men she had ever known, helpless upstairs in a hospital room. Where was the justice in that?

Then she heard the voice.

"You look tired," Stefanos said. He was standing opposite her, his hands thrust casually in his jacket pockets.

"You did do it," she said in a whisper.

He sat down as easily as someone joining a friend for lunch. "Of course. Surprised?"

"Why?" She shook her head to its extremity. "Why him?"

"Did you like the twist? You were afraid for your granny, am I right?"

Rachel said nothing.

"So you and Johnny-to-the-rescue tore through town to get there in time. He's not a very good driver, you know."

"You followed us?"

"I wasn't pleased that you refused to give me my information. And I was not pleased that you called the police. I had to make that clear to you."

"Then you followed him to a church and beat him up, just to send me a message?"

"I hope you got it, loud and clear. Because next time it'll be even louder."

"Next time?"

Stefanos smiled. "There doesn't have to be. You can turn off the message machine right now."

"How?"

"By sharing information. It's simple. And now you know just how much I would appreciate your cooperation."

Rachel shook her head, a conflagration inside her, an explosion of fire that sought expression, even though she didn't know how to let it out.

"You're tense," he said. "I can understand that. Life just isn't fair, is it?"

Someone at the food counter dropped a dish of some kind, and the sharp sound reverberated through the coffee shop. Rachel felt her whole body snap.

"Now our little visit is over," Stefanos said. "We'll be in touch." He stood up. "You know, it's a shame, really, you and me. If circumstances were a little different, you and I might actually get to like each other."

If he had thrown dirt on her she would not have felt different. The thought sickened her.

"You never know," he said. Then he turned and walked out.

Rachel didn't move. Ten minutes, twenty went by. Images, thoughts, and emotions flowed through her in no discernible pattern. She tried to make some sense of things, to see an avenue open up. She tried praying, but the noise in her head was now too loud.

It got louder, poundingly loud, and to shut it off she made a decision. Part of her told her to wait, but the time for waiting was over.

She stood and walked out, leaving her apple and drink untouched.

CHAPTER NINE

THE MOON WAS OBSCURED by nimbus clouds, giving the night a cover of darkness. The street was quiet. Jeff sat in his car and watched the street for half an hour, hesitating.

He felt terrible about this, but he had to go with the hunch, if for nothing else than his sanity. If he didn't try to confirm it, he'd go crazy with doubt. That was the last thing he needed now.

But what if his suspicions were true, what then? That thought was even worse. He had no idea how he would deal with it.

He waited another ten minutes, scanning the sidewalks. Then he decided it was time, now or never. He grabbed the flashlight sitting on the passenger seat and got out.

A distant streetlight cast a pale amber hue. Jeff walked briskly across the street and stopped at the picket fence. The house behind it was dark. No lights in any of the windows.

Looking quickly up and down the street, Jeff slid along the fence line until he reached the driveway. He turned toward the garage, walking quickly now, and stopped at the path that ran along the side. He saw a fence and a gate, and on the other side of the gate, the place Jeff wanted to go.

He flicked on his flashlight and found the latch wire. He pulled it, and the gate opened with a metallic click.

That's when the dog started barking.

It was in the neighbor's yard, and it sounded like one large canine, like a guard dog in search of human flesh to tear into. That wasn't what concerned Jeff. It was the noise. He froze, hoping the dog would stop. A wall divided the properties, and at least the dog couldn't see him.

It continued to bark, pausing only now and then, as if to listen for the next sound, however slight. *Like dog and squirrel,* Jeff thought. *And I'm the squirrel.*

As quietly as he could, Jeff pushed open the gate and walked through on his toes. The dog did not concede anything and continued to bark his alert.

Jeff decided to get it over as soon as possible. He shined his flashlight into the garage window and peered inside.

There were two cars there. One he knew well, the other he had only seen once. But that was the one he had come to find.

It was sleek, and black, and a Lexus.

The dog barked again, with renewed zeal, as if it had just heard another sound to wake the dead about. Jeff turned to leave when he felt the touch of metal against his ear.

"Don't move," Sam Zagorsky said.

"Leave a message."

Beep.

Rachel hung up the phone. She didn't want a recorded message hanging out there. Somehow the wrong person would get it. Somehow.

Where was he at this hour? And why did she have the feeling that something wasn't right, that Jeff Bunnell might actually be in harm's way, but worse—that she couldn't do a thing about it. Forces were in place, but they were a shadow menace, something she couldn't identify.

As she sat heavily on the sofa in the living room, in the semi-darkness dispelled only slightly by the light filtering in from the kitchen, Rachel felt a sense of déjà-vu. She'd felt this same mixture of feelings before.

When? The swirl of memory brought it all back. It was just after she found out Stevie was using drugs and confronted him in the park. They'd had another argument, this time in his room.

"How much are you using?" she had demanded.

"None of your business," he spat back at her.

"You little idiot! Don't you know that stuff'll kill you?"

"Get out of my room."

"Where you getting the stuff?"

"Get out!" He pushed her, slamming her into the wall. Without thinking, Rachel slapped Stevie across the face, hard. It stunned her, and it stunned her brother. She had never laid a finger on him before. She opened her mouth to say "I'm sorry," but the words stuck in her throat as tears formed in her eyes. Stevie, his hand on his face, ran out of the room. Rachel heard her father call his name, then the sound of the front door being thrown open.

She ran to the door and out onto the front lawn. She looked around but saw no one. "Stevie!" she yelled into the night. "Stevie!"

But there was no answer.

She had to talk to him, but the shadows had swallowed him up. Where was he? Where would he go?

Rachel came back to herself as she sat by the phone now. Where was Jeff? She needed him now. Where was he?

"You shouldn't have come, Jeff," Sam said. He pointed the gun at Jeff's face.

Jeff, seated on a bench in the garage, shook his head. "Why, Sam?"

"You don't know these guys," Sam said.

"Why don't you call it off right now, go into protection?"

"He'd find me. He'd find my family."

"Who?"

"The Man. That's what they call him. He found Dedenok, didn't he?"

"He was the one who did Dedenok?"

Sam said nothing. The gun shook slightly in his hand.

"I should have guessed sooner," Jeff said. "You remember when you showed me how Dedenok clipped you on the head?"

Sam frowned, then nodded.

"You said you got hit here." Jeff put his right hand on the right side of his head. "Only one problem. You remember Dedenok didn't use his right hand. If he hit you from behind, it would have been with the left."

Sam said nothing, but his eyes got a little wider.

"So I figure," Jeff continued, "someone else was in on it. He knocked out Dedenok with trichloromethane while you helped. And then he clubbed you on the side of the head to make it look right."

For a moment Sam looked down at his feet. Jeff looked sideways toward a workbench to his left. A large crescent wrench lay just within reaching distance. "Why'd you get sucked in, Sam?"

His voice distant, like it was coming from the past, Sam said, "You know how it is. You look at your wife and your kids and you want them to have some of the good things. Some of the good things you can't get on an agent's salary."

"But Sam . . ." Jeff's tone was quietly rebuking.

"What of it?" Sam said quickly. "You think any side in this is squeaky clean? You think we don't have the same stuff going on over on our side of the fence?"

"No, Sam, I don't. We have our problems, but we don't traffic in narcotics. We don't kill people who are inconvenient to us. At least most of us don't."

The remark straightened Sam up. "I'm sorry, Jeff. I always liked you. But I'm in too deep."

"You won't kill me, Sam."

"I already tried once."

"But you won't do it here, at your home."

"We don't like burglars here in Altadena."

"How's it going to look?"

Sam shrugged. "I'll take my chances. You were bagged because of the Dedenok thing. You got mad. You came here to have it out with me. You snuck around the house, dogs started barking, what was I to think?"

Jeff shook his head. "Sam, don't do this." He read a note of hesitation in Sam's face. That's when the door connecting the house to the garage swung open.

"Sam, I heard—" It was Janie Zagorsky in a bathrobe.

Jeff saw Sam turn his head toward the door. Without another thought, acting purely on instinct, Jeff rolled off the bench as he grabbed the crescent wrench from the work table. On the floor of the garage he rolled again and heaved the wrench as hard as he could into Sam's chest.

Sam cried out in pain as he fell backward onto the hood of the black Lexus.

Janie Zagorsky screamed.

Jeff sprang at Sam, laying on a midsection tackle that would have pleased his high school football coach. At the same time he reached up with his left hand and grabbed hold of Sam's right wrist.

The gun fired.

Jeff heard Janie scream, "Stop!" as he and Sam fell to the ground. For an instant Sam was on top of him. Then Jeff threw a leg over Sam's body and rolled him over. Jeff straddled Sam's body and pounded Sam's wrist on the cement floor. Sam grunted in pain, then released the gun.

Jeff snatched it, but Sam threw his arm around Jeff's neck, headlocking him.

"Please stop!" Janie cried.

Sam's arm squeezed tighter around Jeff's windpipe, and Jeff felt the last of his air leave him. Lightning exploded in his head. He knew he would be out in seconds.

He turned his hand inward and fired the gun. The sharp report echoed through the garage. Sam grunted, then fell backward.

Janie screamed again.

Jeff scrambled to his knees and looked down at Sam. A blotch of red was spreading on his left side, just below the heart. Jeff looked at Sam's eyes, and his look told him Sam knew it was all over. "Sorry, Jeff," Sam said. His eyes closed.

"What did you do!" Janie screamed, rushing over. She pushed Jeff aside and fell to her knees by her husband. "Sam!"

That night she dreamed of Stevie. He was running away from her, through a fog, over some sort of countryside.

On each side of her were headstones. It was the world's largest graveyard.

She called to him, but he didn't stop. She tried to run faster, but her step got slower. Her feet were in mud. The mud was pulling her down.

She was pulled down to her knees. Some of the headstones started to move. Things were going to come out of them, she knew in her dream-knowledge, and that is when she woke up with a scream.

A moment later Abi appeared at the door, flicking on the light. "What on earth?" she uttered.

Groggily, Rachel said, "Abi, I'm sorry."

"I heard you scream."

"I had a dream."

"Oh, you poor thing." Abi sat on the bed and began to stroke Rachel's hair. "What was your dream about?"

"Stevie."

"I'm so sorry."

Rachel glanced at the clock radio near her bed. The red numerals said 4:35. "I might as well get up. I have an important hearing today in court."

"I'll make you some coffee."

"If I fall asleep in the shower, call 911."

CHAPTER TEN

SITTING ON THE BENCH, Judge Carl Montross seemed even more imposing than he did in his chambers. Rachel thought that if he spread his arms out his billowing black robe would take up the entire back wall of the courtroom. He would at least block out the lights, or so it seemed, even though he was quietly reviewing the papers before him, reading glasses pressed down on his nose.

The courtroom was also silent, though fully packed. The media was here in force. Even though Jaroslav Supevsky wasn't in court this day, it was the Supevsky trial. And Jessica Osborn Holt had promised some fireworks.

She was sitting at the defense table, tapping the eraser end of a pencil with one of her red-plated fingernails. Every now and then Rachel glanced toward her. Once she caught Holt looking back at her with eyes made of cold, blue steel.

Alan Lakewood spoke with Rachel at the rail that separated the audience from the lawyers. "You all right?" he asked.

Rachel nodded.

"You look a little preoccupied," he said. "And tired. Am I working you too hard?"

"No."

"Well, I'll have to load you up a little more then, huh?" He had a smile in his voice. Rachel smiled weakly and nodded.

"All right," Judge Montross said, tossing his glasses on the bench.

"Here it comes," Lakewood said to Rachel. Rachel sat down.

Montross said, "We have here a motion to dismiss the indictment on the ground of outrageous government conduct. Ms. Holt, do you have anything to add to your papers?"

"Yes, Your Honor," Holt said. She stood up, grabbed a legal pad, and strode to the lectern between the two counsel tables. "It is quite clear that the government has unfairly targeted Mr. Supevsky in this matter. The government has been after him for years, has never mounted a successful prosecution, and yet this pattern of abuse and intimidation continues. Your Honor, my client is a productive member of the community—"

Someone audibly snickered in the gallery. Holt whirled around, a look of utter contempt on her face.

"I want no editorial comments from the audience," Judge Montross bellowed. "Continue, Ms. Holt."

"As I said, this man has led a peaceful, productive existence ever since he moved here, yet the government has not ceased to make his life miserable."

The judge was impassive. "Ms. Holt, this is a murder we're talking about here. Someone is dead, and the government says your client had something to do with it."

"Sure," Holt intoned. "The government can say anything it wants and often does. But that is precisely the point. The government has the power to investigate ad nauseam. But instead of going after real criminals, the government keeps coming after the same man, and this is simply another example of it."

The judge looked at Alan Lakewood. "Mr. Lakewood, you have a response?"

Lakewood took no notes with him to the lectern. "Our written response will suffice, Your Honor. I'll only add that as long as the same man continues in a criminal enterprise, we will continue to, as Ms. Holt says, come after him."

"You see, Your Honor?" Jessica Osborn Holt said, as if she'd caught a four-year-old with his hand in a cookie jar.

"Ms. Holt, please," said Judge Montross. "I am perfectly capable of distinguishing rhetoric from an admission of guilt. That's why they made me a judge."

The courtroom responded with titters of laughter, and Judge Montross did not object. "Now, I've reviewed the papers and the arguments, and I am going to deny the motion, Ms. Holt. I see nothing outrageous here."

"There is one more thing," Holt said.

"Yes?" said the judge.

"It came to our attention only this morning. I wasn't able to include it in my papers."

Immediately Alan Lakewood was on his feet. "I object to this, Your Honor."

"To what?" the judge snapped. "We haven't even heard what it is yet."

"But we've received no written notice—"

"Sit down, Mr. Lakewood. Ms. Holt, what is this all about?"

With a look of smug satisfaction, Holt said, "Your Honor, we have received information from a reliable source that a member of the government's team has engaged in obvious outrageous conduct. We'd like the opportunity to conduct an examination to determine the full extent of this conduct."

Judge Montross looked down from his perch. "That's a quite an accusation, Ms. Holt. I assume you can put some substance behind it?"

"I can, Your Honor."

"Just what sort of outrageous conduct are we talking about here?"

Jessica Osborn Holt paused, then said, "Witness tampering."

A murmuring vibrated through the courtroom. Rachel herself felt an audible puff of air escape her. She knew, as did everyone in the courtroom, what this charge meant. If Holt actually had evidence that the prosecution had tampered with a witness, tried to influence testimony or suborn perjury, it would blow the Supevsky case sky-high. More likely than not Supevsky would walk, and whoever it was who meddled with the wit would be looking at prison time.

"Ms. Holt," Judge Montross said. "I think you had better give me an offer of proof."

"Of course," said Holt, stepping dramatically to the lectern. "The offer of proof is sitting right there."

Rachel looked up and saw Jessica Osborn Holt's finely manicured finger pointing directly at her. "One Rachel Ybarra, Your Honor."

This time Rachel was barely aware of the mumbling in the courtroom. All sound seemed to leave her head, leaving only the pounding of her own heartbeat. It was like a kettledrum.

Apparently too stunned to respond, Alan Lakewood merely turned, his mouth slightly open, and looked at Rachel with an expression of pure puzzlement. Rachel managed only to shake her head.

"Rachel Ybarra is a paralegal with the U.S. Attorney's Office," Holt explained.

"I'm aware of that," said Montross.

Holt nodded. "We believe Ms. Ybarra has attempted to coerce and influence the testimony of the government's key witness."

Looking unmoved, but definitely interested, Montross said, "What are you proposing, Ms. Holt?"

"Your Honor, it would be a simple matter to have Ms. Ybarra take the stand right now and allow me to examine her."

Alan Lakewood had a look of sheer bemusement on his face, reflecting what Rachel felt. He looked like he was about to speak, but no words came out of his mouth.

Judge Montross scowled. "That's ridiculous, Ms. Holt. Pointing a finger at someone is not an offer of proof."

"We're just after the truth," Holt said.

The judge looked toward Alan Lakewood, who immediately said, "May I have just a moment, Your Honor?"

"By all means," Montross said.

Lakewood turned and motioned Rachel. Feeling as if every eye in the world was on her, Rachel rose and walked through the gate, coming to a stop next to an obviously stunned Alan Lakewood. Her right leg started to shake. She couldn't stop it.

Lakewood put his head next to Rachel's. "What's this all about?"

"I have no idea," Rachel said.

"Witness tampering?"

"No way. I haven't done a thing."

"Does she know about Deanna Natale?"

"How could she?"

Lakewood shook his head. "This is a smoke screen."

Rachel nodded. "It has to be."

"She's just trying to inject a phony issue into this thing. The question is, will Montross buy it?"

"How can he when I haven't done anything wrong?"

"You need a lawyer."

Rachel hesitated a moment. "No," she said.

"This is serious."

"Let's take care of it right now. I haven't done anything wrong."

"Are you sure?"

"I'll have to answer her questions at some point. Let's do it now and show the judge she's full of air."

Smiling, Lakewood said, "You've got good instincts. Okay, let's do it." Lakewood stood up and addressed the court. "Your Honor, Ms. Ybarra is prepared to take the stand."

Rachel looked at Jessica Osborn Holt and thought she saw a momentary look of surprise on her face. But it quickly faded into her characteristic glower.

"Ms. Ybarra," Montross said. "You understand you have the right to representation by counsel?"

"I do, Your Honor," said Rachel, standing.

"Are you willing to waive that right?"

"I am."

"All right then. Let's swear you in."

As she walked forward, Rachel was sure the courtroom could hear her heart trying to escape her chest. She barely heard the clerk as she took the oath. When she sat in the witness box, she was suddenly cognizant that the room was packed and every face was turned her way. She stated her name for the record and then looked at Jessica Osborn Holt, who stood at the lectern. She looked like a tiger pacing in front of its cage.

"Ms. Ybarra," Holt began, "you are employed by the United States Attorney's Office, correct?"

"That's right."

"As a paralegal?"

"Yes."

"You're currently a law student?"

"Yes."

"At what school?"

"USC."

Casually, Holt said, "A pretty fair school." Rachel shifted uncomfortably at this seeming informality. Holt either had some surprise Rachel was totally unaware of, or she was posturing in an attempt to make Rachel think so. Either way, it was working. If Holt wanted to make Rachel squirm, she was off to a good start.

After a short pause, Holt said, "You are Mr. Lakewood's assistant is that correct?"

"Yes, I am."

"And you are specifically helping him with regard to this matter, the United States against Jaroslav Supevsky."

"That is one of my duties."

"Do you have any others at the moment?"

Holt had scored, and Rachel knew it. She did not have any other duties. Now she would have to admit it, and it would look to the judge like she was dissembling.

"No," Rachel said quietly.

"So you *are* in fact devoting all of your time to this case, correct?"

"Yes."

"And what are some of the things you do for Mr. Lakewood?"

Alan Lakewood stood. "Objection, Your Honor. This is getting into privileged matters."

Montross nodded. "That's right, but the witness can answer in a general fashion without giving away any specifics." He looked at Rachel. "Just tell us in general what you do for Mr. Lakewood."

Rachel drew a breath and thought for a moment. "Well, I review motions and go over documents. I do a lot of legal research. I participate in meetings. That sort of thing."

"What about interviewing witnesses?" Holt snapped.

"No," said Rachel defensively.

"Never?"

Rachel suddenly knew that Holt was going to ask about Deanna Natale. But how could she? Her side had not been given the identity of that witness. Yet Holt had to be aware, or she wouldn't be pressing her on this point. Rachel's legal mind snapped to attention, and in the seconds before her answer she drew the distinction between actually interviewing a witness, which is what the investigators and attorneys did, and merely being present with Deanna, which is what she did. It was a close distinction, but as her Criminal Law professor had once said, the law is about picking nits.

"Never," Rachel answered.

Jessica Osborn Holt paused and stepped from behind the lectern. She stood to one side and set her arm on it, leaning casually, looking like the proverbial cat who caught the canary. "Does the name Deanna Natale mean anything to you?" Holt asked.

Immediately Lakewood was on his feet objecting. "This is privileged information, Your Honor!"

Montross shook his head. "What's privileged about it? Ms. Holt has a name, and she's asking about it."

"But she can't . . ." Lakewood's voice trailed off.

"Why not?" Montross asked.

Lakewood looked flustered as he sat down. Judge Montross looked at Rachel. "You may answer."

"Yes," Rachel said, not volunteering anything more.

"And Ms. Natale is going to be a witness in this case, is she not?"

Rachel glanced at Alan Lakewood, asking with her eyes what she should do. Lakewood shook his head slowly, resignation etched all over his face.

"Well, Ms. Ybarra?" Holt said.

"Yes," said Rachel.

"A little louder, please," said Judge Montross.

"Yes!"

With the confidence of a dog trainer holding a docile canine on a leash, Holt walked to her counsel table and picked up a sheet of paper. She brought it to the lectern and laid it down. "On June 18th, did you have occasion to visit the Sleepy Wheel Motel in El Centro?"

This is unbelievable, Rachel thought. How could she possibly know this? Rachel had no choice but to answer. "Yes."

"And at that time you met with Deanna Natale, is that correct?"

"Yes."

"This wasn't the first time you met with her, was it?"

Rachel looked at the judge for a moment. He looked back at her, with no hint of comfort in his face. Rachel faced Holt again. "No."

"When did you first meet with Deanna Natale?"

"In May."

"Where?"

"In Connecticut."

"And what was the purpose of that meeting?"

Again, Lakewood protested. "This is getting into work product and client confidentiality, Your Honor."

Montross nodded. "It is, Ms. Holt. I won't allow a fishing expedition."

"Very well, Your Honor," Holt answered. "I'll move along to the specific information I have. Ms. Ybarra, at this meeting on June 18th, is it not true that you attempted to influence how Ms. Natale would testify?"

Heat rushing to her cheeks, Rachel said, "Absolutely not."

Holt did not back down. "Isn't it true, Ms. Ybarra, that you in fact attempted to use religion to coerce her testimony?"

"No, I—"

"Did you not in fact attempt to lead Ms. Natale in a religious conversion—"

"Objection!" Lakewood shouted.

"—and in fact force her to pray with you?"

"Objection!" Lakewood repeated.

"Quiet!" Montross commanded. He did not look pleased. "When I have an objection, Ms. Holt, I expect you to stop until I rule, is that understood?"

"I'm sorry, Your Honor," said Holt contritely.

"Now, I'm going to overrule your objection, Mr. Lakewood, because Ms. Holt apparently has specific information. The witness can affirm or deny. That doesn't violate any privileges."

"I'll ask the question again," said Holt. "Did you or did you not force the witness, Deanna Natale, to pray a prayer of religious conversion?"

"I didn't force her to do anything."

"Did you pray with her?"

"I . . . yes."

"And was this a prayer of religious conversion?"

Feeling naked and exposed, Rachel could only say, "Yes."

Murmurs arose from the gallery, and Judge Montross called for order. Holt looked up at the judge. "Your Honor, the witness has admitted to leading a witness to a religious conversion. This is a blatant abuse of her position as a member of the prosecution team. The United States Supreme Court has recognized, in numerous decisions, the power of religion in the lives of our citizens. As Justice Field stated in *Davis v. Beason*, religion has reference 'to one's views of his relations to his Creator, and to the obligations they impose of reverence for his being and character, and of obedience to his will.'

"Your Honor, it is quite obvious that Ms. Ybarra has tried to position her side as the side of God, thus coercing favorable testimony from the witness. That is the power of religion over people. But used in this fashion, it is nothing less than tampering with a witness before trial. Under *United States v. Russell* and its progeny, Your Honor, outrageous government misconduct like this is grounds for dismissal. As that case states, it should be an absolute bar to the government invoking judicial process to obtain a conviction.

"And," Holt added as a seeming footnote, "though I am loathe to ask, it seems that a sanction is in order. Ms. Ybarra needs to learn a lesson she apparently hasn't been taught in law school."

Whisking her paper from the lectern, Jessica Osborn Holt returned to her chair.

For a long moment a silence hung over the courtroom. The only sound came from Judge Montross, tapping his glasses as he pondered what to do next. Finally he looked at Alan Lakewood. "You want to ask any questions, Mr. Lakewood?"

"Your Honor," said Lakewood, standing, "I'd like to request that we put this matter over for a day. We obviously need some time to research the law on this."

"That's fine," Montross said. "We'll take this up again tomorrow morning. And then I want to resolve all motions and get the trial going, understood?"

Holt and Lakewood responded affirmatively. With that Montross stood and left the bench.

Feeling shell-shocked, Rachel made her way back to the counsel table. Jessica Osborn Holt was already on her way out of the courtroom, no doubt to a waiting cadre of eager reporters.

"How bad was it?" Rachel asked Lakewood, who was stuffing his briefcase.

"Bad," he snapped. "How come you didn't tell me about this?"

"It didn't seem relevant to the case."

"Well, obviously it is now. What were you thinking?"

"I was thinking about doing what you told me to do," Rachel said tersely.

Lakewood slammed his briefcase shut. "What I told you to do?"

"You wanted me to relate to Deanna Natale, get her comfortable enough to testify. That's exactly what I did."

"By turning her into a Christian?" His voice was harsher than Rachel had ever heard it. "Come on. We better get to work. We've got a case to save, not to mention a promising legal career."

CHAPTER ELEVEN

BY MIDAFTERNOON Rachel felt like her insides had been sucked out by an industrial vacuum cleaner, leaving a sagging sack of skin in its wake. For two hours she had gone over her dealings with Deanna Natale with Alan Lakewood. For another two she had been tracking down every case she could find on outrageous government conduct and witness tampering. The little relief she felt came from the lack of any case in which religion had been deemed an illegal weapon in the hands of government officials.

On top of all that, she kept replaying the morning in her mind, each time the picture of Jessica Osborn Holt getting larger and more threatening. That alone was enough to take all her energy away.

She was alone in the library, so she put her head down on her arms and closed her eyes. She almost fell asleep. Then she heard the sound of someone sitting across the table from her. It was Kim Adcox, one of the up-and-coming lawyers in the office.

"So you went through the Holt meat grinder, eh?" Kim said.

Rachel tried to smile, but her mouth wouldn't cooperate. "Don't I look it?"

"Don't let it get you down. Holt's heading for a fall. Who knows? Maybe you'll live to see it."

"I just want to live, period."

Kim laughed. "I heard a little bit about the hearing. What Holt is suggesting is ridiculous."

"The judge didn't seem to think so."

"Montross? I wouldn't worry about him. He's not a big fan of Jessica Osborn Holt."

"I have to admit, though, she made me look like a blithering idiot."

Kim slid a booklet across the table. "Here's some reading for you. I did a law review article on, guess what, religious freedom in the workplace. It's not exactly on point, but I think there might be some good cases in there for you to look at."

Rachel took the article reprint and looked at the cover. "Thank you, Kim. I really appreciate it."

"We have to pull together. You never know what's going to happen in these crazy, high-profile cases. Like that agent that got shot."

"What agent?"

"Didn't you hear? One of the FBI agents on the Supevsky's detail got killed last night. Something like Zig. . . ."

"Zagorsky?"

"That's it."

Stunned, Rachel looked at Kim Adcox but didn't see her.

"But the really weird part," Kim continued, "is that he was shot by another agent."

The room and everything in it started to fade from Rachel's perception.

"This really looks bad," Kim said. "What a thing to happen, huh?"

Rachel closed her eyes and tried not to get sick.

Ten minutes later, hardly aware of how she got there, Rachel was in her office, on the phone. Jeff's answering machine picked up. It was torture to listen to the recording, short as it was. Finally the beep came, and Rachel said, "Jeff, this is Rachel Ybarra. I don't know if you're there, but if you are—"

A click on the line, then Jeff said, "Hello, Rachel. I'm screening my calls."

"I just heard something about—"

"Zagorsky? Yeah, it was me."

"Are you all right?"

"I have a little post-traumatic stress disorder. I'm shaking, and can't seem to stop it."

"I'm coming over." Rachel did not even wait for a response before hanging up.

Thankfully, the drive to Jeff's apartment building was not obstructed by the usual snarl of L.A. traffic. Rachel even managed to find a parking spot on the street, a two-hour zone without a meter.

Her feet flew across the sidewalk. Jeff buzzed her in after she rang his bell.

He hadn't shaved, and his eyes were heavy-lidded. If she hadn't known him better she would have thought he had been drinking. They sat in the living room, in the hazy afternoon sunlight that filled the room.

"It's a nightmare," Jeff said. "I can't believe it, even now."

"Tell me what happened. Everything."

He did, starting with the murder—for that is what he knew it was—of Paul Dedenok. Then he traced it down through his galling discovery, that his former partner, Sam Zagorsky, had sold out and tried to kill him. Instead, it was Sam who was dead by Jeff's hand.

"Are the police going to charge you?" Rachel asked.

"They may. Then again, this may be taken out of their hands. It's a federal matter, too, one agent shooting another. But the police did the initial questioning. They questioned me and Sam's wife. She saw the whole thing. She saw Sam holding a gun on me and then saw me jump him. That corroborates self-defense. But she's not too happy with me, and they may take her nuances to another level. What's worse is that I'm an agent, he's an agent, and somebody is going to have to take the fall in the papers. Even if it's seen as self-defense, the FBI gets a big, fat, black eye. I won't be making any new fans inside."

Jeff put his head in his hands and breathed deeply.

"Let me fix you some coffee," Rachel said.

"I'll do it," Jeff said.

"No. You sit." Rachel stood and walked into the kitchen. Unwashed dishes and pans lay in the sink like old junk. She searched through the cupboard until she found a can of Folgers and a box of coffee filters. She started the brew in a much-used Mister Coffee machine and then went back to the living room.

"There's one part of this I want to know more about," she said. "This unidentified man who Sam said killed Dedenok."

"Yeah. He called him The Man."

"Did he describe him?"

"No, why?"

Rachel paused, drew a breath. Now was the time. "Because I might know him."

Jeff's expression changed from tired to confused. "What are you talking about?"

Rachel told him exactly what she was talking about, and it came out in a torrent. The pent-up emotion of weeks came pouring out.

"This is the same guy," Jeff said when she was finished. He told her about Froug, and the threat that had almost driven him crazy.

"I'm sure it's the same guy," Rachel concurred. "He's working for the *legal* team now. He wants information. And he got it. Zagorsky is the one who told him about Deanna Natale, and for that I was put through the wringer." She gave Jeff the short version of her courtroom encounter with Jessica Osborn Holt.

The accounts seemed to wake up Jeff. "Okay," he said. "We've got to move very carefully now." He stood and paced in small circles. "He's a threat, obviously, but more to me than you. He wants you alive so you can feed him the information the defense needs to beat this case. He wants me dead."

"What are you going to do?"

"I'm not sure yet, but I'm not going to stay here. I'll get myself a room somewhere, and then I'll contact you."

"What about the police? If you disappear now, it will look like flight."

"I know. But I need time. I have to try to find out who this guy really is. And then I have to figure how to smoke him out."

"Jeff, this guy's dangerous."

Jeff put on a tired smile. "Danger is what I live for."

It was the way he said it that made her laugh—casually, but tongue-in-cheek. He broke the tension in a way that made her feel reassured in some unspoken way. And so it was the most natural thing in the world when he put his arms around her, laughing too, and pulled her close to him. Naturally, too, her arms enclosed him as she put her head on his chest.

They stayed entwined for a long moment. "When this is all over," Jeff said, "I want to get close to you."

Tilting her head back, Rachel said, "I want that, too."

He kissed her then, and for that moment the world was no longer a dangerous place.

Jessica Osborn Holt was not intimidated by anyone. She had made herself that way, first out of a need for survival, and then a need to dominate. The drive that had gotten her to where she was now had been forged on the anvil of hard experience.

But now, sitting in her office overlooking the ocean, she had to admit to herself that there was an exception. The man who would soon be here scared her in a way that reminded her of when she was a little girl, a prisoner in a dungeon, awaiting the tormentor.

Much of that time was still hazy to her, but the five years she spent in analysis had brought enough of it back to piece together the essentials. The memories always started with the smell—stale alcohol in the house and on her father's breath.

When the smell was strong, she knew what was coming. There was nowhere to go. She was eight years old, as best she could recollect, when the beatings started. Why her father chose that age to begin, she didn't really know. It might have had something to do with her mother. She did not have more children after Jessica, and when that became an accepted fact in the house, her father seemed to tip over the delicate edge that had been holding him above the canyons of aberration.

He had wanted a son. He told her that again and again. But she was his only child, and nothing she ever did was enough to please him. And plenty of things she did do displeased him.

When he was displeased, he got the belt. He beat her with the buckle end. He sent her to the basement to await her punishments and would not allow her to turn on the lights.

He died when she was fourteen, but by then the internal damage had been done. Jessica herself recognized this. She knew why she could never love a man. Her failed first marriage had been a mistake but also her last-ditch effort to see if she could overcome that part of herself that had been beaten into raw hatred. It couldn't. Nothing could—not drugs, not alcohol, not Eastern mysticism. Only ambition and the temporary elation of victories in court gave her any serenity.

She would always be on the run from her past. She knew it, she accepted it, and she used it to fuel her drive. Her will was stronger than she had ever encountered in anyone else, man or woman.

With the exception of *him*.

What exactly was it about him? Not that he was a hired killer. She had known killers before, had *represented* them in fact, and she had never been awed by any of them. Always she had felt superior, and not just because she was their lawyer, but on some existential plane. She was just more *aware* of life and existence—that had been the one good result of her sojourn in India. It opened up her awareness so her killer instincts could push through to a higher level.

And that was what she sensed about him, too. He was more than a killer. He was a shaper of lives and destinies. He was not just a hired gun but a seer who happened to kill people for a living.

In other words, he was just like her. And that was why, when he finally strode into her office, she felt that emotion so foreign to her, so alien that she almost couldn't identify it.

The emotion was fear.

"Sit down," she said, indicating a chair.

Grigory sat down, smiling. He was dressed in a white summer suit with a black tee shirt under the coat. He would have fit in at a Hollywood premiere, rubbing elbows with Tom Cruise.

"We need to discuss a few things," Holt said.

"Then discuss," Grigory said.

"How are things?"

"Things?"

"With Rachel Ybarra."

"How should they be?"

"Is she talking to you?"

"She will."

"You weren't able to get the name of their secret witness out of her."

Grigory took a deep breath. "It would have happened. But the issue became, as you lawyers like to say, moot."

Holt shook her head slightly, and Grigory said, "You don't agree?"

"Oh yes, that issue is moot. But others won't be."

"And you're worried about them, aren't you?"

Trying to sound bold, Holt said, "I'm worried about you."

"Me?"

"Yes, pushing too far. Overstepping. Becoming exposed."

"That will never happen. And you know it will never happen."

"Do I?"

Grigory stood now, making Holt shift uncomfortably in her chair. "Of course you do. And you wouldn't mind if it happened anyway. You want to win this case more than anything else. You want to win every case more than anything else. That's your nature. You will take every advantage you can. In this case I'm your advantage."

"I can win without your help," Holt protested.

"You doubt that. I have been provided to you, and you're afraid of what would happen if I weren't here to help."

"You're way off."

"Am I?" He stared at her, challenging her to contradict him.

"Just don't overreach. Don't push her too far."

"She has to be pushed."

"Why?"

"Because she thinks God is on her side. That's a hurdle that has to be overcome, slowly but methodically."

"What do you intend to do?"

"I have some ideas."

At that Holt shuddered, as if she were back in a cold, black basement in a house in Mobile, Alabama.

"Now why don't you just tell me," Grigory said, "what sort of things you want me to get out of her when she's ready to talk?"

The sounds of night traffic on the 405 Freeway melted into the thumping in his ears. Jeff took several deep breaths to calm himself, then stepped to the front door of the Federal Building and inserted his GSA card into the lock system. The door clicked open. They hadn't retracted his code.

That gave him hope, but only for a moment. There was still the matter of the duty agent on the seventeenth floor.

Jeff rode the elevator, got off, then waited several minutes, just listening. Finally, with another deep breath, he walked down to the security door at the end of the hall. He inserted his card, and once again the door opened. Jeff stepped inside to the duty station. The agent on duty was Dean Mills. He was on the phone, taking one of the many calls he would get during night duty, but when he looked up and saw Jeff, he almost dropped it.

Jeff waited patiently for him to finish the call. As he did, he looked around at the place he knew so well. He had four years invested here. But now, standing there in the dead of night with a disturbing silence around him, he felt like an outsider.

"Jeff," said Mills, hanging up the phone, "I didn't expect to see you."

"Hi, Dean. How's the graveyard?"

"Fine, Jeff. What can I do for you?" His tone was clipped, even a little strained.

"Just coming in to do a little quick research," Jeff said, stepping toward a door.

Mills immediately stood and put his hand up. "I can't let you, Jeff."

For a moment the two men stared at each other. Jeff forced a smile. "What's up, Dean?"

"I'm sorry, Jeff."

"What, I'm persona non grata?"

"You're under investigation."

"Yeah, but I'm innocent."

"So you say. And I hope it's true. But we still can't allow access to you. You should know that."

Jeff thought he saw real tension in Mills's face. "Dean, listen. It's like this. I have some information that may get me out of this. I need some access on OCIS, that's all. If I get this information, it could clear me."

Mills shook his head slowly. "I wish I could, Jeff. I really wish I could."

"Dean, this may be my only chance. Look, there's a hitman who is known as The Man. He's the guy who popped Paul Dedenok. And he's stalking someone involved in the Supevsky case."

"Put it through channels, Jeff."

"I *am* channels! I can't hand this off. It's *my* life; it's my career on the line. Is it so much to ask?"

"I have a career, too, Jeff."

"Dean, look. You remember awhile back you said you'd do anything you could to help me?"

"Anything legal."

"This isn't breaking and entering here! Come on."

"It's violating an order."

"To exonerate an innocent man. You do believe I'm innocent, don't you?"

Dean Mills looked at the floor and said nothing.

"I can't believe this," Jeff said.

"Listen, Jeff—"

"Thanks, pal." Jeff turned and quickly walked out the way he came in. He didn't respond to Mills calling out his name. When the door slammed behind him, Jeff thought it sounded eerily like the final bang of a prison door.

Manny Mendoza looked better tonight, if having clean bandages was better. And he was sitting up and watching the TV that hung from the ceiling of his hospital room. Rachel thought his eyes were a little blank. Maybe he was just tired.

"Come in," he said when he saw her at the door. His was the first bed. There were two others, both curtained. Rachel heard groaning from the last bed. "Cheery, isn't it?" Manny said.

"How you feeling?"

"Like Fred Astaire in *Royal Wedding*."

Rachel stared blankly at him.

"You know," he explained, "the one where he dances up the wall and on the ceiling?"

"Right."

"Just what I want to do." He paused and read Rachel's face. "That's called humor."

Pulling up an orange vinyl chair, Rachel sat by the bedside. "When are you going to get out?"

"A few days, probably."

"That'll be good."

They sat in momentary silence. "I've been watching the news," Manny said finally. "The Supevsky case is coming up. I heard them mention your boss's name."

"Alan?"

"You call your boss Alan?"

Rachel smiled. "All right, Mr. Lakewood."

"That's the guy. Anyway, that's what you've been working on, isn't it?"

Rachel allowed her silence to be the response.

"You're going to be famous." Manny winced as if in pain.

"Take it easy," Rachel said. The patient in the third bed groaned again. A nurse, a large woman with the look of a striking dock worker, lumbered into the room and headed for the groaning patient.

"Friendly atmosphere," Manny said. "Rachel?"

"Yeah?"

"Did my getting beat up have anything to do with your case?"

Rachel looked at her hands and nodded.

"You know who it was?"

Again, she nodded. A knot of guilt blocked any words from coming. It was like a wound being reopened. The wound was Stevie.

Looking up at the ceiling, Manny asked, "Are they going to get him?"

"I don't know."

"Rachel?"

"Yes?"

"You going to be okay?"

She put her head in her hand.

"Hey, hey," Manny said, putting his own hand on her arm. "Listen to me. This guy, you got the law on him?"

"An FBI agent is working with me."

"Okay. Now all you got to do is put on the whole armor of God. Remember?"

"Ephesians 6."

"That's right. That's what I'm doing, baby. How can we be afraid?"

"Easy."

Manny laughed slightly. It looked to Rachel like the old joke—it only hurts when I laugh.

"I want you to do something about this guy," Manny said.

"What?"

"Quote Scripture at him."

For a quick moment, Rachel felt like the request was absurd. Quote Scripture? It was a fuzzy, Sunday school thing to do, and this was real life. Then immediately she felt disappointed—in herself. She was ashamed she didn't have the faith of the man in the bed, nor the belief in the power of the Word.

"You remember how Jesus dealt with Satan?" Manny said. "He answered, 'It is written,' and then boom! Scripture. The Word, baby. That's power."

"I know."

"You know what happened to me when I led my first Bible study? I could just feel the enemy dead set against it. I felt it all that day. The oppression, baby. It was real. I was down at the old church and felt the darkness all the way up to the time we started. Did I ever tell you what happened?"

"I don't think so."

"I was at the front, and in walks the last person I expected to see, a guy who was my enforcer when I rode with the Bandidos. A guy who had three murders under his belt. He walked in and in a funny way mixed with all the people. Remember, I was teaching a lot of former gangbangers and prostitutes and things like that."

Rachel nodded. Manny did have a special ministry to the lower depths of society.

"So this guy, we called him The Eyeball 'cause he had one eye, walks straight up the aisle and opens his jacket and shows me a piece. He's got a gun right there in his pants, and he's smiling, the way he always did. I knew he was there to kill me."

Manny paused a moment, the last words seeming to take a good deal of effort to say. Then he took a breath and continued. "I was frozen in place, baby. I was scared and didn't know *what* to do. I was thinking, *what happens if he opens up on me?* It's going to scare everybody, and then they'll never come back! And right then and there a verse pops into my mind. *You will trample down the wicked; they will be ashes under the soles of your feet on the day when I do these things, says the Lord Almighty.* And I said it out loud. I said it right to his face."

Like a child listening to a story, Rachel said, "What happened?"

"He smiled at me, the killer smile, and then he turned around and walked out. Two weeks later he came back. This time he didn't have a gun. This time he stayed and asked me about Jesus. He said he hadn't been able to sleep since that night. He accepted the Lord."

Rachel shook her head in amazement. Manny Mendoza's Christian life seemed like one miracle after another. But amazing as it was, it didn't prepare her for what he said next.

"Here's the thing, Rach," Manny said, taking her hand and holding it firmly. "That verse of Scripture? It's from Malachi 4."

"Yes?"

"I never memorized that verse. I didn't know that much about Malachi at all. But it came to me, and I said it, word for word. I know because somebody heard me say it and came up to me and told me where it was from. He showed it to me in his Bible."

Rachel squeezed Manny's hand and for a moment felt like the power of his faith was generating heat in her body.

"Scripture, baby," he said. "Okay?"

"Okay, baby," Rachel said.

The night was clear as she drove home, though her thinking was not. At least the visit with Manny had been a good one. She had seen fight in his eyes, and he had not blamed her. She thanked God for that and said a prayer for his healing.

The lights were out at home, which meant that Abi was already in bed. Rachel slipped in quietly through the back door, turning the knob so the door wouldn't make any noise. It was almost 9:30 by the clock in the kitchen.

She went immediately to her room and undressed, slipping into her soft bathrobe and favorite pair of slippers.

In the kitchen she started some water boiling for tea, then went to the living room to catch the ten o'clock news. She was not much of a television watcher, but she did try to keep up on the local coverage, especially where the trial was concerned. And she never knew when Jessica Osborn Holt might be appearing in front of the cameras, delivering her spin.

She flicked on the lamp by the TV, and that's when she saw him. She screamed in shock.

"Evening," Stefanos said.

He was sitting casually on the sofa, his legs crossed, his hand in his lap. The hand held a gun.

"Startle you?" he said.

"What are you doing here?" It sounded trite as soon as she said it, as if there was going to be some rational response, some communicative exchange.

"You sound surprised to see me."

"How did you get in here?"

"Through the door, how else?" He looked at her from head to foot. "Nice robe."

Rachel suddenly felt unclean, like a thick film of grime was covering her body. "Please get out."

"I like that," Stefanos said, shifting slightly, as if to make himself more comfortable. "Very polite. *Please* is a nice word."

"And keep your voice down. I don't want you to wake up my grandmother."

"Oh, I don't think Granny's going to be disturbed."

She shuddered. "What have you done to her?"

He lifted the gun and pointed it at her. "Sit down," he said. The feigned civility was gone from his voice.

Rachel didn't move. "Where is my grandmother?"

Stefanos stood up, the gun now level with her chest. "If you want Granny to live, sit *down*."

She sat. Her body was shaking. For a moment the two seemed frozen in time, like eternal enemies caught in a painting. Then the silence was broken by a high, piercing scream.

The tea kettle.

Instinctively, Rachel stood. Stefanos pushed her down roughly. "Stay here," he said. He disappeared from the room. A moment later, the whistling stopped.

When Stefanos came back in Rachel said, "Where's my grandmother? That should have awakened her."

"No," he replied. "Granny's out for the night."

"Did you hurt her?"

"Me? What gave you that idea?"

His repartee made Rachel's stomach turn. In some ways this mental torture was worse than physical pain. He was a crazed cat playing with a docile mouse.

"Tell me what you want," Rachel said.

"I want what I've always wanted, your trust."

Rachel closed her eyes.

"I want you to trust me. Trust me to do what I say. If you cooperate with me, no harm will come to you or Granny. Turn on me again, and it's all over. Can I make it any plainer than that? What have you got against me?"

It was a question that was so absurd Rachel didn't know whether to laugh in his face or turn away from him. She said nothing.

"Good," he said, like they'd made a deal. "The trial is starting next week, and I'm going to need to know a few things. Like the order of your witnesses, the lines of questioning, strategy. That sort of thing, you know?"

With no response to give, Rachel sat silently.

"By the way," Stefanos said. "How's your friend in the hospital?"

A surge of anger brought Rachel to attention. "How can you do this?"

A broad grin took over his face, like a grotesque clown smile. And then he made his move. Later Rachel would think this was entirely rehearsed beforehand, played out in a grand scale for her benefit.

He walked over to the wall where, above the piano, hung a painting of Christ with his disciples. It had been done by one of Abi's sisters, Rachel's great aunt Frederica, who had died fifteen years ago. It was a wonderful painting, mostly for the expressions on the disciples' faces. Aunt Freddie, as she was known, had captured the longing, love, and fascination that must have been in the disciples' hearts as they walked with their Teacher. Rachel had loved looking at that painting ever since she was a little girl.

Stefanos lifted the painting off the wall. Still grinning, he placed the gun in the waist of his pants and took out a switchblade knife from his pocket. He clicked the blade open.

"No!" Rachel cried.

Holding the painting on his left hand, Stefanos sliced it down the middle, an ugly ripping sound filling the room. Then quickly, like a mad surgeon, he made four complementary slits from each corner. Finished with his work, he tossed the remains on the floor.

Now, knife uplifted, he walked toward her. She did not try to move. She knew it would be useless. He bent down and placed the end of the knife on her left cheek. Rachel felt a pinprick of pain, like the sting of a bee.

Stefanos said, "You will provide me with a list of the order of your witnesses and a summary of what each of them will say. You will have this ready on Sunday evening. If you don't, Granny will go to sleep again. Only this time she won't wake up."

He straightened himself, folded the knife, and put it back in his pocket. "When this is all over," he said, "you'll understand why I had to do this. And then you and I can get to know each other all over again."

Glaring at him, Rachel said nothing.

He started for the door. "Don't bother, I know my way out."

Just before he reached the door, Rachel felt a surge of fire inside her, not rage exactly, but something intensely similar. She stood up and said, "If God is for us, who can be against us?"

He paused, his hand on the doorknob. He looked back at her, and his face was twisted in a way she had never seen before. He had always been good at the cool mask. For the briefest moment that mask was off. His mouth curled up in what was almost a sneer.

Then, without a word, he was out the door.

Rachel ran to Abi's room. She threw the door open and hit the light switch.

Abi was snoring softly in her bed. But why hadn't she awakened at the noise and conversation? Then Rachel knew. Knocked out. Like Paul Dedenok.

Rachel knelt at the bedside and put her hand on Abi's head.

CHAPTER TWELVE

JEFF FIRST BECAME AWARE he was being tailed as he turned his car down Lankershim Boulevard. It was a black sedan, and it wasn't making any secret of its intentions. Instead, it flashed its lights at him—on, off, on, off—in an obvious signal to pull over.

Pull over to what? A bullet in the brain? Did the Mob think he was that stupid?

He pushed the gas pedal down, gradually increasing speed. He opened up about a five-car gap.

The black car sped up.

The traffic was moderate here, near Universal studios. And traffic lights. If he should hit a red, Jeff thought, that might give the gunman a chance to jump out and do him right there in the intersection.

Jeff almost rear-ended a blue Honda. He jammed on the brakes, screeched, and swerved. Then, with a quick check in the mirror, he shot by the obstructing vehicle on the right. If a cop or CHP officer saw this he'd be pulled over in an instant. Not a bad thought if you were trying to avoid getting plugged by some unknown assailant. But no law enforcement officers were around. Never when you need one, Jeff thought.

The light ahead of him was yellow. He looked in his mirror and saw the black car dealing with the same Honda. There was no way it would make the light.

Jeff shot through the intersection.

He switched lanes and had a clear route to the next light up ahead. Breaking the speed limit by a healthy sum, he gave a quick glance in the mirror.

Unbelievably, the black sedan was coming after him. Nothing as tepid as a red light was going to stop it. The car flashed its lights again, and something else—an arm sticking out of the driver's side window, waving.

Jeff reached under the seat and pulled out his gun, laying it on the passenger seat. Then he took a hard right at the intersection, gunned his car again, and began improvising.

He took a sharp turn down a side street, another turn a block away, then another. He emerged on Laurel Canyon and jumped into the flow of traffic.

Too much traffic. Jeff had to ram on his brakes to keep from driving into the backseat of a Coronado in front of him. Then he got wedged in when the second lane backed up at the light.

Stuck.

He turned his head this time to look out his back window. No sign of the black car now. Maybe he'd lost it.

He hadn't. The car turned the same corner Jeff had moments before. It was only three cars behind him in this automotive line.

The light changed to green. The Coronado didn't move. Only then did Jeff realize the driver was leaning over and talking through the passenger window. There was a newsstand on the sidewalk. The guy was ordering a newspaper!

Jeff rammed his car horn. The driver of the Coronado looked back at him and then gave him the customary Los Angeles salute involving a single, upraised finger.

Jeff looked back at the black car and saw a man jump out and begin running in his direction.

A guy from the newsstand was just delivering the paper. They wouldn't be moving soon enough.

Grabbing his gun, Jeff threw open his car door, jumped out, and knelt. He pointed the gun over the trunk of his car at the man running toward him.

The man stopped and threw up his hands. That's when Jeff recognized him.

"What are you *doing?*" Jeff screamed, his gun still at the ready.

"Jeff, what do you think, huh?" Dean Mills yelled back. "I want to talk to you!"

By this time several people at the newsstand and on the street had noticed the odd little scenario being played out before them. Several of them ran, scattering like ants. One man uttered an expletive and dove behind a bus stop bench.

Jeff felt a drop of sweat roll down his forehead into his right eye. The salt sting woke him up. He stood, lowering his weapon. He looked around at the people on the sidewalk and in cars, looking at him from various positions of safety or panic. He felt like a guy caught on *Candid Camera* or *America's Dumbest Criminals*.

Dean Mills stepped toward him. "I knew you were jumpy, Jeff, but this is a little ridiculous."

"Dean, man, what do you expect? You were tailing me."

"Right, because nobody knows how to get in touch with you!"

Angry honking rose from the street. Jeff's car was blocking a line of seven or eight cars. Mills said, "Meet me at that Burger King down there. And leave your gun in the car."

Jeff heaved a sigh and got back into his car, then drove to the Burger King a block away. He pulled into the parking lot at the far end, waiting for Mills. A minute later, Mills parked next to him.

Jeff got out and leaned on his car. "I'm sorry," he said as Mills joined him. "I didn't know what to think."

"That was painfully clear. I saw my life flash before my eyes."

"How'd you find me?"

"I got good news for you. Your car theft system works beautifully."

Jeff shook his head. "But how'd you get access?"

"I work for the FBI, Jeff. Ever heard of it? You don't think we know people?"

That's when Jeff started to laugh. "I'm not a very good fugitive."

"You got that right." Mills's tone turned serious. "Jeff, you're in this pretty deep. I gotta tell you it doesn't look good."

"I know, Dean, but what are my choices here? I've got a story but no hard facts. And no witnesses."

Mills nodded. "But it looks like you're running away."

"Is that what you tracked me down for? To tell me how I look?"

"No." Mills hesitated. Then he opened the passenger door of his car. He reached in and pulled out a manila envelope, closed the door, and turned back to Jeff. "I don't have to tell you I'm putting my neck on the line with this."

He handed the envelope to Jeff. Jeff started to open it, but Mills stopped him. "Not here," he said.

"What is it?" Jeff asked.

"That research you wanted."

"You did it?"

"Yeah."

"But what did you search for?"

"You mentioned the guy's a.k.a., remember? The Man."

"Right."

"I ran it through a couple of systems and came up with this." Mills tapped the envelope with his index finger. "It ain't much, but you wanted it, so there it is. Now look, we both know I'm not supposed to have this material out on the street. So I'd appreciate it if you'd take good care of it and burn it up as soon as you can."

The tension in Mills's voice was evident. "Dean, I don't know how to—"

Mills put up his hand. "Don't thank me. Not yet, anyway. You and I may have to open up a gas station together soon."

Jeff laughed. "Can I at least buy you a Whopper?"

"No, thanks," Dean said. "I'm going back to my day job. One other thing. You better disengage your car theft system, you know? Even Inspector Clouseau could find you with it turned on."

"I'll do it."

"And Jeff . . ."

"Yeah?"

"Take care of yourself."

"I will, Dean. Thanks."

Forty-five minutes later, after a run through L.A. traffic and several looks over his shoulder, Jeff let himself into the small apartment in the building owned by his sister and brother-in-law. Guava Manor wasn't elegant. It was in a rundown part of the Valley. And for that reason it was perfect—out of the way, unobtrusive, and even a little cozy.

Jeff sat in an old, stuffed chair by the window and opened the envelope Dean Mills had given him. The first page was a search summary:

Search Term:	"The Man"
Dates:	All
Section Code:	24
Result:	Grigory Viazmitin, a.k.a. "The Man."
Last known whereabouts:	N/A

The next page was more intriguing, a copy of an affidavit for a search warrant, sworn by an agent in the New York Organized Crime Unit back in 1984:

> Your affiant, Agent Raymond Friesen, #4798, has been an agent with the Federal Bureau of Investigation for more than seven years. For the past 19 months I have been assigned to the Organized Crime Unit. My primary assignment has been the collection of intelligence and investigation of organized crime activities, specifically, the activities of Russian Mafia.
>
> I have received formal training in the investigation of organized crime activities from the Federal Bureau of Investigation and the New York City Police Department. I have attended a number of seminars dealing with the operations of the Russian Mafia.
>
> During the course of this investigation I have received information from a confidential reliable informant (CRI). The CRI is someone who has been known to law enforcement officials and the FBI for more than three years. The CRI has provided agents of the FBI with information that has resulted in the arrest and conviction of six individuals for various criminal offenses. Presently, the CRI is an active member of a local crime "crew."
>
> Through his activities in this group, the CRI has received information and instruction regarding "hits," or contracts for murder. One of these was the murder, currently unsolved, of a reputed

> head of a Jamaican "posse." According to the CRI, the hit was carried out by one Grigory "The Man" Viazmitin.
>
> The CRI has been present at a residence located at 110 Benoit Street, Brooklyn. The CRI stated that this was the residence of Grigory Viazmitin. The CRI observed several weapons in the residence.
>
> Your affiant believes that items located within the premises will tend to connect the premises, persons, and locations to be searched with the items to be seized and the case being investigated.

An attachment to the affidavit summarized the results of the search. Nothing had been found. The premises had been vacated.

That was all Dean had given him. It was a mere thread, but Jeff knew he had to pull it. He grabbed the phone and dialed a number from memory.

A moment later he heard her voice. "Hello?" Amy Alford said.

"Is this New York's most famous reporter?" Jeff asked.

"Jeff?"

"Surprised?"

"Surprised enough to hang up."

"Don't."

"Give me one good reason."

"Paris?"

A pause. "What are you talking about?"

"It's romantic."

"Then I haven't got time."

"Remember in *Casablanca?* Bogie tells Ingrid Bergman, 'We'll always have Paris.' The pleasant memories."

"We didn't have Paris, Jeff, we had Burbank. And the memories aren't pleasant."

"I know. I didn't handle it too well."

"No, you handled it like a—" Amy uttered a choice expletive.

Jeff winced. "I wrote you a letter."

"I tore it up."

"Not one of my better efforts?"

"Why are you calling me?"

"I'm in trouble, Amy."

In the silence, Jeff wondered if she was smiling. But there was no derision in her voice when she asked, "What's wrong?"

"Off the record?"

"Fine."

"I shot another agent."

"Oh, Jeff." She sounded genuinely concerned.

"He was on the take. It's a long story, but bottom line is I'm under investigation, and I'm hiding out."

"I want this story, Jeff."

"Still off the record."

"Why?"

"I need to do it my way. Tell you what, though, I'll give you an exclusive when it's over."

"Even if you're doing twenty-five to life?"

"Yeah, even then."

"All right, Jeff."

He gave her the bare outline of his situation, then told her about Viazmitin. "I remembered you had a contact at Main Justice. Do you?"

"I can't give away my professional secrets."

"You do then."

There was a long pause, then Amy said, "And?"

"Would you see what you can find?"

"If I do, will you owe me forever?"

"At least for a year."

"Done."

Jeff put his head back on the soft chair and closed his eyes.

The phone awakened him.

"Jeff?"

"Rachel, where are you?"

"He was here, Jeff."

His grogginess left him. He sat up in the chair, feeling the twinge of a stiff neck. "When?"

"Last night. He knocked out my grandmother."

"Rachel, hang up."

"What?"

"Just do it." Jeff hung up himself. If The Man had been there he could have put in a bug. He hoped Rachel would figure that out. And he hoped their little conversation hadn't been picked up.

Fifteen minutes later the phone rang again. "Jeff," Rachel said, "I'm at a convenience store. You think he might have bugged my phone?"

"Right."

"This is crazy."

"*He's* crazy, remember?"

"What do we do?"

Jeff told her about the profile Mills gave him. "I have a friend on the *New York Times*. She does investigative stuff and has a source at the Department of Justice. It's not much, but it's something."

"He wants a witness list by Monday. We haven't got much time."

"Sit tight."

"Jeff, that's one thing I *can't* do. I have to do something."

"There isn't anything you can do right now."

"Maybe there is."

Jeff didn't like the resolute sound in her voice. "What are you thinking?"

"I've got to go."

"Wait a minute—"

"I'll call you." The phone went dead.

Jeff sat motionless for a moment before slamming the receiver down.

Because it was the weekend, there was only beach traffic on Wilshire. Rachel found a two-hour parking spot on the street with no problem. When she entered the building a lone security guard was on duty at the

Monitor Bank. But she knew that big-time lawyers working on big-time cases usually worked on Saturdays. And with the start of the trial on Monday, Rachel knew there was a good chance Jessica Osborn Holt would be prepping at her office, no doubt with a video technician capturing her opening statement rehearsal.

"Help you?" the security guard said.

"I'm just going up to see if Jessica Osborn Holt is in."

"Oh, she's in. Came in this morning."

"I'll just go up then."

"She expecting you?"

"I don't think so."

"I'll have to call up. Can I have your name?"

"Tell her Rachel Ybarra from the U.S. Attorney's Office is here."

The guard punched an extension and held the phone to his ear. "A Rachel Ybarra is here to see Miss Holt. She says she's from the U.S. Attorney's Office."

Rachel bristled at the "she says." It made her sound like a con artist. The guard sat silently for a minute or so, then said "Okay" before hanging up. He looked at Rachel. "Eleventh floor."

"Thank you." Rachel walked to the elevator, her heart doing dance kicks.

She got out on the eleventh floor and walked down the hall to Suite 1130. It was locked. She knocked. A moment later the door opened, revealing a young man in a tieless white shirt. "I'm Rachel Ybarra," she said.

The young man merely grunted as he motioned her in. Then he said, "Take a left and go all the way down."

Rachel headed in that direction. Apparently the young man, probably a summer clerk, was the only other person in the office.

At the end of the aisle was an open door for the corner office. Even before she reached the door, Rachel heard Holt's voice say, "Come in, Ms. Ybarra."

Rachel entered an office where everything seemed to be made of oak or maple. An antique grandfather clock ticked relentlessly in one corner, next to a huge, glass-enclosed bookcase that covered an entire wall. Inside the glass serried rows of leather-bound books stood at attention, like crisp literary troops.

Jessica Osborn Holt sat behind a huge desk, stacks of papers and files and legal pads covering the surface. In contrast to the office design, which was classic legal, Holt was dressed in workout clothes, as if she'd just come from an aerobics class. She finished writing something, then tossed her pen on the desk and looked up. "Well, I didn't expect this little visit."

"I'm sure," Rachel said.

"Lakewood know you're here?"

"No."

"Maybe we should call him."

"No."

"I don't want you to get into any more trouble." She said it with a slight smile.

Rachel said, "No trouble."

"Why don't you sit down? Can I get you some coffee?"

"No, thank you." Rachel sat in a leather chair. It was cold and stiff.

"I'll have some." Holt hit a button on her speaker phone. "Michael? One cup of coffee please, for me."

A voice answered, "Right away, Ms. Holt."

Holt leaned back in her chair. "You like working for the U.S. Attorney?"

"Yes," Rachel said.

"Too bad."

"Why's that?"

"Because you'd make a really fine defense lawyer. You'd have to learn not to manipulate witnesses, though."

"I didn't manipulate her, and you know it."

"No, I *don't* know it," Holt said sharply. "That's for the judge to decide."

The young man who had let Rachel in entered the office, carrying a black coffee cup. He gave Rachel a sideways look as he handed the cup to Holt. Rachel thought he looked a little embarrassed.

"Thank you, Michael," Holt said. "Close my door on the way out, will you?" He did. Holt took a sip of coffee, then placed the cup on her desk.

"Understand there was nothing personal about it. You crossed the line with a witness, and it's my duty to bring that to the court's attention. Do you understand that?"

"How did you get the information?" Rachel said.

"Excuse me?"

"Who told you about my conversation with Deanna Natale?"

Holt paused, reached for her coffee, and took another sip. "That's privileged information."

"I know how you got it."

This time Holt froze, looking steadily at Rachel. "You want to share that with me?" she said finally.

"You used an FBI agent as a mole."

"Ms. Ybarra, do you realize what you're saying?"

"I know exactly what I'm saying."

"I don't think you do."

"I also know about The Man."

"What man?"

"The one who has been assigned to threaten me."

Jessica Osborn Holt stood up. She moved like a kickboxer. At any moment Rachel expected Holt's leg to shoot out and break a board. "You're way off here," Holt said. "And I don't like being insulted."

"What's being insulted," Rachel said, "is my intelligence. You can't pretend to be blind to what's going on. The information this goon is asking me for is what a lawyer would want if she needed an advantage at trial. You're pulling his strings."

"What you're suggesting is highly unethical. . . ."

Rachel stared at Holt.

" . . . and could get a lawyer disbarred."

"That's what I intend," Rachel said. "But I may reconsider if you call him off."

With a large sigh, Jessica Osborn Holt looked out her window. "You know, you can see the Catalina from here on a clear day. We don't get many of those anymore, but when they come, it's an incredible view."

"I want you to call him off."

"And if you turn your head just so, you can almost get a glimpse of the Channel Islands too."

"Miss Holt—"

"If you work hard and take some risks, you can have an office like this someday too." Holt turned around slowly, her hands clasped behind her back, and looked at Rachel. "But it won't happen if you go around making wild accusations against respected attorneys."

"Call him off," Rachel snapped. "If he comes anywhere near my grandmother again, so help me, I'll see to it that everyone knows what I know."

"Knows what? Have you gotten this far in law school without understanding that it takes evidence to prove a charge?"

"I can get it."

"I don't take kindly to being threatened. So let's just give a word to the wise. You won't say anything. If you do I'll bury you."

The cool dispassion with which she said it made Rachel shake slightly. But it passed quickly, and in its place Rachel felt a new resoluteness take hold in her. She looked directly at Holt and said, *"He who plots evil will be known as a schemer."*

"Excuse me?" Holt almost laughed.

"Proverbs," Rachel said, as she turned and walked out the door.

CHAPTER THIRTEEN

IT TOOK HER TWO HOURS to cool off.

The day was comfortably warm, with a few clouds floating in a clear sky. Rachel sat on a lawn chair in Abi's backyard and sipped an Abi lemonade—heavy on the fresh lemon. She had the feeling that the peace she felt was not going to last much longer.

Abi called her from the back door. "You have a phone call," she said, "I think it's that nice young man."

Rachel hurried inside and picked up the kitchen phone. "Jeff?" The moment she said it she knew she'd made a terrible mistake.

"Sorry to disappoint you," Stefanos said.

Rachel's insides shifted.

"Who is Jeff?" Stefanos asked.

"A friend."

"I'm interested in your friends. I'm interested in everything about you."

"What do you want?"

"I want to know about Jeff."

"Why did you call?"

"To find out about Jeff."

Rachel gripped the phone like a weapon. "I saw Jessica Osborn Holt today."

"Is he your boyfriend?"

"I saw Holt."

"I'm jealous."

The conversation was going nowhere, fast. Rachel thought about hanging up, but he would keep calling or, worse, come to the house.

"If I thought you had designs on another man," Stefanos said, "I'd be very hurt."

"I doubt that."

"And if Jeff turned out to be, oh, a law enforcement type, that would make me very upset. I'd think you were trying to get me into trouble."

Did he know?

"He wouldn't be a law enforcement type, would he?"

"My personal affairs are none of your business."

Stefanos laughed. It seemed forced. "I decide what my business is."

Emboldened, Rachel said, "No, you don't. You're working for Supevsky. And Jessica Osborn Holt. They're calling the shots, not you."

The pause on the line told Rachel she had touched a nerve. Then he said, "I don't work for Jessica Osborn Holt."

"Really?"

Another pause. "You're not trying to get me to say things, are you? You wouldn't be taping this conversation, would you?"

Rachel wondered why she hadn't thought of that.

"And besides," Stefanos said, "I wouldn't want our love talk to be broadcast to the world, so I'm very careful, maybe a little shy, about what I say."

"Say whatever you want."

"I'll save it for our date. You do remember our date, don't you?"

"Is there anything else?"

"Tomorrow night. We're going to have a little meeting, remember?"

"No."

"I'll call you with the details. Just remember, I want to see you alone. I want to have you all to myself when I look at the gift you're going to give me."

There was a short pause and then a *click*. The phone line went dead.

Rachel stood there for a long moment, not moving.

Rachel went to the convenience store again to call the number Jeff had given her. It took him seven rings to answer.

"I just got in," he said. "I have something."

"He called me."

"Again?"

"He wants a witness list."

"We can't talk like this. I want you to meet me."

"Where?"

"L.A. library, downtown. Make sure you're not followed."

"Where will you be?"

"By *Moby Dick*."

It only took twenty minutes for Rachel to get downtown. She carefully surveyed her rearview mirror and was sure she wasn't being followed. She parked in the lot under the library—a bargain on Saturdays at one dollar—and took the elevator to the main court.

The security guard gave her a smile as she entered. He was an old guy who looked like he could have been with the library since the Depression. She asked him where the fiction wing was. He pointed her toward the escalators and told her to go to the third floor.

She ascended two floors, entered the Literature/Fiction room, and began looking for M, for Melville. She scanned two aisles and then heard a voice whisper, "Over here."

She turned and saw Jeff sitting at a table, a book open in front of him. She had the urge to run into his arms but opted for the chair instead.

Jeff hadn't shaved. He looked tired. He closed the book. "*Moby Dick*," he said. "About a tortured soul with an oversized ego going for the big kill."

"I never actually read it," Rachel admitted.

"Me either. But I did see the movie. And that's the basic plot. Which makes this whole thing very interesting."

"Why?"

"Because our man may be another Ahab." Jeff reached into his pocket and pulled out two sheets of folded fax paper, stapled together. He unfolded them, laid them on the table, and smoothed them with his hand. Then he pushed them toward Rachel. "A fax from my New York friend."

She looked at it and read the name. "Grigory Viazmitin."

"That's our boy."

"How do you know?"

"Read it."

The two-page memo was a summary of what the CIA knew about Viazmitin. It wasn't much, but it lined up with what he himself had told Rachel about KGB and a superassassin. There was a little bit about his background, too. He had come from a city called Samara. He was apparently recruited early by the KGB.

There was reference to some criminal activity in the Brighton Beach area of New York, with suspicions that Viazmitin had been involved. But no one could get any hard evidence. The closest they had come was a search warrant based on information from a confidential informant. But when the warrant was served on the apartment, it was empty. And no one had seen or heard of Viazmitin again.

"I had a friend of mine do one more cross-check," Jeff said, "based on the search warrant affidavit. And you know what I came up with?"

Rachel shook her head.

"Supevsky. The hit back in Brighton Beach was allegedly done on Supevsky's orders. That gives us a connection between Viazmitin and the man about to go on trial. It fits."

Suddenly Rachel felt like every eye in the library was looking at her, almost as if she had shouted through the stillness and disturbed the entire building. She glanced around quickly. No one was looking.

"What do we do?" Rachel asked.

"I don't know," said Jeff. "But whatever we do, we better do it together."

"That's fine by me," Rachel said. "But you need to be very careful, Jeff. I don't want you to end up dead."

Jeff smiled and put his hand on hers. "Thanks for the sentiment," he said.

CHAPTER FOURTEEN

SUNDAY.

Rachel took Abi to church, but worship was an exercise in futility. Rachel's mind kept jumping from image to image, thought to thought, with no coherent pattern. The singing was spirited, and the choir was on. But it all washed over her like so much noise.

Abi seemed to sense her discomfort. She kept patting Rachel's hand and nodding her head at her as if to say, *It's going to be all right*.

By the time the associate minister stood up to preach, Rachel was considering slipping out the back. She wasn't doing anyone any good here. But Abi patted her again, and she decided to stick it out. The service dragged by, and it was actually a relief for her to get home and start to work on the witness list.

It took two hours to put the list together and get the words exactly right. When Rachel finished, she printed out the list and put it in a sealed manila envelope.

She tried to lose herself in a book for the next couple of hours, with only partial success. When the call finally came, it seemed like she had been waiting for months.

"Had a nice day?" he asked.

"I have the list for you," Rachel responded.

"I asked you about your day."

"Where do you want me to meet you?"

"Rachel," he said, his voice smooth and mildly reproachful, "can't you be a little friendlier?"

"You really expect that?"

"Start with this morning. Did you take a shower?"

"Stop it."

"Did you have a hearty breakfast?"

"You want the list or not?"

"Go to church?"

She paused a moment, then said, "Yes. Want to hear about it?"

He laughed. "Of course I do. In person."

"Where?"

"A place you know well."

"Yes?"

"Your little oasis in the wilderness."

She waited.

"The little chapel on campus," he said.

Rachel tensed. How did he know about that? Had he followed her there once? The very thought sent icy streams through her body.

"It's a little drab," he said, "but it has a certain irony about it, don't you think? You get to deal with the devil in the house of the Lord, or something like that. Be there at 5:30."

He hung up.

Rachel looked at the clock. She had one hour.

She was in the chapel at 5:20. The afternoon sun was setting, its dusky rays barely shining through the small, stained-glass window.

She was alone.

She sat in a front pew and tried to focus her thoughts. Why had he chosen this place? She came up with two reasons, one obvious, the other hidden under the surface.

First was his desire to show her he knew her every move, even the secret place she treasured so much as an escape from the world. If he could invade that place, he could show her his control, his power. That was essential to him.

The second reason was his obvious rebellion against God. This was another chance for him to show his contempt. He had jokingly referred to himself as the devil. Perhaps, in his own mind, that wasn't far from the truth.

She checked her watch. It was a few minutes past 5:30. Maybe he wouldn't come after all. That wouldn't be out of the question. He could make her run all over town if he wanted to put her through more cat-and-mouse games.

The chapel door creaked open.

He appeared as a shadow at first, the fading light behind him. When the door closed, it was almost like he had materialized from apparition to physical body.

"Shrines to human frailty," he said, looking around him. "What a waste."

Rachel stood and faced him. "Can we get this over with, please?"

"Not so fast. Let's take advantage of the moment."

She held out the envelope for him. He took it without looking at it, then tossed it on a pew. "Do you feel it?"

Rachel said, "You have the list, can I please—"

He raised his hand. "Do you feel it?"

"Feel what?"

"The change. There's a change taking place between us."

"It's time for me to go."

"I'll be in charge of your time. You don't feel it?"

"I don't know what you're talking about."

Grigory took a step toward her. "Rachel, the one thing we know about life is that it changes. You, me, all of us. Nothing is constant."

"May I go now?"

"It's like sand on the shore. No pattern, no predictability, except the inevitability of change."

He was sounding to her like some philosophy student who had scrambled his brain on drugs and now wandered the streets making obscure speeches to no one in particular. The difference was that he was dangerous.

She thought for a moment of making a run for it. If he reached out and grabbed her, she could break free, get out the door. She could take away his comfort, for a moment at least.

But she didn't. He was playing some sort of game with her, a psyche job. Maybe she could play it too. And she had an ace in the hole. She knew who he was. At some point she'd turn that card over. Not yet.

"You know what I think?" she asked.

"I'm very interested in what you think."

"I think you'd rather be someone else."

"Who?"

"Anyone. Anyone but yourself."

"Not true."

"I can give you that opportunity."

He looked at her, saying nothing.

"I can arrange a deal for you," she said. "I can get you into the witness protection program."

For a moment he looked surprised; then he started to laugh—a long, lingering laugh that became a parody of itself. Finally he stopped and said, "Can you just see it? Can you see me in Dirt, South Dakota, mowing my lawn and saying 'Howdy' to the neighbors?"

"It's better than what you've got now."

"You have no idea what I've got now. I've got everything I want, except one thing."

She didn't have to respond. She knew he would tell her, and she also knew *what* he would tell her.

"I don't have you," he said.

The feeling of slime creeping over her body began to take hold. Instinctively, she took a step backward.

Grigory, The Man, took two steps forward.

Rachel felt herself bump the tiny stand at the front, the one that held a large Bible. She put her hands behind her and used it for support.

"I'm used to getting what I want," he said. He took another step toward her.

She didn't move. The only way out was through him. "How can you even think it?" she said, not so much with contempt as with incredulity.

"I can think a lot of things. I like to think." One more step, and he was less than an arm's length from her.

"You're crazy," Rachel said.

"Would you like to see just *how* crazy?"

He leaned forward, his face coming down slightly toward hers. At that moment she had a flash of memory, from that scene in the second *Jurassic Park* movie, where the giant T-Rex leans over and looks at the hero in the window.

"Aren't you even a little curious?" he said.

She could smell his breath. It was antiseptic, chalky. *"The Lord is my shepherd,"* she said.

He raised his head up slightly. At first a sneer distorted his face, then a slow, hellish grin replaced it. He suddenly seemed poised and coiled and ready to do something. She didn't know what, but she feared it would be more loathsome than any act she could have previously imagined.

A creak sounded behind him. He whirled around.

The door was opening, and in came two young people, a man and a woman. They had backpacks slung over one shoulder, student-style. When they stepped into the chapel they paused for a moment, staring at Rachel and The Man.

"Excuse us," the young man said. He took a step backward as if he were going to leave.

"No, it's okay," Rachel said quickly. "We were just leaving."

The Man looked back at her, but she didn't return the look. She stepped past him, brushing his shoulder. He didn't try to stop her.

The students at the door still did not move, as if they sensed something was not right. Rachel looked at them and composed her voice, saying, "It's nice here, isn't it?"

They mumbled assent as Rachel continued out the doors. She turned left quickly, walking toward the main drag, where the foot traffic would be heavy. She kept walking without looking back until she reached the stream of summer school students walking to and from classes. That's when she allowed herself a glance back toward the chapel.

She saw no one, only the encroaching shadows of twilight.

Part Three

The Fallen

If I were dying my last words would be: Have faith and pursue the unknown end.

—Oliver Wendell Holmes, Jr.
Justice, United States Supreme Court

CHAPTER ONE

JUDGE CARL MONTROSS SAID, "There's a little too much noise coming from the members of the fourth estate." He scanned the faces of the reporters in the gallery. "Confine your comments to the papers and airwaves."

A few people in the audience laughed. Nervous laughter, Rachel thought. At any time Montross could severely limit their numbers and access.

She also knew Montross could limit or even scuttle her own legal career, even before it got started. He was about to make his ruling on Holt's motion to dismiss the case for outrageous government conduct—her conduct.

Across the courtroom, Jessica Osborn Holt, dressed in red, sat relaxed and composed, her legs casually crossed in front of her. It was as if she knew something no one else knew. That prospect sent a small shiver from the back of Rachel's head down to her feet. That's when she noticed her left foot, almost by itself, was tapping the carpet.

"It seems we've been presented with a novel legal issue here," Judge Montross began. Alan Lakewood and Rachel turned all of their attention to the judge. "It has been alleged that a paralegal, Rachel Ybarra, working for the United States Attorney's Office on a high profile case, has attempted to coerce favorable testimony from a key witness. Specifically, the defense alleges that religion has been used as the tool of this coercion. The theory being advanced is this. Religion touches upon the most meaningful part of our lives.

"Thus, when Ms. Ybarra engaged the witness in a prayer that asked God for mercy and salvation, she turned the allegiance of the witness toward herself in a profound way, and since Ms. Ybarra works for the government, in essence tried to make sure the testimony would be slanted favorably toward the government's case."

Montross paused for a moment as he looked toward Jessica Osborn Holt. Rachel thought she noticed Holt nod toward the judge, like he was her old chum.

"This is certainly a new one on me," Montross continued. "Witness tampering usually involves the passing of money or threat of physical harm. Can a prayer be viewed as a threat? In other words, is such prayer as powerful as the defense would have us believe? My answer to that is yes."

In the short pause that followed, Rachel felt the eyes of the reporters shift toward her, even though her back was to the gallery. She felt the color draining from her face.

"I agree with Ms. Holt," Montross said, "that religion plays a powerful role in the life of people and used in the fashion described here can have a profound effect."

The words "agree with Ms. Holt" hit Rachel like a slap across the face.

"However . . ." Montross let the word linger, as if pausing for dramatic effect. ". . . I find that this was not outrageous conduct on the part of Ms. Ybarra."

Relief washed over Rachel like an ocean wave. *Not* outrageous conduct. That's what he said!

"Ill-advised, yes," the judge said. He looked at Rachel, and his piercing eyes seemed ablaze, but in an almost paternalistic way, as if he were a father castigating a teenager for driving too fast in the family car. "She needs to learn that this sort of thing is not proper when preparing a case for trial. But she is not a lawyer, not yet, and nothing in the declarations filed here evidence any ill-intent on her part. It was a mistake, but this is something Ms. Holt may bring to the attention of the members of the jury, and they can decide what weight to give it. I am not dismissing this case. Anything further?"

It was over. Rachel was stung, but that would wear off. She would get to practice law someday.

Holt and Lakewood both said they had nothing else to bring up. Montross said, "All right, then. We will start picking a jury at 1:30." He stood and walked off the bench.

A few reporters scurried to the rail, vying for Rachel's attention with shouted questions and flailing arms. Lakewood ushered her out, cutting off the questions with a terse, "No comment."

By the time they got back to the eleventh floor, Rachel was physically and emotionally drained.

"I feel like spaghetti," she said.

"But we won," Lakewood assured her. "Holt's little distraction didn't work. Now we can concentrate fully on the trial. You won't have to bother with these things again."

Right, she thought bitterly. No bother at all.

"By the way," Lakewood said, "Deanna Natale wants to see you."

"Why?"

"Probably just scared. I want you to go see her, but this time don't talk about religion, okay? We don't need another objection from Jessica Osborn Holt."

Deanna Natale had been moved to a hotel in Glendale, a fifteen-minute drive from the courthouse. There were three agents in the room with her, and they were not leaving. Rachel felt a little like a laboratory rat as she sat down with Deanna near the window.

The prosecution's star witness smiled wanly and put out her hands to Rachel. "I just needed to talk to you," she said.

"That's fine," Rachel answered. "I'm here." She felt Deanna's hands shaking slightly.

"What's happening in the trial?" Deanna asked.

"It's just getting started this afternoon. They're going to pick a jury."

Deanna sighed heavily, as if the news of the impending trial was a sudden, fearful burden. "Then it's close."

"Yes."

"I wish it was over."

"It will be, soon enough."

"What's going to happen to me?"

"You'll be sworn in, and you'll tell your story. That's all."

"What about the other side? What about the lawyer, what's-her-name?"

"Jessica Osborn Holt."

"Won't she question me?"

Rachel nodded. "On cross-examination."

A look of fear came into Deanna's eyes. "Won't she try to make me look like a liar?"

Rachel patted Deanna's hand. "That won't work, not if you stick with what you've told the investigators. And the jury will be on your side."

"They will?"

"Yes," Rachel assured her. "That's the way it is most of the time. Jurors look at witnesses like one of them."

"But I'm not," Deanna objected, "not really."

"Everybody has baggage in their past."

"Not like mine."

"Don't worry, Deanna. Remember, God is going to be . . ." Rachel stopped midsentence.

"Yes?" Deanna said anxiously.

"I'm sorry, Deanna, I've got be very careful what I say to you."

Deanna frowned. "Why?"

"Because you're a witness for us. I can't try to influence you in any way."

Shaking her head, Deanna said, "But I *want* to talk to you about God. I want to."

"I know you do."

Deanna's shoulders sagged. "Will he help me, Rachel? Just tell me he'll be with me." Her hands, which had not let go of Rachel's, squeezed harder.

Rachel squeezed back. "Of course he will." The words just came out. Rachel could feel the eyes of the FBI agents scrutinizing her. But she no longer cared. If she couldn't give a scared witness, who was a new Christian, some small comfort, then the law, in the famous phrase, was an ass.

"You just put your trust in the Lord," Rachel said, "and he'll make your path straight."

⟡⟡⟡

The three of them sat in the back of a limousine with darkened windows.

Jaroslav Supevsky opened the bottle of Dom Perignon and poured some into a champagne glass. He handed the glass to Jessica Osborn Holt.

He poured another and handed it to Grigory Viazmitin. Then he poured one for himself. He placed the bottle in the ice bucket on the built-in wet bar and raised his glass. "To victory," he said.

The trio sipped their wine.

Holt felt the bubbles burn in her throat. This was an odd ritual to be going through, but she had learned to accept the unexpected from her client. "Isn't this toast a bit premature?" she asked.

"How can I lose?" Supevsky said. "I have the world's greatest criminal lawyer on my side and the world's greatest former Soviet agent working for me. If there is any guarantee of victory, it is in this car."

"I'd still prefer to wait until after," Holt said.

"Oh, come on," Supevsky said. "Drink your wine. When you start picking jurors, you'll have a little glow."

Supevsky laughed. It seemed to Holt that his jocularity was a little bit forced, almost as if he were blustering on her behalf. She wondered how much he really trusted her to get him off with a not-guilty verdict. If that trust had been total, he wouldn't have had this assassin sitting with him.

"When we have our jury," Supevsky said, "I think it would be a good idea to get one on our side from the beginning."

Holt looked at him with surprise. "Meaning what?" she said.

"Meaning he or she should be convinced that a certain outcome would be in his or her best interest."

Glancing quickly at Grigory, Holt knew exactly what Supevsky was proposing. "No," she said. "No way. That would be going too far."

"I don't see it that way," said Supevsky. "I like sure things."

"Jury tampering is bad. It could blow up in our faces."

"You don't give Grigory nearly enough credit, Jessica."

"No," Holt insisted. "No jury tampering."

"Is it any worse than tampering with a clerk at the U.S. Attorney's Office?" There was an edge in Supevsky's voice that made Jessica Osborn Holt very uncomfortable.

"Look," she said, "just leave the trial to me, will you?"

"I've never left anything that concerns me to anyone else in my life." His convivial manner was gone now, replaced by a cold stare. Coupled with the unemotional eyes of Grigory, the atmosphere was becoming decidedly cool. Jessica Osborn Holt, who had built her entire professional life around calling the shots, now realized she was not in total control.

"Now," Supevsky said, "we have some concerns about this law clerk. Grigory is convinced she's told an FBI agent about him."

"And why does he think that?"

"He has his reasons. The question is, What do we do about it?"

Holt felt an icy finger run down her spine. "What are you thinking?"

"Elimination."

Her breath leaving her, Holt managed to say, "You can't be serious."

Supevsky finished his champagne in one gulp. "There is a new world being created out here, and I am helping to create it."

"But the Feds. You can't mess with—"

"Don't keep telling me what I can't do. You don't understand, you don't have the vision. You don't have Grigory."

Holt looked again at the impassive killer.

"It's elegant, really," Supevsky said. "This FBI agent is implicated in the killing of another. A suicide is not out of the question. Grigory, as you know, is good at staging such scenes. That would be a simple matter."

For a moment Holt felt a small, inner prompting, like a faint voice from a distant shadow, calling out in protest. This, after all, was another human life in the equation. She had gone along with Dedenok because that was an obvious move and he was a dirty snitch. But this was an FBI agent, and things could get awfully murky.

The voice faded almost as quickly as it had come. She was, after all, making nearly a million dollars on this case, and the champagne was the best. She smiled, took a sip of sparkling wine, and said, "Simple, no doubt."

Rachel was putting the finishing touches on a memo when she heard the knock on her office door. But she wasn't expecting Ron Ashby.

For the last two weeks he had been quiet, almost too quiet, around her. It was such a sudden shift that she began to suspect he was cooking up some juvenile scheme to spring on her. But she decided she was paranoid—an acceptable emotion under her present circumstances—and gave him no further thought.

Until now.

"Busy?" he said.

"Yes," Rachel said, "as a matter of fact, I am."

"Supevsky?"

"Yes."

Ashby walked around her desk so he could see her computer screen. His manner reminded her of a little boy cheating on a test.

"Do you mind?" she said.

"I don't mind at all," said Ashby.

"I have to get this done."

"But I'm here to help."

"I don't need your help, thank you."

"You don't have any choice."

Rachel whirled around in her chair and stared up at him. "What are you talking about?"

"Oh, I'm sorry," Ashby said, sounding anything but. "I thought you knew."

"Knew *what?*"

"That the Supevsky file's going to be handed over to me."

The words were like a fist, a body blow, leaving her short of breath. "Who said?"

"Lakewood," said Ashby, with more smugness than she'd ever seen in any one person.

"He hasn't told me anything like that." Rachel stood up, but she knew it had to be true. A guy like Ashby, with his perfectly knotted ties and no-hair-out-of-place head, wouldn't make such a bold pronouncement without having it backed up. But why hadn't Lakewood told her?

"Excuse me," she said, and brushing by Ashby she left her office and charged down to Lakewood's office. His door was closed. She gave a quick knock and heard him say, "Come in."

Lakewood wasn't alone. In one of the chairs sat a man she recognized but couldn't place at first. Then suddenly she remembered. He was one of the three FBI agents who had been protecting Deanna Natale.

"That'll be all for now," Lakewood said to the agent, who immediately got up and, without a smile or acknowledgment to Rachel, left the office. "You probably know what this is about," Lakewood said.

"I think so."

"You had strict instructions not to talk to Deanna Natale about God or anything like that."

"I know, but—"

"And you did not follow those instructions."

"No, I didn't."

"I'd like to know why."

Rachel felt that she could tell him everything, and nothing. How could she possibly make him understand? Alan Lakewood wasn't a religious bigot, that much she knew. But he was a career professional who was able to place everything outside of the box of his profession. Maybe that's what you had to do as a lawyer, but if it was, she hadn't learned that lesson. She didn't know if she could.

"Sir," Rachel said, lapsing into formality, "Deanna Natale is our witness, but she's also a person who is reaching out. I can't ignore that."

"You have to!" Lakewood said with a flash of anger. "This can all blow up in our faces." He stood up and gestured wildly with his hands. "Can't you just see Jessica Osborn Holt on cross-examination? 'Did Rachel Ybarra tell you God was on your side?'"

"I never said that!" Rachel protested.

"It doesn't matter exactly what you said; you gave the impression. And Holt will ask the questions in the most damaging way she can. And then there's the judge! Boy, he's going to love hearing that you were God-talking again after that motion by Holt."

"But he ruled against her."

"That doesn't mean he sanctioned what you did. He only found it wasn't outrageous conduct warranting a dismissal. He clearly wasn't happy about it. And now you've opened the door again."

"Then he can hold it against me."

"I'm your boss! He's going to hold it against me too. That's why I'm letting you go." He looked out the window.

"I'm off the case?"

"Yes."

Rachel's legs suddenly felt like rubber. She was being sacked. She had never been fired from anything in her life. Now, in one of the most prestigious offices in the nation, a place where she hoped to spend a career, she was being told she had blown it.

Rachel stood there for a moment, unable to think of anything to say. She knew it was hopeless to argue her case now. And even if she did, Lakewood was making sense. Holt could definitely use this against them. The answer to the argument in her head was not clear, and Rachel had always thought the law would be clear if you thought about it hard enough. It wasn't now.

Lakewood turned to her. "You'll be sure to give all your files to Ron Ashby."

The sound of the name gave her a nauseous feeling, but she managed to say, "Of course."

There was an uncomfortable pause, then Rachel said, "Is that all?"

"I'm sorry," Lakewood said quietly. "But for the good of the case—"

"You don't have to explain," Rachel said, shaking her head vigorously. Feeling like she might burst into tears or throw a chair, she quickly turned around and practically ran out of Lakewood's office.

CHAPTER TWO

ART YBARRA WOULD NEVER have imagined he could do what he was about to do to Ernie Sanchez. But then again, he never imagined life would turn out the way it did.

He considered himself a man's man, which meant you did not let your emotions get the best of you. Growing up on the streets of East L.A., he'd learned to harden himself. That was how you survived with the gangs, and in a way, the whole world was filled with gangs.

He was proud of the fact that he'd forged a good life for his wife and two kids. He delighted in them, especially the son, Esteban. The kid was going to be a star athlete. He was going to make the big bucks, live the real American dream. The girl, Rachel, was a cute little thing, quick with the mind, just like her mother.

He let his wife take the kids to Mass, and he even went on occasion. Religion was okay, as long as you didn't take it too seriously. It might even do some good along the way. If it kept his kids in line, great. Let the priests and the nuns have their way.

That way came to sudden stop when Maria died suddenly of cancer. Cancer! At only thirty-eight years old. What good had the church been after all? She was the faithful one, the pious one, and what kind of help was her religion anyway?

That ended Mass for the family.

It also brought to Art Ybarra a challenge he wasn't ready for, something his work ethic and skilled hands couldn't do on their own—raise two children without a mother. He did what he thought was best, but it obviously wasn't good enough.

Esteban—everybody called him Stevie—fell into drugs and was cut down on the streets. Someone was to blame. Art had the notion that he himself was to blame, but that was not something a self-made man could comprehend. He had to find another way to deal with it, and it seemed like his daughter was the obvious choice. She had taken on the role of surrogate mother, hadn't she? Well, she botched the job.

And there was something else. Stevie and Maria were dead. But Rachel had become some kind of born-again Christian! She didn't just walk away from the Catholic church; she fell into some sort of super enthusiastic cult that preached all about a good God and everything's rosy, and it was just like hysterical salt rubbed in an emotional wound.

The pain of that wound was real, and Art Ybarra found his solace in alcohol. He could handle his beer; he could even drive drunk. He could wake up the next day with a slight headache but then go to work and do an honest day's labor. When evening came, and with it the shadows of the past, he always had the beer and TV.

Sometimes he took his beer down at The Boxcar, a local saloon with a satellite for sports and a predictable group of drinkers.

On this night, into his fourth beer and third shot of tequila, Art sat at the bar watching baseball, feeling a dull warmth starting to take hold, when Ernie Sanchez took the stool next to him.

"Hey, man," Ernie said, at the same time raising his hand to the bartender.

Art grunted a greeting, keeping his eyes on the screen. Eric Davis of the Baltimore Orioles was up. Art liked Davis. He was a gamer.

"Hot out tonight," Ernie said. When Art still said nothing, Ernie gave him a fist on the shoulder. "What's up?"

"Nothing," Art said.

Ernie's tone changed slightly. "Maybe I should go find another spot, huh?"

"Fine."

"Hey, what's wrong with you, man?"

"Be quiet."

Ernie shook his head. The bartender served him a beer, and Ernie took a third of it in one gulp. "I want to talk to you," Ernie said.

"Why?"

"I got a favor to ask."

Art scowled. Usually Ernie was short of cash, and Art figured that's what this was all about. He'd lent Ernie money before, and Ernie was good for it. But he wasn't in the giving mood tonight.

“Forget it,” Art said.

“Hey, man,” Ernie said in protest, “you ain’t even heard me out.”

“You want money.”

“No, I don’t.” Ernie exhaled a disgusted breath, then swore into his beer.

Art turned his gaze to him. “What’d you say?”

“Nothing, man.”

“You call me something?”

“Watch your game.”

Art motioned for the bartender to bring him another beer. Eric Davis got a hit, stretching a single into a double. When his beer arrived, Art started drinking without comment.

Finally Ernie said, “I got a problem.”

Art didn’t respond.

“DUI,” Ernie said.

“Too bad.”

“Yeah, too bad,” Ernie mimicked. “I can’t afford this. I gotta get me a lawyer.”

Art shrugged.

“So I was thinking,” Ernie said, “your daughter. She’s a lawyer, ain’t she?”

The sudden thought of Rachel burned Art’s mind, taking him out of the alcoholic somnolence he had just started to enjoy. “She ain’t no lawyer.”

“Yeah, she is, you told me.”

“She’s a law *student*, is what I told you.”

Ernie sagged a little. “Then what the hell good is she?”

Only later did Art realize that Ernie had made one of his Ernie-type jokes, the kind that are supposed to be funny but aren’t. He’d heard Ernie say things like that dozens of times. But this time he didn’t hear it that way. He heard it like the start of a fire in his gut.

A blind, red rage took hold of Art Ybarra. He was barely aware of what he was doing. His right fist shot out and caught Ernie flush in the face. Art felt the crackling of cartilage under his knuckles. Ernie fell back off the stool and hit the floor with a sickening thud.

Art jumped on top of him, flailing with his fists as Ernie, bleeding from the nose, tried to cover up his face. A string of swear words poured out of Art's mouth. He was hardly aware of what he said. He only knew they were flowing, and he had no desire to stop them.

The next thing he knew he was on his back, thrown off by several hands. The bartender and two other guys were standing over him. One of the guys had his foot, which was inside a heavy work boot, pressing down on Art's arm, holding it to the floor, sending searing pain up through his shoulder and neck. Voices were shouting, but Art couldn't make anything out. He was in a haze and afraid to come out.

It took ten minutes or so for Art to come to himself. When he finally started to think again, he saw he was alone at a table near the wall. Ernie was at the bar holding a towel over his face. The bartender was helping him.

Shaking his head, Art got up and staggered to the bar. As soon as he got there, the bartender stepped between him and Ernie.

"That's it," the bartender said. "You're out of here."

Art said, "How is he?"

"Out," the bartender said.

"I'm drunk."

"Get out."

Art leaned to the side. "Ernie, you okay?"

"Shut up," Ernie said, his voice muffled by the towel.

"Ernie, listen—" Before he could say another word, the bartender, bigger than Art by at least six inches, grabbed him by the shoulders and started pushing him toward the door. Art shook free. "Okay!" he said. He weaved toward the door by himself.

The night air was hot and moist. Art fumbled in his pocket for his keys, dropped them, and almost fell over trying to pick them up. He got them back in his hand and made it to his truck. Operating out of habit, he started it up and burned rubber out of the parking lot.

Things were happening too fast in his brain. He drove without really seeing, letting his senses run on autopilot, his mind a jumble of images.

Outside the truck, lights of all colors seemed to be flashing indiscriminately, and Art wasn't sure if they were traffic lights or liquor store signs, street lights or neon. He only knew, or thought he knew, he was driving in the general direction of home.

Then the unmistakable lights hit him in the eyes. They flashed in his rearview mirror—red, blue, red, blue, red, blue. The cop must have been trailing him since he pulled out of The Boxcar. The cop must have known he had a prime drunk driver in his sights.

Art Ybarra pulled over to the curb, skidding his tires against it, and cut the engine.

The only good thing was that Toni Galvan had insisted on taking her to dinner. And once they were seated at the Italian restaurant, Rachel felt slightly better. It didn't do anything for her appetite, but her spirits were temporarily lifted. Toni was a good listener and a comfort.

"I just can't believe he'd let you go like that," Toni said.

Rachel shrugged. "I'm trying to see it from his point of view. I guess he did what he thought was best."

"Will you quit taking his side!" Toni slammed a piece of garlic bread down on her plate. "You were hosed! You can carry this forgiveness thing too far."

"You want me to get angry?"

"Yes. Fight back."

"How?"

"I don't know, raise a stink. Get a baseball bat! Something!"

Laughing, Rachel put her hand on Toni's arm. "You know who you sound like?"

"Who?"

"Jessica Osborn Holt."

Toni reeled at the suggestion, then smiled. "You're right. Sorry."

Rachel was silent for a moment. The thought of Jessica Osborn Holt made her queasy. Holt would soon be loving the fact that Rachel was out.

"You know," Toni continued, "I can't help feeling . . ."

"What?"

". . . that Ashby had something to do with this."

"How?"

Toni nodded. "Call me paranoid, but that slimeball has been slithering all around the office, looking for ways to knock off anybody in his way."

Rachel stuck her fork in her linguini and twirled it without picking it up. "I don't know. He's slimy, that's for sure, but I don't think he has any influence with Lakewood."

"Well, anybody that works with him better watch his or her back. Anyway you slice it, you were treated pretty shabbily."

"I've got to believe it's for the best."

That brought a look of shock to Toni's face. "How can you say that?"

"I have to."

"But why?"

"God works all things for good."

Shaking her head, Toni said, "You really believe that?"

Rachel tapped her head with her finger. "I believe it up here," she said. Then she pointed to her chest. "I want to get it back down here."

Toni thought for a moment. "It would be nice to believe," she said with a faraway voice. "I still think you need a baseball bat sometimes. God understands."

"Oh, yes?"

"Sure. Remember, I'm Jewish. I know about God using plagues and all that. That I can understand."

"Hey, Toni?"

"Hm?"

"Thanks." Rachel put her hand out, and Toni took it with a look of pure understanding. "You've been a pal."

"Let's stay that way, huh?"

"You got it."

They spent the next few minutes talking like what they someday might be—old friends. Rachel even managed a few bites of linguini. When her cell phone rang, Rachel reached for it as if it might be a page from the office.

It wasn't. It was an Officer Logan at the Montebello police station. "Can I have your name, please?" he said.

"Why?" Rachel asked.

"We found this number in the wallet of one Arturo Ybarra. Are you related?"

"What's wrong?"

"Are you related, ma'am?"

"Yes, yes, I'm his daughter."

"All right. He's down here at the jail. If you want to come get him, you can."

"Why? Can I talk to him?"

"He's in no condition to talk right now, ma'am. We're here all night."

The line went dead.

"What is it?" Toni asked.

"My dad. I have to go." Rachel started to get up.

"Hey," Toni said, putting a hand on Rachel's arm, "call me if you need me, okay?"

"Thanks."

The drive to Montebello seemed endless. When she finally pulled up in front of the station, she felt like she'd just swum a fifteen-hundred-meter race.

Inside, the police station had an oddly antiseptic smell, almost like they made an effort to keep things too clean. Rachel told the desk sergeant who she was. "I'm here to see Arturo Ybarra."

"You got ID?" the sergeant asked tonelessly.

She showed him her driver's license. "What's he in for?"

"Deuce," the sergeant said.

"Drunk driving?"

"That's what I said. Wait over there, please." He nodded toward the wall. Rachel paced toward it.

A woman was sitting on a hard bench with a young boy, maybe seven or eight. "See," she said, "this is what will happen to you if you gang it up." The boy seemed uninterested. A few moments later a uniformed officer appeared with a teenager. The woman stood up and screamed at him, "You no good! That's what you are! You no good!"

Another fine, family portrait, Rachel thought despondently. Then she turned the thought on herself. What was she being critical about? She was about to fish a drunken father out of the can, one who probably didn't want to see her anyway.

The police officer led Art Ybarra to the front desk. To Rachel he looked like a man who might be hanging out on a street corner. His hair was a mess, his shirt had a tear, and he obviously hadn't shaved. And he walked with a shuffle and slight limp. He looked like a man defeated.

The desk sergeant handed Art a large envelope. Then, turning to Rachel he said, "His Notice to Appear is inside. Make sure he does."

Her father looked at the floor and didn't move. For a moment Rachel didn't move either, waiting for him to acknowledge her. He didn't.

"You don't want to go?" the sergeant said. The officer who had led him in laughed.

Rachel went to her father and took his arm. "Come on, Pop."

Art yanked his arm out of his daughter's grasp and motioned toward the door with his other hand. Rachel walked toward the door, and he followed her.

When they were out in the night air, Art said, "Why'd you come here?"

"They called me, Pop," Rachel explained. "You had my number in your wallet."

"Ain't you working?"

Looking at the ground, Rachel said, "I was on a case, but I got taken off."

"Why?"

"Because they think I blew it."

"Did you?"

"Maybe."

Art grunted.

"Pop, are you all right?"

"No."

"Let's go home."

"They took my truck."

"We'll get it in the morning."

"I'm gonna lose my license."

"Let's go home, Pop."

Art didn't move. He ran his fingers through his hair and shook his head. "They're gonna take my license away."

"Come on."

Refocusing on his daughter, Art snapped again, "Why'd you come here?"

"Because you're my father!" Rachel said, just short of yelling. "And I love you."

For a moment Art stopped his agitations. He looked into Rachel's eyes with a mixture of surprise and longing. Then, quickly, it was gone. He looked back at the ground, shook his head, and said, "Let's go."

They didn't speak again until Rachel opened the door of the Ybarra house and flicked on the lights. "Let me put some coffee on," Rachel said.

"Don't bother."

She did. She set a pot brewing in the kitchen, then came out to the living room. Art was slumped on the sofa, looking into a blank TV screen. Cautiously, Rachel sat down on the other end of the sofa. "It'll be okay, Pop," she said softly.

Art shook his head slightly and continued to stare. From the side he suddenly looked like a child, scared and vulnerable. The shock of that juxtaposition filled Rachel with a sudden, intense, and unidentifiable emotion. It was a mix of everything she had felt about her father from the time Stevie died and the incredible ordeal of the last several weeks. Without any ability to stop it, Rachel erupted into tears.

Sobs poured out of her. She buried her head in her hands and let herself go, trying in that surrender to let everything out, once and for all.

Suddenly she got up and ran out of the house. As she got in her car she thought she heard her father's voice calling her name, but when she looked toward the house, she did not see him.

She almost fell asleep on the drive home to Abi's. She had not expended so much emotion in years, not since the awful days surrounding Stevie's death.

By the time she made it to the Hollywood Freeway, it was almost ten o'clock. All she wanted to think about was a warm bed.

Her cell phone rang, startling her out of her drowsiness. Who would be calling her at this hour? She was sure it would be him, The Man.

She hesitated.

It rang again.

It could be Jeff. She hadn't spoken to him in two days. Maybe there was trouble.

Another shrill ring.

She picked it up.

"Did I catch you at a bad time?" The Man said.

"What do you want?"

"Please, must you be so harsh?"

"We don't need to speak anymore."

"Oh, but we do."

"No, you don't understand. I was let go. From the case. I can't be of anymore help to you. You can leave me alone."

There was an ominous pause. She imagined him laughing at her naïveté. "Rachel," he said, almost cooing her name. "You know this isn't the end for us."

She had known but couldn't bring herself to admit it. "Why not?" she asked, wanting to hear the worst.

"I think you know. My position in this case needs to be handled delicately. If you were to make our relationship known to certain parties, it would defeat my whole purpose, wouldn't it?"

Of course it would. She had briefly entertained all sorts of thoughts about going to the FBI and spilling the entire scenario. But his fearful hold on her was still strong. Others were involved—Abi, Deanna, Jeff, Manny. She couldn't endanger them.

"I can't give you anymore case information," Rachel said. "I just don't have it."

"You can always get it."

"Look—"

"Maybe you don't take our relationship as seriously as I do."

His oily tone made her skin crawl. "I won't say anything," she said, "but I can't help you anymore."

"But you can."

"No."

She was nearly at her off-ramp. The thought of going back to Abi's with him on the line was almost as loathsome to her as having her on his arm.

"Rachel, you'll have to let me explain."

"No. I don't want to talk to you anymore."

"But I want to talk to *you*."

"No."

He sighed. "Am I going to have to pay your grandmother another visit?"

Anger suddenly flashed into her head, and she didn't care. "You are disgusting."

"Now, now."

"Leave me alone."

"I can't do that. I don't want to do that."

Rachel's body shook.

"You'll see," The Man said, as if he were comforting an old friend. "It will all turn out for the good."

That jolted her. It was almost like the devil quoting Scripture. It was *exactly* like it. If she hadn't been clear about it before, she was now. This was pure spiritual battle. She was engaging a demonic force. Manny was right.

"*Every knee shall bow,*" she said, tightening her jaw.

"Excuse me?"

"*And every tongue confess.*"

"Rachel—"

She disconnected him and threw the phone on the floor. A moment later it rang again. She didn't pick it up.

CHAPTER THREE

ALAN LAKEWOOD STOOD, walked to the lectern, and faced the jury. Rachel scanned the faces of the fourteen—twelve jurors and two alternates. They seemed alert and interested.

Several externs from the office were in the courtroom, along with the media. There weren't any empty seats.

Toni Galvan, next to Rachel, said, "This is it."

Rachel nodded with little enthusiasm. This had once been her case. Now Ron Ashby, sitting in the front row near the U.S. Attorney's table, was taking the notes.

"Good morning, ladies and gentlemen," Lakewood said. He pointed at Supevsky. "The defendant sitting over there is a man who is used to getting what he wants. It doesn't matter what law, what social institution, or what person stands in his way. Such things don't matter one bit to Jaroslav Supevsky. Money and power are the only things he cares about. So when a man named Dimitri Chekhov became a problem for the defendant and his thriving drug business, he didn't think twice about eliminating that problem.

"Ladies and gentlemen, when all of the evidence is in, we believe it will prove to you beyond a reasonable doubt that Jaroslav Supevsky is guilty of contracting the torture and murder of Dimitri and Sarah Chekhov."

Lakewood paused and looked down at his notes. Jessica Osborn Holt was writing vigorously on a legal pad. Supevsky stared straight ahead.

"One thing I'm going to ask you to keep in mind from the very start," Lakewood continued. "One murder victim in this case, Dimitri Chekhov, was not a fine, upstanding citizen. We make no attempt to hide that fact. He was, you will learn, a Russian immigrant who built up a substantial limousine business. He did a lot of legitimate work, but he also did something all of us despise. He ran drugs. You will learn a lot about that drug trade because that was the motive for murder in this case. You will learn that Jaroslav Supevsky wanted a piece of that trade, and Dimitri Chekhov was not willing to give it to him.

"I bring this to your attention now, because the one thing you are not to do is hold the victim's drug trade against him. Regardless of what you feel about Dimitri Chekhov, he was murdered through a cold, premeditated, professional hit. Murder in any form, of any person, is something we simply don't countenance in this country."

Jessica Osborn Holt shot to her feet. "Objection! That's prejudice, Your Honor. My client is an American citizen. Mr. Lakewood is trying to paint him as an outsider."

Judge Montross glared down at her. "No speeches, Ms. Holt, if you please. Rhetorical flourish is allowed during opening statement."

Toni leaned over to Rachel and whispered, "She's not shy, is she?"

Rachel shook her head.

"Continue, Mr. Lakewood," said Judge Montross.

Lakewood nodded. "We will detail the specifics about this drug distribution business. We will tell you why the defendant did not like what Mr. Chekhov was doing. Then you will hear from a witness about the plans the defendant made to hire two killers to take care of Mr. Chekhov. You will hear how those killers captured and tortured Mr. Chekhov's wife and then Mr. Chekhov, and then how they killed them both, set fire to Mr. Chekhov's house, and burned the bodies beyond recognition."

Supevsky still showed no sign of emotion. He seemed defiantly calm.

"The case is really that simple," Lakewood said. "It is not a complicated story, but it is a story that has its beginnings all the way back in the Soviet Union."

"Objection!" Jessica Osborn Holt shouted again.

"Overruled," Montross said sternly.

Holt stayed on her feet, allowing the jury to get a full view of her expression of disgust.

"Sit down," Montross ordered.

Only then did Holt reclaim her seat. Toni whispered to Rachel, "Does she want the judge mad at her?"

"Yes," Rachel answered. "She wants the jury to think everyone is against her."

Lakewood spoke for thirty more minutes, outlining the government's case and summarizing the evidence he would present. He ended his opening statement by referring to the Russian underworld.

"It's a brutal, remorseless, violent, and deadly form of enterprise," Lakewood said. "And the defendant wanted to be the top dog. Well, ladies and gentlemen, the dog has had his day. When you review all of the evidence, we're confident that you will find him guilty as charged."

As Lakewood returned to counsel table, Toni said, "Short and sweet."

Rachel nodded and watched as Jessica Osborn Holt took her time walking to the lectern. It was theatrical and studied, the calm before the storm. Holt knew how to rivet attention. She carefully placed a notepad on the lectern and then looked at the jury. And looked. She seemed to study the face of every juror. Every juror looked back at her.

Holt still did not speak. She walked silently and deliberately to the U.S. Attorney's table where a puzzled Alan Lakewood and equally bemused Agent Emmitt Jefferson sat. Without a word she reached down in front of Lakewood and picked up one of his documents.

Lakewood appeared too shocked to say anything. Holt walked back to the lectern and held the document up. "Ladies and gentlemen," she began, "this is the government's indictment against my client, Jaroslav Supevsky."

She paused, waving the document around in the air. Then she walked to her own counsel table, reached under it, and pulled out a wastebasket. She set the wastebasket on the table. Then with the intensity of an angry Shaquille O'Neal, she slammed the indictment into the basket.

"It's *trash!*" she shouted. "This whole farce is trash!"

Lakewood shot to his feet, "Your Honor," he said with a voice that did not have to add the word *objection*.

Montross was rubbing the bridge of his nose. "Rhetorical flourish," he said with resignation, and with his hand motioned for Lakewood to sit down.

"It's *not* just a rhetorical flourish!" Holt said to the jury. "This prosecution stinks from top to bottom. It's a bigoted, selective prosecution of a decent American citizen. And it's garbage."

"Stick to the evidence, Miss Holt," Montross instructed.

"The evidence will *show* you that it's garbage," she said. "You are going to hear that garbage spewing from the witness stand. You are going to see a case presented to you by the government that is not even worthy of being called a case. You will hear witnesses testify, but I remind you that you are not to form an opinion until I have a chance to cross-examine those witnesses. When I do, ladies and gentlemen, let me assure you that you'll get a much different picture than the one painted by the government."

Holt spent another twenty minutes painting a Norman Rockwell portrait of her client, complete with a reverence for Christmas and Thanksgiving. She finished by saying, "Don't let the government of the United States railroad an innocent citizen, ladies and gentlemen. In an attempt to make it seem like something is being done about organized crime, a scapegoat has been chosen, a victim, simply because he is a Russian immigrant, a man who escaped communism because he thought he could build himself a better life in a free country. Don't let that dream die for Jaroslav Supevsky. You're the only hope he has."

Jessica Osborn Holt held a pose for a moment, then walked back to her seat. Rachel saw a few reporters nodding their heads, as if they were thinking what a great performance Holt had just turned in.

"We'll take a ten-minute recess," Judge Montross announced, "and then you can call your first witness, Mr. Lakewood."

"Good morning, sir," Alan Lakewood said to Emmitt Jefferson, who had just taken the oath, stated his name, and was now seated in the witness chair.

"Morning," Jefferson answered.

"Would you tell the ladies and gentlemen of the jury how you're employed?"

"I'm a special agent with the FBI."

"How long have you been an agent with the FBI?"

"Twenty-one years. Twenty-two years next month."

"Where do you work currently?"

"In the Los Angeles office of the FBI."

"And how long have you been assigned to the Los Angeles office?"

"Approximately seven years."

Rachel mentally checked off these preliminary questions as Lakewood continued to qualify his witness.

"Tell us briefly about your educational background," Lakewood said. "Where did you go to college?"

"I went to the University of Illinois."

"What year did you graduate?"

"In 1971."

Jessica Osborn Holt was impassive, tapping a pencil on her desk. To Rachel she looked like a cat waiting for an owner to walk away from a parakeet cage.

Alan Lakewood asked, "Have you received any special training with the FBI?"

"Yes, sir. I've been trained as a police instructor with the FBI and as an airplane pilot for the Bureau. I've also spent the last few years concentrating on organized crime."

"Such as the Mafia?"

"Objection," Holt said from her chair. "No foundation."

"Overruled," said Montross.

Jefferson, a well-trained witness, did not have to be asked the question again. "Yes," he said, "the Italian and Russian Mafia, to name two."

"What sort of training have you received?"

"I took a six-week course from Professor Judith Lydaker at UCLA. Professor Lydaker has taught and written extensively about Russian migration and crime. I've also taken seminars on organized crime at the John Jay College of Criminal Justice in New York and at Main Justice in Washington."

"Can you please describe for us some of the background of the Russian Mafia?"

From Jaroslav Supevsky came an audible snort, a dismissive exhalation that was clearly heard throughout the courtroom. Montross glared at him but said nothing.

"By the early 1980s," Jefferson began, "Russian immigrants had inundated the Brighton Beach area of New York. It's estimated that the Russian population there was approximately thirty thousand, which was almost half of the total Russian immigrant population in the entire United States. Virtually all of these former Soviet citizens were schooled in crime."

"And why is that?"

"Because crime was a way of life for them in the Soviet Union. The ability to make a better life for themselves and their families was all related to how well they could illegally divert goods and services."

"In a so-called black market?"

"Yes. This pattern of behavior was enforced with violence, bribery, and blackmail."

"And many Russian immigrants who came here used that pattern themselves."

"Correct. And many didn't. Many became law-abiding citizens. But others began forming criminal networks called *molina*."

"What does that word mean?"

"Well, it's a Russian word for a certain hand gesture."

"Can we call it an antisocial hand gesture?"

"Very antisocial."

Here Lakewood paused. Rachel thought for a moment that Jessica Osborn Holt was going to offer Lakewood an antisocial gesture of her own.

"Agent Jefferson," Lakewood said, "are there differences between the Russian Mafia and, say, the more familiar Italian Mafia?"

"Yes," Jefferson replied. "The Italian Mafia, or La Cosa Nostra, is a product of Sicilian culture and has a formal structure."

"Like in the *Godfather* movies?"

A few titters of laughter could be heard in the courtroom. "Right," Jefferson said. "You have heads of families, and consigliaries, and caporegimes, and soldiers, and so on. Each role is defined, and there are rituals involved in stepping into a role."

"What about Russian Mafia?"

"No rules. The object is to know your competition and deal with it."

"Violently?"

"Usually."

"Why is that?"

"Because it sends a message to other, potential competitors—don't mess with me."

"What are some of the methods used in sending this message?"

"All sorts. Anything that works. Torture, shootings, setting bodies on fire—"

"Objection," Holt said, standing. "All this is cumulative and prejudicial."

Montross nodded. "I'll sustain the objection at this point. Mr. Lakewood, bring your questions back home."

Lakewood cleared his throat. "Agent Jefferson, what are some of the outward signs that a Russian immigrant might be associated with this type of behavior?"

"Illegal weapons is one thing we look for. Associations with other known criminals. Connection with businesses that are a front for criminal activity. That sort of thing."

Lakewood flipped a page of his notes. "Turning your attention to May 28 of this year, did you have occasion to search the residence of the defendant in Beverly Hills?"

"Yes."

"Was that search conducted pursuant to a warrant?"

"Yes."

"Did you review that search warrant before you participated?"

"Yes, I did."

"When did you start working on the search of the defendant's residence?"

Jefferson took a pair of reading glasses from his inside coat pocket. "May I review my notes?"

"Certainly."

Looking down at the pages of a notebook, Jefferson said, "I entered the residence at approximately 4:30 in the afternoon."

At this point Lakewood turned to the judge and asked for permission to put up a graphic. Permission was granted. Lakewood pulled a four-by-four poster board from the side of his counsel table and set it on an easel near the jury box. It was a diagram of the interior of a home. The poster was titled "Supevsky Residence."

Resuming his place at the lectern, Lakewood said, "Do you recognize this, sir?"

Jefferson studied the graphic. "It appears to be a diagram of the interior of Jaroslav Supevsky's home."

"Does it look accurate to you?"

"Yes, it does."

"All right. Do you recall the first place you went to search?"

"Yes, it was the study."

"Where was that located in the house?"

Jefferson got out of the witness chair and walked to the diagram. With his finger he pointed to a room just off the front entrance. Lakewood said, "Will you please take a red pen and put an 'S' where you just pointed?"

Jefferson complied, then sat in the witness chair again.

"What did you recover from the study?" Lakewood asked.

"We were authorized to search for documents that might be associated with the murder of the victim. We seized a number of documents, business records and the like, to review."

"And when you took all those documents, what did you do with them?"

"I took the documents and placed them in a plastic bag. I also placed an evidence card, which generally described the documents or the items. I initialed that card and dated it; it also had the file number on it. Then I closed the bag and sealed it with evidence tape."

"What did you do once you sealed the bag with evidence tape?"

"I entered a brief description of the items in a written log."

"Did you initial the tape on the bag after you sealed it?"

"Yes, I did."

In the gallery, Toni whispered to Rachel, "What's this all about?"

"Chain of custody," Rachel whispered back. "Lakewood had to show that the evidence hasn't been tampered with."

Toni nodded. They watched as Lakewood placed a large envelope on the rail in front of Emmitt Jefferson.

Lakewood said, "Would you please look in the envelope in front of you and take out Government's Exhibit 12, the plastic bag you just described?"

Jefferson did as instructed, pulling out the bag. "I have it."

"Do you recognize that?"

"Yes, sir. This is the plastic bag I used for the documents I retrieved from Mr. Supevsky's study."

"How do you recognize it?"

"It has the evidence tag in the bag and also has my initials, E.C.J., on the evidence tape that I used to seal the bag."

To Judge Montross, Lakewood said, "The Government offers 12A into evidence, Your Honor."

"Any objection?" Montross said to Holt.

"No objection," she replied.

"Received," said Montross.

"Thank you, Your Honor," Lakewood said. Then to Jefferson: "Looking at that bag, does it have a Q number on it?"

"Yes, it does."

"What is the Q number marked on that bag?"

"The Q number is 25."

"Does that indicate the documents in the bag are part of a series?"

"Yes. Each document in this bag has a 25 number. The first document would be 25–1, the second would be 25–2, and so on."

"Let me direct your attention to a document in the envelope marked Government's Exhibit 17B. Do you see that?"

"I do."

"Do you recognize 17B?"

"Yes, I do."

"Is that a document you took from Mr. Supevsky's study?"

"Yes, it is."

"Does it have the Q number marking that you've previously described?"

"Yes, it does."

"What does it say?"

"Q number 25–10."

"Your Honor, move to admit Government's Exhibit 17B into evidence."

Montross glanced at Jessica Osborn Holt. He didn't have time to ask her if she had any objection because she stood up and said, "Object to foundation, Your Honor."

Montross said, "You want to question the witness?"

"Or I'll withdraw the objection if you'll make him subject to recall."

"Why do that?" said the judge. "He's here. You might as well *voir dire* him now."

With a slight look of consternation, Alan Lakewood gathered his notes from the lectern and returned to the counsel table. Jessica Osborn Holt, without any notes at all, walked to the side of the lectern and leaned on it. She gave all the appearances of someone who had deep concerns about what just took place.

"Agent Jefferson," she said, "you claim this 17B is a clean copy?"

"Yes."

"What does that mean?"

"Well, when the documents went to the lab, apparently they were processed."

"Excuse me," Holt snapped. "What do you mean by *apparently?* Don't you know?"

"I assume they went to the lab."

"The infamous FBI lab?"

"Objection!" Lakewood said, but the phrase was already out. Rachel knew what Holt was up to. She wanted to taint the physical evidence by her questions alone. Stories about incompetence in the FBI forensic labs had been around for years.

"Sustained," Montross intoned. "Ms. Holt, keep your questions objective."

"Of course, Your Honor," Holt said, sounding as innocent as a child. To Jefferson she said, "So you *assume* the documents went to the FBI lab, where they *apparently* were processed?"

Shifting slightly, Jefferson said, "I'm not a lab technician. I wasn't there."

"Obviously. Now you're saying that 17B is a copy?"

"A clean copy, yes."

"Of the original document?"

"Yes."

"As far as you know. We're assuming here, right?"

"Yes."

"So let me see if I follow this. You are telling the jury that you seized documents from Mr. Supevsky's house, put them in a bag, and logged them; then they were apparently sent to Washington to be processed?"

"That's right."

"Is the processing you're talking about for fingerprints?"

"That's my understanding."

"And from your experience as a special agent, you know that pieces of paper can yield fingerprints if subjected to certain processes. Correct?"

"That's correct."

Holt picked up what was apparently a blank piece of paper from the lectern and held it in the air. "So, for example, if I were to touch this white piece of paper I'm holding up with my thumb and forefinger, it could be chemically treated, and the fingerprint would show up. Right?"

Alan Lakewood stood up. "Objection, your Honor. This is beyond the scope of *voir dire* of this witness."

"Overruled," Montross said.

Jefferson answered, "It's possible. Not always."

"When it's subject to processing with a chemical solution to cause fingerprints to come up, then the document will be discolored. Correct?"

"It may become discolored, correct."

Holt took her time placing the blank piece of paper back on the lectern. "Now, Agent Jefferson, is it your understanding that the document you call a clean copy is a copy that was made *before* the fingerprints were taken?"

"I don't know how the clean copy was made."

"So you can't tell us whether the clean copy was something the FBI went and got from a third party or whether it came from Mr. Supevsky's house, or where it came from at all, correct?"

"I'm not the one that could speak for that."

Holt snapped, "Just answer the question, sir."

"I am answering the question," Jefferson shot back, anger seeping into his voice.

Holt looked at the jury, a look of contempt on her face. Shaking her head, she said, "No further questions," and sat down.

Toni Galvan whispered, "What do you think?"

"She's making the FBI look bad," Rachel explained, "even though they did nothing wrong."

"She's pretty good, isn't she?"

Rachel couldn't disagree.

Lakewood continued his direct examination of Jefferson. The crucial pieces of evidence were the documents, several of which turned out to be receipts from White Wings Limousine Service, the company owned by Dimitri Chekhov. This established a connection between Supevsky and the murder victim. From her work on the case, Rachel knew Lakewood would fill in the nature of that connection with other witnesses.

Now it was Holt's turn again to question the witness, this time on cross-examination.

"Agent Jefferson," she began, "have you ever been in business for yourself?"

"Business?"

"Yes. Have you ever owned a business?"

Jefferson thought a moment, then said, "I had a lemonade stand when I was a kid." The moment he said it, Rachel knew it was a blunder. Even though a couple of audience members laughed, it gave Holt an opening that she immediately charged through.

"You find something funny about all this?" she barked.

"No, I—"

"You find something funny about a man on trial for his life?"

Montross jumped in. "That's enough, Ms. Holt."

Defiant, Holt said to the judge, "I demand that you admonish the witness."

"Ms. Holt, let's move on."

Holt slapped the lectern with her hand, producing a loud *pop*. "This is important, Your Honor."

"Move on, Ms. Holt."

The attorney took a breath and returned her focus to the witness. "Aside from your lemonade stand, Agent Jefferson, have you ever been in business for yourself."

Quietly, Jefferson said, "No."

"I didn't hear you."

"No," he repeated.

"So you don't know anything about entertaining clients, do you?"

"Not really."

"But surely you've heard that limousines are useful for that purpose?"

Lakewood interrupted. "Your Honor, this is beyond the scope of direct. Agent Jefferson is not being offered as an expert on business practices."

"That's for sure," Holt said.

"Quiet!" Montross snapped. "The objection is overruled."

"Now," Holt said, "Mr. Supevsky owns a nightclub on Sunset Strip, doesn't he?"

"Yes."

"It's a popular place, is it not?"

"I believe so."

"Various stars and celebrities have been known to go there, haven't they?"

"I've heard that they do."

"And if, say, Mr. Supevsky wanted to entertain such a person, and if he were to hire a limousine for that purpose, that would be perfectly understandable, wouldn't it?"

"I don't know if that's what he did."

"Are you afraid to admit it would be understandable?"

Lakewood said, "Objection. Argumentative."

"Sustained," said the judge.

"I have no more use for this witness," Jessica Osborn Holt said, returning to her chair with a sigh of disgust.

CHAPTER FOUR

LAKEWOOD LOOKED ANGRY. He had summoned Rachel to his office over the lunch break. She entered to find him with Ron Ashby and Emmitt Jefferson. Ashby gave her a dismissive look before returning his gaze to his boss.

"We didn't make any gains," Lakewood said, pacing. "I only hope the jury didn't buy the fog Holt was spewing." He paused, rubbed his face, then added, "That's what she's good at, though."

Jefferson seemed haggard. "I'd like to see her put away for a few years." With a burst of frustration he said, "I let her get to me!"

"Don't worry about it," Lakewood said. "She has that effect on a lot of people. The thing now is strategy. I think we've got to go for the throat." He turned to Rachel. "That's why you're here."

With no idea what he meant, Rachel nodded.

"I'm going to put Deanna Natale on the stand tomorrow," Lakewood said. "She will make or break this case either way you look at it, and there's no use saving her for the end. Holt got some momentum going today. I want to stop her dead in the water."

Jefferson nodded. "Dead would be just fine with me."

Ron Ashby snorted a congenial laugh, like he was one of the boys. Rachel still wasn't sure why she had been called in. Lakewood explained, "You need to be here to escort her to the courtroom. She's scared enough as it is."

A sense of relief filled Rachel. She hadn't been sure if she would be allowed to see Deanna again. Her look must have spoken clearly, because Lakewood continued, "Holt knows enough about you already that it doesn't matter anymore. Nothing we can do now. She's going to try to tar you and the witness as much as she can, but we'll beat her to the punch."

"How?" Rachel asked.

"By taking the sting out of Holt's cross-examination. I'll question Natale about you and what went on. If the jury hears it from me first, it will lessen the impact when Holt brings it up."

"Brilliant," Ron Ashby muttered.

"So," Lakewood said, "I'll want you here in my office early tomorrow morning, and we'll go from there. Deanna Natale has been asking to see you anyway. After the trial you'll be free to talk to her all you want. Okay?"

Rachel nodded.

"Good," said Lakewood. "All right, let's get some lunch. We've got four witnesses for this afternoon. Oh, Ron . . ."

Ashby sat up. "Yes?"

"I need that memo we spoke about, on privilege."

"I'll work through lunch," Ashby said.

Lakewood nodded. Jefferson and Ashby stood up to leave. Rachel turned, but Lakewood called her back. When they were alone in the office he said, "I got a call about you."

Puzzled, Rachel waited for an explanation.

"You know a guy named Art Ybarra?"

"My father called you?"

Lakewood nodded. "Called me a couple of choice names, too."

Feeling herself blush, Rachel put a hand on her cheek and said, "I'm so sorry." She wondered what Lakewood must think of her now. What could her father have been thinking? Was he drunk?

Then Lakewood did something absolutely unexpected—he smiled. "Yeah, it seems your father thinks I'm lower than pig slop because I bounced you off this case. He said anybody who'd drop the smartest person in this whole office must be a few french fries short of a Happy Meal."

"He said *that?*"

"That's my paraphrase. What he said was actually a little more . . . colorful."

"I am really sorry. He should never—"

"Sure he should have. He's sticking up for his kid. My dad did the same for me when I was cut from the freshman football team. He marched down to the school office and told the coach to his face that if ignorance ever went to forty dollars a barrel, he wanted drilling rights on his head."

Rachel couldn't suppress a laugh. "And you made the team?"

"No, I had to run extra laps every day after school. The point is, that's what dads are for. So I understand yours. And I also think he's right about you." Lakewood sat on the edge of his desk. "I was hasty yanking you off the case. I was mad, that's for sure. This case means a lot to me."

"I know it does. It means a lot to me, too."

Lakewood gave her an understanding nod. "You can still do your part by putting Deanna Natale at ease tomorrow. Be there for her."

"I will."

"And give my best to your dad next time you see him, huh?"

With a broad smile, Rachel said, "Sure."

Rachel called Jeff from her office. It seemed like forever since she had last talked to him.

"How's the trial going?" he asked.

"Not as well as planned."

"That happens. You okay?"

"I'm hanging in there. I want to see you."

"Same here. Any contact from you-know-who?"

"None. I don't know whether that's good or bad. I can't hear him or see him, but somehow I feel his presence."

"Let's not talk about it over the phone. Meet me somewhere . . . Chubby's. You know it?"

"It's a coffee shop, right?"

"Woodley and Ventura. I know the guy; it's quiet. How soon can you come?"

"I have some work to finish here. I can be there by four."

"I'll be waiting for you."

That sounded so good. Somehow everything would be all right if she could just be with Jeff.

She tried to work for the next two hours, managing to finish up some research on a fraud case for another AUSA. The subject was dull, and she realized that just about every other legal subject was going to be dull after what she'd been through. How could anything compete with hired killers, secret witnesses, and a plot to move drugs from Mexico?

At 3:30 she put the finishing touches on her memo, printed it, gave it a proofread, then handed it to the attorney. He thanked her tersely.

When she left the courthouse, it almost felt like an escape. By the time she got to her car in the open lot, she was sure she was under surveillance.

Jeff left the apartment at his sister's complex at exactly 3:47. It was only a five-minute drive to Chubby's. He had plenty of time. The drive itself would be a pleasant one. He was going to see Rachel.

He had spent the previous hour fussing about his looks. Like some school kid on prom night! Amazing. He had showered, shaved for the second time, messed with his hair, and put on some fresh clothes. He took the stairs two at a time, heading for his car.

The two men stopped him when he turned into the parking structure.

"Jeff Bunnell?" asked the taller of the two men. He had a buzz haircut.

"You guys are from Washington," Jeff said, matter-of-factly.

The tall man nodded, showing his FBI credential. "You're a hard man to pin down."

With a shrug, Jeff said, "Training."

The tall man didn't smile. The shorter man, the one with sunglasses over a full face, cracked a small one.

"Let's go," the tall one said.

"I'm going to meet someone," Jeff said. "How about I come in later?"

Now the tall man smiled. "You can't be serious."

"I am. I know I can't avoid talking to you guys. But I have to meet someone I really do. What do you say? Give a fellow agent a break?"

The two men looked at each other, and Jeff saw in their looks what the answer would be. The tall man looked back at Jeff and said, "Get in the car, Agent Bunnell."

"You arresting me?"

"Just get in the car."

When she finally pulled up near Chubby's Coffee Shop, Rachel wondered if *he* was watching her. He had known her every move before, or so it seemed. She was beginning to make friends with paranoia.

Once inside the diner she felt better. It was just a few minutes past four, and the afternoon crowd was long gone. An old couple was sitting in a booth by the window and a guy who looked like a construction worker was at the counter. That was it. A waitress with gray hair and a pale, blue uniform asked Rachel if she wanted a table for one.

"Two," Rachel said.

The waitress grabbed two menus and led her to a booth near the front doors. "May we sit in the back?" Rachel asked.

The waitress shrugged and walked to the last booth in the house, near the kitchen doors. As restaurants go, it was the least desirable location. It was perfect for Rachel. She sat with her back to the kitchen so she could see the entire restaurant.

The waitress plopped two water glasses on the table and asked if Rachel wanted anything while she waited. Rachel shook her head.

For the next several minutes Rachel tapped the table with her fingers and watched the front door. A man came in and asked for change, then left. The old couple by the window paid their check and shuffled out.

At 4:20 Jeff had still not arrived.

Rachel took out her cell phone and dialed the number Jeff had given her. She heard his recorded voice: "Leave a message."

Figuring he must be on his way, Rachel hung up.

Five minutes slogged by like ten, and ten like twenty.

He wasn't coming. Something was terribly wrong.

All sorts of possibilities zipped through her mind, including the conjecture that Grigory may have found him. She told herself not to panic, but it was useless. She prayed silently for Jeff's protection.

The gray-haired waitress came back to the table, a look of consternation on her face. "You still going to wait?" she asked.

"Yes," Rachel said, with the slight hope he might still arrive.

"You want to order something?" It was more of a demand than a question.

"I'll have a Coke."

The waitress rolled her eyes and walked away.

"Can I make a phone call?" Jeff asked.

"To your lawyer," the tall agent, whose name was Reed, said.

"I don't need a lawyer."

"Your choice."

"I want to call someone else."

"Sorry."

The three of them—Reed, his partner, and Jeff—were seated around a metal table in an interrogation room. How many times had Jeff been in such a room asking the questions? Now he was answering them.

Reed's partner, Agent Giesler, worked the tape recorder while Reed gave Jeff his Miranda rights. Jeff waived them. He was less concerned about the interrogation than Rachel. He was sure he wouldn't be held, and the sooner he got this over with the sooner he could contact her.

"You worked with Zagorsky how long?" Reed asked.

"About four months."

"How'd you two get along?"

"Great."

"No tension there?"

"Why should there be tension?"

"You know, different strokes, personalities."

"We got along fine. You're going nowhere."

Reed paused a moment and took a sip of coffee from a Styrofoam cup. Jeff thought he gave a knowing glance to Giesler, like they were waiting to spring something.

"You were on witness protection with him, weren't you?" Reed asked.

"Of course. Paul Dedenok."

"The one you lost."

That was a needle. Reed was apparently enjoying this. Jeff didn't think that merited a reply and said nothing.

Reed continued, "You were holed up in the Bonaventure Hotel."

"That's right."

"We questioned some of the staff there, Jeff. One of them was a maid, a woman named Astasio."

"So?"

"So she remembers you."

Jeff frowned. He had no recollection of any maid in particular, nor any reason to think he made any sort of impression on one. "Why should she remember me?"

"Oh, they remember people, Jeff. You order room service and don't leave a tip, they remember. You swipe a towel, they got you marked."

"I didn't steal any towels."

"But you did threaten Zagorsky."

There it was, the accusation Reed had obviously been building toward. "That's crazy," Jeff said, trying not to sound guilty.

"She gave us a statement," Reed said. He opened up a file folder and took out a sheet of paper, glancing at it as he spoke. "Says she was outside your room when she heard heated words being exchanged. At one point a voice screams 'Shut up!' She knocks on the door. You answer, and you don't look happy. You blow her off and shut the door. But she says your voice was the one doing most of the screaming."

Reed tossed the statement on the table and said, "Ring a bell?"

It did. Jeff remembered the short blowup he'd had with Zagorsky over Rachel. He had indeed lost his temper, but it lasted no more than a minute. "Is that what you're hanging on to?" Jeff said incredulously.

"It contradicts your story, Jeff."

"Story?"

"You tell us one thing, a witness tells us another."

"You guys are reaching on this. Why? Why single me out?"

With a sigh, Reed sat back in his chair. "You've got to admit, Jeff, your actions of late have been a little, well, odd."

"Like?"

"Like taking another apartment. Like trying to sneak into the office at night. Like not telling anybody where you are."

"You calling that consciousness of guilt?"

Reed shrugged. "Your words."

"I wanted to buy some time, that's all."

"Time for what?"

"To do my own investigation."

"Why didn't you get the Bureau involved?"

"I made a promise."

"To?"

"Someone."

"Jeff, you're not helping me here."

"I can't tell you any more."

"That's disappointing, Jeff." Reed looked anything but disappointed. He had a case-closed expression.

"What about Janie?" Jeff said. "She backs me up."

Reed looked at Giesler. Giesler raised his eyebrows.

"Well what?" Jeff said. "She change her story? What?"

"Let's just say," Reed said, "that we'd like to compare her recollection of events with yours. Why don't you start by telling us exactly what happened the night you went to Zagorsky's house."

Jeff looked at the faces of his fellow agents. They weren't "fellows" anymore. They were accusers. They were guns from Washington with obvious orders to clean house. They weren't interested in hearing his story; they just wanted him to supply the rope they would tie around his neck. Jeff felt a rush of anger trying to break through, but he told himself to stay calm.

"I'll take that phone call now," Jeff said.

"I told you, Jeff, no phone—"

"I want to talk to a lawyer. This interview is over."

Rachel was through waiting at 5:35. The coffee shop was almost filled with a dinner crowd, and the waitress who had seated her an hour and a half before was looking at her with daggers. Rachel tossed a five-dollar bill on the table and walked out to the street.

She paused on the sidewalk and dialed Jeff's number again. Once more she got the machine. This time she left a short message: "Looking for you. Call me when you get in."

As she walked up Woodley toward her car, she wondered if she should just drive over to Jeff's and wait for him. But how long would he be? Especially if he was in some sort of trouble? Maybe he'd lost her cell phone number and had called Abi's. Rachel decided the best thing to do was go home and wait.

She unlocked her car, which was parked on the street where the residential section began. No one was out. It seemed like a nice, quiet neighborhood.

It was when she put the key in the ignition that she sensed something was wrong. In the millisecond it took her to recognize the thought, her mouth and nose were covered, her head yanked back, and breath taken away. In another millisecond she was sure she was going to die. Then came blackness.

CHAPTER FIVE

RACHEL AWOKE WITH THE SMELL of salt air in her nose, an acrid emanation that seemed to come up from some dismal sea. She tried to open her eyes, but the lids kept falling back down. She'd had surgery once, arthroscopic on an injured knee, and coming out of the anesthesia was just like this.

She kept struggling to open her eyes and sensed a new feeling, almost of weightlessness. Her neck was stiff, like she'd had it in an awkward position for a full night. She tried rolling her head around, and the shot of pain brought her to further wakefulness.

She was in a house. It was dark, though she sensed daylight outside. Windows, but they were covered by heavy curtains. She heard the very faint but unmistakable keening of a sea gull from what seemed like a distance of miles.

The ocean. Was she somewhere near the ocean? In a house by the ocean? Weightless.

How?

She discovered she was sitting but could not move. She was bound. Heavy tape of some kind was wrapped around her body and the chair she was secured to. Her hands had some other type of restraint behind her.

The last thing she remembered was getting in her car. Jeff. She had been there to meet Jeff. He hadn't shown up. And then . . .

Then what? Something covered her face.

Him. He must have been in her car. How was that possible? But he had done it. He had been waiting for her . . . maybe for Jeff too. At once she was thankful Jeff hadn't arrived.

Slowly she gained more of her senses. She pushed against her bonds, but there was no way out. She attempted to lean forward and, by wriggling, to move the chair. But it became obvious that the chair itself was secured to the wall. She was utterly powerless.

The slow, methodical ticking of a small clock became louder and louder as she focused on it. What time was it? How long had she been knocked out? It had to be at least one night. Could it have been more?

A creeping desperation took hold of her. Deanna! What about her testimony? What about Lakewood?

Or had it already happened? Had the case come crashing down around Lakewood's ears while he silently cursed her absence?

What day was it?

"Does anybody know where Rachel is?" Alan Lakewood ran his fingers through his hair. He didn't need this, not this morning. Not with the report of a neurotic witness. Deanna Natale was apparently ready to flip out. She had been asking for Rachel since four in the morning.

Ron Ashby shrugged. "Not a word," he said.

"Well this is just great." Lakewood said. Maybe there was an explanation. Maybe. But he wasn't in the mood to think one up. "Let's go," he said to Ashby, grabbing his briefcase and pounding out of the office.

They took the stairs to the twelfth floor and entered the Brosio Room, where Emmitt Jefferson sat with a very gaunt-looking Deanna Natale. She had her hands wrapped around a mug of coffee, her eyes downcast. At least, Lakewood noted, she was wearing the clothes they had bought her a few days before.

"How we feeling, Miss Natale?" Lakewood said in his best, comforting tone.

Deanna looked up. Despite her makeup, dark circles were visible under her eyes. "Where's Rachel?" she said.

"We're working on that right now."

"Why ain't I seen her?"

Lakewood sat in one of the chairs. "As we've explained, Miss Natale, there are some legal reasons for that. But Rachel has every intention of being here today for your testimony. She'll be in the courtroom, I'm sure."

"I want her there."

"We know."

"I'm scared."

"We know that, too."

"What's gonna happen?"

"I'll be asking you some simple questions, nothing that you haven't answered before. All you have to do is tell the jury the same things."

"What about the other lawyer?"

"Yes, she'll ask you questions, too."

"They won't be easy, will they?"

"No. That's called cross-examination. But all you have to remember to do is tell the truth. And just answer the specific question with a yes or a no. Or if you don't know the answer, say 'I don't recall.' That's all. You don't have to be afraid if you tell the truth."

Deanna seemed to tremble. To Lakewood she looked like a butterfly clinging to a branch on a windy day. He was not filled with confidence.

"Will he be in the courtroom?" Deanna asked.

"Supevsky?"

Deanna nodded.

"Yes," Lakewood said. "The defendant is always present."

Deanna closed her eyes tightly, as if she were trying to keep her emotions from pouring out of them. For an instant, Lakewood considered calling the whole thing off. But he knew that option was closed to him. Deanna Natale, for all her liabilities, was the one link he had that went directly to Supevsky's intent to kill Chekhov. And there was always the possibility that the jury would sympathize with Deanna. If she appeared vulnerable, and Holt overplayed her hand, it could all work in their favor.

It had to work in their favor.

"I need Rachel to pray for me," Deanna said in a halting voice.

"I'm sure she is," Lakewood said. "Wherever she is, I'm sure she's thinking about you."

Rachel Ybarra prayed for Deanna Natale, Alan Lakewood, Abi, and Jeff Bunnell. It was a comfort to do it. Secured to a chair so she could not move, Rachel found her only power in prayer. And comfort. She remembered the Psalm that went something like, *Why are you downcast, O my soul? Why so disturbed within me? Put your hope in God, for I will yet praise him, my Savior and my God.*

Manny had once said that there was a powerful form of prayer, where you praise God even in your darkest trials. She tried that now. If ever there was a time for persevering in faith, this was it.

She repeated Scripture in her mind, prayed, and wondered how long she would be here alone.

The relentless ticking of the clock became like torture. She had no idea how much time was truly passing. And the tape was beginning to irritate her arms, causing them to burn and itch. If he had intended to torment her, and of this she had no doubt, he had done his job well.

She began to test the rope—what she thought was nylon rope—around her wrists. There was a certain give in nylon, and maybe she could . . .

She heard the sound of a door opening, then the click of it shutting slowly, and steps into the room.

Grigory walked to the chair opposite Rachel and sat down. "Sleep well?" he said.

When Rachel spoke her words came out thick and slow. "What do you want?"

"We'll have time to discuss that. But I'm sure you're thirsty and hungry. How about breakfast?"

So it was morning, she thought. She had been out for one night. Grigory got up and walked into what she assumed was the kitchen. As he made the noises of someone preparing a meal, he carried on a running conversation. "You'll have to excuse me for bringing you here on such short notice. I was improvising a bit myself. But your visit makes a lot of sense, for both of us."

She heard the refrigerator open, something being removed, then a pouring sound. The refrigerator door closed. Grigory said, "Do you like the house?" Rachel didn't answer. After a moment he continued, "I designed it myself, along with a colleague from KGB. He now sells security systems all over the world. I told him I wanted a place that could be secured from the inside as well as the outside."

He came back into the living room, holding a tray with two glasses of orange juice and some muffins and croissants. He placed the tray on a small coffee table. "I also wanted it soundproofed. We have a little noise seepage, but there's no one around to hear any of it. Juice?"

Without waiting for an answer, he picked up a glass of orange juice and walked it over to Rachel. He set the edge of the glass on her lower lip and tilted the glass slightly. Rachel didn't open her mouth. "Come on, now," Grigory cooed, "let's not be petulant."

He forced the glass into her mouth and poured. Rachel started to gag, coughed, and turned her head quickly to the side. Juice spilled down her chin and onto her lap. "Now that's too bad," Grigory said. "It was fresh squeezed."

He placed the glass back on the tray and went to a cabinet, opened it, and looked over a stack of CDs. "Do you like classical?" he asked. "I have Bartók, *Duke Bluebeard's Castle*. Let's see. Ah, Stravinsky. Do you know *Rite of Spring?*"

His matter-of-fact, friend-of-the-family manner was chilling. Rachel was sure he wasn't going to kill her. She would already be dead. No, he still wanted something out of her, and this was his means of getting it.

"Prokofiev I keep for the kiddies," he said, continuing to clack his way through the CD collection. "You may think me a sentimental fool, but I actually like *Peter and the Wolf*. I have some fond memories." He turned around and faced her, holding up a CD in an orange box. "You may be shocked, but you know who I really like? Your own George Gershwin. Have you heard the piano rolls?"

Rachel sat motionless as Grigory placed the disc in the player. A moment later jazz piano music filled the room. "Gershwin made piano rolls of his pieces, and through the wonder of technology, they are here brought to life. It's like having Gershwin himself playing the piano right here in this room. Isn't that wonderful?"

He sat down again and picked up a croissant from the tray. He opened a small jar of jam and, with a small knife, spread a little of the red preserve on the pastry. He took a small, almost dainty bite, and said, "I enjoy having someone to share this with. Many of the people I come in contact with have no appreciation for the finer things. It means a lot to me that you're here, Rachel."

The mockery in his voice was only slight, keeping her wondering if, in some small way, he meant it—meant to have her here to "share" part of his life. That was the most terrifying thought of all. A rash of possibilities, odd and distorted pictures, came to her in torturous waves. She realized at once that was exactly what he wanted. The torment of uncertainty, the wild designs of her own imagination, were self-inflicted and thus all the more effective. This must be just a hint, she thought, of what it was like to be a prisoner of an agency like the KGB. They had, as the cliché went, ways of making you talk.

It occurred to her then that talking was the one way she could avoid thinking about the things she didn't want to contemplate. Perhaps it would even buy her time, eventually offer her a way out. It was a scant hope, a dim light wrapped up in the shadows of her uncertainty, but she told herself that hope was always something God-given and not merely a delusion.

"Grigory Viazmitin," she said.

For the briefest instant, The Man's eyes reflected a subtle vulnerability. But just as quickly he reasserted control. "Very good," he said. "Your FBI friend?"

He had tossed his own shocker back at her. She was not as adept at hiding her surprise. He said, "Yes, I know all about him. In fact, I was hoping to meet him at that little diner. He didn't have the good manners to show up, did he?"

"He knows what he's doing."

"Perhaps. But it makes me very upset."

"What does?"

"The fact that he knows. I am very disappointed that you've dirtied our relationship like that."

"We don't have any relationship."

"You know we do."

"When will it end?"

"Perhaps never."

"It will end. And soon."

"That would make me very unhappy." He looked at his watch, then back at Rachel. "About now she's taking the stand."

Deanna.

"You know who I'm talking about, don't you?" Grigory said.

Rachel waited.

"They did a good job of hiding this one," he said, "but I understand she has her own liabilities. It wasn't necessary to take any drastic action with her. She'll self-destruct on the witness stand. I understand she was quite fond of you."

Her torment multiplied. *What must Deanna be thinking now,* Rachel wondered, in the swirl of the courtroom lights, facing press, public, and the man who had used her as a personal plaything? *Oh God, help her now. . . .*

CHAPTER SIX

DEANNA NATALE SAT on the witness chair and placed her hands, tightly entwined, in her lap. Alan Lakewood stepped to the lectern and said, "Good morning, Miss Natale."

Her response was barely audible. Judge Montross said, "You'll have to speak up, ma'am."

Looking terrified, as if the voice had come from heaven, Deanna nodded vigorously at the judge. "Try pulling the microphone closer to you," Montross suggested.

Lakewood waited while she adjusted the mike. She did indeed look nervous, like she would jump out of her own skin at any moment. Lakewood proceeded with a soft, comforting voice. "How are you feeling?" he said.

"Nervous," the witness answered.

"This is a little hard for you?"

Deanna nodded. Montross said, "You have to answer orally, ma'am."

"Oh," she said, "um, yes."

"This courtroom is a pretty imposing place?" Lakewood asked.

"Yes."

"Well now, you just relax. All we're interested in is the truth here, and that's all you have to tell us."

Jessica Osborn Holt said, "Object to that self-serving statement." Today she was dressed in regal blue.

"I'll allow that," Montross said. "We are, after all, interested in the truth, aren't we Miss Holt? Now, Mr. Lakewood, go into your examination."

"Thank you," Lakewood said. "Now, Miss Natale, when did you first meet the defendant, Jaroslav Supevsky?"

Once she launched into her account, Deanna Natale seemed to relax a little. Lakewood marched her through the narrative, which she had given a couple of times before, first to the FBI and then to Lakewood himself. She recounted how she had been working as an actress in "adult movies" in New York when she was told by one of her producers that a very influential man wanted to meet her. She complied, as she always did, with those in authority over her.

Asking carefully worded questions, Lakewood guided Deanna through the affair with Supevsky and then focused in on some of the most important details for the jury.

"Did he beat you?" he asked.

"Yes."

"Often?"

"All the time."

Holt interrupted. "Vague, Your Honor."

"I'll clarify," said Lakewood.

Montross said, "Go ahead."

"When you say 'all the time,' Miss Natale, you don't mean every moment, do you?"

For the first time Deanna Natale looked more confused than nervous. "No, not every second. But it seemed like every day."

"How would he beat you?"

Once more, Holt said, "Objection. Irrelevant and prejudicial."

"Overruled," said the judge.

"You may answer," Lakewood said.

Deanna licked her lips and drew a breath. "With a whip."

One of the jurors, number seven, a woman, gasped.

"Was it a large whip," Lakewood asked, "like one would use on horses?"

"No. It was more smaller."

"Like a riding crop?" When Deanna looked confused, Lakewood added, "You know, those small whips a jockey might hold?"

"Yes," Deanna said, "that's it."

Lakewood noticed Supevsky leaning over and whispering something to Holt.

"And where would he whip you?" Lakewood asked.

"All over."

"On the face?"

Deanna shuddered slightly, and a tear cascaded down her cheek. "Yes," she said just above a whisper. Lakewood paused to let the jury ponder that answer. He could sense from their faces that most were on Deanna's side, and those that weren't were at least interested. That was all he could have asked for at that point.

Next, Lakewood had Deanna talk about the drugs that Supevsky supplied her with. Haltingly, she admitted she had been a regular user of marijuana and, on occasion, had snorted cocaine, but that was as far as she went. Until Supevsky.

"Did he ever force you to take drugs?" Lakewood asked.

"He wanted me to try smack," she said.

"Heroin?"

"Yes."

"And did you?"

"Yes."

"And what happened as a result?"

"I got hooked."

"Are you still hooked?"

"I've been in Methadone treatment. I've been clean for over a year."

Lakewood took a moment to review his notes. The direct had gone as well as could be expected. But Lakewood sensed Deanna was tiring. He had two choices. He could call for a recess and allow her to recover, or he could press on with the final, crucial portion of the testimony. Sizing up the situation, he decided it was best to go for it. It was best not to interrupt the flow of the narrative at this point. And the judge would almost certainly call for a short recess after the testimony.

"Miss Natale," Lakewood said. "Does the name Paul Dedenok mean anything to you?"

"Yes," Deanna said. "He was a soldier for Juri."

"Objection!" Holt shouted. "That's clearly an unsubstantiated opinion."

"Sustained," said Montross.

"Let me phrase it this way," said Lakewood. "Did you know a man named Paul Dedenok?"

"Yes," said Deanna.

"And how did you know him?"

"He was always around. I saw him lots of times at Juri's club."

"Objection," Holt said. "Assumes facts not in evidence."

"Sustained," Montross said.

Lakewood expected that. "Miss Natale, you're referring to a club on Sunset Boulevard, is that correct?"

"Yeah."

"What is the name of the club?"

"Nazimova."

"To your knowledge, who owned the club?"

"Objection, Your Honor," Holt said. "No foundation."

"Sustained," came the judge's answer.

"Let me ask you this," Lakewood said. "Did the club have an upstairs apartment?"

"Yeah."

"And who lived there?"

"Juri used it."

"Did anyone else use it?"

"No. He kept it for himself."

"All right," Lakewood said, assured that the jury had enough information now to conclude that Supevsky owned the club, or at least had a controlling interest. "Now getting back to Paul Dedenok. Did you ever speak to him?"

"Yeah, sure."

"Did he ever tell you what he did for a living?"

Once more Holt was on her feet. "Objection, Your Honor, calls for hearsay."

"Mr. Lakewood?" Montross said.

"This is an exception to the rule, Your Honor," Lakewood explained. "We're not offering it as proof of the matter asserted but as evidence of the witness's state of mind."

"But of what possible relevance is her state of mind?" Holt said.

Montross ran his finger across the bottom of his chin a few times, then said, "I'll allow it. Go ahead, Mr. Lakewood."

Lakewood asked, "What did Paul Dedenok tell you he did for a living?"

"He said he was something in Russian."

"He told you something in the Russian language?"

"Yeah."

"Did you understand the word?"

"No. I asked him what it meant, and he said 'soldier.' Then he showed me a gun and smiled."

"He showed you a gun?"

"Yeah. He had it under his coat, in one of those shoulder things."

"Shoulder holster?"

"Yeah."

Lakewood nodded, then asked a series of questions to establish that one night she was in the Club Nazimova "partying," when she suddenly got the idea to run up to Supevsky's apartment and invite him down.

"What gave you that idea?" Lakewood asked.

"Well, I was a little suspicious."

"Of what?"

"I thought he might have another girl up there. I knew he had others, but he told me I was special." Her voice choked off at the end.

"And you wanted to see for yourself, that's all?"

"Yeah."

"Now the club is connected to the upstairs apartment by a secure stairway, right?"

"That's right."

"How did you gain access to the stairway?"

"I got the key." Deanna suddenly smiled with a little girl's mischievous grin. "I took it off of Medilich."

"That would be Kolya Medilich?"

"Yeah."

"Another soldier?"

Deanna said, "Yeah," just as Holt shouted, "Objection."

"Sustained," said Montross. Looking at the jury, he said, "You will disregard the witness's answer."

Lakewood continued, "How did you get the key from this man Medilich?"

"It wasn't hard. He'd had a few."

"He was drinking?"

"Vodka. You know, like a Russian."

A wavelet of laughter washed over the courtroom. Deanna smiled self-consciously.

"And what happened next?" Lakewood asked.

"I sort of flirted with him at the bar. And while I was doing that I took the key out of his jacket pocket. I was having fun, you know?"

"And Medilich didn't notice?"

"Not then. When he found out he was really hacked."

"You mean angry?"

"That's what I mean."

Lakewood nodded. "So did you then access the stairs?"

"Yeah. I snuck over there, unlocked the door, and went up."

"And what happened then?"

"I was halfway up the stairs when I heard voices."

"Did you recognize the voices?"

"Yeah. It was Juri and Paul."

"That would be Supevsky and Dedenok?"

"Yeah."

"And their voices were loud?"

"Juri's was loud. He was real upset."

"Did you hear what he was upset about?"

"Something to do with his operation. He was upset about this guy taking away some of his trade."

"Trade in what?"

"Drugs."

"Did Mr. Supevsky mention any names?"

"Yeah. Dimitri Chekhov."

"And what did he say in connection with the name Dimitri Chekhov?"

"That he wanted him subtracted."

"Was that his exact word, 'subtracted'?"

"Yeah, you know, like kill?"

Holt stood up. "Objection, Your Honor, speculation."

"Let me ask it another way," Lakewood said. "What did you understand the term 'subtracted' to mean?"

"Same objection," Holt said.

"Sustained," Montross said.

Lakewood took a moment, then asked, "What did you hear next?"

"I heard Juri say to Paul, 'Find somebody to do it.'"

"And did Dedenok say anything in return?"

"He said he knew a guy who would be perfect."

"Did he mention a name?"

"No, just something about The Man."

"So Dedenok said he would find this man in order to kill Chekhov?"

"Objection!" Holt shouted.

"Yes," Montross said, "sustained. Jury is to disregard counsel's last question."

Lakewood turned to a new page of notes. "Miss Natale, I want to switch subjects for a moment and ask you about a person who works for our office. You know Rachel Ybarra, don't you?"

Deanna's face softened into a smile. "Yes, I do."

"Would you describe for the jury how you met?"

Deanna told the jury about the visit Rachel made to her mother's place in Connecticut. She also recounted the conversations they had about testifying in this case.

Now Lakewood was ready to ask about the interchanges Rachel and Deanna had about God and religion. He would have to be careful here. If he spent too much time with it the jury would get the idea that there was more to the issue than there really was. That would play right into Holt's hands.

"Did you and Miss Ybarra have any discussions about religion?"

"Yes, sir."

"What was the nature of those discussions?"

"Rachel told me she was a Christian and said that God could help me get through all this. I never had anybody talk to me about God like that. It didn't seem put on. It was real to her, and I wanted what she had."

"Did you become a Christian as a result?"

Nodding excitedly, Deanna said, "Yes, I have accepted Jesus as my Lord and Savior."

"Now, Miss Natale," Lakewood said slowly, "in all of these discussions, did anything that Miss Ybarra said or did influence what you have told us in this courtroom today?"

"Um, I'm not sure."

Lakewood felt a tiny fist grip the inside of his throat. "What I mean, Miss Natale, is this: Did anything Miss Ybarra said or did change your testimony in any way?"

"I don't think so."

This wasn't the categorical disallowance Lakewood was looking for, but it would have to do. He stepped to the side of the lectern and directed his full attention to the witness. "Miss Natale, are you absolutely sure about the words used by Jaroslav Supevsky and Paul Dedenok, which you have testified to today?"

Deanna Natale said, "Yeah. Absolutely."

"No more questions," said Lakewood.

Montross glanced at the clock. "We'll take a fifteen-minute recess," he said. "And then Miss Holt can begin her cross-examination."

Lakewood glanced at Jessica Osborn Holt. She had the look of a tiger just before feeding time.

Grigory took a long, noisy bite out of a crisp apple. He savored it, then said to Rachel, "You need to eat."

Weak from her ordeal, Rachel wanted to assent. But she wasn't ready for capitulation. Though tied up and in no position to bargain, she was not going to give him any satisfaction by doing what he said.

"How long am I going to be like this?" she asked.

"Uncomfortable?" Grigory said, his cheek filled with apple.

"What do you think?"

"You need to open yourself up."

"What are you talking about?"

"Experience."

"Are you going to let me go or not?"

"You fascinate me."

She suddenly felt like a laboratory rat under the gaze of a mad scientist. The way he was talking now convinced her, if she hadn't been before, that he really was crazy. She could half understand a man doing the bidding of others, even if it meant killing other human beings. But that same man having some sort of rational conversation about life and experience, that was outside the boundaries of her imagination.

"I don't want to kill you, Rachel," Grigory said. "I will if I must, but I'd much rather avoid it. There are alternatives."

"Please . . ." She was pleading for a stop to the verbal games as much as for her freedom.

As if considering all of the choices, like a hungry man perusing a menu in a fine restaurant, Grigory said, "You could come live with me, for one."

Rachel felt a dull ache in the pit of her stomach. She looked for signs that he was merely mocking her but found none. He was serious.

"How can you even think that?" she said.

"I think a great many things, Rachel. Things far beyond what others even dare to imagine. I find you interesting because you've stopped your thoughts at the level of God, of superstition. You've cut yourself off from experience, Rachel, but I can help you out of that nightmare."

"I'm not in any nightmare." It struck her as soon as she said it that she was, that this was her nightmare.

"Are you familiar with Heidegger?" Grigory asked.

"Excuse me?"

"The philosopher."

"I've heard of him."

"He tells us that we all come into this world abandoned. There is no separation of mind and matter, no consciousness apart from the world. So we simply have to choose our own, unique vocation. That's what I've done."

"We are not abandoned in this world," Rachel said strongly.

"You don't feel abandoned?"

"No."

"Even now?" He indicated her restraints with his hands.

"No."

"We could do so much more together. I've been thinking about giving up the life, Rachel. I have a place in Switzerland just waiting to be permanently occupied. Have you ever been there?"

Rachel just stared at him.

"I'll take you. You'll love it. And you'll begin to see life as it really is."

"You can't believe I'd ever go with you, can you?"

Grigory rose and walked slowly, agonizingly slowly, toward Rachel. She couldn't avert her eyes from his. They were suddenly and fearsomely filled with an intensity she had not seen before. It was almost as if he were trying to will her into his world.

He reached out and put one hand under her chin. Rachel tried to move her head, but he held it fast. Then he bent over and put his lips on her cheek. They were cold and wet. Then he stood.

"I'll teach you," he said. "You'll see."

Frozen by disgust, Rachel said nothing.

"I'll do something to show you how much I care about you," Grigory said. "You'll see, after it's done."

She couldn't imagine what he was thinking, but she knew it was not good.

"You like this FBI agent, don't you?" he asked.

A glacial fear covered her. She didn't have to hear the details to know what he was thinking. "Don't, please . . ." she said. Her words sounded hollow. She knew her pleading would have as much affect on him as a command to a wild animal.

Grigory said, "This merely confirms how far we have to go together. Once he's out of the picture, as they say, it will get much easier."

"You are crazy," she said.

"Or more sane than anyone you know. Why don't you think about it?"

He began to turn, as if to walk away. "Wait," Rachel said. "Where are you going?"

Turning back, he said, "Did you know it was the Quakers who were the first to try their hand at prison reform?"

Rachel didn't even try to form an answer. What good would it do? He was in another zone.

"It's true," he said. "They came up with the idea of the penitentiary. A place to practice penitence, you see? They thought that complete isolation would do the trick. So they built a huge prison in Philadelphia, the city of brotherly love. Prisoners were not allowed to speak to one another, to see one another. They were kept in their cells, alone, with nothing but a Bible. Rachel, did you know that?"

She didn't know that. She was a law student, not a criminologist.

"The idea, you see, was that when forced to confront their own sin, these prisoners would see the error of their ways and return to the innate goodness that was in them. Instead, you know what happened? Most of them went insane. So much for the value of religion."

He lifted his coat and adjusted the concealed weapon that was under his arm. It was obviously a deliberate move, just so she could see. "But I like the idea of reflection, Rachel. So while I'm gone I'm going to give you the same opportunity the Quakers gave their prisoners. I'm going to let you reflect. I want you to begin to *see.* I'm going to help you see."

Now when he turned and walked out, it was resolute. Rachel knew he was going for Jeff. "No!" she implored, but it was useless. She heard him walking through the kitchen and opening the door. Then she heard the door close and some clicking sounds, no doubt the security system designed to keep intruders out—and prisoners in.

She became aware of a throbbing inside her. She would have to use the bathroom soon. Yet he had left her this way, no doubt by design. He was going to try to break her down, and indignity was one way to do it. That was why he'd kissed her in a way suggesting that he could, and probably would, take more later. For now he was content to let the torment build, inexorably, by leaving her alone with only her thoughts.

She could understand why those prisoners had gone insane.

She vigorously shook against the tape and the rope around her wrists.

CHAPTER SEVEN

JESSICA OSBORN HOLT walked slowly to the lectern and gently placed her notes on it. She raised one finger to her lips in a contemplative gesture, then fixed her gaze on Deanna Natale.

Lakewood sat well forward, literally on the edge of his seat, ready to protect his witness with an objection, should it become necessary. And he was sure it would become necessary. This was the big moment of the trial. What Jessica Osborn Holt did on cross-examination would spell the difference between victory and defeat, conviction and acquittal. He was sure she would spare nothing in going after Deanna Natale, who looked like the proverbial deer caught in the headlights of an oncoming truck.

But Holt surprised him when her tone was gentle, almost comforting. "Miss Natale," she began, "I have to ask you a few questions now on cross-examination. Do you understand that?"

At once Lakewood knew this was a masterful, strategic decision. Holt recognized how vulnerable Deanna was, that she was an extremely sympathetic figure to the jury. An attack with fangs bared ran the huge risk that the jury would turn on Holt as a bully. Knowing that, Holt was opting to kill with kindness. This would be a much harder cross-examination to check with objections.

"Yes," Deanna said, looking shocked but also relieved at how the questioning started.

"I don't have many questions for you, and then you can go, all right?"

Deanna nodded. "Okay."

"Good. You need any water, anything like that?"

"No, thank you."

"All right, then. You mentioned during direct testimony that you were a pornographic actress, is that correct?"

"Adult films, yes."

"How many did you appear in?"

Rolling her eyes in obvious embarrassment, Deanna said, "I don't know, fifty or sixty, maybe."

"And did you use a screen name?"

Hesitantly Deanna said, "Yeah."

"Was your screen name Tanya Tempest?"

Deanna nodded.

"You have to answer out loud," Holt said sympathetically.

"Yes," said Deanna.

"And the name Tempest was chosen because you had a particular specialty, isn't that right?"

Deanna looked puzzled, then glanced at Lakewood as if to ask for help. He remained impassive. The last thing he needed now was for the jury to think he was sending her signals.

"Do you understand the question?" Holt said, still sounding more like a psychological counselor than a hostile attorney.

"Umm, no."

"Isn't it true that you made movies mostly involving sadomasochism?"

Looking down at her hands, Deanna, almost in a whisper, said, "Yeah."

"You made pornographic movies that had to do with acts of bondage and beatings, isn't that right?"

"Yeah."

"Miss Natale, I know this is difficult for you, but if you could just keep your voice up."

"I'm sorry."

"Now wasn't your particular specialty dealing with whips?"

Deanna glanced quickly at the jury. The look on her face was telling. It was the look of someone afraid that her answer would damage a newly minted friendship through the revelation of an awful secret. Deanna looked back at her hands and said, "Yeah."

"Both inflicting and receiving beatings with a whip, correct?"

Deanna nodded.

"Out loud, please," said the judge.

"Yeah."

"This is not to pass judgment, Miss Natale," said Holt, "but only to get at the facts. Isn't it true that you liked it?"

Deanna shook her head.

"Please, Miss Natale," Montross reminded.

"No," Deanna said.

"Isn't it true that you liked taking those beatings?" asked Holt.

"No, it isn't."

"Isn't that one way that you tried to deal with your past, a past you felt guilty about?"

Lakewood objected. "No foundation," he said.

Montross said, "Sustained."

Holt did not flinch. She was still asking questions in tones that made her seem almost apologetic about having to put the witness through this ordeal. "Isn't it true, Miss Natale, that you actually requested Mr. Supevsky to use a whip on you?"

Deanna looked around the courtroom, then said, "I may have at first, but then—"

"Your answer is yes, then?" Holt pressed gently. "You were the first to suggest a whip being used?"

"I thought he'd like it."

"Is your answer yes or no?"

"Yes."

Holt nodded, indicating to the jury she had the answer she wanted. Lakewood knew it was effective. Whatever shock value there had been in Deanna's revelations about being beaten was now sufficiently muted. The jury might even hold a reserve of resentment for Lakewood for not bringing out this information himself. He hadn't, though, because he didn't know about it. Obviously, Supevsky told her.

"Now, Miss Natale," Holt continued, "you testified on direct examination that you are a heroin addict."

"I'm clean now."

"Clean for about a year, is that correct?"

"Yes."

"But once a heroin addict, always a heroin addict, right?"

Deanna nodded sadly. "Yeah."

"And on the night in question, the night you allegedly overheard the conversation between Mr. Supevsky and Mr. Dedenok, on that night you were still an active user, weren't you?"

"Yeah."

"Did you shoot up that night, Miss Natale?"

Deanna thought for a moment, but her hesitance looked more like an avoidance than an attempt to remember. "Yes."

"You stated, I think, that you were down in the club partying. Is that right?"

"Yeah."

"And by partying you mean having a good time."

"Sure."

"Including drugs and alcohol, right?"

"That wasn't the whole thing."

"But it was part of it, wasn't it?"

"I guess."

"We don't want you to guess, Miss Natale." Holt's voice was now showing a bit more sternness, as if she were a parent questioning an evasive child. She still wasn't hammering Deanna, but Lakewood sensed that Holt was perfectly in tune with the perceptions of the jury. Deanna was starting to equivocate, and as she did, Holt's tone shifted accordingly. "Now please tell us," Holt said, "if drugs were part of your party scene?"

"Yes."

"You said you had shot up with heroin, is that right?"

"Earlier, yeah."

"Did you take any other drugs that night?"

"I think so."

"Tell us what drugs you took, Miss Natale."

"I'm not sure."

Holt took a step away from the lectern, like a boxer leaving his corner. "You're not sure what drugs you may have taken that night?"

"No, it was a party."

"With drugs freely flying everywhere?"

"It wasn't like that, exactly."

"You're not sure what it was like, is that what you're telling us?"

The questions were coming faster now, and Deanna was starting to look even more confused than she had previously. "Well, yeah."

"But, Miss Natale," Holt said sharply, still managing not to sound mean. "You are so sure about what you may have overheard on the staircase. Why aren't you sure now?"

"I . . . don't know," Deanna said.

"I see," said Holt. "Would it be fair to say you smoked some marijuana that night?"

"Yeah, there was some."

"You're just not sure, right?"

"Yeah."

"And what about alcohol? Did you have anything to drink?"

"I may have."

"But you can't remember, is that it?"

"Not real clearly."

Holt, putting on a look of consternation, returned to her notes. "You mentioned that you were 'flirting' at the bar with one Kolya Medilich, is that right?"

"Yeah."

"I think your exact words were that you were 'having fun.' Is that correct?"

"Sure, we always had fun."

"At the bar?"

"Sometimes."

"You said Medilich was drinking vodka, is that right?"

"Right."

"What were you drinking, Miss Natale?"

"I don't know, maybe some Cuervo."

"That's tequila, right?"

"Yeah."

"So in this state, Miss Natale, after having taken heroin, marijuana, tequila, and other things you may not even remember, after all this, you say you managed to pick the pocket of a trained security man, enter a secret stairway undetected, just in time to hear this conversation between—"

Lakewood jumped up. "Objection! This is argument, Your Honor."

"I'm asking the witness to summarize," Holt insisted.

"Hold on," Montross said. "I'm going to sustain the objection. Any inferences from the testimony of the witness can be argued during summation. But I don't want any arguments here, Miss Holt. The last question will be stricken, and the jury is admonished to ignore it."

Fat lot of good that does, Lakewood thought bitterly.

Holt sighed, then asked, "Miss Natale, you gave a statement to the FBI on this matter some months ago, is that correct?"

"Um, yeah."

"It was a statement that was later put into written form, and then you signed it, right?"

"Yeah."

"And you signed it under oath, do you remember that?" Holt emphasized the last word, but Lakewood couldn't object to a tone.

"Yeah," Deanna said.

"The oath was to tell the truth, the whole truth, and nothing but the truth, correct?"

"I think—I mean, yes."

"The same oath you took today before you began to testify, right?"

"Yeah."

Holt looked to the judge, "May I approach the witness?"

"Yes," said Montross.

Grabbing a report, Holt strode to the witness box and laid it on the rail in front of Deanna.

"Miss Natale, I ask you to look at that document and tell us if you recognize it."

Deanna took a moment to look through the three pages in front of her. "That's my statement."

"The one to the FBI, which you swore to?"

"Uh-huh."

"Is that a yes?"

"Yes."

Holt walked back to the lectern. "In that sworn statement, Miss Natale, is there anything about killing anyone?"

Deanna didn't even look at the document. "Juri talked about killing Chekhov."

"Where is that in the report, Miss Natale?"

This time she did look. She took a full minute to scan the pages, then looked at Holt and said, "Juri talked about subtracting him."

"Oh yes, we all remember you think subtracting means kill, don't you?"

"Yeah."

"Where does it say that in the statement?"

Deanna shook her head. "That exact word isn't in there, but—"

"Isn't it true, Miss Natale, that you didn't come up with this interpretation until just before this trial?"

"No!"

"It's not in the statement, is it?"

"No."

Deanna opened her mouth to say more, but before the words came out Holt said, "Isn't it true that subtract means to take away something?"

"Well, sure."

"And isn't it true that what Mr. Supevsky meant was merely that he did not want to do business anymore with Mr. Chekhov?"

Deanna slowly shook her head. "No, he wanted to kill him."

"I see," Holt said, now allowing her voice a full expression of chastisement. "In your drugged-out condition you not only could hear but you could also interpret the words coming from inside that apartment. Is that what you're telling us?"

"Objection," Lakewood said. "Argumentative."

"Sustained," said the judge.

"Let's move on," Holt said, picking up the pace so the questions were coming faster. "You testified that Mr. Supevsky said to find somebody to 'do it,' isn't that right?"

"Yes."

"Do what, Miss Natale?"

"Kill Chekhov."

"Where does it say that in your statement?"

Deanna looked at the paper with a look of desperation. Finally she said, "It doesn't say that exactly."

"Oh, but you knew, standing out there on the stairs, exactly what he meant, didn't you?"

Deanna did not answer. She looked petrified.

"Isn't it true," Holt asked, "that you have made all this up to get back at Mr. Supevsky?"

"No, it's not!" Deanna said. "I didn't even want to testify."

"Ah, but you're here," Holt said, as if the last answer was the perfect segue. "You changed your mind, didn't you?"

"I guess—I mean, yes."

"And that change came as a direct result of the actions of a member of the U.S. Attorney's Office, right?"

"You mean Rachel?" Deanna asked.

"Rachel Ybarra, correct."

"She helped me."

"In fact, she helped you by talking to you about God."

"Yes."

"She prayed with you?"

"Yes."

"She encouraged you to pray?"

"Yeah."

"And because of her you found religion, right?"

"I found Jesus, yes."

"You found Jesus," Holt repeated, as if to make it sound like the least plausible of scenarios. "And has Jesus led you into this courtroom to wreak vengeance on Mr. Supevsky?"

"I . . ." Deanna cut herself off. Holt let her dangle.

Finally Holt swept up her notes from the lectern and said, "No further questions, Your Honor."

CHAPTER EIGHT

EXHAUSTED, RACHEL LET HER HEAD drop so her chin touched her chest. She wondered if she might pass out. Her head felt like it had been cleaned out with a leaf blower, and her body ached in several places at once. The irritation caused by the heavy tape had gotten progressively worse.

She had no way of knowing the time, but it felt like she'd been tied up for days. And for the first time in all of the bizarre events that had surrounded her since she first met Grigory, she felt like she was losing hope.

Grigory would have to kill her eventually. It was what he might do before her execution that she could not stop thinking about. He was capable of anything.

She wasn't afraid to die. To die is gain. She believed that. But there were too many people around her who cared, who would be devastated by her death. Abi, of course, would have a hard time recovering, if she recovered at all.

And then there was her father. She needed to talk to him again, to set things right. For the first time since Stevie's death that door was open. He had made a call to Lakewood on her behalf. He was not a man who could say he was sorry. He showed his regret through action.

She remembered when she was seven or eight and her father had come home drunk and screamed at her. His voice was louder than any sound on earth, she thought. It made her body shake and froze her to the floor, releasing her only when her tears came in such a torrent that she had to run for fear of bursting like a balloon right there in front of him. She hid in her room that night, daring not to come out, even for food. The next day, Saturday, she didn't get out of bed. When her father came into the room she pretended to be asleep.

Next thing she knew she was swept up in his strong arms. At first she thought she would be beaten. But then he softly guided her head to his shoulder, stroked her hair, and without saying anything took her out and put her in his truck. Then he drove her to the International House of Pancakes, her favorite restaurant, the place she went only on special occasions, like her birthday. Her father told her to order anything she wanted, and she ordered the Swedish pancakes. They were the best she'd ever had.

Her father never mentioned the incident from the night before. But she knew he was sorry, and this was his way of saying so. It was the last tender moment she could remember having with him.

Now she wanted escape so she could tell him how much she loved him.

In the circle of her thoughts, the image of Jeff returned—another reason for living and another reason for terror in the pit of her stomach. Was he dead even now, even as she thought about him?

With one mighty pull and a scream of determination and agony—which reverberated and sounded to her like an Olympic weight lifter—Rachel pulled against the rope with her right hand, feeling the burn of the cord as it tore into her skin, wondering if the small bones were breaking, then suddenly feeling the incredible sense of release when her hand actually pulled free.

She cried with a mixture of joy and relief. It was only a small victory—she was still held fast to the chair by the heavy tape around her torso and arms—but it was a *victory,* and she thanked God.

The wait had been too long.

Grigory, with a sense forged over years of experience, knew Agent Jeff Bunnell would not be returning any time soon. It had been easy enough to confirm the apartment he was staying in, but what was not easy was figuring his whereabouts.

Perhaps he was detained now. Perhaps the FBI itself had caught up with him and was questioning him about the Zagorsky affair. That was inevitable, Grigory mused. Zagorsky had been a man born to be caught. Bunnell, on the other hand, would find a way out. And when he did, Grigory would have time to catch up with him.

The time here had not been wasted, however. He had Rachel to think about. She was an odd experience for him, and he wanted a chance to reason it through.

He had never thought he was capable of love. He didn't believe in love. What people called love was merely a chain reaction of chemicals in the body. The mind, being a chemical product itself, thought that by observing the reaction and giving it a label it had somehow come into contact with an objective state. And the poets had elevated it to a position of high worship.

What nonsense. Chemical states were nothing more than accidents. What mattered is that some accidents are more enjoyable than others.

He would enjoy having Rachel Ybarra and bending her to his will and desire. What was odd to him was why he had picked her. He decided it was because of her intelligence and capabilities. She was like him in a way—one committed to peak performance.

But she also had this fixation on God, and that presented a unique challenge. What would it be like to take someone's simple faith and destroy it? To be in a position to build something new, to replace the one truth with another, his own? It would be almost like cloning himself, and that was as close to immortality as any human being would get.

Immortality. Was that, for him, the ultimate desire?

Perhaps he did not know himself as well as he thought. Thus Rachel was, in a strange way, a door, a passage to a new level of knowledge. Knowledge was power. And power was very, very enjoyable.

He started his car and headed back toward the beach house.

The deputy district attorney was young, well-groomed, intense, humorless, and no doubt ambitious. That was how Jeff sized him up. It was the last attribute that concerned him. A nice, fat, juicy murder case had just been dropped in his lap from the FBI. This guy was going to run all the way with it.

Jeff's lawyer, Mark Garrigas, was well-known in the criminal law community. Jeff testified once as a government witness in a case Garrigas defended. Garrigas grilled Jeff on cross-examination. It was tough but fair. The guy did not hit below the belt. At the time Jeff had thought that if he ever got in trouble himself, Garrigas would be the one he'd want defending him.

That time had come.

He was being arraigned in state court, a venue he was unfamiliar with, but one in which Garrigas had achieved remarkable success. At fifty-one, Garrigas was at the zenith of his career. It was going to cost Jeff every penny he had, but this was no time for scrimping.

This was a murder charge. When the FBI guys had finished interrogating him, they had handed him off to the district attorney's office. What went into that apparently high-level decision Jeff didn't know. Maybe it went all the way back to Main Justice and a desire to keep free from any hint of bad ink. Let the state handle it, get rid of a bad egg, and the Bureau wouldn't even have to dirty its hands.

So after a night's incarceration, Jeff Bunnell, former rising star in the nation's premiere law enforcement agency, was forced to his feet in the courtroom of Judge Sherise Weston to answer the charge with "Not guilty."

The deputy district attorney, whose name was Targament, immediately asked the court to hold Jeff without bail.

Garrigas argued eloquently about his client's spotless background and the "amorphous" evidence, and asked for Jeff to be released O.R.

The Solomonic Judge Weston split the difference and set bail and $500,000, which meant that Jeff was going to be spending a good deal more time in the slammer.

Judge Weston set the preliminary hearing in exactly one week. Then she called the next case.

Before being carted away, Jeff met with Garrigas in the last two seats of the empty jury box. "There are two things I need you to do," Jeff said.

"Name them," his lawyer answered.

"Get in touch with my mom. She lives in Riverside. She can arrange for a bond."

"Done."

Then Jeff gave Garrigas a phone number. "Find Rachel Ybarra. Tell her where I am and that I want to see her."

"Girlfriend?"

"I think she's the only one who can help me."

"And what am I? Chopped liver?"

"Besides you."

Garrigas turned serious and put a hand on Jeff's knee. "Don't worry, kid."

Five minutes later Jeff was in the lockup, shackled and staring at four bare walls. It should have been, he realized, a moment of unadulterated despair, with no hint of hope. But he had hope. Like the child he once was, he was trusting God in a way that defied rationality. From the depths of his being he felt a renascence of the faith he had once had, an assurance that had grown cold over the years but never left.

This is what it must be like, he thought, for those who find God in prison. Something about the four walls and the grinding wheel of government sanction makes a man think. He knew, of course, that many claims about being born again in prison were bogus, mere dog-and-pony shows for the parole boards. But imprisonment held something compelling for the open heart.

Facing a murder charge now, alone with his thoughts, Jeff allowed the feeling of surrender to wash over him, and it did, in warm waves. It picked him up and carried him, like a man floating on a tropical cloud. He closed his eyes and felt, for the first time in years, connection with a power greater than himself.

And then he thought of the one person he wanted to share this with—Rachel. He didn't care if he was locked up or not. As soon as it was possible, he wanted to tell her all about it.

It took what seemed like a good twenty minutes, but by leaning and stretching, Rachel was able to get her right hand down to feel the tether on the leg of the chair, a link chain of some kind that went right into the wall. An elaborate enterprise for some, she thought, but not for him. For Grigory it would have been a pleasure to hook this up.

The iron chain was solid. There was no way to break it. Perhaps if she were able to get enough leverage, she could pull it from the wall. That would depend, however, on how strongly attached it was, and she had no doubt it would be secure. How many times, she wondered, had he restrained people just like this?

The only other possibility was the chair. It was, as far as she could tell, a basic wooden chair, the kind you'd find in a million dining rooms. She couldn't actually see any of it. The tape kept her from being able to lean far forward, and she couldn't swivel her head around far enough to catch sight of the backrest. She could feel only part of the legs with her hands, and it was a smooth, varnished feel.

She thought about the wood. If the right tension was applied, might it break?

She heaved her body forward against the tape, moving the chair absolutely nowhere but engendering a sharp pain in her neck. She ignored it and kept driving forward. Not even the feet of the chair moved significantly.

After five minutes she rested momentarily and tried leaning against the tension of the chain. The chair held. She tried again but didn't even hear the strain of the wood.

Hopeless.

The throbbing in her body increased, and she was sure a childlike humiliation was imminent. That spurred her on, and with one, huge convulsion she put all she had left into her enterprise. She heard herself groaning, as if she were outside of her body, listening. Her wild jerking gave her the sensation of being on a giant roller coaster.

Then, suddenly, something gave, and she felt herself fall. She hit the floor on her right shoulder, and her head banged on the hardwood. Searing pain shot through her body. For a moment she lay on the floor stunned, unsure of what happened. And then she realized that the legs of the chair had slipped under her, and though she had changed positions, she was still tethered to the wall.

From this bizarre fetal position Rachel began a series of slow movements, running a new series of calculations through her head. From where she lay she felt she had cut off half her body, making escape even more difficult. She even thought about Grigory's face when he came back, how he would smile and mock her for such a feeble attempt.

Rachel kicked outward and felt her feet contact the wall. The wall was now her floor. By pressing, she was able to create a new tension with the underside of her thighs as a fulcrum. Kicking off her shoes, she put both feet firmly on the wall and pushed.

Pain like a wildfire consumed her right side, from her shoulder to her waist. She felt like she was grinding herself into the floor, like the absurd cousin of the cartoon Tasmanian Devil. But if this didn't do something, nothing would. She would be forced to lie there like an overturned turtle, helpless and lying in the middle of the road.

Harder and harder she pushed, beyond what she thought were the limits of her capacity. In her swimming days, doing the long races, her coach had called this "the wall," that obstacle that distance athletes hit when the body declares its desire to shut down immediately. Only by breaking past the wall does the athlete find new reserves of energy and will.

She thought of the wall now, remembering the times she had hit it herself, how it burned to keep going, but how she kept on going anyway.

Pushing, pushing, she felt the strain on her ankles, up her calves, to her thighs, where the edge of the chair dug in. Something was giving, but she wasn't sure whether it was herself being turned into the amazing elastic woman or the chair or just her imagination.

Whatever it was, it caused pain. She felt like she could hold the effort maybe ten more seconds.

Or less . . .

She took in a huge breath and gave one more, all-out thrust with her legs.

Crack.

She spun around, the back of her head hitting the wall. It felt like someone banging a two-by-four across her skull.

That's it, she thought, her initial rumination being one of surrender and resignation. No more. Nothing left. Spent.

But then she moved one leg, and the other, and the chair moved outward, away from the wall.

She was still attached to the back of the chair, and the back was still attached to the seat. But one chair leg was snapped off, the one held by the chain to the wall.

Like a baby snake, Rachel squirmed along the floor, trying to find enough leverage, without being able to use her hands, to get to her feet.

CHAPTER NINE

"SO WHAT'S YOUR ASSESSMENT?" Alan Lakewood said. He had nibbled only the corner of his ham sandwich, which sat lonely and isolated on a napkin on his desk. Ron Ashby, who sucked Minute Maid Orange Juice out of a can through a straw, looked perplexed.

"I . . . think it's okay," Ashby said.

"What trial have you been watching?" Lakewood snapped.

"Okay, Holt scored some points. But you never know."

Lakewood shook his head. "It was a *disaster!*"

Ashby clearly flinched and almost choked on a squirt of orange juice.

"My sense is we've lost the jury," Lakewood said. "And I can't think of any way to get them back."

Nor, apparently, could Ron Ashby, who looked at the floor, his mouth still covering the straw.

"I want you to go over the transcript tonight," said Lakewood. "I want you to comb over the cross and see if you can find anything that would merit a mistrial. We may have to try this sucker all over again."

"I'll do it," Ashby said anxiously. A little too anxiously. A few drops of juice dribbled out of his straw and onto his chin. Lakewood rolled his eyes and dismissed Ashby with a wave of his hand.

After Ashby left, Lakewood put his head in his hands and unsuccessfully fought back a headache. He was a fighter and usually an optimist, but he could not help feeling that, once more, he was going down to defeat at the hands of Jessica Osborn Holt. That nightmare was repeating itself, and a new incubus was drawing awful pictures to come.

Holt, holding a news conference on the courthouse steps, exulting in victory.

Holt, the darling of the talk shows.

Yes, Larry, I think the government blew it. They clearly had no case. I don't know why Alan Lakewood ran with this, unless it was sheer desperation for a big win.

And he would have to deal with the question of his future in the office.

He could see himself relegated to a string of nothing cases, entrapped in a position that went nowhere. He could kiss any thoughts of the federal bench goodbye too. A dull, gray career would masticate him until he was spit out into an ignominious retirement.

Lakewood's temples throbbed. He considered asking Montross for a recess, but that would be a dead giveaway. The jury would know that Holt had scored a knockdown and that Lakewood would be in his corner, licking his wounds.

No, like it or not, limping or crawling, back in the courtroom he'd have to go.

Rachel walked around like a comedic mummy, bumping into things as she inspected the house and assessed her options. The first thing she tried was the kitchen door, which was the exit Grigory had used. True to his word, it was secured from the outside. By turning her back she got her hand on the knob and tried it, but the door would not budge.

Her next thought was extrication. She immediately looked for a knife. Would he keep a knife in the house, especially when leaving her alone? She wondered about that as she reached backward for the drawers and started pulling them out.

The first three she tried were empty. The fourth one opened with the familiar jangle of silverware. She looked down and, indeed, saw a plastic holder with a modest set of eating utensils. Nothing there would do for her plight, however, unless there was a sharper knife in the back of the drawer.

She pulled again, and the drawer flew out, dropped to the floor with a crash. The sound startled her, like the report of a gunshot from behind. Spoons, forks, and table knives spread out in a crazy jumble. Her heart pounded under the armor of tape she wore.

She looked down on the floor she saw it—a black-handled steak knife. Rachel emitted a small squeal of victory, slowly dropped to her knees, reached down behind, and found the knife. Her hand closed around it, held it, readied it.

And then she realized she had no way of reaching the tape. Her hands were too low, their movement restrained.

Grunting with frustration, she struggled to her feet and tried to think of something else to do. If she could figure out a way to affix the knife somewhere, she could move back and forth perhaps and cut the tape that way. But she could find nothing to secure the knife.

With an irritated groan she dropped the knife. Now what? Was she doomed to wander stupidly around her prison until Grigory returned? She thought about breaking a window, but even as she approached the living room, she knew what she would find there.

Heavy curtains, with unforgiving shutters on the outside cutting off light. The windows themselves would not be made of glass. They would be made of some high security unbreakable material.

That is what she found. She could not escape from the inside of the house. Her escape would have to come from the outside. And the outside was reachable by phone.

But there was no phone.

Looking desperately around the living room and in the kitchen, Rachel realized that the house had no connection to the outside world.

She was imprisoned, incommunicado.

Just before yielding to some final despair, she noticed a wire running along the wall and floor. A phone wire. It had to be. She followed it from the kitchen out to the living room, where it disappeared behind a sofa. Rachel put her foot behind one side of the sofa and pushed. The thing hardly moved. She put more effort into it, feeling the strain on the inner part of her thigh. But finally it was moved enough so she could see the course of the wire.

It came to an end at a phone jack.

So the place was wired for a phone after all, though whether it was active or not was another matter. And still she could find no phone.

She sensed time running out. Time for Jeff, time for herself. Grigory would be finishing his work or, if not, returning to torture her further.

Whether it would do any good or not, she determined to search the house quickly, one final time. Something might turn up. What, she didn't know. But anything was better than waiting.

She began in the bedroom with the chest of drawers. She pulled them all out fully, letting them fall to the floor. She didn't care. Let the place look ransacked.

The drawers contained a few items of men's underclothing—T-shirts, briefs, socks. The thought that she was looking at the intimate wear of Grigory Viazmitin sickened her. She made a quick examination of each drawer, then moved to the closet.

A few shirts were hanging there, with nothing else on the bar. Stuffed in one corner was, of all things, a vacuum cleaner. A picture of Grigory engaged in domestic chores was both hilarious and grotesque. But what else did she expect, she thought, in a monster's house?

She was about to close the door when she noticed a small protuberance sticking out from behind the vacuum cleaner like a rat's tail.

A wire.

She kicked the vacuum with her foot, and it fell over like a wounded soldier. And there on the floor, now revealed, was a phone.

It was an older phone, one of the original Touch-Tones. The question now was whether it was in here in the closet because the phone service had been discontinued.

She had to find out, and with the same contortions she had used up to now, she bent and picked it up and hurried back to the living room.

Now she put all her weight into shoving the sofa all the way out from the wall. When she finally had enough room, she got on her knees and, by feeling behind her, plugged the phone wire into the wall jack.

The moment she connected she heard the faint sound of a dial tone. The phone lay on the floor, the receiver off the hook, and it was working.

Working!

Rachel shrieked.

She waddled on her knees to the phone and tapped 911 with her finger.

She hadn't even thought about getting her head down to the receiver when she heard the dispatcher's voice. She bent down and spoke into the mouthpiece.

"I've been kidnapped," she said.

"What's your name, ma'am?" the voice, a woman's, responded.

"Rachel Ybarra."

"Are you in physical danger?"

"I will be. He's going to come back."

"Who is?"

"Grigory."

"Is this the kidnapper?"

"Yes. Send someone."

"The address is on-screen. We'll send someone."

"Hurry."

"Can you continue to talk?"

"Please hurry."

Grigory opened his car window and let the warm sea air blow through his hair. This was a sensual pleasure, and he laughed. Then he thought, *I am not like other men*.

It's a thought he often had, and it usually gave him the greatest pleasure of all. He was invulnerable. He could do no wrong.

Yes, he had made mistakes, small ones, in the past. All a part of his bank of experience. The question was always, what do you do with your mistakes? Do you let them set you back or let them make you stronger?

He always grew stronger.

For a long moment, with wind and sun on his face, he exulted in the thought that he was stronger than anyone.

The first step, Grigory decided, would be to take her physically. Her will was strong, and she would continue to resist him if it were just a matter of bodily restraint. Over the years he had learned to size up his subjects quickly, to get a reading on their inner strength in even the first few seconds. Very rarely had he been surprised, and almost never did his initial reaction have to be radically revised.

Rachel Ybarra was one of the strong ones, though her strength was a surface strength, based on her faith. To strike at the heart of that without wasting too much time, he would have to cut to the chase, as it were, and inflict on her the ultimate act.

Then her mind and will would be softened to the point at which he could work with her.

The afternoon sun was hot, the way he liked it. As he drove up the coast highway he felt relaxed, calm, and in control. That's when he made his decision.

He would close up shop here on the West Coast. He had been paid well by Supevsky, but he sensed it was time to bolt. He had several offers coming in from Europe. Best to take one of them up and spend some time relaxing in the shadow of the Alps.

Relaxing with someone else.

Rachel would come with him. He would have no trouble convincing her.

He took the turn off the main highway and headed toward the semi-private road that would take him to the house near the shore, where no one would hear her screams.

Once more Rachel turned to thoughts of getting out of her cocoon. The only thing she could think of was heat, and the only heat was the stove. An electric stove. Flame would have been better, easier. But nothing was easy. This didn't surprise her.

She managed to turn on a front burner and waited until it glowed red. That was the easy part. Now came the challenge. Leaning forward, she let her front side make contact with the burner. She could feel the heat through the heavy tape. It was faint at first; then it felt as if someone had put a hot iron on her stomach and left it there. Small wisps of smoke rose from her torso, and an odor like burning rubber hit her nose.

She pulled back to check herself. Looking down she saw a small fissure in the dull gray layer of tape, blackened around the edges. But it was a perforation she could not utilize. She had to get it open at the bottom or top, so she could apply pressure and break out.

She looked for a way to touch the bottom of her restraint to the stove, but that involved more contortions than she was capable of. She bent from the waist and set her shoulder near the heat. It came perilously close to her face. She managed to burn a small amount of the tape before having to stand up again. Her cheek felt a slight burn. It was evident she would have to suffer some pain, perhaps major, to get out of this.

It took her two seconds to accept that price.

She began a slow, repetitive cycle of burning and relief, burning and relief, trying to work her way down from shoulder to arm, finding progress excruciatingly slow and acutely painful. The pain didn't matter. At least she was doing *something*.

When she sensed the breach had reached halfway down her right arm, she felt, for the very first time, a loosening of the bonds. She was by no means free, but she was closer. At some point, assuming continued success, she thought she would be able to free one arm, and then it would be a short order to free the rest of her body.

And then maybe she could figure out a way to smash out of this house and really be set free.

Through the heavy walls she thought she heard the sound of a car engine.

It was him. It had to be.

She had no other choice than to accept that fact, even if it turned out to be wrong.

She leaned on the burner, ignoring the pain, muttering, "Come on, come on!"

The bitter smell intensified, but she felt a further loosening.

The sound of the car engine grew closer.

Hearing herself groan, feeling the burn but no longer caring, sweat now covering her face, she all but fell on top of the stove. Writhing, she tried to get the burner to contact as much of the tape as possible. She sensed somehow that this was it, the final moment. If she wasn't free in the next few seconds, she never would be. He would be in the house, and it would be over, all over.

She stayed on the heat until she physically could not stand it anymore. Jumping backward, she strained with all that was left within her against the hot, gooey surface that enclosed her.

Her right arm flew out.

She had half a body back.

From just outside, she heard the sound of a car door closing.

A weapon. She needed something to defend herself. A cold, despairing prescience creeped inside her—after this entire ordeal, to be finally loose, only to have him walk through the door and see her there, helpless.

She looked around desperately. The place was spare, and she knew it was purposely so. There were two kitchen chairs, but she couldn't do anything with them with just one arm, an arm she realized was now moving from numbness to tenacious ache.

On the stove . . . yes, she *had* seen it. An old-fashioned iron frying pan.

She grabbed it, then stood behind the door.

And waited.

No footsteps. No sound. Nothing.

Where was he?

Still no sound. She put her head nearer the door.

A seagull wailed in the distance. It sounded like a dirge.

And then the door opened.

Officer Bob Myers of the Ventura Police Department loved country music. His favorite song of all time was the Willie Nelson-Waylon Jennings ditty, "Mamas, Don't Let Your Babies Grow Up to Be Cowboys." This was the cause of no small amount of embarrassment to his wife, who was ten years younger than he and had grown up on Aerosmith. She tended, at social functions, to keep the subject away from popular music, and if her husband even seemed on the verge of whistling, she put the kibosh on it right away.

So when Officer Myers was driving in a squad car as he was today—alone, on routine patrol—he let his voice have full reign.

Even when answering a 911.

In fact, he noticed a long time ago, the speed at which he drove influenced his choice of song. When the pace was leisurely, it might be a George Strait ballad. On his way to a call with sirens blaring, it could be the latest Garth Brooks.

Now, heading toward the stretch of private beach, he was humming an old Conway Twitty.

Myers didn't know this part of the county too well. The people on this stretch liked their privacy. Old Hollywood money built some of the homes that still commanded seven-figure prices. And usually it was quiet.

But this call was serious, probably some sort of extreme domestic violence thing. Maybe a girlfriend being held against her will. Maybe a drunken boyfriend with a busted heart. Whatever. It would probably make a good country song if you really wanted to dig into it.

He turned down the frontage road with guitar music sounding in his head.

She had only a split second, she knew. That's all it took, but in that micromoment she conjured up the image of a professional assassin with years of deadly experience, deflecting her desperate blow, grabbing her wrist, and maybe breaking her arm.

The picture burst like a camera flash as she swung the iron pan.

It landed with a solid crack across the front of Grigory's face.

The moment it hit she knew it was on the mark, perhaps even deadly. Grigory did not even issue a sound, but crumpled to the floor, seemingly lifeless. Rachel was immediately sickened. Yes, he was evil, but she had never come close to hurting another human being like that.

Rachel knelt down and reached under his coat, removing his gun from its holster.

Grigory didn't move.

Rachel stood and had one thought.

Jeff.

She had to know. Was he all right? Was he alive? She ran to the living room, picked up the phone, and dialed Jeff's number. Holding Grigory's gun at the ready, she looked back through the door and could see his body lying there.

The phone rang once.

Please be home . . . please be home. . . .

The phone rang again.

Grigory moved!

Rachel's chest tightened. She dropped the phone and held the gun in both hands and, pointing it outward, ran to the kitchen.

Grigory sprang to his feet. His eyes were red with blood, as was half his face. An ugly laceration ran across his forehead.

Teeth clenched, he practically growled at her. "You think . . . you can do this . . . to me?"

He took a step toward her.

She took a step back, pointing the gun at his chest. "Don't move."

"You really think . . . your God . . . will save you?"

He advanced another step.

"Do you?"

Rachel tried to steady the gun in her trembling hands. "I said stop."

For a split second his bloody lips parted in a mocking smile. And then he charged.

Rachel pulled the trigger.

Nothing happened.

Then he was upon her, in one move knocking her backward off her feet and ripping the gun from her hand. She slid on her back across the floor. He pounced on her, jerking her head back by the hair. He had her pinned.

"My darling Rachel," he hissed, "before you fire a gun you must release the safety." She saw him make a move with his thumb on the gun and heard a muted *click*. "Understand?"

She said nothing. He yanked her head back even further. "I asked you a question!"

"Yes. . . ." A cracking, shooting pain blasted Rachel's neck.

Her eyes met his. They were on fire. "I offered you real life! I was going to give it to you. And you do this?" He bared his teeth. They were stained with blood. "Do you want to know what I'm going to do? The same thing I did to Dimitri Chekhov."

She twisted in his grasp.

"I have never killed without pay," Grigory said, "but Supevsky won't have to pay me for this one. And then you know what I'll do?" He waited, seeming to enjoy the moment. Then he said, "I'll do the same thing to your beloved agent."

Jeff! she thought. *Still alive.*

"How does that make you feel, Rachel? I'll make it look like suicide, like with Dedenok. They'll think your agent killed himself because he was so distraught over killing a fellow agent. How does that make you feel?"

He put his bloodied face so close to hers she could smell the blood. She closed her eyes.

A voice said, "You let go and get up. Now."

Rachel didn't recognize the voice, but it had the tone of authority. Grigory still had hold of her head, so she couldn't turn to see.

"Let go," the voice commanded.

Grigory did not move. Rachel saw his eyes dart one way, then the other. She could feel his muscles tense, like a cat before it pounces. She knew then he would turn and shoot whoever it was.

"You got one more chance," the voice said sharply. "Get up. Now!"

Relaxing his grip on Rachel's hair, Grigory began slowly, almost imperceptibly, to roll off Rachel. His other hand held the gun against his body, hidden from the voice.

Rachel's move was instinctive. Still half-bound by the tape, it was all she had—an old swimmer's kick, the dolphin, which she had used swimming the butterfly. With one, vigorous undulation, her lower body flailed, her knees entering Grigory's stomach. She felt his weight leave her completely, while the force of the kick sent her over on her stomach.

She sensed rapid movement and then heard a shot.

And another.

And one more.

She half expected another shot, the one that would end her life.

The very first thing Jeff did after getting bailed out was drive to Abi's house. He'd made a phone call from jail to try to get hold of Rachel, but Abi was near hysterics. Where was Rachel? What was going on? Could he come over?

He found Abi red-eyed and weak. It became his first order of business to calm her down.

Jeff sat her in the kitchen and insisted on making her a cup of tea. She spoke to him in a nearly unbroken string of incomprehensible sentences. Jeff finally sat next to her and put both his hands on her shoulders.

"She's all right," he said, trying to convince himself as much as Abi.

"Where is she? This isn't like her."

"You know she's responsible. There's an explanation somewhere."

"But where is she?"

"We'll find out."

He wondered if they would. For twenty minutes he sat with her, until he was sure her blood pressure was stabilizing. He was about to leave to file a missing persons report when the phone rang.

Abi picked up. As she listened, her face turned white. She could hardly speak. She mumbled something, then Jeff put out his hand. Abi gave him the phone, saying, "She's in a hospital!"

Jeff inquired. It was the Ventura Police. And yes, Rachel Ybarra was in the hospital, being checked and questioned in connection with a kidnapping that had ended in a death.

"Come on," Jeff said after he hung up. "We're going to take a drive up the coast."

Alan Lakewood looked at his Egg McMuffin with a mixture of nausea and despondency. Try as he might, he could not bring himself to place any part of it in his mouth, though he knew he had to eat. He couldn't go into court this morning without some reserves of energy. He would need every ounce of stamina he could muster.

He felt like the cat on the poster, the one with the kitten barely clinging to a bar that says, "Hang in there, baby." In a few moments his claws were going to give way. He was going to fall off into the rabid jaws of Jessica Osborn Holt.

Emmitt Jefferson gave a knock on Lakewood's door. It was fifteen minutes before the start of the afternoon session.

"Anything?" Lakewood asked, knowing what the answer would be.

Jefferson shook his head. "No more witnesses, Alan. What do you think?"

"You don't want to know what I think."

"That bad?"

Lakewood sighed. "There's a gestalt that goes on in the courtroom. You know when you've lost a jury. Not that there aren't some surprises. But they're rare. I don't see any exception here."

"So what do we do?"

"There's only one thing. When Holt puts on her case, I go full bore into her witnesses and try to blow them out of the water. Cross-examination can turn a case around, and that's what's going to have to happen here. Meanwhile, maybe a rebuttal witness will turn up."

Jefferson nodded. "I've seen you cross-examine before. If anyone can do it, you can."

"Thanks, pal, but you're on my side of the fence. Those jurors are sitting on Holt's side."

The two took the elevator together. Lakewood sensed even among the reporters on the second floor a feeling of inevitability, like the crowd at a basketball game when the stronger team starts to take over. The sportscasters called it the "Big Mo," for momentum. The few reporters who tossed questions at Lakewood did so with a certain relish, closing in for the kill.

With each step Lakewood took, however, he worked himself up into a fighting mode. Lakewood had never quit anything in his life, and though it was bleak, he wasn't going to quit now.

He still had cross-examination.

Taking his seat at counsel table, Lakewood took out his trial notebook and opened to his notes on cross. He was ready.

Montross entered, called the court to order, and asked for the jury. Lakewood studied their faces as they marched in and sat. They seemed grim. No one looked at him.

"Good afternoon," Montross said to the jury, which responded in kind. Then he said, "Mr. Lakewood, do you wish to call another witness?"

Alan Lakewood stood. "No, Your Honor. The government rests."

Montross nodded, and Lakewood thought he saw a hint of shock in his expression. The judge then looked at Jessica Osborn Holt. "Ms. Holt, you may present your case."

Holt took her time rising to her feet. She waited until all ears were trained on her. "Your Honor," she said, "it is our position that the government has failed to prove its case beyond a reasonable doubt. We're ready for closing argument."

For a moment Lakewood wasn't sure he heard her right. But then he saw a self-satisfied look on her face and knew he'd just been sandbagged.

Montross, looking slightly bemused, said, "All right. No more witnesses. We'll schedule closing arguments for nine o'clock tomorrow."

The judge thanked the jury, told them to be back in the morning, and began the standard admonishments. Lakewood heard none of it. He was lost in a fog where there was no sound.

When Jeff and Abi burst through the door Rachel was lying in bed, spooning the last bit of hospital-issue pudding in her mouth. She dropped the cup and spoon on her tray and put her arms out.

"Abi, Abi, Abi," she said as her grandmother took her embrace. She held Abi close and closed her eyes. Her grandmother seemed too overcome to speak.

Jeff smiled. In spite of everything going on—and still to come—he was with her. Rachel turned to him and put her arms out again. Jeff fell into her caress. They were silent for several moments.

"So what's this all about?" Jeff whispered.

"There's so much," Rachel said. "I want to tell you everything."

"Sure. What's the doctor say about getting out?"

"I'm ready. But the police want to ask me more questions."

"Police?"

Rachel nodded toward the door. Turning, Jeff saw a uniformed officer enter the room. He put his hand out to Jeff. "Bob Myers," he said.

"The man who saved my life," said Rachel.

Jeff pumped the cop's hand. "How?"

"Suppose we talk out here?" Myers said.

Rachel nodded. "You go ahead. Abi and I have a lot to talk about."

In the hallway, Myers gave Jeff a summary of what he'd been able to piece together from his own observations and the initial questioning of Rachel. Jeff took it all in like a thirsty man drinking water.

When Myers finished the summary, Jeff said, "Where is the body now?"

"I'm assuming the coroner's got it."

"Did the ME take prints?"

"Yeah."

"Get them to Interpol."

"Already in process. Miss Ybarra put me on that."

Jeff smiled. "Smart girl."

"She got a pretty bad scare."

"Thanks, Officer, for being there."

Myers nodded. "You have a vested interest?"

"It's not vested yet," Jeff said, "but if I have anything to say about it, it will be. If you'll excuse me, I've got to get her back to L.A."

Myers laughed. "Son, that's one place I'd never be in a hurry to get back to."

CHAPTER TEN

PACING BACK AND FORTH in the Brosio room, Lakewood went over his closing statement once more. He had been up until two o'clock that morning rehearsing, rehashing, and refining. Now, at 8:30 a.m., with the conclusion of the trial just a half hour away, he was trying desperately to keep his mind from becoming mashed potatoes.

His words began to sound artificial to him, in no small part because he hardly believed them himself. Even though he was convinced of Supevsky's guilt, his personal opinion was not relevant and was precluded by law from being stated. No, only comments on the evidence were admissible, and it was difficult if not impossible to come up with something compelling there.

All he could do was state the case in the best possible terms and hope for a hung jury. He no longer considered conviction a possibility. With a deadlock the government could at least try this case again. But if acquitted, double jeopardy would attach, and Supevsky would be free.

His knees began to feel weak. That would be all he needed—to collapse in front of the jury. He wondered if they'd laugh, cry, or applaud.

The wall phone buzzed. It was the reception desk. "Rachel Ybarra is here to see you," the receptionist said.

Lakewood almost dropped the phone. "Rachel!"

"She says it's crucial."

"All right, send her in."

Lakewood gathered up his notes and took a deep breath. If Rachel were here just to offer some apology, he would ask her to leave. He didn't have time.

With a short knock, Rachel entered the room. Even under makeup it was clear her face and neck had bruises. She also had a slight limp. "You all right?" Lakewood asked.

"I'm here."

"What's going on?"

"Chief, you are not going to believe what I'm about to tell you."

Relaxing in the attorney's lounge of the Federal Courthouse, Jessica Osborn Holt felt like the proverbial million bucks. She was dressed in what she called her "Jury Blues," an ensemble of deep cerulean that a fashion consultant once told her was her best color for persuasion. Indeed, she had never lost a case when wearing this outfit. It was a good luck charm.

Not that she needed luck. She knew she had the jury. Absolutely knew it. After taking apart Natale on the stand, it was all over. The icing on the cake was the look on Lakewood's face when she announced she would not put on a case. He was itching to cross-examine, and she had forever removed that option from him.

Victory was sweet.

She checked her watch. It was precisely 8:44, and that's precisely when her PCS phone rang.

"You're a minute early," she said.

The voice on the other end laughed. "I like to keep my appointments," said Ken Soble. "Especially when they involve screen rights. So, have we got a deal?"

"You like to get right to the point, don't you?"

"That's why I'm where I am."

"One million, plus points."

Soble whistled. "You pick that number off Mars somewhere?"

Chuckling, Holt said, "I'm letting you off easy. I'm not putting in any casting approval, though this would be a nice change of pace for Julia Roberts."

"You think big. I like that."

"So, do we have a deal?"

"Seven-fifty, plus two points."

"I'll take eight, and three points."

"Done."

"Oh, and Ken," Holt added. "That's gross, not net."

Soble chortled. "You're good, but not that good. You can have one point gross."

"Deal."

After a short pause Soble added, "And by the way, this is all contingent."

"On what?"

"On your getting the verdict, of course. If you lose the case, no deal."

"If that's all your worried about, forget it. It's in the bag."

With a quick flick of the thumb, Jessica Osborn Holt disconnected one of the more powerful producers in Hollywood, dropped the phone in her handbag, and checked her watch once more. She had a full five minutes before she had to walk down the hallway toward a nice, three-quarters-of-a-million-dollar bonus.

Rachel, seated in the front row next to the wall, watched Jessica Osborn Holt stride into the courtroom and take her place at the defense table. Holt looked every bit the confident lawyer. There was almost a swagger to her. The media, in full force for closing arguments, seemed to hang on her every move. No less than three courtroom artists began immediately to sketch Holt in her eye-popping blue suit. By noon, Rachel was certain, one of the pictures would be on CNN, sending Holt's image all over the world.

But what, exactly, would the story be? The only thing Rachel knew was that Jessica Osborn Holt was about to get one of the shocks of her legal life.

Rachel hoped Holt would not see her in the gallery, but then Holt turned to scan the courtroom seats. Her eyes connected with Rachel's. The look on Holt's face, for an instant, was complete stupefaction. Recovering quickly, Rachel knew, was one of Holt's trial skills, and the lawyer quickly looked away, as if Rachel's presence were of no concern.

But Rachel knew that Holt realized something was about to come down.

It happened just after Carl Montross took the bench and asked Alan Lakewood if he were ready to have the jury come in for closing argument.

"Your Honor," said Lakewood. "The government would like to reopen its case for a final witness."

Immediately, Holt was on her feet shouting, "Objection!"

Montross put his hand in the air. "I can hear you, Ms. Holt. I'm only ten feet away."

Some reporters laughed. Rachel didn't. She could feel the legal tension in the air because she knew what was at stake. This case could go either way, depending on how the judge ruled.

"Your Honor," Holt persisted, "the government rested its case. You dismissed us yesterday to get ready for closing arguments."

"Yes—"

"And now the government comes back, knowing it has lost the case—"

"Ms. Holt—"

"The government gambled and lost, Your Honor, and—"

"Ms. Holt!" Montross's voice thundered through the courtroom. "You have made your objection. You don't need to embellish further. And I should note one thing. I don't view trials as a game of chance. Yes, there's a certain amount of gamesmanship involved, but as the judge I have discretion to cut through all that if I think it's in the interest of justice. Is that clear?"

Jessica Osborn Holt said nothing.

"Good," said Montross. To Lakewood he said, "Now, Mr. Lakewood, there is a basis for the objection. Trials have an orderly process. Why should I allow you to reopen?"

"Your Honor," said Lakewood, "you have the discretion to serve the interests of justice. We wish to reopen for another witness because that witness was unknown to us until now."

Montross tapped his chin. "Who is this witness?"

Turning to his left, Lakewood motioned toward Rachel with his hand. Rachel, feeling like the entire world was watching her through some ubiquitous television feed, stood up as Lakewood said, "Rachel Ybarra."

With a yelp of outrage, Holt said, "His assistant! Your Honor, how can he stand up here and say he didn't know about her before?"

"Good point," said the judge with a tone of strict admonishment.

Lakewood said, "We did not know about her as a *witness*, Your Honor. Her testimony only became relevant over the last twenty-four hours."

Holt laughed derisively and shook her head. Rachel sat down, feeling the eyes of every reporter in the room. One of the sketch artists was now looking at her.

Judge Montross leaned back in his chair. "You'd better give me your offer of proof, Mr. Lakewood."

With a nod, Lakewood said, "Rachel Ybarra will testify to the following facts, Your Honor. Two days ago she was kidnapped by one Grigory Viazmitin and held against her will at a location near Ventura, California."

In the pause that followed, Rachel watched Jessica Osborn Holt. She seemed to tense up into a giant fist even as she stood listening. It was odd that Holt had not resumed her seat. It made the scene seem more like a heavyweight bout than a legal argument.

"Ms. Ybarra will further testify," Lakewood continued, "that she was able to free herself from her bonds and call 911. She will tell the jury that just before the police arrived she struggled with Viazmitin, who proceeded to make several statements that corroborate our case against the defendant."

"Your Honor—" Holt started to say.

Montross silenced her with a raised hand. "The first problem I see is with identity, Mr. Lakewood. Who is this Grigory guy?"

"He was, to use the vernacular, a hit man."

"Oh, please!" Holt said, sounding slightly desperate for the first time.

"Even assuming you get past that," Montross said, "we have a little evidentiary problem, don't we?"

"Hearsay," said Holt.

"There are exceptions under Rule 804," Lakewood said. "The statements were against the party's penal interest. Viazmitin implicated himself in criminal activity."

Holt shot, "We have no way to cross-examine on that issue, Your Honor. This violates the confrontation clause of the Constitution. Every accused has the right to cross-examine witnesses against him."

"Except," Lakewood said, "when the testimony falls under a hearsay exception and the witness is unavailable. Viazmitin is dead, Your Honor. You can't get any more unavailable than that."

Several reporters laughed. Rachel smiled. That last comment was just like the old Alan Lakewood—casual and confident. He was feeling good again.

"Ms. Holt?" said Montross. In asking for a response, he indicated that he was taking the argument seriously. When Holt began to speak, she actually stuttered at first.

"Your Honor," she said, "I . . . it's . . . this is outrageous."

"No doubt you think so," said the judge, "but I need a legal argument."

"It's the interest of justice!" Holt said, slapping her palm on the table so vehemently that the water pitcher moved an inch.

A slight smile scurried across Montross's face. "You know, I'm reminded of what Abraham Lincoln once said. 'If the facts are against you, argue the law. If the law is against you, argue the facts. If both are against you, pound on the table and scream for justice.'"

Once more the courtroom filled with laughter. Rachel kept her eyes on Holt. The back of the lawyer's neck turned red, in sharp contrast to her suit.

"Ms. Holt," Montross said, "you're screaming for justice, but the way I see it the Rules of Evidence allow for this testimony. You'll have your chance to cross-examine the witness."

Then Judge Carl Montross looked out into the gallery and locked eyes with Rachel. "Ms. Ybarra," he said, "prepare to take the stand."

Jeff Bunnell still couldn't relax. He knew he should feel a huge sense of relief—after all, the evidence gathered in Ventura would completely exonerate him. But he had been through one of those extremes of life that does not allow for quick recovery. It would be some time before he got that California laid-back feeling again.

At least he was back in his temporary apartment, not having to worry about anyone hassling him. The only worry he had was for Rachel. He was divided about going down to the courthouse to see if she would get to testify. He had decided against it because he didn't want her to be nervous in any way.

But he could hardly stand the wait, and different scenarios kept playing in his mind.

What if she didn't get to testify?

What if she were held up to ridicule on cross-examination?

What if the media portrayed her as some wild woman with a crazy story?

What if? What if? What if?

Twice he started to get dressed to shoot down to the courthouse. He made it only to Levi's and socks before he decided again to stay put.

She would call him when it was all over.

A thought hit him as he was standing in the middle of his living room. He immediately whirled and rushed into his bedroom.

It was there, on the floor where he'd left it, staring him in the face.

CHAPTER ELEVEN

WITH RIGHT HAND RAISED, Rachel heard the oath and said, "I do." She sat down and took a sip of water. Her throat felt like sandpaper.

Alan Lakewood led Rachel through her incredible story, with only a few questions asked here and there for clarification. She did well until she got to the point where she tried to recall Grigory's exact words. Seeming to sense a problem, Lakewood immediately asked, "You were under extreme stress at the time, were you not?"

Holt quickly objected on the ground that Lakewood was leading the witness. Montross sustained the objection. Rachel knew that was the correct ruling, but now at least she was alerted to the problem.

So when Lakewood asked her what her condition was at the time of the struggle, she replied, "I was very weak. I thought I'd almost pass out a few times."

"And when Viazmitin was holding you down, what was his condition?"

"He was bleeding."

"From the wound you inflicted?"

"Yes."

"And where was he physically when he said these things to you?"

"Right in front of my face."

"All right. Tell us what, in essence, he said to you."

Once more Holt was on her feet. "That calls for a vague answer, Your Honor. Either she remembers the words or she doesn't."

"I'll rephrase it," said Lakewood. "To the best of your recollection, Ms. Ybarra, tell us what he said."

"Well, he first said he was going to do the same thing to me as he did to . . ."

Lakewood waited. Rachel looked to the ceiling. "I'm sorry, I just blanked on the name. It was the victim in this case."

"Dimitri Chekhov?"

"Objection!" shouted Holt.

The judge said, "Mr. Lakewood, ask your question another way."

Lakewood nodded. "Are you sure about the name now, Ms. Ybarra?"

"Yes, I am. It was Dimitri Chekhov. I'm sorry."

Jessica Osborn Holt groaned. Rachel expected the judge to say something, but he was silent.

"Please go on, Ms. Ybarra," said Lakewood. "What did Viazmitin say next?"

"He said that he did not kill people without being paid for it, but that Supevsky wouldn't have to pay for this one."

After allowing the answer to sink in a moment, Lakewood asked, "Are you absolutely certain he used the name 'Supevsky'?"

"Yes."

"Anything else?"

"He said he was going to do the same thing to an FBI agent."

"Did he use a name?"

"I don't think so, but I knew who he meant."

"How did you know?"

"Because it's someone I'm acquainted with."

"What's his name?"

Before Rachel could answer, Holt objected again. "What possible relevance is this?" she asked the judge.

Rachel waited for the ruling but was surprised to hear Montross ask her a question himself. "Ms. Ybarra," he said, "did Viazmitin ever name this FBI agent?"

"I don't think so, Your Honor," Rachel said.

"Then we don't need to speculate," Montross said. "Objection sustained."

"Anything else that Viazmitin said?" said Lakewood.

"Yes. He said in regard to the agent that he would make it look like a suicide, like he did with the witness who was going to testify in this case."

"Anything further?"

"He said the world would think that Jeff . . . I'm sorry, the agent . . ."

"Objection!" Holt said. "Move to strike. In fact, at this point, I'm going to move for a mistrial."

Rachel could see reporters scribbling like crazy.

Montross looked less than pleased. "Motion for mistrial denied. The witness's last answer will be stricken, and the jury is admonished not to regard it in any way. Continue, Mr. Lakewood."

Lakewood leaned on the lectern. "What did he say about the agent and what the world would think?"

"That he was so upset about killing a fellow agent that he killed himself, and then the world would think he really was guilty."

"Guilty of what?"

"Murder."

Lakewood paused and then asked Rachel to continue her narrative. She finished the story, ending with her stay in the hospital.

At that point Alan Lakewood turned his witness over to Jessica Osborn Holt.

The defense lawyer virtually ran to the lectern, as if she couldn't wait to begin her assault. Rachel took another sip of water. The glass shook in her hand.

"Ms. Ybarra," Holt said tersely, "you are a paralegal with the U. S. Attorney's office, right?"

"Yes."

"In fact, you're the one who tried to influence a witness in this case."

"Objection," Lakewood said quickly. "Argumentative and beyond the scope."

Montross thought a moment. "I am going to sustain the objection as being argumentative. However, I won't preclude this issue because it goes toward possible bias. You may continue, Ms. Holt, but watch the phrasing of your questions."

"All right," Holt said, conceding nothing. "You know a witness in this case, Deanna Natale, right?"

"Yes."

"You met with her a few times, right?"

"Yes I did. I was—"

"Just answer my questions as I ask them please. You met with her?"

"Yes."

"You prayed with her, right?"

"Yes, but—"

"But what, Ms. Ybarra?"

"But I wasn't trying to influence her."

"You spoke to her about God."

"Yes."

"You even, as the saying goes, led her to Christ, am I right?"

"Yes. . . ."

"And you did that because you thought it would change her life, didn't you?"

"For the better."

"And you don't think that's trying to influence someone?"

Rachel said nothing. Holt quickly added, "Is your religion powerless or isn't it?"

Lakewood objected, and Montross sustained, but Rachel sensed some damage had been done.

"Now," Holt said, "let's turn to your memory troubles with regard to what this supposed hit man supposedly told you."

As Holt flipped her notes, Lakewood objected again, Montross sustained the objection again, and Holt again seemed unfazed.

Holt asked, "When you tried to recall what name this alleged hit man used in reference to what he was going to do to you, you couldn't, could you?"

"I blanked for a moment," Rachel explained.

"You blanked until Mr. Lakewood prompted you, right?"

"It refreshed my recollection."

"Ah," said Holt with pronounced incredulity. "And when you spoke about the supposed setup of the witness who was a suicide, you couldn't recall that name at all, could you?"

"I didn't at the time."

"Can you recall it now?"

Helplessly, Lakewood watched as Rachel sat silently. "No," she said finally.

"Okay," Holt said. "You couldn't recall two names that were supposedly mentioned to you while you were in this supposed struggle. But you had no trouble at all recalling the name of my client, did you?"

"No."

"Isn't this what is called selective memory?"

Lakewood said, "Objection!"

"I'll withdraw the question," Holt said.

She was making points with the jury, Rachel knew. Even her objectionable questions were on the mark, and though Montross was sustaining the objections, the questions were having a cumulative effect. One of the effects was a sinking feeling in Rachel's stomach.

She heard a slight sound at the back of the courtroom and turned to look. And there, just inside the doors, she saw Jeff.

He was looking at Lakewood, who had also turned, and was indicating something in his hand.

A marshall went to Jeff and began moving him back outside the doors. There were no seats left in the courtroom. Just before he slid out of sight, Jeff indicated to Lakewood again.

"Your answer, Ms. Ybarra?" It was the judge's voice. Rachel had completely missed the last question.

"I'm sorry, Your Honor," she said. "What was the question?"

Holt rolled her eyes, then snapped, "Isn't it true, Ms. Ybarra, that the only source of information about what this supposed hit man said is you?"

"Well," Rachel said, "there was the policeman, Officer Myers."

"But he only came in after these things were supposedly said, didn't he?"

"Um, yes."

"And you know as well as I do that he didn't hear those words."

"I guess he didn't."

"You *guess?*"

"No, he didn't."

"And so it remains a fact that the only source of information about what was said is you, right?"

"Yes."

"Now, Ms. Ybarra, you have testified that you were in a terrible struggle with this supposed hit man. Is that correct?"

"I was."

"And I believe you said he was bleeding?"

"Yes."

"And that he had his face right in yours?"

"Yes."

"While he was holding you down?"

"Yes."

"Threatening you?"

"Yes."

"Would it be correct to say you were in fear of your life, Ms. Ybarra?"

"Yes." Rachel did not like the staccato sound of her repeated answers.

"You've never been in that situation before, have you?"

Rachel thought a moment. "I've been in fear before."

"Ms. Ybarra, were you ever pinned to the floor by a bleeding hit man before this?" Holt's voice was clipped and derisive.

"No, of course not."

"And yet despite this, and despite being unclear today about two important names, you're absolutely sure about what this bleeding hit man told you, is that what you're saying?"

"I'm pretty sure."

"Pretty sure?"

"Well, yes."

"How sure, Ms. Ybarra?"

Rachel felt her body temperature rising. "I'm . . . I'm sure about the substance of what he said."

"No chance of a mistake?"

"No."

With a look of incredulity, Holt said, "You are beyond making a mistake, Ms. Ybarra?"

"Objection," said Lakewood. "Argumentative."

"Sustained," said the judge. "Rephrase."

Holt said, "There is absolutely no chance you could be mistaken?"

"Well I guess there's always a chance, but—"

"And if you are mistaken about what was said, then we'll never know, will we?"

"But I'm sure about the substance."

"That's not what I asked, Ms. Ybarra. Listen carefully. If you have made a mistake, we'll never know the truth, will we?"

Looking at the floor, Rachel said, "I haven't made a mistake."

Holt looked at Judge Montross. "Your Honor, I move to strike the answer as nonresponsive."

Montross, seemingly with reluctance, said, "The answer will be stricken. The jury is instructed to disregard it."

"Nothing further," Holt said, returning to her table.

Rachel cast a quick glance at the jury members. Their faces were solemn. One woman, juror number seven, met her eyes for a moment before quickly looking away.

"Any redirect, Mr. Lakewood?" said the judge.

"Your Honor," Alan Lakewood said, "may we take a fifteen-minute recess?"

Montross looked at the clock. "I'll give you ten," he said.

Everyone stood as the jurors shuffled out. Rachel waited until the judge was off the bench. She wanted to talk with Lakewood, but he was already racing out the courtroom doors. In fact, just about everybody seemed to be racing out the doors.

The only person looking at her was a courtroom artist, busy with his sketch.

Technically, no one was supposed to smoke inside the federal courthouse, least of all a judge. These totems of jurisprudential majesty were symbols of respect for law, not disdain. Which mattered not in the least to Carl Montross. These were his chambers, and he was going to smoke a cigar if he wanted to.

And he wanted to.

Back when he had been a federal prosecutor, and you could still smoke in the building, Montross would use a stout stogie as an aid to legal creativity. He always felt there was something to the Kiplingesque notion that a sense of calm inhered to a cigar, and he used that calm to strategize about his cases. And he never lost. Not one.

Now a judge for life, Montross used the smoke break to relax and reflect on what he might do in his courtroom.

This Supevsky trial was one of the strangest he'd ever presided over. That was what also made it exciting. He didn't particularly like Jessica Osborn Holt, but she was one crackerjack trial lawyer. And she had made mincemeat of that poor legal assistant. He remembered the conversation he'd had with Rachel, when he warned her about Holt. Now that prediction had come true.

He was sure the jury would acquit now, or at least hang. A hung jury would be a plus for the government, because that meant Supevsky could be tried again. But he wondered if the government would try him again. Based on the evidence he'd seen so far, it was a paper-thin case.

An outright acquittal would be bad for Alan Lakewood. Very bad. But that was the reality of life in the U.S. Attorney's Office. If he lost this case, there would probably be no Judge Alan Lakewood.

Montross took a leisurely puff on his cigar when his phone buzzed. It was his clerk. "Alan Lakewood would like to see you," she said.

"Lakewood?"

"Along with Jessica Holt."

Perplexed but curious, Montross said, "Send them in."

Within seconds Lakewood and Holt entered his chambers, Holt looking irritated and Lakewood looking stunned.

"Don't tell me," Montross said. "You two are getting married."

Holt shook her head, "Now that's not funny." She coughed a little and waved her hand in the air.

"Sorry," Montross said, stubbing out his cigar. "I'm feeling frisky. What's this all about?"

"I'm just as in the dark as you are," Holt said.

"I'm in possession of something you need to hear," said Lakewood. "And Ms. Holt needs to know about it."

Lakewood sat in one of the two leather chairs in front of Montross's desk. Holt remained standing, her arms folded.

"I'm in receipt of new evidence," Lakewood said.

"Oh, please!" Holt said. "Haven't we had enough phony dramatics?"

Raising his hand, Montross said, "Dramatic or not, the issue is relevance and timing. I assume you just got this new evidence?"

"Yes," Lakewood said.

"Go on."

"I received it from FBI agent Jeff Bunnell."

Holt gasped. "What could he possibly have to say?"

"It's not his testimony," Lakewood said.

"Well, what is it?" Holt countered.

Alan Lakewood, in spite of himself, smiled.

Rachel was set upon by several reporters in the crowded hallway. She waved them off, looking around frantically. One reporter, a woman, grabbed Rachel's arm and spun her around, shouting, "Fifty thousand for an exclusive!"

"Please," Rachel said, taking back her arm and physically making her way through the crush of journalistic humanity. She was about to sink even further when she felt another hand grip her arm and pull. Turning, she saw the source.

"Come on," Jeff said. With his other hand he pushed through the reporters until he and Rachel popped out to relative freedom by the elevators. He led her down the hall to the attorney's waiting room. It was empty and quiet inside, like a refuge in a storm.

"But you're not a lawyer," Rachel said with a smile.

"They don't know that, do they?" Jeff said.

She threw her arms around his neck and pulled him into her, holding him with all her strength. "This is crazy, crazy," she said. "Don't let me go."

"I don't intend to."

They held the embrace for several minutes. Then Jeff took Rachel by the hand and sat her down near the window. "Tell me what happened," he said.

She recounted her testimony in excruciating detail. "I think I got reamed," she concluded. "I was a stammering idiot by the end."

"That's what Holt's paid to do."

"I could see the jurors' faces. I think it's all over."

Jeff put his hand on her cheek and stroked it softly. "Don't be so sure."

"What are you talking about?"

"In a few moments, if it hasn't happened already, Jessica Osborn Holt is not just going to hit the roof, she's going to blast a hole right through the top of the building."

"What's going on?"

"I love the fact that you're a very resourceful woman."

"What does *that* mean?"

"You tried to call me from that beach house, right?"

"I dialed your number, that's all. Then Viazmitin got to me."

"You must have dropped the phone."

"What?"

"My answering machine picked up."

Rachel puzzled for a moment, then realized what he meant. "It recorded what happened?"

"Every bit of it. We have Viazmitin's voice confessing everything."

Rachel closed her eyes and shook her head. When she opened her eyes Jeff was smiling at her, and without another thought she put her hand on his neck, drew him close, and planted what she was sure was the most passionate expression of affection the attorney's lounge had ever seen.

"We should come here more often," Jeff said.

Rachel's smile grew, then suddenly faded. "Wait a minute. How do we know the judge is going to admit this?"

"He *has* to," Jeff said.

Rachel shook her head. "Judge Carl Montross doesn't have to do anything."

"Then we'd better go find out."

They stood and practically sprinted out the door.

When Montross entered the courtroom, Rachel had the feeling that time had stopped. She was crammed in the back corner, but at least she was in. It had seemed like hours before Montross took the bench, even though only twenty-five minutes had passed. Usually punctual, the judge had taken more time.

Obviously, thought Rachel, to consider his ruling.

She tried to read the attorneys. Both Lakewood and Holt were sitting stock still at their respective tables, not betraying any emotion by their body language. Next to Holt, Jaroslav Supevsky was also motionless.

Next to Alan Lakewood sat Jeff Bunnell. As the judge took his seat, Jeff turned and looked for Rachel. When their eyes met, he winked.

"Back on the record in United States versus Supevsky," Montross said. "Ms. Holt, you wish to make a statement for the record."

"Yes, Your Honor," said a subdued Holt. "Your Honor has indicated in chambers that he is going to allow the introduction of a certain audio tape. I am stating my objection. It is prejudicial, speculative, and meets no exception to the hearsay rule."

Jessica Osborn Holt sat down.

"Objection overruled," said Montross. "Let's have the jury."

CHAPTER TWELVE

THE HOUSE WAS FILLED with salsa—both the musical kind and the fresh tomato-cilantro concoction Abi made. She'd also made fresh *ceviche* for the first time in years. Rachel had forgotten how much she loved it.

In the living room Jeff filled a fresh tortilla with a mound of *ceviche* and rolled it up, holding it carefully over his plate. As he took a bite, a stream of juice shot out the opposite end of the tortilla and pooled on the plate, almost sloshing over the side.

Manny Mendoza laughed. "You eat like a total gringo," he said.

"I feel like a total gringo," Jeff responded. "What have I wandered into?"

"My world," Rachel said, taking Jeff's free arm and squeezing it. "And welcome to it."

Lydia Mendoza, seated next to her husband, said to Jeff, "Come on, I want to hear the rest of it."

Jeff put his plate down on the coffee table. "Well, there was nothing Holt could do. As soon as I authenticated the tape, they played it for the jury."

"How was the quality?" Manny asked.

"Like a recording studio," Jeff said. "Every word was clear."

"That couldn't have pleased the lawyer," Manny said.

"Like I said, there was nothing she could do. The judge made his ruling, and the tape was played."

"So," Lydia inquired, "is that it?"

Rachel said, "Tomorrow will be closing argument, and then the case goes to the jury."

"They have to convict," Manny said.

"No," said Rachel, "they don't. Remember, they heard a lot of evidence before this."

"You think there's a chance he'll go free?" Lydia said.

At that moment Abi entered from the kitchen. "Are you all still talking about that crazy trial? This is a party for my granddaughter. I don't want to hear anymore about lawyers!"

Everyone laughed. Jeff looked at the painting on the wall—a painting of Jesus with his disciples. It had a curious pattern across it, almost like it had been cut. "You like it?" Rachel asked.

"I do," said Jeff.

"I think I like it even more now," Rachel said. "It's a survivor."

"What do you mean?"

Smiling, Rachel said, "Just wait till I tell you."

The doorbell rang.

"I'll get it," said Rachel, rising. She flicked on the porch light and opened the door.

It was her father, dressed in a sport coat and clumsily knotted tie.

"Pop!" Rachel said, running into his arms.

"Hello, Rabbit," Art Ybarra said.

From inside Abi said, "Who is it?"

Rachel took her father's arm and led him into the living room. "Look who's here!"

Everyone stood up. Abi put one hand to her mouth.

"Hello, Little Mama," Art said. Then he went to her, put his arms around her, and pulled her to him. Rachel heard the muffled sound of Abi's soft crying in his shoulder.

"Hey, none of that," Art said. "He said this was a party."

Abi wiped her eyes. "Who?"

Art motioned toward Manny with his thumb. "This guy. The preacher."

"I confess," Manny said. "I was the one who called him. I hope you don't mind." He looked at Rachel.

"No," Rachel said. "It's perfect. Absolutely perfect." And for the next few hours, it was.

Everything seemed to come full circle the next morning when Rachel found herself standing in Alan Lakewood's office. "You feeling okay?" Lakewood asked, taking his familiar seat on the corner of his desk.

"Today I am," Rachel said.

"I've been in this office seventeen years, and I have never seen, nor do I expect to see, anything like this case again."

Rachel smiled and shook her head.

"That should be good news for you too," Lakewood said.

"Why?"

"Because when you come to work full-time, every case you get will be a piece of cake."

Rachel wondered if she heard him right. "Full-time?"

"When you graduate I'm going to recommend you to the office. That is, if you want the job."

Her expression must have been a mixture of surprise, disbelief, and utter confusion because Lakewood quickly said, "It's true. You deserve it. First off, I owe you an apology for overreacting about you and Deanna Natale. Chalk a little of it up to the willies. I was under some stress with this case, wanting it real bad. Anything that could have disturbed it was bound to be a tick in my briefs, and I don't mean legal."

Lakewood stood up and walked around his desk. "And you were doing what I asked you to do, which was to keep her up and ready to testify. While you did that you formed a bond, and that isn't a bad thing. Coloring it that way was wrong on my part and smacks of religious prejudice."

"I didn't take it that way."

"How *did* you take it?"

"Like a slap upside the head."

Lakewood laughed. "Which is what I need." He picked up some pages off his desk. "The second thing is this memo that Ron Ashby prepared for me, under pressure I might add."

Puzzled as to the significance of this item, Rachel was silent.

"It is a brilliant piece of writing," Lakewood said, "and the research is excellent."

"That's . . . great."

"It is also reminiscent of other brilliant work I've seen." Lakewood looked directly at her and raised his eyebrows. He was talking about her. "So I did a little checking. You remember when Ashby took over for you?"

How could she forget it? "Yes."

"He took your files, including your computer files."

"I gave him all the files and my computer disks."

"Do you remember giving me one of those disks?"

Rachel thought a moment. "No."

"Well, maybe it was a mistake," he said. "But one of your research memos came to me in an envelope with a disk inside. I tossed the disk in that basket." He indicated a wire basket on the top of a filing cabinet by his door. It was overflowing with papers. "When I read Ashby's memo, it had a certain style to it that I hadn't seen in him before. Remember, I've been reading these things for years."

Rachel nodded, still perplexed.

"I remembered your disk," Lakewood said, "and on a hunch I popped it in my computer. Guess what I found?"

Rachel shook her head.

"Yep," Lakewood continued, "some rough drafts of other memos, including most of the memo Ashby handed me. He plagiarized your work."

"I just can't believe that. How can you be sure?"

"I've also spent a lot of years cross-examining witnesses, most of them a lot tougher than Ron Ashby."

"He confessed to it?"

"Took me all of about two minutes to get it out of him."

"He didn't have to do that. He may be a lot of things, but he's not dumb."

"He may be a lot of things we don't want in this office. I advised him to go back to Berkeley and retake his ethics class."

"He's gone?"

"As of yesterday. Which means I'll be needing someone to take his place." Lakewood looked at his watch. "I've got to get down for closing argument. Shall we go together?"

Alan Lakewood seemed relaxed and confident before the jury.

His closing argument was not a long one. He had once explained to Rachel that he liked to keep things simple and focus on one big issue. In this instance it was the tape recording.

"What more do you need, ladies and gentlemen?" he asked rhetorically. "The statement is clear. It doesn't have any double meaning. And it establishes everything we need to prove our case beyond a reasonable doubt. The defendant, Jaroslav Supevsky, hired Grigory Viazmitin to brutally—and that's a key word, *brutally*—murder Dimitri and Sarah Chekhov."

Pausing at the lectern, Lakewood leaned casually on it and then said, "The judge is going to instruct you on the law you are to apply in this case. You, ladies and gentlemen, are then going to go back in the jury room and decide on the facts. When you put those two things together—the facts and the law—you can reach only one conclusion. I'm confident you'll find it. Thank you."

Lakewood sat, and then it was Jessica Osborn Holt's turn. Throughout the argument Rachel tried to read the faces of the jurors. She couldn't. The only thing she was certain of was that they were paying attention to Holt because it was impossible not to.

It was quite a performance. Holt went from theatrical and outraged, to quiet and indignant, then back again. She held back nothing and spoke right up to the noon hour.

"This case has been a stinking cesspool of lies, half-truths, and manipulation of evidence," she told the jury. "You know that, deep down in your heart of hearts. And what stinks needs to be cleaned up. You, the jury, are the only ones who can do that."

Holt turned to the judge and suggested it was a good time to break for lunch. Montross asked Holt how long she had left. Holt thought another half hour, and then Alan Lakewood said his rebuttal would be about the same.

The judge adjourned court for the lunch break.

At a few minutes past one, the receptionist paged Rachel to the twelfth floor. When she got there, Babs told her a "Dena Natalie" wanted to see her. Through the glass Rachel saw a lonely figure sitting at the other side of the building, looking out the window.

Rachel walked out the security door and hurried across the hallway. "Deanna?"

Deanna turned to Rachel. Her eyes were red. "Hi," she said.

Rachel pulled up one of the visitor chairs and sat down. "How are you?"

"I'm sorry for disturbing you like this."

"You're not!"

"Did I blow it?"

Rachel took Deanna's hands in hers. "No. There was a lot more evidence you don't even know about. So don't worry."

"But I do," Deanna said tremulously. "Do you think God's disappointed in me?"

"No way."

"I tried, but I looked stupid."

"Juries understand what witnesses go through."

A faint smile appeared on Deanna's face. "You've been so good to me. I hope I didn't mess up your life too much."

"Don't even think that. You've made my life better. I've seen you become a new creation."

"I wish I felt like it. I feel like a total loser."

"Listen to me," Rachel said firmly. "A wise old Christian lady once said, 'God don't sponsor no flops.' It's true. Will you believe it?"

Deanna's eyes were wet. She squeezed Rachel's hands. "I'll try."

"I'll help," Rachel said. "Are you going back home?"

Deanna nodded. "Mom needs me."

"The most important thing for you to do is find a good church. I'll talk to my pastor. He knows churches all over the place. I'll bet he can find one for you."

"Rachel?"

"Hm?"

"Will you write to me?"

"Of course I will."

"Will we always be friends?"

"More than that, Deanna. Sisters."

Two days later the jury returned its verdict—guilty.

Rachel wasn't in the courtroom to hear the verdict, but she was outside on the courthouse steps to hear the impromptu news conference held by Jessica Osborn Holt. As always she was news, and the gaggle of reporters and cameras testified to this unalterable, Los Angeles fact.

"I will file an appeal," Holt fairly shouted. "Of course an appeal will be filed. This case is a travesty. An injustice. It almost pains me to be standing here in the shadow of what is supposed to be a temple of justice and have to say these things."

"Aren't you just mad because you lost?" a reporter shouted.

Rachel could see the fire flaring in Holt's eyes. "I didn't lose! The system of justice lost! The American people lost! And this case is not over. It won't be, as long as I have anything to do with it."

Toni Galvan, standing with Rachel, said, "Heard enough?"

"Oh yeah," Rachel said. "Let's go get a burger."

They walked across the street to the food court.

The sun, dropping toward the sea, was still warm over Los Angeles. Rachel cut through the water in the USC pool with a sharpness she had not felt in a long, long time.

Today she would not just beat the Russians for the gold, she'd set a new world's record.

When she touched the edge, invigorated and refreshed, she imagined a packed arena bursting into wild applause. And then she heard some.

It was the sound of one man clapping.

Jeff stood at the edge of the pool, applauding rhythmically. "Nice finish," he said.

"How long have you been there?"

"Admiring you? Not long enough."

Rachel climbed out of the pool. "How did you know I was here?"

"I'm an FBI agent, remember? Fully reinstated by the way."

Rachel tossed her head back and said, "Yes!" Then she threw herself into his arms. After a long embrace she took a step back. "I'm sorry!"

Jeff looked down at his shirt, now wet and sticking to his body. "That's okay. I like this look." He reached out with one arm and pulled her to him. "In fact," he said, "I'd like to make it permanent."

ACKNOWLEDGMENTS

FINAL WITNESS COULD NOT have been written without the aid of some very generous people. My law school classmate, Jeffrey Isaacs of the United States Attorney's Office, was of inestimable help. He was unselfish with his time, suggested several possible avenues for my federal trial to take, sharpened the legal arguments, and lent me some excellent written materials.

Al Menaster of the appellate division of the Los Angeles Public Defender's Office was likewise of great assistance. He not only knows law and courtrooms, he is also one of the country's leading experts on legal fiction. I thank him for taking the time to look at mine.

Retired FBI agent Steve Moss provided specific details about the Bureau and also the human side of being a federal law enforcement agent. I'm also grateful to another law school classmate and friend, Jan Norman, one of L.A.'s best criminal lawyers, and to Scott Carrier of the L.A. County Coroner's Office.

My editor, Len Goss, and Mark Lusk, both of Broadman & Holman Publishers, gave me needed encouragement and support.

As always, my first editor was my wife, Cindy, who does not fail to call them as she sees them. I'm never happier than when something I write pleases her, and when something doesn't, I get out the blue pencil.

ABOUT THE AUTHOR

JAMES SCOTT BELL IS a former trial lawyer and the author of *Circumstantial Evidence* (Broadman & Holman). He studied writing with Raymond Carver at the University of California, Santa Barbara, and graduated with honors from the USC Law Center. Now a full-time writer, he is the author of several books on the law and has appeared as a commentator on *Good Morning, America*, CBS radio, and *Newsweek* magazine. He lives in southern California with his wife, son, and daughter, and is currently at work on his next novel.